Dick Nelson

THE _Trojan Horse_ Conspiracy

THE **INFILTRATION** AND **DESTRUCTION** OF **AMERICAN DEMOCRACY**

DICK NELSON

outskirtspress

DENVER, COLORADO

Outskirts Press, Inc.
http://www.outskirtspress.com

PB ISBN: 978-1-4327-9508-5
HB ISBN: 978-1-4327-9511-5

Library of Congress Control Number: 2012910784

Outskirts Press and the "OP" logo are trademarks belonging to Outskirts Press, Inc.

PRINTED IN THE UNITED STATES OF AMERICA

Preface

Scattered throughout ancient Greek and Roman literature are descriptions of the Trojan War, a ten-year conflict between the Greeks and the City of Troy. In Homer's *Illiad* and *Odyssey*, Virgil's *Aeneid,* and the verses of the Cyclic Epics, the story is heavily infused with elements and characters of Greek mythology. According to these ancient writings, the Trojan War began when Paris, the son of the Trojan king, fell in love with Helen, the wife of Spartan king Menelaus, and took her back to Troy.

When diplomacy failed, the Greek alliance attacked Troy with a powerful army, disembarked from their fleet. Failing to breach the city fortress, they opted instead to pretend a withdrawal. Faking the traditional peace offering, they constructed a huge wooden horse, beautifully crafted by a Greek artisan, and left it at the gates of Troy. The Trojans, delighting in their victory, moved the prize inside their gates and celebrated.

What they did not know was that the giant horse was hollow, and dozens of armed Greek soldiers were hiding inside. As soon as night fell, and the Trojans had relaxed their guard, the soldiers climbed down from the horse and slaughtered the sleeping Trojans, including their leaders. At a pre-arranged signal, the Greek fleet returned and Troy was taken.

While this all happened around 1200 B.C., the concept of covertly infiltrating a strong adversary also was recognized in other lands. Around 500 B.C., Chinese general Sun Tzu wrote the following in his treatise *Art of War:*

> What enables the wise sovereign and the good general to strike and conquer, and achieve things beyond the reach of ordinary men, is *foreknowledge.* Now this foreknowledge cannot be elicited from spirits; it cannot be obtained inductively from experience, nor by any deductive calculation. Knowledge of the enemy's dispositions can only be obtained from other men. Hence the use of spies...

This concept was used by the Greeks with the ploy of the Trojan Horse, and has survived the centuries and evolved to modern times. One might characterize America as the modern Troy, and its Communist adversaries as the wily Greeks.

With the ascendency of the mysterious man known to his fellow conspirators as Pegasus, the time of reckoning had arrived—with a vengeance. The "American Experiment," described in the 19th century political analysis of Alexis de Tocqueville, may finally be over. The great American Eagle has lost his ability to fly and hunt. He now cowers helplessly in his deteriorating nest, soiling himself, hoping that someone will feed and protect him.

This is the story of a few courageous Americans, who tried to set things right before it was too late. It may be the product of my imagination—*or is it?*

The land is as the garden of Eden before them

and behind them a desolate wilderness... Like the noise of chariots on the tops of mountains shall they leap, like the noise of a flame of fire that devoured the stubble, as a strong people set in battle array... The earth shall quake before them; the heavens shall tremble; the sun and the moon shall be dark, and the stars shall withdraw their shining. ---The Book of Joel

Dick Nelson

Prologue

The muscular man shivered as he slipped quietly into the cold, dark alley off Kowloon's Ki Lung Street. Plumes of ghostly steam rose from the manhole covers and merged with the damp morning fog, illuminated by the pulsing glow of the adjacent bordello's neon sign. He was clad in black, using a shop doorway as cover. Navy Lieutenant Brad Tilsdale, a member of the U.S. Naval Special Operations Group's SEAL Team One, known popularly as "SEALs," was violating his superior's orders by meeting with a local Chinese "asset." The standing orders were to use only "safe" houses, and never to conduct field contacts of this type.

The Chinese national, code-name "Panda," was a recent immigrant from the People's Republic of China to the adjacent Hong Kong Territories. He told Tilsdale that he had actu- ally worked at the Communist Chinese nuclear facility in Lanzhou, and had valuable intelligence that he would trade for asylum in the U.S. He made clear that he would only deal with Tilsdale, and no one else. Tilsdale concluded that the potential value of "Panda's" information was worth the personal risk. If he could successfully bring him in for debriefing, it would be a major intelligence coup, as nothing specific was known about Lanzhou and how much uranium had been enriched for nuclear weapons.

In this Cold War era, Kowloon was a hotbed of Chinese and Western spy activity. Still part of the British colony of Hong Kong, the valuable port city would not be turned over to the People's Republic of China until 1997. The major powers all found that rich intelligence sources abounded in this heavily populated territory, and LT Tilsdale was sure that he had discovered a man with great value to the U.S. intelligence community.

Tilsdale stiffened, holding his breath. The sound of a bottle hitting pavement echoed down the alley. On a building above, Major Zhu Sung of the Chinese People's Liberation Army, Special Intelligence Unit, was watching Tilsdale through an infrared night scope. Capturing an American intelligence officer would be of great value to his superiors in Beijing, and he was determined to take this American alive. The hunter was being hunted.

Out of the foggy depths of the alley, a man emerged, walking toward Tilsdale. The pre-arranged signal was for the man to blink a flashlight twice, followed by Tilsdale's response of three flashes. The man stopped, giving two flashes. Tilsdale gave his three flashes in response and approached the man, whose face was still not visible.

When he was fifteen feet away, Tilsdale reached to the small of his back and pulled out his favorite weapon, the Randall Special No. 1 Fighting Knife, with a razor-sharp seven-inch carbon steel blade. A Navy SEAL is always pre-pared for the unexpected. He gave the code-word in Chinese. *"Yǔ?"* [Rain?]

The man responded correctly, *"Fēngbào."* [Storm.]

The code-word was correct, but Tilsdale sensed danger. Then he detected movement from the shadows on his right and left—a trap!

The man known as "Panda" suddenly lunged at him. Without hesitation, Tilsdale side-stepped and plunged the blade of his Randall into the man's kidney, twisting it out for the next assailant, who came at him with a club. Using the figure-eight double-slash technique, he blocked the swing of the club and sliced the man's face across his eyes, followed by a vertical knife-thrust into the underside of his jaw.

The next man threw a casting-style fishing net over Tilsdale's head, and tackled him from behind. Reaching around his left side, Tilsdale drove the knife deep into the man's sternum, a death blow. As he rolled free of the net, he sprang to his feet to confront Major Sung, a martial arts expert, who was running toward him to complete the capture.

Blocking three vicious kicks to his head, Tilsdale spun quickly to his left, driving his extended fingers into Sung's diaphragm. While Sung gasped for air, Tilsdale struck him with a powerful hand-edge blow to the larynx. Sung stag-gered, holding his throat. Tilsdale swiftly broke the Chinese officer's spine with a sickening snap, slamming the man backwards and down over his bent left knee.

Tilsdale recovered his Randall and ran quickly down the alley toward the harbor ferry terminal. Boarding the ferry for Victoria, Tilsdale positioned himself carefully to detect any Chinese "tail." Finally relaxing, he thought to himself,

What the hell—a good body count is better than no score at all.

Back at the U.S. Consulate, the CIA Resident was not amused. "I specifically told you not to engage any assets by yourself," growled the Agency veteran. "That's the trouble with you goddam SEALs—you think you are bullet-proof. You almost got yourself killed. Worse yet, you almost got kidnapped. You know what the CHICOMs would have done to you? Let me tell you, son, there are a lot of things worse than death, and you would have met them face to face. The Chinese do not fuck around. We *still* have not heard from some of our people they took during the Korean and Vietnam wars, you know. You could be sitting in the basement of the MSS [Ministry of State Security] right now, with bamboo splinters pushed under your fingernails and electric wires attached to your eyelids!"

"Yes, Sir, but I thought it was worth the gamble. How much would the Agency give for accurate information on Lanzhou and their nukes?"

The agent glared at him. "You're right. But if we lost you, it would mean a pile of paperwork for me! And you know how I hate paperwork! Look, I know you tried, but I am going to transfer you back to the embassy in Tokyo. Don't worry, I will not mention anything about this incident—I'll just say that your cover was 'blown,' and that we need a new operator for your slot who is not known to the bad guys. OK?"

"Fine, Sir. Thanks." Tilsdale was disappointed. The SEALs were routinely attached to the CIA to provide "muscle" for missions that needed it. This had been a choice assignment, and Tilsdale hated to lose it.

The U.S. Embassy in Japan was located at 1-10-5 Akasaka, in Tokyo's Minato district, near Exit 13 of the Rippongi Dori expressway. Upon his arrival, Tilsdale received a frosty reception from the Naval Attaché, Rear Admiral Evans. "Jesus Christ, Brad—what the hell were you thinking? In the first place, the Naval Academy should never have assigned our graduates to cowboy units like the Swift Boats and SEALs. The taxpayers have invested too much in you guys to risk losing you. This is a perfect example of what happens when you guys go off free-lancing on my nickel. If the Chinese had been able to grab you, there would have been hell to pay, and I probably would have been recalled to Washington."

"Sorry, Sir. It seemed like the thing to do at the time." Tilsdale was getting fed up with the Navy's "cover-your-ass" mentality, which had prevailed since the Vietnam war. The senior officers worried more about their careers than the mission. He had decided that it was time to leave.

"Well, you were wrong, and your next fitness report will reflect it."

"That won't be necessary, Sir. I am resigning from active duty. I am accepting a job with the FBI."

"Really? God help them! You better not pull stunts like this with those guys. They all march in step over there, and they don't tolerate this kind of behavior. I'll give you six months, and you will be looking for another job, because you refuse to go by the book. Get the hell out of here."

"Aye, aye, Sir. Thank you for the inspirational talk."

The admiral looked up, fuming at the insolent comment. "Goodbye, Mr. Tilsdale. And good riddance."

This was not the first of Tilsdale's daring exploits. The CIA, DIA, and the FBI had noticed his work on several large counter-intelligence cases. Although Tilsdale did not fit into the Navy's rigid command structure, the intelligence community was always looking for players of his type. All three services tried to recruit him when he left active duty, but the FBI won. His life's course would now be charted in a different direction, one that would merge in unforeseen ways with the twisted destiny of his country.

Chapter 1

Genesis

It was the winter of 1980-81, and a cold, blustery day in Beijing. The Russian KGB officials were becoming angry at their hosts' delay in arriving for the meeting. They had been sitting in the large conference room at the Ministry of State Security just off Tiananmen Square for an hour. Yuri Andropov, Chairman of the Soviet KGB (*Komitet gosudarstvennoy bezopasnosti*) was irate. He stared out on the Square and the gate to the Forbidden City, wondering how many Chinese had died there over the centuries at the hands of their rulers. *People have no value to the Chinese,* he thought, *as they can so easily manufacture more, like stinking rabbits.*

"We have flown thousands of kilometers to get here, through this miserable Chinese weather, and have put up with these primitive conditions, and now they let us sit here drinking tea!" he complained.

The doors suddenly opened, and the Director of China's MSS walked in, accompanied by translators and staff. The Chinese officials gave the Russians the customary embrace. "Welcome to the People's Republic of China, Mr. Andropov,"

said Director Li Kenong in broken Russian. Had they known about it, the fact that the heads of the Soviet and Chinese secret services were meeting would have been important information to the CIA and Britain's Secret Intelligence Service, known as MI-6. The Soviets and the Chinese

had been careful to keep this
conference secret, including the
travel plans of Andropov and his
staff. The Russians were carefully smuggled into the Ministry
from a nearby Chinese Air Force
base in unmarked cars.

"Thank you, Director. We are
honored to be here." A veteran of
many dangerous political meetings, Andropov studied the faces
and body language of his Chinese counterparts, calculating
their hidden motives and the power relationships between
each of them.

"Please be seated," Li Kenong said. "Would you like any
refreshments?"

Andropov motioned for his translator. "No, thank you.
We would like to discuss the subject of this meeting, which
each of our governments has ordered. These discussions
must be kept at the highest level of secrecy, for obvious reasons. Shall I begin?" he asked. An expert in diagnosing organizational dynamics, Andropov had already figured out that
Li's late arrival probably indicated that the Chinese hierarchy was not in full agreement.

"I assure you," Li said through the translator, "Premier
Zhao Ziyang wishes to make this project the highest priority, but we would like to review its details."

"As do we, Director." Andropov had to suppress a smile,
because he had just been through the same internal wran-
gling with the Soviet leaders. Many felt that his plan would
never work. "Allow me to frame the problem that requires
a solution. The United States has a new President, as you

know. Unfortunately, they got rid of that weak idiot, Carter, and now we have a real 'cowboy' to deal with—the Hollywood actor, Reagan. Our window of opportunity to take action may be closing."

"Comrade Andropov, we are very concerned," said Li. "Let me be candid. China intends to establish itself as the dominant power of the Asian-Pacific region, both economically and militarily. At the same time, we want to do away with this atmosphere of suspicion and distrust between *our* two countries. We do not want more border violence or armed confrontations with the Soviet Union, such as we have had in the past. We acknowledge *your* position as a trans-continental power, with important assets in the northern Pacific. However, my government has instructed me to offer a geopolitical arrangement—an alliance—in which we can each pursue our global expansionary interests, while living within our respective spheres of influence. We believe that, other than your current facilities in northern Asia, such as Vladivostok, Petropavlosk, and Siberia, *we* should hold primary rights of influence in the central and southern Asia regions, below your Pacific coastal area. By the same token, we recognize *your* rightful sphere of influence to be Europe and the Middle East."

Highly-placed KGB agents within the Chinese government had predicted this offer, so Andropov was prepared for it. "Our governments are in agreement," said Andropov. "But what about Africa and the Americas?"

"We can easily carve out territories in Africa between us, or we can joint-venture our activities. However, the Americas are a different story. There, we *both* have the capitalist Americans to deal with. You already got a bloody nose when you tried to establish a presence in Communist Cuba in the early Sixties. We were quite surprised that Kennedy, the Americans' playboy President, was able to force your withdrawal without even firing a shot." Li could not suppress a smirk.

Andropov reminded himself that Chinese names begin with the family, or surname. "Comrade Li, that was admittedly a failure of our political leadership at the time, who fell for Kennedy's clever bluff. Our national security organizations were shocked, especially after we had been successful in forcing Kennedy to abandon the Bay of Pigs invasion of Cuba in 1961. Nevertheless, we *did* achieve the withdrawal of American ICBMs from Turkey, which were a real threat to us. But while we are on the subject of backing down from confrontation, I seem to remember *your* government did not do so well with your Taiwan Strait hostilities, and you still have not taken back Taiwan from that pip-squeak puppet government." The Russian smiled.

"Let's not trade insults, Comrade," said the Chinese official. "As the Americans say, we have other fish to fry here."

"Agreed."

"Our mutual problem is America. Neither of us can pursue our long-range goals as long as America is strong and aggressive. The Americans *must* be neutralized. The question is, how do we accomplish that?" The Director motioned to his staff members, who passed a document to each of the Russians. "Neither of us can risk a nuclear exchange with the Americans and their allies in NATO. Their warhead superiority, especially when you consider their missile submarines, is overwhelming, and any conventional military confrontation would quickly escalate from conventional to nuclear."

"No doubt. We have managed to obtain some of their

NATO war plans, and they intend to use tactical nuclear weapons against our forces, if we push across the border into a NATO country. That would quickly escalate to total nuclear war."

"Yes, the same is true for us," replied Li. He wanted the Russians to know that the Chinese espionage apparatus was also active. "One of our spies at their Department of State learned that they would defend Taiwan and respond to our invasion with nuclear weapons. They know that they do not have the ground or air forces to stop us, so that is their only option. We do not wish to lose our cities to these weapons. We must find other means."

"Since we originated this plan, let me quickly review the details," said Andropov, passing a large document to the Chinese officials. The document was marked "самый секретный" (*Samiy Sekretny,* or Top Secret) in large red characters.

"The essence of the strategy is to infiltrate the American government and political system with our agents, and to force them to abandon their self-protective, aggressive posture. This is a long-term process, and can only be accomplished by our nations maintaining our respective commitment to its success. It is not very costly, compared to developing weapons systems or engaging in armed conflict, but it can only succeed by both of us implementing the program, including through our successors, until it is all in place.

"The proof that this can work is found in our mutual experience in assisting and supporting the North Vietnamese during their war with the U.S. The Soviet Union and the People's Republic of China provided the Vietnamese with the necessary weapons, training and supplies. But more important, we showed them how to influence the American media and convince them that the war was lost. As you recall, General Giap's Tet Offensive in early 1968 was a military disaster for the North Vietnamese, but was a public relations victory, thanks to the hysterical American media. Remember General Giap's statement in his memoirs? He admitted that the Americans defeated the North Vietnamese on the battlefield, but they were saved by the American media and the Left-wing anti-war movement.

"We even convinced the Americans' top TV journalist, Walter Cronkite, to buy our charade that the Vietnam War was lost. Their President Johnson, himself, gave up his office as a result. This proves that, with the Americans, you do not *need* to assassinate their leaders. When our agents eliminated John Kennedy in 1963, even though we were hugely successful and got away with it, he was replaced by a stronger and more aggressive man—Lyndon Johnson. You never know for certain what you will get as a replacement, or what that person will do in office. We learned our lesson."

Li nodded. "I was always curious. Just how *did* you do that, without getting caught?"

"That was a long-term situation, which began in an unexpected way. It started with some of our KGB agents in Japan, who were watching the American U-2 spy plane base in Atsugi, Japan. Oswald, whom the Americans erroneously identified to be Kennedy's sole assassin, was in the Marine Corps and assigned to the base radar and electronics facility. We learned of his unstable personality and tendency to get in trouble with his superiors, and thought he might be susceptible to recruitment. That would allow us to penetrate this secret base. During that time, shooting down their U-2s was a top priority for us, because they were over-flying our territory on a regular basis."

"Yes, and ours, too," added Li.

Andropov nodded. "Our agents were more successful than they ever expected. More accurately, they were just lucky. They not only recruited Oswald as a spy, but then they actually induced him to defect to the Soviet Union. Like the Americans, we, too, had trouble controlling him. He had significant psychological problems, which apparently related to his childhood. We assigned one of our female KGB agents to shadow him, and he wound up marrying her—a great surprise! Now we controlled the best possible surveillance agent—his wife!

"When he was allowed to return to the U.S. with his Russian wife, we were shocked. The American CIA probably thought it would be easier to debrief him if he were back in their territory, so they pulled strings with their State Department to let him in. He immediately became involved with various radical organizations, some of which actually had back-channel ties to U.S. intelligence.

"Our government was still very bitter about the embarrassment of the Cuban Missile Crisis, and we thought Kennedy might try to avenge his debacle with the Bay of Pigs invasion of Cuba by trying it again. We were given a 'green light' sanction to take him out, *provided* we could do so without our involvement being discovered.

"Obviously, we could not risk being identified as the perpetrators. That would cause immediate nuclear war. Even the Americans would not tolerate having their leader assassinated by a foreign power. Accordingly, we used our agents that had been planted within their labor unions, and engaged the unions' connections with certain American crime figures. The unions in Illinois and other states had stuffed ballot boxes for Kennedy, giving him a narrow win in the 1960 election against the anti-Communist Nixon. We had provided significant financing for that effort. However, Kennedy turned out to be problematic in his own way, with respect to Cuba. He was too easily manipulated by the CIA. After the humiliation of the 1962 Cuban Missile Crisis, our top leadership wanted him eliminated.

"We had learned that Kennedy had a secret life as a chronic womanizer. Even in the White House, he had female visitors. We took advantage of this through our new 'contract partners,' the Mafia. We helped the Mafia with their drug supply lines and supported their control of the unions. We made sure that Kennedy was supplied with sexual encounters, including a girlfriend of the head of the Chicago Mafia, Sam Giancana. At that point, we and Giancana felt that we had developed some blackmail possibilities. We became very concerned when, with Kennedy's blessing, the CIA approached Giancana in a plot to assassinate Fidel Castro. We were lucky that we already had Giancana in our pocket. But that was the last straw for our Soviet leadership. They wanted to accelerate Kennedy's assassination timetable.

"I was instructed to form a project team. We began to study his itinerary, and learned that he was going to Dallas, Texas, for a political appearance in November of 1963. The lack of sophisticated law enforcement in that part of the U.S., combined with strong sentiments against the liberal Kennedy Administration, made Dallas an attractive choice for our operation, which was called 'Operatsiya Molniya,' or Operation Lightning. The stupid Americans even made his motorcade route public. Their security was a joke. However, we had very few assets and agents in the Dallas area at the time.

"One of my staff remembered that the defector, Oswald, lived in the area. We could not entrust such an important task to this unbalanced character, so we decided to use Oswald only as a decoy, or as the Americans say, 'a patsy.' On the promise of his becoming a 'spokesman' for local radical groups, combined with financial support from our anonymous agent-donors, Oswald sought out employment along the Kennedy motorcade route. We had one of our agents meet Oswald and his wife at a Russian language club gathering, and offer them a cheap room at her house. This provided Oswald and his wife with a safe-house.

"Our agents convinced him to take photographs of Kennedy on the motorcade route, for which he would be paid. The agents told him that the photographs were needed for propaganda materials, in support of radical causes. We bought him a cheap camera. Oswald obtained a low-level job at the Texas Book Depository, overlooking Dealey Plaza, on Elm Street.

"Our agents had been successful in convincing Oswald that he might be attacked by government agents, and that he needed to carry a loaded pistol for protection. We continuously stoked his anger about Kennedy's invasion of Cuba, and made him believe that Kennedy's agents were looking for him. We forged his signature and left a paper trail to show that he had mail-ordered a Carcano rifle, equipped with a scope.

"At the same time, through our Mafia connections, we sub-contracted for three expert shooter teams from Europe. As far as the shooters knew, the Mafia was running the operation, and the apparent motive was to stop the investigation of organized crime being pushed by the Kennedy Administration. The shooters were experienced 'hit' men who worked for the Mafia drug rings in Marseille.

"We used triangulated cross-fire to make the shots. We disguised one team as Dallas Police officers, and had the shooter fire from behind a fence on a grassy knoll. Another shooter was on the railroad overpass, dressed like what Americans call a 'hobo,' or vagrant. The operation leader was near the street, and dropped an umbrella as the signal to fire simultaneously. Then there was a third shooter, using a telescopic-sighted Carcano rifle from the 6th floor of the Texas Book Depository building.

"Kennedy was hit twice, including a fatal head shot." Andropov chuckled. "This was all done while poor Oswald was having lunch. In his typical incompetence, he had failed to be ready to take photographs, and was actually sitting in the employee lunchroom when the motorcade went by. When he heard that a shooting had occurred, he panicked and ran from the building, thinking, in his usual paranoia, that the U.S. government was after him. Our 'disposal' team had been directed to kill Oswald, but he avoided them through the back door."

Andropov continued. "After the shooting, we used several fake police officers to remove the hobos from the area, including our shooting team, so that it would appear that they were being arrested. The shooter on the grassy knoll left in what appeared to be a police car, and the one in the Book Depository planted his rifle in a 'sniper's nest' near an open window. Using transfer technology, we applied a handprint and some fingerprints of Oswald to this rifle.

"The police also failed to catch Oswald before he left the building. Using a backup plan, one of our agents, dressed like Oswald, killed the officer that stopped him for questioning on a residential street. This was done to enrage the local police, who we hoped would kill Oswald when they found him. Oswald was finally taken into custody in a movie theater, and his prints were matched to the rifle.

"We had ensured that the police received a description of Oswald as the shooter, and intended that Oswald would be killed by police. We now had a problem. He was still *alive*, in police custody, and subject to interrogation. We desperately looked for a way to eliminate him before he talked. He was already telling the police that he had been 'set up.' Some people in the Kremlin were in a panic.

"We consulted again with our Mafia contacts, and learned that they had a strip-club operator in the Dallas area, named Jack Ruby. His Mafia boss contacted him and gave him a mandatory 'contract' to kill Oswald.

"There was very poor security within the Dallas Police headquarters, and Ruby was able to prowl the halls looking for a chance to shoot Oswald. The opportunity never developed until the police were transferring Oswald to the county jail when they walked him past Ruby, who fatally shot Oswald."

"But how did you keep all of the witnesses and involved players from talking?" asked Li.

"We eliminated almost all of them. In as many cases as possible, we made the deaths appear to be accidental or from natural causes, like auto accidents or heart attacks. As you know, there are several drugs that can cause cardiac arrest, and leave no chemical trace by normal testing."

"Yes, we have used those also—usually through one of the doctors from the Ankang Institute," said Li.

Andropov continued. "The few witnesses left are terrified and afraid to talk. But we terminated all of the shooter team. Then we had trouble with Giancana and Hoffa, head

of the Teamsters Union. Giancana, who was being investigated by John F. Kennedy's brother Robert, threatened us
with exposure if we did not eliminate Robert Kennedy. At
the same time, Hoffa threatened to go public with what he
knew about Giancana's activities.

"We used a similar plan and a fake shooter to take out
Robert Kennedy in 1968 in the kitchen of a hotel in Los
Angeles. The 'patsy' in that case was Sirhan Sirhan, an Arab.
The real shooter, who used a pistol of the same caliber with
a silencer and fired through an air vent grill in the back of
the room, escaped in the confusion. He used explosive bullets to prevent ballistics analysis. We later hired some Mafia
hit men to eliminate both Giancana and then Hoffa, whose
body was disposed of in a local sausage factory.

"We were extremely lucky, as I see it. Vice President
Johnson hated the Kennedys and was delighted to become
the President. He did not want the distraction of a lengthy
investigation into the JFK or the RFK assassinations, even
though he suspected our involvement. His FBI and Secret
Service were obviously negligent, so both of those organizations also wanted to avoid further revelations. The CIA was
worried that some of their unauthorized 'black ops' would be
discovered, so they, too, wanted the investigations to stop.
It was amazing—everyone that could tie us to the assassinations wanted to bury the investigations and pin them on
Oswald and Sirhan.

"The government created a 'show trial' for the JFK
assassination called the Warren Commission, which white-
washed the assassination plot and pinned it all on Oswald.
We could not believe our good fortune, and there were a lot
of congratulations and vodka consumed in Lubyanka Square
[the KGB headquarters] when this ridiculous report came

out. To this day, the official finding contends that Oswald was the lone assassin and acted alone."

"Quite fascinating, Comrade," said Li. "However, I think you would agree that this was a very high-risk operation. My leadership does not want to engage in such adventures. However, we do want to achieve the same results, but by more subtle means."

Andropov did not like receiving a lecture from the Chinese, whom he viewed as operating a primitive, Third-World country. "Alright, Comrade Li, that is why I am proposing our joint long-range infiltration operation. We need to begin immediately. May I describe our plan in more detail?"

"Of course, please proceed," said Li.

"First, as we saw from the influence that the media had in ending the Vietnam War, we need to gain control of their media."

Li frowned. "How can we possibly do that? Their media is run by huge corporations. Are you proposing that we acquire them?"

"No, of course not. We will take them over from within, by injecting a Left-wing, anti-American ideology into their journalistic ranks. This will take time, but we believe that in 15-20 years, their news content, both in their print and electronic media, will project an international Socialist message that will chill American expansionism, and leave a sizeable vacuum for our respective national interests."

"How do you propose to do that?" Li asked.

"We use those fundamental strategies that have kept both of our governments in power. First, we start with the U.S. education system. Within a decade, we can populate their college campuses with a growing cadre of Left-leaning, or even Marxist professors. We must particularly focus on their journalism schools. Some of the students undoubtedly need financial support, and by using on-campus agents, we can identify those with the most compatible ideologies and assist them through various front organizations and scholarships. In America, it is money that brings power. We must be prepared to spend money on steering these young people into positions of power wherever the news is published, whether it is on the radio, on TV, or in print. If we can control the message, we control American voters, and thereby we can significantly influence their government."

"We will agree to that, but it would appear to be a very long-term solution," Li commented.

"Perhaps not as long as you might think," said the Russian. "But let's look at the next element. We need to attack them economically."

"That is easier said than done. They won World War II on the basis of their economic engine, and it is stronger than ever, even after their President Carter."

"True, but we have come up with a two-pronged strategy, and you are part of this," said Andropov. "The entire world, and every modern war, still runs on oil. We have a significant amount, and we can influence the production and price in many parts of the Middle East. You, on the other hand, are a nation that needs significantly more supplies of oil to fuel your country's expansion."

"Quite right," said Li.

"We propose that you begin aggressively to lock up oil supplies with the world's producers. Many of them are nations in political chaos, or are already friendly to us. A major problem for the U.S. is their Middle East supply. The Iranians hate them, and the Arab nations distrust them because of their support for Israel and perceived suppression of the Palestinians. We can do a lot to stir that up, as we are already doing through our agents in Lebanon, Syria, Egypt, and Iraq. As you remember, we were able to persuade the Arabs to embargo oil shipments to them in the early Seventies, and that almost shut them down. Their navy and air force had serious fuel shortages, as a result."

"But is that enough? They seemed to get through that."

"Yes, but we orchestrated that disruption at a time when the North Vietnamese began to invade South Vietnam, and we could not afford to have them come back in with their ground and air forces. In 1973-74, with the political distraction of Nixon's Watergate scandal, combined with the Arabs cutting off America's oil, we rendered them incapable of conducting distant military action against our North Vietnamese allies. This was a good example of the power of that black gold. We wound up with a staunch ally in Southeast Asia, and new naval and air bases."

"I have to admit, that *was* brilliant," said Li. "I have a suggestion on this topic. We need to use our combined educational and media assets to convince the American public that carbon-based energy sources, such as oil and coal, are destroying the planet, and that they should not invest in the search for, and exploration of such sources. The gullible Americans are easily seduced by emotional, 'do-good' symbolism. We could show how the polar bears and penguins are dying from an increase in the Earth's temperature, with the ice packs melting out from under them." The two spy chiefs laughed at the thought.

"I think you have a good idea. We will take a look at that," said Andropov, motioning for one of his staffers to jot down a note. "So far, Comrade Li, we appear to be in total agreement." Li nodded.

"We must also undermine and destroy their manufacturing base. That is the cornerstone of their power, and we *must* weaken or eliminate that."

"We have studied that in detail," said Li. "We believe that we are in an excellent position to usurp their manufacturing in a massive way. We have a cheap labor force, and unlike the Americans, we don't have unions to deal with, nor do we have their layers of stupid regulations. Even with the cost of shipping, we can still manufacture most of their consumer goods at a cost well below their domestic suppliers. At the same time we take away their manufacturing infrastructure, we will be hurting them by a massive trade imbalance, which directly subtracts from their Gross National Product. Last, but not least, we will artificially suppress the exchange value of the *yuan*, our currency, which will add pressure for them to buy from us, and avoid their own expensive manufacturers. This will also put pressure on them, over time."

Andropov nodded his agreement. "Their government also has a tendency to overspend, creating large deficits. They need to finance those deficits by selling U.S. government notes and bonds. You will be in an excellent position to channel your profits from trading with them back into their government securities, making them increasingly dependent on you as their major creditor. When that number is large enough, they will never dare to attack you militarily, no matter what you do with Taiwan. Unfortunately for *us*, the only things *we* trade with them are spies, insults, caviar, and vodka." They both laughed at the thought.

"I agree, Comrade Andropov. However, this will still take 10-20 years to acquire enough of their debt instruments to give us control of their economy. I mean no disrespect, but even if everything goes perfectly, we will not achieve these items until around 2001."

"Well, let me describe the more difficult goal, and the crown jewel of our plan—the infiltration and subversion of the American political system. The prior topics merely provide us with background support for *this* important item. Taking all of these strategy measures together, we believe that we can neutralize, and perhaps, through our surrogates, even take political control of the U.S. government within twenty years or less, without firing a shot."

Li frowned. "I don't see how you can do this. This sounds too easy, as if someone has used excessive imagination," said Li.

Andropov stared coldly at his counterpart. "A lot of work has gone into this component, Comrade. Please wait until you see the details before you form an opinion," said Andropov. "However, we have all had a long day. I request that we wait until tomorrow morning to review that item." After dealing with the Chinese all day, Andropov needed a double vodka and a few hours' sleep. He stood up. "*Spokoĭnoĭ nochi, tovarishch.* [Good night, Comrade.]"

Li rose. "*Wǎn'ān.* [Good night.] *Wǒ huì kàn dào nǐ de míng tiān, tóng zhì.* [See you in the morning, Comrade.]"

Chapter 2

Birth of the Trojan Horse

The next morning, the Soviet and Chinese delegations met again in the palatial conference room of the Ministry of State Security. Andropov and Li sat across from each other, sipping tea and exchanging small talk.

"Shall we begin, Comrade Director?" asked Andropov.

"Yes, please do," Li replied.

"Let me use a historical metaphor that we all can relate to. Remember the famous story in Virgil's *Aeneid* about the Greek war with the City of Troy?" Andropov had read the KGB report on Li, which mentioned that he was fascinated by the history of warfare.

"Yes, of course. The Greeks, even with their hero Achilles, were unable to breach the walls of Troy."

"As you recall, they pretended to withdraw their fleet, while leaving about 40 soldiers inside a large, hollow replica of a horse. When the Trojans saw their withdrawal, they assumed the horse was a peace offering, and brought it inside the fortress walls. During the night, the Greek insertion force crawled out of the horse and opened the gates for the Greek army, which had sailed back under cover of darkness." Andropov lit his pipe, looking more like a history professor than the ruthless spy chief that he was.

"The point of this symbolic story for us is this—the Greeks won the war and captured Troy by a clever ruse. They showed that it only took a few soldiers to bring down the enemy fortress, *if* they could gain entry without being detected. Their stunning victory was gained by trickery, after their massive frontal attacks had not succeeded."

"I see. You obviously would characterize the U.S. as Troy, and us as the Greeks," Li said with a smile. But what *is* the Trojan Horse in our case, Comrade?"

"That is the key question, Comrade Li. It is more a matter of *who* the 'horse' is, than *what*. I believe that the key to success with this plan is the careful selection and grooming of a sleeper agent, who will constitute 'the horse,' facilitating our planting of dozens, or even hundreds, of agents at high levels within the U.S. government. Our most knowledgeable and creative strategists have been studying this, and constructing various hypothetical scenarios."

"Since you recently gave us an overview of this concept, we have also been studying it. We can not see how an agent at that level could possibly survive the intense scrutiny of working in their bureaucracy." Li shook his head.

Andropov smiled. "You assume that their state security is as good as ours. In fact, it is incredibly lax. We believe that the 'horse' must be inserted directly into their political sphere, not the bureaucracy. In that arena, anything is possible, as long as their gullible electorate will vote for the candidate. I'm sure you are aware that they have even had *criminals* serving in their political government positions."

"Oh, yes! This demonstrates how defective their form of government really is. Ordinary citizens cannot be trusted to put the right people in office. This is why our form of government is superior," Li said smugly.

Andropov ignored the self-serving accolade. "We propose the selection and development of a candidate for President of the United States," said the Russian.

When the translator finished, Li and his staff stared at Andropov, dumbfounded. "Surely you are not serious, Comrade!"

"We are absolutely serious. It will do little or no good to put someone in their Congress, the federal bureaucracy or the President's Cabinet. We need someone who can move things in the right direction with only *his* signature. That is their President, and no one else."

"So how can you *possibly* hide his connection with us? Their media will pounce on this, and he will never get elected."

Andropov chuckled. He had anticipated all of these arguments. "Comrade Li, we will have no direct links with the 'horse.' He will be carefully programmed by the joint efforts of your Ankang psychological group and our Pochevsky Institute. These are the world's experts in mind alteration and psychological programming. I think the Americans call this 'brain-washing.'" Andropov knew that it would be important for the Chinese to be equal partners in this effort.

"What would be the basis for the programming?" Li asked.

"This individual must be selected and groomed from a young age to believe fervently in international Marxism and liberal causes, and to believe that capitalism is evil."

Li laughed. "Comrade, I often wonder how many of our respective government leaders *actually* believe in Marxism. They are too busy plotting and figuring out how to eliminate their internal rivals and save their own skins," said Li.

"Very true. However, we must imbue *this* individual

with an iron-clad belief in the ideology of international Socialism, Communism, Marxism, whatever you want to call it," said Andropov. "That is how we will control him and channel his actions. Comrade Li, we have also concluded that the ideal candidate should have no allegiance to the Americans' core religion, Christianity. The scientists at the Pochevsky Institute believe that, ideally, he would be devoid of strong religious beliefs of *any* kind, which would interfere with his Socialist programming. An agnostic or atheist would be ideal. Please refer to page 34 of the document we have given you."

The two groups turned to the page, which showed a bi-lingual list of factors in Russian and Mandarin, the preferred Chinese dialect:

Candidate Qualification Requirements

1. *Racial makeup*. The candidate should be part Caucasian, but of mixed race. Optimum racial factors for guaranteeing votes in American elections in the future would include a parent of African or Hispanic descent. These two are expected to be the largest non-white groups within the U.S. in the future, and will tend to vote blindly for a candidate of their race, without regard for his politics. In addition, they are the easiest groups to manipulate with Socialist political messages.

2. *Gender*. Although Americans pretend to be ambivalent about gender in picking their leaders, our analysts found that they tend to distrust the toughness and stability of female candidates, especially in a

crisis. Therefore, the candidate should be male in order to attract as many voters as possible.

3. *Parental influence.* Both of the candidate's parents must strongly believe in Socialism. The candidate should be raised by a single parent, if possible, to prevent conflicting guidance. Assuming the candidate has a white parent and a non-white parent, the non-white parent should be eliminated early in the candidate's life. To avoid leaving an ideological "trail," the remaining parent should be eliminated before the candidate enters politics.

4. *Environmental factors.* It is considered essential that the candidate be taught that he is a citizen of the world, not the United States. He must be exposed to an international, multi-racial environment and be taught that capitalism is unfair and corrupt. He must believe that the wealth of the U.S. is created at the expense of poor people in other countries. Ideally, he should grow up in a multi-racial environment.

5. *Education.* No expense can be spared in educating this candidate properly. He must be funded and guided to attend the most prestigious American universities. However, he must be carefully channeled into Leftist plans of study, under the guidance of teachers or professors that believe in Socialism. This is one of the most important ingredients that will determine the success or failure of the candidate. In addition, it is essential that he become a highly effective communicator, especially in oral presentations

such as speeches and debates. In this regard, he must eventually achieve dramatic orator skills on a par with Lenin, Hitler, or Reagan. As with those historical figures, what he *knows* is not as important as what he can effectively *communicate* in a persuasive message.

6. *Immediate family*. Optimally, this candidate will marry a woman of his non-white racial category. The hypocritical Americans still find the marriage of a white and non-white as somewhat distasteful and threatening. His marital life should be exemplary, and his children should be attractive and well-behaved. To have otherwise would be a distraction from the image we wish to create.

7. *Associations*. An important part of his programming will be the influence of his close associates and friends. As a first criterion, they should all be from the Americans' Democratic Party. Republicans will find many things about this candidate to dislike, and he would not fare well in that conservative political environment. Secondly, as many of these associates and friends as possible should be ardent, radical Socialists that hate the U.S. and are willing to work toward its downfall.

8. *The chameleon factor*. The candidate must be intensively trained in the political art of rhetorical maneuvering and "double-talk." He must never allow himself to be tied down to a particular, well-defined position on any important issue. His use of

words will virtually create and define him, and using words unwisely can destroy him. Depending on the group to whom he is talking, he must be able to modify even his speech patterns, accents, and content to match the audience group's aspirations, fears, and prejudices.

9. *The U.S. sponsor.* There must be a central, powerful figure of great wealth that advances the candidate's career toward the Presidency. This is the safest way for us to keep from being linked to him. This sponsor is our surrogate, and must be totally trustworthy. The sponsor, whether an individual or a corporate entity, should believe in Socialism and have no loyalty to the U.S. Funds in support of the candidate should be channeled through the sponsor, to hide their true origin. Suggested code-name: ZEUS.

10. *Point of insertion.* When the candidate is ready to be inserted into the American political system, the point of entry must be sympathetic to the candidate, especially with respect to his mixed race. The geographical entry point must be sufficiently corrupt and susceptible to various external influences, including bribes and kick-backs. It must also heavily favor his political party, the Democrats. Our studies indicate that there are two areas that meet these criteria: New Orleans, Louisiana and Chicago, Illinois. The former is not preferred, because it is in the American South, which is more conservative and rarely elects non-whites to high office. The best

choice is Chicago, which has a large non-white population, rampant corruption, and is controlled by the Democratic Party political machine, which we have been able to infiltrate in the past.

Li looked up at Andropov, smiling. "Comrade, this is remarkable work. We are ready to provide any support that we can. We are committed to be your partners in this effort."

Andropov was under no illusions about the devious nature of the Chinese. Ever since those unstable days of Chairman Mao Tse-Tung, the Chinese presented the Soviets with a dilemma. While they cloaked themselves in Marxist propaganda, the Soviets viewed the Chinese as obsessed with their own nationalist aims, using Socialist labels as a cover for their true intentions. Still, as the Americans liked to say, they were the only "game" in town, and it was essential to have them on the same side in this risky venture.

"I think it is advisable to have a code-word for the candidate," said Andropov. "I propose that from this point forward, we refer to him only as 'Pegasus.'"

"Very clever. I see the analogy. In Greek mythology, Pegasus was that flying horse, the ally of Hercules. I hope we fare as well as Hercules did," said Li.

"Good, then Pegasus it is! The plan shall be code-named 'the Trojan Horse project,'" Andropov concluded. "Comrade Li, we must leave now and get to work. I would like to see you alone before we leave."

"Of course, Comrade. Please join me in my study."

Li's Russian translators found this odd, because Li spoke little Russian, and Andropov spoke only a little Mandarin. The two retired to Li's study alone, and the door was closed. A nervous young woman jumped to her feet and bowed to Li.

"This is Li Quan Ming, my sister's daughter. She speaks fluent Russian, and can be totally trusted," said Li. "With your permission, she will translate for us."

Andropov recognized that with the Chinese, family connections are the most trustworthy. *If only Russians had such loyalty,* he thought. "Certainly, Comrade."

Quan Ming began to translate the conversation. "As you certainly must know, Comrade Li, information leaks about this project will doom it to failure. We must restrict knowledge about it within our governments to the highest levels. All it would take is one of our bureaucrats getting drunk at a bar or whispering details in his whore's ear."

"I agree. What are you saying?"

"With the exception of your niece here, all of the translators on both teams should be liquidated. These people have heard and seen too much—all of the project details."

Li's face hardened. "Yes, I see your point. We will eliminate ours, and we expect you to take care of yours."

"Of course. And thank you for speaking with me about this." Andropov's mind was clicking through a plan to murder the Russian translator team as soon as they returned to Moscow. As Quan Ming translated, her eyes widened. She wondered if *she* were living on borrowed time, even though her uncle was Director of State Security.

Li stared at Tiananmen Square below. "Isn't this interesting? Already, people are being sacrificed for our project. One of our ancient philosophers once said that no good plot can succeed without total secrecy and a few murders."

"Goodbye for now, Comrade," said Andropov, moving toward the door.

"Goodbye, and please have a safe trip home," said Li.

Chapter 3

Finding the Foal

After his return to the KGB's headquarters in Lubyanka Square in Moscow, Andropov and his small project staff composed an inquiry, to be sent in code to KGB agents in the U.S.:

"Highest priority. Review all of your local U.S. contacts and search for a young American male with the following characteristics:

- Age: 18-24
- Race: mixed; either half-Black or half Hispanic
- Parents: one White, the other Black or Hispanic
- Political orientation and ideology: Leftist or Socialist
- Intellectual capacity: extremely high
- Communication skills: excellent
- Personality: self-centered, but charming; narcissistic; supremely confident; poised.
- Report names, addresses and particulars on any candidates that you locate to KGB Headquarters, Bureau 252, Demographic Research Project. Refer to this project only as Pegasus. Encode

all communications with S-5 communications protocol.

CLASSIFICATION: MOST SECRET"

Agents throughout North America began searching through their networks and acquaintances for candidates with these parameters. As always, one agent had become sloppy. Perhaps he had been in America too long.

He had written out the selection criteria message on a piece of notepaper and left it on the seat of his car. When he returned from a local California college campus and parked his car, an FBI surveillance team was able to take a photograph with a powerful telephoto lens from their stakeout office, several floors above. The FBI agents had been watching the KGB agent, known to the FBI as "Goldmine," for over one month. A digital enlargement of the photo showed the notepaper on the vehicle seat. Further digital enhancements allowed the FBI analysts to read the text and have it translated.

Special Agent-in-Charge ("SAC") Bradford Tilsdale ran the domestic counter-espionage unit in the FBI's huge Los Angeles field office, located in Westwood, near the UCLA campus. One of his surveillance teams had just forwarded a report on the photographed document, with a translation. He studied it, wondering what it meant. It seemed odd that a routine demographic study would be classified "most secret," which was normally reserved for extremely sensitive intelligence matters. There was a knock on the door. A member of the counter-espionage unit entered.

"Boss, Goldmine has been burrowing into student files at UCLA. He seems intent on locating a kid that matches that KGB message, and is using his campus contacts to search through student records. He is also talking to people for follow-up info on candidates. Are they trying to recruit an agent here, or what?" asked Agent Billings. In fact, Goldmine's search was only one of many that were going on throughout the U.S.

"I don't know, Jeff. My instinct tells me that something is just not right here, and there is more to this." Tilsdale's instincts were highly respected within the intelligence community. He possessed a Sherlock Holmes type of intuition, combined with the deductive reasoning skills of a computer. When Tilsdale zeroed in on something, everyone took notice. Several KGB and MSS spies had been caught by this gifted man, including one within the FBI itself.

What Tilsdale did *not* know was that one of his own superiors within the FBI Washington headquarters was a highly placed "mole," working secretly for the KGB. His code-name within the KGB was "Cerberus."

Sitting in his Washington office, Cerberus read the report from Special Agent Tilsdale with alarm. Whenever a "most secret" message can be compromised by the rival intelligence service, disaster is not far behind. Cognizant of his orders to stay dormant except in an emergency, Cerberus decided that the KGB should be informed about this development. He picked up the phone, and dialed a "blind" number, listed to a fictitious clothing store in nearby Maryland.

Knowing that his phones, like all of the communication systems within the FBI, were monitored or bugged, he allowed the called number to ring seven times, and then hung up. This was the signal for the next call to be forwarded to his senior KGB contact at another location. He dialed the number again. This time a woman answered.

"Good afternoon, Capitol Menswear. How can I help you?"

"Good afternoon, I was wondering if you have any wool suits on sale?"

"Yes, of course. Can you come in today? The sale ends tomorrow."

"Yes, thank you. I will be there," Cerberus said. He had actually written the protocol for investigating suspicious calls from or to FBI headquarters, and was confident that any agent monitoring the call would find it routine and not check it out further.

As an Assistant Director for Counter-intelligence, he could come and go as he wished without arousing suspicion. "Nancy, I'll be out for the afternoon. I need to buy some clothes for my European trip."

"Very good, Sir. Don't forget to pick up some matching shirts and ties," she advised. FBI secretaries developed a strong personal loyalty to their bosses, and protectively hovered over them like mother hens.

Cerberus drove out of the underground garage, waving to the security guards. He turned right on Ninth, then right again on Constitution. He headed for the Roosevelt Memorial Bridge and Arlington. Exiting the highway, he made his way to North Irving Street, the location of the KGB's most carefully disguised safe-house. It contained the most sophisticated satellite communications equipment in the attic, which could not be intercepted by the trackers at the National Security Agency. It also had a "bug-proof" basement with shielded walls. Two under-cover KGB agents, a husband and wife, maintained a visible residence there, pretending to be retired. He parked his car in a commuter lot several blocks away and walked down an alley, where the safe-house van was waiting. He jumped in.

During the short drive, there was no conversation. In the clandestine services of every nation, an operator tried to know as few people and as little information as possible, in case he was caught and interrogated. The driver moved the van into the garage and closed the garage door. Cerberus got out and entered the house. As he stepped carefully down the stairs to the basement, he was surprised to find the KGB Resident from the Soviet Embassy seated at a desk. He had expected someone of lesser rank. Several burly security officers stood near the far wall.

"Cerberus, *what* could be so important that you risk your cover to come here?" demanded the Resident.

"Colonel Zorinsky, I have just learned that one of your agents in Los Angeles has been compromised, and a KGB headquarters message has been obtained by the FBI. I don't know anything about the operation involved, but it apparently has something to do with a project named Pegasus."

The KGB officer looked like he had just seen a ghost. "Who is the FBI supervisor in charge of surveillance of our Pegasus agent?" asked Zorinsky. The Colonel only knew that Pegasus was a code-name for a very important project of some sort. KGB field officers had been liquidated for lesser sins. He was pleased that this was not technically his responsibility, which was held by someone in KGB headquarters in Moscow.

"A very good man, and a brilliant counter-intelligence expert. His name is Tilsdale."

"Can you reassign him without repercussions?"

"I suppose so, but it must be done in a way that makes it look like he is getting a promotion or a choice assignment. Tilsdale is an unusual personality. He loves his work more than his personal life. That's probably why his wife left him a few years ago."

"Well, please see to it immediately. I will take care of that stupid agent of ours in Los Angeles. *His* next assignment will be Siberia." Cerberus smiled. Neither actually knew the full importance and mission of Pegasus and the Trojan Horse project. Had they known, they would have been terrified.

"Do you have anything else?" asked the Russian.

"No, not at this time. I need to get back to the office and figure out what to do with Tilsdale in order to stop his surveillance. Can you get that Los Angeles KGB agent quickly reassigned?"

"Yes, I will do that. I am informed that we have a backup agent to replace him, a female professor on the faculty of that college. What is it called again?"

"UCLA."

"Oh, yes. Well, have a safe trip back."

"Thank you," said Cerberus. He climbed the stairs, entered the garage and got into the van. After retrieving his car, he began the drive back to Washington, feeling a sense of relief. He knew exactly how to stop Tilsdale's investigation. He could not suppress a smile at the irony of his solution.

Zorinsky was nervous. He ordered a report to be sent back to KGB headquarters. His instincts told him this was going to be trouble for someone, and he wanted to position himself on the safe side of it. Always the pragmatist, Zorinsky issued an order for the KGB field agent in Los Angeles, called "Goldmine" by the FBI, to be called back to Moscow. The man would be lucky if he were *not* sent to Siberia, Zorinsky mused. Better to scapegoat this problem to the lowest denominator, which was the field agent.

He was pleased with the quick response by Cerberus, even if using this mole was somewhat dangerous. Early information from Cerberus had enabled Col. Zorinsky to assign surveillance on Special Agent Tilsdale, starting in Los Angeles. Zorinsky knew all about Tilsdale, who had severely damaged the KGB network in the U.S. by his counter-espionage efforts. Senior officials within the KGB had wanted to "eliminate" Tilsdale, but Cerberus advised Zorinsky not to do this, since he was Tilsdale's boss. Killing Tilsdale would put the U.S. intelligence spotlight on Tilsdale's supervisor and subordinates, and Cerberus did not want that extra scrutiny. "Sometimes, even *you* have to resist your temptations," Cerberus reminded Zorinsky.

Chapter 4

Cerberus

In Roman and Greek mythology, Cerberus was the three-headed dog that guarded the gates of Hades, and prevented its residents from returning across the River Styx. The "Cerberus" known to the KGB acquired his code-name directly from Andropov, who, when plotting the proper role for Cerberus, felt that the name symbolized his plan with this human asset.

Cerberus, whose real name was David H. Dallinger, Jr., had been carefully recruited by the KGB during his undergraduate days at Princeton. Coming from a wealthy and well-connected New England family, he had every opportunity that a young man could want. As with many in the U.S. intelligence community, beginning with "Wild Bill" Donovan's Office of Strategic Services (OSS), he was a typical, polished product of the Ivy League university culture. He also had a romantic fascination with Leftist politics, on an intellectual level. Dallinger was a history major, but also had studied Russian, French, and German, and was fluent in those languages.

As a student during the Vietnam War years, he had become a secret member of several radical campus organizations. As with all intelligence services, the KGB field agents were always looking for new, young talent. The American college campuses were, and are, active "incubators" of radical-Left thinking and a rich source of potential candidates.

The KGB recruiters had noticed how clever and manipulative Dallinger was, never exposing himself and his identity in various violent incidents. He skillfully guided some of the most successful operations, like those conducted by the Weather Underground, Students for a Democratic Society, and the Black Panther Party. The best covert agents are "puppet masters," and accomplish their objectives by inducing others to take the risks while they remain hidden in the shadows. Dallinger clearly had this natural ability.

Dallinger maintained a charade of ambivalence about politics, as he joined the John Birch Society, the Federalist Society, and the Young Republicans in order to cover his true beliefs. He enjoyed sitting in the background when these conservative campus groups met, listening to their Right-wing ranting with amusement. *It is vital to know your enemy,* he said to himself. Any background check of his campus days would yield only an innocuous picture of a politically conservative and patriotic student. His Leftist activities were carefully buried by his new sponsors and his own careful planning.

Through intermediaries, the KGB had provided him with a summer trip to Europe after his graduation. It included a stop in Vienna, which like Lisbon and Madrid, was infested by spies from every country. This was where global spy business was conducted and sinister plans were hatched. During the trip, Dallinger was invited—alone—to visit the palatial home of a mysterious billionaire, located near the posh area of Lainzer Strasse. This was the home of one of the world's most dangerous and powerful KGB affiliates.

Victor Zebrotny had a lifelong alliance with the Soviets, dating back to his youth in Nazi-occupied Europe. He was born to a wealthy Jewish family in Prague, which with Communist Party assistance, narrowly escaped being herded into the growing number of Nazi death camps. Using all of their financial resources to bribe officials and obtain transportation, the family made it to neutral Portugal, which had been accommodating an influx of Jewish refugees.

Young Victor worked tirelessly with the MGB, predecessor of the KGB, to hunt down Nazi agents in the Iberian Peninsula. By the end of the war, he had gained the confidence of senior KGB officials. His wartime experiences had turned him into a strong believer in the Soviet Union and its ideology, which were the natural enemies of Nazi Germany. As written in the ancient Chinese proverb, "The enemy of my enemy is my friend."

The First Directorate of the KGB [foreign intelligence], and its organizational successor, the SVR, quickly recognized Victor's brilliance with financial matters and realized he could provide an excellent cover for the projects of their financial subversion unit. This unit was staffed by dozens of economists and financial experts. Its mission was to de-stabilize the economic structure of a foreign country through currency manipulation or failure of its banking system. Victor was seen as a potential surrogate in those important operations. He was also destined to become "Zeus," the covert sponsor and puppet-master of Pegasus, and key to the Chinese-Soviet Trojan Horse project.

As Victor proved his loyalty and financial expertise in ever-larger KGB missions, he was allowed to make millions for his personal wealth. He relocated to Vienna, with easy access to the corrupt banking system of Switzerland. This would become his operational base, from which he would disguise himself as a world-class philanthropist, giving millions of dollars to charities and Leftist social causes around the world, while carefully concealing his connection with the KGB. He needed the KGB, and they needed him.

During a two-week stay at Zebrotny's Austrian compound, the young man who would become Cerberus became enthralled with the eloquent billionaire's mastery of Socialist history and global politics. When he spoke, everything seemed to fit together nicely, and was completely logical. The American government was a threat to world peace and prosperity, and the only force standing in the way of American expansionism was the Soviet Union—the last fortress of true Socialism. Near the end of his stay, Zebrotny asked Dallinger if he would like to meet an important Soviet official. Dallinger was delighted that he could have such an opportunity.

Zebrotny introduced him to Andropov, and the three spent hours discussing Socialist solutions to the world's problems. Finally, Andropov turned to Dallinger and said, "We need someone of your intellect and commitment to Socialist ideals who is willing to help us prevent the atrocities of capitalism on the world. If you will help us—confidentially, of course—we will support you with the financing and technical assistance that will enable you to make a positive mark on history."

"I am humbled that you would ask me," said Dallinger. "But what can I do?"

"We think long-term," said Andropov. "We will sponsor you to get a law degree from a top university, and help you get an important government job. From that point, you will become our secret watch-dog within the U.S. government, and be in a position to prevent them from persecuting our allies and representatives in the U.S." Andropov deftly "sugar-coated" the description of a "mole." He did not want to scare this young man off, or offend his sensibilities at this delicate point.

Little by little, Andropov set the hook. Using Zebrotny's shell corporations, the KGB financed Dallinger during his Harvard Law School years. As always, Dallinger excelled intellectually and won a job with the FBI upon graduation. He was now committed, and there was no way for him to back out. The KGB owned him.

Dallinger displayed a superior grasp of covert operations, and his FBI superiors—ironically—carefully groomed him toward the specialty of counter-intelligence. With KGB training, he had learned how to "beat" the annual polygraph examinations, and background checks found nothing out of place in his personal or financial life. Dallinger was burrowed into the Bureau's infrastructure, to be used at the KGB's discretion.

As with all double-agents, Dallinger soon became aware that he had gone down an irreversible path, from which there was no return. Always the pragmatist, he resigned himself to make the best of it. He became obsessed with the intellectual challenge of his predicament. He was immersed in a deadly cat-and-mouse game, and had to outsmart his Bureau adversaries, using his own cunning and instincts against their sophisticated investigative tools and experts. Brad Tilsdale was one of those experts that worried him, who had to be successfully deceived. Controlling Tilsdale was one of the most valuable services he could render to his masters at the KGB.

Chapter 5

Deception and Damage Control

Victor Zebrotny's favorite meeting place with his senior KGB contacts was in the ski resort of Salzburg, where he had acquired a second huge mansion that overlooked the ski slopes. It was impossible to conduct surveillance on him and his guests in this mountainous location, which is why KGB Chairman Yuri Andropov preferred to meet him there. Every year, Victor and Yuri would meet and go over the past year's operations, together with plans for the future. This is where Victor first learned of the role he would play in Project Trojan Horse, and his sponsorship of the young man called Pegasus.

"Yuri, I am honored that you would think of me for this role," said Victor.

"Victor, you have earned your place in this important project," noted Yuri. "We are going to thoroughly indoctrinate this bright young man, and then push him through the American political system. We envision that he will emerge on the political scene sometime after 2000. He will need your financial backing to gain his education, and to position himself within the local Chicago political system.

Undoubtedly, he will need your money—*our* money—to buy off corrupt politicians in order to execute the plan." His pointed reminder of how Victor had become so rich brought a smile to Victor's face.

"That should be no problem," said Victor. "But why stop there? I suggest a concurrent infiltration of their political media sources, which can add support to his rise to power."

"Victor, that is an excellent idea, and it shows how correct we were in entering into our alliance with you years ago. We are already working on that."

"Yuri, you know how much I despise American capitalism and social policies. Also, their election of Reagan, a neo-Conservative, is an outrage. We need to change that country and bring it peacefully into the new world order. Their adventurism can no longer be tolerated!"

The KGB Chairman thought how fortunate he was to have developed this man for the KGB. "Well said, Victor! I agree with your ideas. Just keep me advised, please." Andropov failed to mention that the KGB, which trusts no one, had kept a close eye on Zebrotny since the start of their relationship. "Now, where is that French champagne you were telling me about?"

Back in his office at FBI headquarters, Dallinger placed a call to Special Agent Tilsdale on a secure telephone line.

"This is Special Agent Brad Tilsdale."

"Brad, how are you? I have enjoyed reading your latest workups."

"Fine, Sir. We are getting some interesting stuff on that Pegasus case."

"Well, great. But I have something much more interesting, and it's really made for someone of your talents."

"Really? Can you tell me about it?"

"Not on the telephone. Catch the red-eye flight, and be in my office by 10:00 a.m. tomorrow. Plan on staying about three days."

"I understand, Sir. I'll see you tomorrow." Tilsdale hung up, and sat staring at the wall. Something did not feel right.

One of Tilsdale's agents drove him out to Los Angeles International Airport to catch a late-night flight. The agent noticed that his boss was much quieter than usual. He obviously had something on his mind.

Tilsdale was met at the ticket counter by the American Airlines manager, and escorted into the back office, where he presented his identification. "Will you be carrying a firearm on board, Sir?" asked the manager.

"Yes." Tilsdale was dressed in casual clothes, including a light windbreaker. He pulled his jacket back to show a Glock pistol in a shoulder holster. Most FBI agents still carried the standard-issue .357 Magnum Smith & Wesson revolver, with a six-shot capacity. The Glock Model 17 was a new Austrian-made, 9mm automatic. Its reliability, combined with its impressive 17-round magazine, made it the perfect weapon for Tilsdale, a master marksman, especially with "hot load" hollow-point ammo to increase its stopping power. Equipped with tritium "night sights," he carried the pistol in a Galco Miami Classic shoulder-holster. The Glock's compact silhouette made it easy to conceal, which Tilsdale and his counter-intelligence team found to be a useful characteristic.

The airline manager filled out a special form and Tilsdale signed it. This was to be provided to the captain of the flight, so that he would know that an armed officer was in the cabin. The flight attendants would also be informed, in case they spotted his weapon. Airline crews were accustomed to this situation, because federal, state and local law enforcement officers, including Sky Marshals, routinely carried their weapons while traveling. Tilsdale viewed the seating chart, and selected a seat in Business Class, on the aisle. This would give him a clear view of the cockpit door. He had always been concerned that airliner cockpits were not sufficiently secure, and that someone who wanted to bring the plane down could force an entry.

The airline customer service manager escorted Tilsdale through security, and he proceeded to the gate. By instinct and training, he found a seat against the wall, where he could observe people as they waited or walked past, and no one could approach him from behind. You never know when you might see a "wanted" subject, especially in a transportation terminal. Without even realizing it, his eyes shifted from person to person, scanning for anything unusual or a face from a "wanted" poster.

Finally, the flight was boarded, and he lined up with the crowd going down the jetway. As he stepped through the big door of the DC-10, the flight attendant smiled at him. "Welcome aboard, Sir." She looked at his boarding pass, and recognized the code for an armed law enforcement officer. "Seat 12B, Sir. Straight ahead."

Tilsdale sat down, placing his briefcase beneath the seat in front of him. No one really noticed him, because like many FBI agents, he did not stand out in a crowd. He was in his early thirties, of average height, weight and appearance. However, even when he appeared to be resting, watching the in-flight movie, or eating, he was acutely aware of what was going on in his environment. Few details or audible conversations escaped him. His ex-wife hated this part of him, because she never had his full attention and he never relaxed.

After takeoff, Tilsdale began thinking about the unusual directive to travel to Washington. His mind clicked through an inventory of active cases, but none of them would have required his presence at headquarters. He sensed that something else was going on.

When the aircraft reached cruising altitude, the seat belt sign went off and Tilsdale got up to move through the cabin. It was another chance to survey the individuals on board, while they were all facing forward. Without people doing bad things, the FBI would be out of business. People were unpredictable, and you *never* knew what was right around the corner.

Moving down the left aisle in the main cabin, Tilsdale squeezed by the flight attendants and their beverage cart. As he scanned the passengers, his peripheral vision caught a male passenger looking at him. Tilsdale possessed an uncanny sixth sense, enabling him to form accurate conclusions from small bits of disconnected information. He had already become a legend in the hide-bound FBI, as this quality of intuition and creativity was rare. Under the prior, autocratic reign of J. Edgar Hoover, such free-thinking was not encouraged. Being "efficient" and robotically following your superiors' orders normally defined the path of advancement within the Bureau. Tilsdale was an anomaly, and he enjoyed the role of being a maverick.

He continued to the back of the big aircraft in the lavatory area, and looked back at the man, who was seated on the aisle in a coach seat. There was something about the man that triggered his instincts. He passed around the rear bulkhead and headed back to the front of the aircraft via the right aisle. Tilsdale looked straight ahead, avoiding eye contact with the man, but his peripheral vision was focused on the inquisitive passenger as he walked forward. Having lost sight of Tilsdale, the man turned completely around, looking back down the left aisle. *I'm being tailed,* thought Tilsdale. He returned to his seat.

After finishing his Diet Coke, Tilsdale got up and headed to the galley area, where he found the First Flight Attendant. "Miss, let's keep this very quiet and routine. I'm Special Agent Tilsdale, FBI."

"Yes, Sir, I know," she replied, somewhat nervously. "What's the problem?"

"No problem. I just need to see the passenger manifest. I thought I spotted an old friend of mine, but I don't want to look stupid, if it's actually not him. And I would appreciate it if you would not say anything to him."

"Certainly. I've had the same thing happen to me," she said, smiling. "One time I thought I saw an old boy friend from high school in an airport, and I embarrassed myself by asking him how he was."

Tilsdale forced a smile, and said, "Exactly. I don't want to look silly." He studied the name by seat 25C: Mr. Andrew Bermann. *Probably a domestic resident agent,* he speculated, *and most likely a KGB surveillance operator.* "No, I'm sorry. It isn't who I thought it was, Miss. Thank you. Sorry to have bothered you."

"Not a problem! Do you live in Washington?"

"No. Los Angeles. How about you?"

"I live in the McLean area, near Dulles Airport. How long are you staying in Washington?" Eliana Gómez found

Tilsdale attractive, especially since he had the mystique of being an FBI agent. *She is really a strikingly beautiful woman, probably in her mid-twenties,* Tilsdale thought.

Tilsdale always became uneasy with this type of conversation. He disliked it when he had to give out information, and he never trusted anyone completely. "I'm not sure— probably a couple of days."

The attractive brunette's eyes lit up. "Really? Would you like to go to dinner or something?" Tilsdale normally would have refused. He did not make friends or lovers easily, unless he had carefully studied them from a distance to make sure he knew what he was dealing with. However, he saw an immediate benefit to having a visible relationship with her. It would give him a good cover for his trip to Washington, as he could use her as an excuse for being here. *Sometimes you must use what is readily available, including people.* The KGB operative would report this to his superiors, and they might have less curiosity about his presence in Washington. However, Tilsdale was unaware that this was not a routine surveillance by the KGB, that his own superior was a KGB agent, and the tail had been assigned by no less than Washington's chief KGB officer.

"May I call you Eliana?" asked Tilsdale. "I would love to have dinner with you. And my name is Brad," he said with a grin.

Her face lit up. "Of course! Here is my phone number and address. Please call me when you know what your schedule will be," she beamed. Eliana had no idea that she was being used as a cover.

"You can count on it. I'm looking forward to getting to know you better," he said. "I wonder if you could do me a big favor. Did you happen to know what the man in 25C is drinking? In case it *is* my old friend, I need his fingerprints to play a little joke on him. Can you retrieve his glass without getting your fingerprints on it?"

"Wow! This is cool! Sure, I always wear rubber gloves in the cabin when picking up trash anyway, and I'll get his glass and stuff a napkin inside to mark it and keep it separate from the others." She winked, and left to pick up beverage containers in the left aisle. A few minutes later, she returned with a trash bag.

"Here it is," she said, pulling a plastic cup from the bag.

"Could you put it in a sandwich bag or something?" he asked.

Eliana was happy to gain favor with Tilsdale. She carefully inserted the container in a plastic bag and gave it to him.

"Eliana, you are wonderful. Thanks! I guess I had better sit down. I see the seat belt sign is on again."

Several hours later, the DC-10 landed at Dulles, and the "people-mover" vehicles began taking the passengers to the main terminal. This was a feature of Dulles that Tilsdale never liked. Instead of building a standard terminal design, the airport authorities had opted for a space-saving arrangement of parking the aircraft away from the main terminal and running shuttle vehicles that looked like they came right out of a science fiction movie. It was easy to miss a flight, if you missed the last "people-mover" to your aircraft.

Tilsdale noticed that "Mr. Bermann" pushed forward to get on the same people-mover. *That confirms it,* thought Tilsdale. His instinct told him to keep this surveillance to himself, and not even tell his boss at FBI headquarters. He had learned a long time ago that it could be as important to *withhold* information as it is to *obtain* it. He decided to check on "Mr. Bermann" through his personal contacts at NSA, CIA, and DIA (Defense Intelligence Agency), rather than through the Bureau. He could always initiate that internal process, if necessary.

Eliana had rushed to get on his "people-mover," and sat next to him. In the reflected window images of the people-mover, Tilsdale noted that "Bermann" was watching him. *Time to put on a show,* he decided.

He leaned over to Eliana and whispered, "I have to see someone downtown, but how about dinner tonight?"

She smiled and whispered, "I'll be looking forward to it. Six o'clock?"

"Wonderful. See you then," he replied, as the people-mover arrived at the terminal.

As Tilsdale exited the people-mover, he spotted an athletic young man in a suit, scanning the departing passengers. "Mr. Tilsdale?" he asked.

"Good morning, I'm Brad Tilsdale," he said, shaking hands.

"Agent Dave Tucker, Sir. Pleasure to meet you." Tilsdale was well known within the Bureau, and becoming a legend for his ability to solve the most difficult spy cases. Tucker felt lucky to have met this rising star. "I have a car waiting. Would you like to go directly to headquarters, or your hotel?"

"Let's go to the hotel. I need to change clothes." The Bureau still required "business dress" within the headquarters, regardless of your specialty unit.

"Very good, Sir."

The two men walked to a waiting car. Tilsdale placed his luggage in the back seat, and took the passenger seat next to Tucker. "Dave, I have a plastic cup here in a sandwich bag. I want you to take this directly to the headquarters forensic lab annex and have them do a fingerprint analysis. Tell Dr. Robbins that I want the print ID report to be held in his custody in confidential status, for me only. You are not to mention this to anyone, OK?"

"Yes, Sir!" Tucker was delighted to be entrusted with something that Tilsdale was working on. Sometimes promotions can happen from such opportunities.

When the car arrived at the Mayflower Hotel, Tilsdale got out. "I'll get my luggage. Thanks for the ride. And don't forget the goddam cup!"

"No, Sir! It's been a pleasure to meet you!" Tucker drove away.

As Tilsdale picked up his luggage, he pretended not to notice a late-model sedan parked up the street on Connecticut Avenue, with two men inside. *Something is definitely going on here,* he thought. He decided to proceed very carefully, until he understood what *was* going on. The first order of business was to determine who the surveillance team was working for. First, he had to meet with his boss, the Assistant Director.

Arriving at the FBI headquarters, he showed his ID to the security team, and was asked to wait for an escort to the eighth floor, where the offices of the Bureau's senior managers were located. In a few minutes, an agent approached him from the elevators.

"Welcome to Washington, Mr. Tilsdale," said the agent.

"Thank you."

"The Assistant Director is waiting for you." Tilsdale followed the agent into the executive elevator. Arriving at the eighth floor, the agent directed him to the office of the Assistant Director for Counter-Intelligence.

The imperial reign of J. Edgar Hoover ended with his

death in 1972. That had opened up the senior positions for the first time in decades, and under Director William Webster, the Bureau had become more like the other federal law enforcement agencies, instead of the personal fiefdom operated by Hoover.

"Brad, good to see you," David Dallinger said, shaking his hand.

"Thank you, Sir, good to be here."

"Nancy, hold all of my calls. I don't want to be disturbed."

"Yes, Sir," the secretary replied, smiling at Tilsdale. Even the Bureau secretaries knew of Tilsdale's reputation, and viewed him as somewhat of a mysterious celebrity within the buttoned-down agency.

Dallinger motioned for Tilsdale to sit down, as he closed the door. "Brad, what I am going to tell you is rated Cosmic." Tilsdale was surprised. "Cosmic" was a security classification reserved for the most sensitive national security matters, a level above "Ultra," which is above "Top Secret." Only the most threatening security matters received this label.

"Brad, we have a mole, somewhere in the Bureau. We have suspected this for a long time, but the CIA has been losing field operatives who had some linkage or communication with the Bureau. We have to find this individual, and fast. This is a case that was *made* for you, and all of your special skills will be needed. Look, let me be honest. I've been in management so long, I have become more of an expert paper-pusher than a field operative. I wouldn't know where to begin, but you will."

"Well, I appreciate your confidence, Sir, but surely there are other senior agents at headquarters that could handle this. As you know, I have several active cases back on the West Coast, and that is where my team is."

"I know, Brad, but this one has top priority. That comes right from the Director. We want to nail this mole before the other agencies find out about it. That would do enormous damage to the Bureau, as I'm sure you understand."

"Yes, Sir."

"Brad, we want to reassign you to headquarters, working directly for me. This is a very important assignment, and could catapult you into a big promotion. Hell, I might even wind up working for you!" Dallinger smiled. "How about it? Will you take it?"

"The way you put it, Sir, I couldn't say no," replied Tilsdale.

"Great! I want to brief you with what we know so far." Dallinger already had planted evidence within the Bureau, which, he believed, would lead Tilsdale down a blind alley and keep him occupied. In the meantime, he would dismantle Tilsdale's Los Angeles unit, and disperse its agents and cases to other offices. He was sure that would prevent Tilsdale from uncovering the Pegasus matter in Los Angeles. Unfortunately for Dallinger, he did not really know Tilsdale and how his mind worked.

He gave Tilsdale several documents that suggested the mole was working out of the CIA liaison unit, which had about 50 agents. "If I were to guess, someone in this unit has been passing sensitive information to the KGB and then trying to plant false trails in other departments. It's very confusing. This guy must be very good."

"Well, false leads are a two-edged blade," Tilsdale commented. "They often yield clues as to who did the planting. I'll check them out." Dallinger realized that he would need to be careful with this man. Tilsdale was not a typical FBI agent.

"In the meantime, Brad, we want you to move here as soon as possible. This thing is top priority with the Director, for obvious reasons."

"Yes, Sir. I travel light these days, so I can be back here in a week, if that's OK."

"That will be fine."

"By the way, who will be replacing me in Los Angeles?"

"Frankly, in your field, you are not replaceable. We will be transferring your cases and agents to match our field office workload. For budget reasons, that is mandatory."

Tilsdale frowned. He knew that most of the other offices were not equipped or trained to do counter-espionage cases. "Well, Sir, I might suggest that you place most of them with either Seattle or Miami. Those offices have most of the counter-espionage talent."

"Great. We will try to do that. Thanks for that information." Dallinger got up, signaling that the meeting was over.

Tilsdale's head was spinning, as he tried to adjust to the changes imposed on him. In a matter of fifteen minutes, his entire life had changed course. What he did not know was that a career crisis was looming over the horizon. He would soon be forced to make a difficult decision on personal loyalties. In the meantime, he decided to check in with the lab director, Dr. Robbins.

Tilsdale walked through the building and found the entrance to the laboratory annex. The main FBI lab was located on the Marine base at Quantico, VA. The FBI lab unit had achieved international prominence as a top forensic lab, and supported state and local law enforcement requests, as well as those from the FBI itself. Dr. Hal Robbins was a classic scientist, complete with white lab coat, beard and glasses, and was devoted to his work.

"Hi, I'm Brad Tilsdale," he said to the lab receptionist. "Is Dr. Robbins around?"

"Yes, Sir. I'll page him for you," said the woman, studying Tilsdale intently. She had also heard of him, and wondered why he was here.

"Brad, how are you?" asked Robbins, shaking his hand.

"Fine, Doc. Could we talk about something?"

"Sure. Let's go into my office." Robbins led Tilsdale to a large office, piled with file boxes, stacks of books and several computer monitors. "I suppose this concerns that plastic drink container?"

"That's right. Did you find the prints?"

"Oh, yes. Do you want us to run them?"

"Sure, but I am the only person that receives the results, OK?"

"Sure, Brad. It will just take a minute." Robbins picked up the phone and dialed a number. "Henry, we got some prints off a plastic container. Do you have them? OK, go ahead and run them through the system. E-mail the results to me, and do not file them in the main system yet. Leave them in the hold file." Robbins hung up the phone and looked at Tilsdale.

"What kind of case is this, Brad?" asked Robbins. It was not normal procedure to do an ID in this manner.

"Oh, just a routine inquiry. I'm cross-checking some evidence that we may have to use in a court proceeding." *No need to give him the entire story,* thought Tilsdale.

After a few minutes of small talk, the phone rang. Robbins answered.

"Hi, Henry. *Really?* Send them to me by secure e-mail." Robbins frowned.

"Brad, I'll put this up on the screen. Seems odd. The

prints belong to a STASI [East German secret police] agent. All of the NATO intelligence services have been looking for him for years, following several assassinations in Europe. His name is Erich Wolkmann. Where did you obtain his prints?"

"Oh, we just found them on a routine premises search. The evidence is quite old, so we don't need to do anything with this report. I'll have my people deal with it."

"No problem. I have more than enough cases running around here, anyway," said Robbins.

"Thanks, Doc. See you later. And I would appreciate it if you would keep the matter of these prints to yourself. Tell Henry to do the same."

"Certainly." Robbins smiled, but thought, *This is unusual. Why would we worry about sharing this information inside of FBI headquarters?*

As Tilsdale walked to the elevators, he thought, *Why is a Stasi agent tailing me?* The East German secret police organization was controlled by the KGB, and frequently used when the KGB wanted to avoid direct involvement in some matter. He surmised—correctly—that answering this question would answer many more.

Chapter 6

The Candidate

The young man wondered why he had been called to the office of Professor Lydia Baroshta. He had never taken a course with her, and knew very little about her. Lydia, on the other hand, knew quite a lot about this gifted student, Husam Khalil Basi, who went by the name of "Sam."

Lydia had put together an impressive dossier on Sam Basi, including photographs, test scores, grade point average, and known associates. He was a handsome young man of mixed race, and had been raised as a Muslim.

Sam's father, Karimi, had been a wealthy Nigerian from the city of Kano, in the northern Hausa district of Nigeria. Karimi had made his fortune in the Nigerian oil business after moving to Lagos as a young man. It was there that he came under the Marxist influence of the founders of MEND (Movement for the Emancipation of the Niger Delta), a militant insurgent group that sought to redistribute Nigeria's oil wealth. Karimi quickly became the technical expert within MEND, and advised the rebels on how to attack the vulnerable oil fields.

During his work in southern Nigeria, Karimi met and fell in love with an American Peace Corps worker from San Francisco, Alicia Ludbury. Alicia, a beautiful white woman, found her love affair with Karimi to be an irresistible rebellion against the values of her conservative parents, who were horrified to learn of her relationship with a black man. After they married, Alicia became pregnant. She intended to stay with Karimi and give birth in Nigeria. Alicia had become enthralled with the romantic notion of being married to a black revolutionary, and she adopted his Marxist leanings with enthusiasm. She wore her pregnancy like a symbol of ideological honor.

As her delivery date neared, she told her Peace Corps friends that she would be staying in Nigeria and raising her child there. Even in the liberal Peace Corps of that time, this was a shocking revelation. One of her friends advised her that she needed to be careful to maintain her U.S. citizenship, because in the event of trouble in Nigeria, that would be the best way to get her Nigerian husband and her child into the U.S.

Alicia began to be concerned for their safety, when government forces began rounding up rebel operatives and executing them. One afternoon, Karimi returned home and told her to pack up essential items. They were going to a "safe-house," where the Nigerian police could not find them.

After arriving at the house in suburban Lagos, Alicia went into labor. With the help of a midwife, she gave birth to Husam Khalil, a healthy son. As she recuperated from the stress of the birth, Karimi told her that they were in extreme danger, as the rebels had just blown up an oil platform and taken the surviving workers hostage. The Nigerian government declared martial law, and Karimi feared retaliation. He urged her to fly out of the country, back to the U.S. "I'll join you in a few weeks," he promised.

That was the last time Alicia ever saw him. A few months

later, she learned that he had been apprehended and killed by the Nigerian police. More than sorrow, she felt the need to carry on his Marxist ideology.

Using her American passport and the money that Karimi had given her, she bought a one-way ticket to San Francisco, via London and New York. Not understanding the nuances of U.S. immigration law, she decided to create a false birth certificate for her baby, and make him a "pure" U.S. citizen.

After arriving in San Francisco, she rented an apartment near the UC Berkeley campus. She then contacted some old college friends who were connected to the radical Weather Underground, a violent splinter group from the Leftist group, Students for a Democratic Society. She asked one of them how she could establish Husam's birth in the U.S., and was instructed to contact a certain clerical worker—Leona Waller—at one of the big San Francisco area hospitals. She arranged to meet the woman at a coffee shop near the hospital.

"This is very risky for me. I don't want to lose my job," the young woman told Alicia, glancing furtively from side to side.

"I understand. I will pay you for the risk you are taking, but I want my son to receive documentation that proves he was born here."

"I understand. But I will need $5,000, in cash. After you give me the money, I will create a birth file, and forge the necessary records, including a birth certificate. It will look as if you had been in the hospital for two days, and gave birth here."

"OK, I will do it. You will have the money tomorrow." She was relieved that Karimi had wired her $25,000 to become established in San Francisco.

At the second meeting, Alicia handed the woman $5,000

in cash. In return, the woman gave her a large envelope, containing a forged birth certificate for the baby. "I hope it works for you," the woman said. "Good luck." Alicia made a note in her diary of the woman's name and contact information, in the event that errors in the baby's birth documentation became a problem later. Many years later, this diary entry would prove to be evidence that could change history, if it were discovered in time.

"Thank you," replied Alicia. Now there would be no question that her mixed-race son was a U.S. citizen. She felt relieved.

In the next few years, Alicia obtained a Ph.D. and began teaching at UC-Berkeley in the political science department. Succumbing to the influences of one of the nation's most liberal faculties, she became intensely anti-capitalist and began to hate what America stood for. Several of her scholarly writings were published in various liberal magazines and Leftist journals, and she became a star in the growing Left-wing political movement in the San Francisco Bay Area.

All of this had a profound effect on her young son, who attended an exclusive private school in Berkeley. With his mother's coaching, he practiced the Muslim faith, like his father, and became an avid reader of Leftist philosophers and theoreticians. In his mind, the Bolshevik Revolution in Russia was a heroic triumph of justice over tyranny, dwarfing the American Revolution in importance. Even as a young boy, he imagined himself leading crowds of insurgents in armed attacks on the Czar's palace. His mother once pointed at the White House and told him, "That is *our* Czar's palace. We need to remove *this* Czar, too, and redistribute all wealth to the people."

In high school, Sam showed incredible poise and

aptitude with public speaking. He became a state finalist on the debate team, and became interested in law. A voracious reader, he saw from current events how one could use the law and the vulnerabilities of American government to achieve bloodless victories, with lasting consequences. He began to see himself as an advocate and future hero for the poor and downtrodden, a sort of medieval champion of the masses, astride an imaginary white horse.

His mother continued to guide him, and decided that he should attend college away from home. She decided to send him to UCLA, a school where one of her close friends from Leftist organizations had joined the faculty. The friend's name was Lydia Boroshta.

"Excuse me, Professor Boroshta. I believe you asked me to stop by," said Sam.

"Yes, Sam. You have indicated that you would like to pursue a Doctorate in political science, which, as you know, is my specialty."

"Yes, I would. However, I am only a sophomore."

"I know. I would like to know if you wish to compete for a special program that is being funded through a grant. The winner will be transferring to Harvard University in Cambridge, Massachusetts, followed by graduate studies in political science and history. All expenses will be paid by an anonymous wealthy donor, including tuition."

"That is exactly what I would like to do," said Sam. "What do I have to do to apply?"

"I am going to give you a test. Answer the questions in this booklet, and then bring the answer sheet back to me. If you score the highest, you will be the candidate." In fact, she had already concluded that Sam *was* the candidate, and fulfilled all of the parameters that her superiors at KGB-Moscow had identified. Sam was already a talented speaker and debater. He also demonstrated a strong affinity for radical-Left politics, and like many young people, believed that corporate America and capitalism were behind most of the world's ills. She and her colleagues intended to reinforce that thinking.

Lydia, whose codename within the KGB was "Emerald," encoded a MOST SECRET report to her headquarters contact. She used the S-5 communications protocol, which normally would have been adequate to avoid detection. However, a recent breakthrough with the KGB code allowed her encrypted Telex, sent to a KGB drop box in Warsaw, to be intercepted and decoded by the National Security Agency's computers at Ft. Meade, Maryland:

"MOST SECRET: Ref. Pegasus project, top candidate has been identified as a second-year student at UCLA, Los Angeles: Husam Khalil Basi. Subject is Muslim by family background and fulfills all requirements as previously stated. Materials supporting evaluation are being forwarded through Soviet Consulate diplomatic pouch, using courier. After review, please advise next action. /s/ Emerald."

From his Moscow office, Andropov studied the message and the file he had just received. This *was* good news! He had been reviewing dozens of files from his KGB agents, but this one seemed perfect in every way. He called his communications clerk, and dictated a response to Emerald:

"MOST SECRET: Ref. Pegasus, we accept your recommendation. Execute next phase, and coordinate with Miami agents to complete transfer of Pegasus to Atlantis. Well done. /s/ Socrates."

At the National Security Agency (NSA) at Ft. Meade, Maryland, the big gray antennas, shaped like giant bowls, stood guard around the clock. Standing in a silent row, like sentinels, they rarely moved except when they followed an aerial source of radio transmissions, such as a communications satellite. Special electronic "traps" had been secretly  attached to most of the undersea cables and major land communication "nodes," so that no signal would escape the NSA's grasp. After interception, the volume of digital traffic required special tools to "mine" its depths, and only NSA had them.

The NSA super-computers were the most sophisticated in the world, and had been custom-built to handle the massive amount of data collected each day. Within the intelligence community, it was widely believed that the NSA could (and did) intercept all electronic communications around the globe, and could break any code or cipher. The challenge for NSA was to distill this information and quickly produce usable intelligence products for its "customers," like the White House, CIA, State and Defense Departments, DIA, Secret Service, DEA, and FBI.

Once the data was collected, the monolithic rows of huge Cray super-computers, installed in a labyrinth of bomb-proof tunnels beneath the NSA headquarters building, zoomed through the digital elements of the intercepts at lightning speed in search of names, code-words, locations of interest, and "alert words" in over fifty languages. When enough "hits" occurred, the transmission was pulled from the digital universe of intercepts and sent by computer network to Decoding. There, a team of analysts reviewed the "catch" to see if it was worth decoding and pursuing. The Telex messages between Emerald and her bosses at KGB headquarters had been pulled and reviewed, as several key words, or "flags," had been found by the computers. After decoding, they were sent to Analysis.

The senior NSA analyst receiving them viewed these messages with concern. The Soviets were up to something big. If he had known that "Atlantis" was a remote KGB safe-house in the Cayman Islands, he would have been even more concerned. He sent an e-mail to his supervisor, Analysis Director Melissa Clayton, and requested a conference.

The instructions from Moscow meant that Sam Basi was about to go on a trip to meet his destiny. Sam's summer vacation would not be what he expected. Professor Baroshta dialed her agent contacts, and gave a coded message by telephone. That evening, she called Sam. "Hi, Sam. I have great news. You are the winner of the grant program!"

"Oh, wow! This is great! I can't wait to tell my mother!"

"Now, Sam, let me tell you how this works. The donor is a very fussy old guy, and demands complete confidentiality. He doesn't want his generosity to become known. If you tell *anyone* about this program, including your mother, you will be terminated immediately, and you will owe the donor's foundation all of the money that was spent up to that point."

"Oh, OK. No problem. I don't tell my mom very much anyway."

"All right, but don't forget! This is very important, and I don't want to lose you from this great program." Lydia did not explain that "termination" from the program also meant that Sam would permanently "disappear." The KGB did not want another Lee Harvey Oswald problem.

Chapter 7

Detour to Atlantis

FBI Agent Brad Tilsdale was setting up his office in the Washington headquarters of the FBI, when the telephone rang. It was NSA supervisor Melissa Clayton, who had known Tilsdale since he was a Midshipman at the Naval Academy and she was a student at Georgetown University. She had always found him attractive. "Brad? Melissa Clayton. How *are* you? I just found out from a friend at the Bureau that you are going to be in DC now!"

"Yes, that's right. Be careful what you wish for, because you just might get it! Didn't you tell me that?"

"Yes, I did," she laughed. "But I have a problem over here, and wonder if you could take a look at it."

Tilsdale's ears perked up. When NSA asks for help, something important is going on. "Sure, be glad to. Can I come over there? Oops, I forgot. You guys don't exist!"

"Very funny. I am always where *you* can find me, Brad Tilsdale. Hey, get your skinny ass over here!"

Melissa was a no-nonsense lady, and he had always liked her. "OK, I can be there by 1500. That OK?"

"Sure. Ask for me and use my name to get in. Don't show your badge, don't wear a piece [gun], and don't mention you are with the FBI. This is not an official liaison— yet."

"Got it. See ya."

After a one-hour drive up I-295 to the NSA facility at Ft. Meade, Tilsdale rolled up to the outer NSA security gate. He gave his name, and Melissa's authorization got him to the next security gate, where he was required to show his driver's license and give a digital fingerprint. He was approved to go to the visitor's lobby, another secure holding area. The NSA was even more paranoid than the CIA about security. In fact, there had never been an espionage penetration of this agency, while the CIA and FBI had both been compromised several times during the Cold War. Roving K-9 patrols and guards armed with H&K MP-5 submachine guns and .45 semi-automatic pistols roamed the hallways and outside perimeter, and looked like they were serious about their assignments. After all, this was truly the "Fort Knox" of communications intercepts, cryptology, and data "mining." Originating with the American code-breakers of World War II, the NSA was a vital component of America's national security organization, and even its Congressional budget was classified.

Melissa had been a college track star, and had majored in computer science. She joined the NSA soon after receiving her Ph.D. She was still single, and had made it a point to keep tabs on Tilsdale. They had dated in college, and she had always hoped he would marry her. However, the elusive Tilsdale moved around after graduating from Annapolis, and seemed completely obsessed with his career. She was shattered when she learned that he had married a woman from California, but she found out he had divorced the woman a few years ago.

Melissa walked up to the reception desk. "Hello, Brad. You look great." Tilsdale was not physically impressive to look at, but he was obviously in excellent shape. He had maintained his black-belt status and conditioning in *Shotokan Karate,* a martial art he had learned while stationed in Japan, and could easily kill an opponent with a single blow of his hand. His knuckles and the heels of his hands still showed the scars from hand-strike training against wooden boards.

"A little tired, I suppose. Hi, Melissa. It's great to see you." He took her hand and held it a little longer than normal. Melissa still had the body of an athlete, with long legs and flat stomach. *Nice ass,* Tilsdale thought to himself. He wondered if she was still interested.

"Let's go up to my conference room." She led the way, through a maze of security doors that required a special card and a retina scan. They reached a large conference room and entered.

"Make yourself comfortable. Coffee?" she asked.

"Sure. Black with sugar, please."

"Brad, we just processed a pair of intercepts. One communication came from Los Angeles." She handed Tilsdale the message sent by Emerald. "The other one came from KGB-Moscow. They are discussing something or somebody called 'Pegasus.'" She gave him Andropov's response.

Tilsdale normally was able to hide his emotions, but when he saw the word "Pegasus," his jaw dropped. "Holy shit," he mumbled. Now there was a new player: Emerald. There was also a place called "Atlantis." It was obviously a code-word, and he wondered where that was.

"Brad, we normally don't get involved with message content—that's the job of other experts, like you. But it sometimes helps us do our job better if we can understand the context of the message traffic. Is there something you can tell me about this? Should we be targeting this communications pairing?"

"Yes, Melissa. Please put a 'red tag' on this [meaning that NSA would monitor all similar communications and give priority to ones that related to the case content]. And please report all future transmissions to me only. Here's a business card with my pager number. Page me, and I'll call you back on a secure line, or come over to see you."

"I think I would prefer the latter," said Melissa with a sultry smile.

"So would I," replied Tilsdale. "Let's hope there is a lot of message traffic." They both laughed.

Tilsdale rented a townhouse in Georgetown, and completed his move to Washington. As Dallinger continued his secret effort to dismantle the Los Angeles counter-espionage unit, one of Tilsdale's former subordinates advised him that he had been ordered to send the Pegasus file to Washington. An intuitional bell went off in Tilsdale's head. "Are you sending it to me?" he asked.

"No, Sir. I am supposed to send it directly to the ADCI [Assistant Director for Counter-Intelligence]." Tilsdale had that old feeling—it appeared that the game was on.

"I'll tell you what, Jeff. Send it to me first, and I'll take it up to him. If anyone gigs you on this, tell them that's what I ordered you to do."

"Yes, Sir."

A few days later, several sealed file boxes arrived by courier. Tilsdale told his secretary to copy the entire lot, and then to reseal the boxes and send them up to the ADCI, who was, of course, Cerberus. *What exactly is the issue with "Pegasus?"* he wondered. He needed to know more, but he did not want to attract attention—particularly since a mole was operating inside the Bureau. He had to trust someone, but needed to have a contact at a very high level, in order to be able to operate without the mole's knowledge. He needed to find a high-level manager within the Bureau—one that was "street-smart," and that could absolutely be trusted to keep information confidential. He knew Bill Truscott, the DD (Deputy Director and second-highest FBI rank), and had worked closely with him during his first years at the Bureau.

Tilsdale would have preferred to work directly with the Director himself, but the current one—like most—was a political appointee, and not sufficiently knowledgeable about field operations. The Deputy Directors, by comparison, were always "old hands," experienced agents that actually knew how to keep the Bureau running on a daily basis. Tilsdale dialed Truscott's extension.

He knew Truscott's secretary from the old days. "Carol, this is Brad Tilsdale. Is anyone with Bill right now?" Tilsdale did not want to be noticed while he was communicating with the DD.

"Hi, Brad. No, he's free. I'll buzz him for you."

"Truscott."

"Bill, this is Brad Tilsdale. I need to talk to you, off premises."

"OK, let's go over to the Army-Navy Country Club. I'll meet you at the bar at 1400, OK?"

"That's perfect. Thanks!"

A few minutes later, Tilsdale pulled out of the headquarters garage and headed for the George Mason Memorial Bridge. Turning onto 14th Street from Constitution Avenue, he spotted a car tailing him. He deliberately made an illegal left turn, and headed for the Smithsonian, where he quickly parked his car in a reserved spot. A security officer approached to ticket him, and Tilsdale flashed his FBI badge and ID. He told the officer he was on official business, and to leave the vehicle there for his return in a few hours.

Tilsdale quickly entered the Smithsonian, and merged into a crowd of tourists. After moving through several corridors and seeing no tail, he walked quickly to the nearby Metro station and boarded a train for Pentagon City, where he got off. He hailed a cab and proceeded to the Army-Navy Country Club a few miles away. The tail was gone.

Tilsdale knew the Army-Navy Country Club very well. This was where Washington's top military and civilian brass gathered after hours. While he was a junior officer in the Navy, his unit commanding officer, the head of the Special Operations Group, dragged him out to this club nearly every weekend to play golf. The admiral loved to pair up with Tilsdale, who had a "scratch" handicap, meaning he played at pro golfer levels. Tilsdale approached golf like everything he did, constantly strategizing his shots, and using his martial arts training to control his breathing, reflexes, and hand-eye coordination. With Tilsdale as his partner, the admiral delighted in taking on senior Army officers on the huge course, while he rode to victory on Tilsdale's superior play, often betting money on the outcome. He was not happy when Tilsdale joined the SEALs.

Entering the plush club entrance, Tilsdale proceeded to the ornate bar area, where he saw Deputy Director Truscott. The two shook hands, and walked outside to the golfing area where they could not be overheard. "OK, I give up. What is so sensitive that we had to meet out here?" asked the DD.

"Bill, are you aware that I am supposed to be looking for a mole within the Bureau?"

"Yes, the Director and I were informed by your boss. And by the way, why is *he* not here?"

"You know how I operate, Bill. I start solving one of these cases alone, by making no assumptions, and validate the true facts one at a time, until I have no one but the perp [perpetrator] left."

"Yes, and I'm surprised that you even trust *me*!" Truscott marveled at Tilsdale's self-discipline. He never made unnecessary assumptions, which is why he was so good.

"Frankly, Bill, I don't have a choice." They both laughed. "Seriously, I certified you many years ago."

"Lucky me!" said the DD. "If J. Edgar Hoover were still around, he would have your ass for not informing him about this stuff!"

"I know. But he's gone, thank God."

"So let's hear it. What do you need me for?"

"Bill, I need to put together a top-secret team of counter-espionage agents, picked by me. It will take about twenty experienced agents. I want to bring them in from other field offices, so that it does not cause a stir around headquarters. And I want their temporary assignments to be ordered through you, so that there will not be a lot of argument from their bosses."

"All right, you've got it. Have you acquired any leads so far?"

"I think so. But to run them down, and start eliminating people from the list, I need this special team. I am also going to have some consultants from NSA and CIA."

"You *are* treading on thin ice!" said Truscott. The intelligence agencies in this era were very protective of their turf, and did not like to confide in the other agencies. Using people from a sister agency was considered a lack of loyalty, or an admission that your agency was not sufficiently competent.

"Bill, it's got to be this way, or I can't produce results. By the way, I need a secure office for this team, away from headquarters. I want it in a security environment, so that means something like Andrews Air Force Base or Fort McNair. In addition, I want to report only to you. I will make 'shadow' reports to my actual supervisor, the ADCI."

"I know the Commanding General at Fort McNair, so let me give him a call. But Brad—you *must* get results from all of this. I may need to justify this someday, OK?"

"I appreciate that, Bill. I believe I can deliver."

"So do I, Brad. Good luck."

Within days, Tilsdale had been given access to a small office building at Ft. McNair, on the edge of the Potomac. Normal Army security at the gates prevented anyone from surveilling his team members after they entered the base, and a special security detail provided 24-hour watch over the offices. Surveillance cameras and key-coded door locks were added.

Tilsdale recruited his team from various field offices, using the Deputy Director as the source of the orders. He wondered how long it would be before his own boss started asking questions. He did not have long to wait. Dallinger began to notice how much time Tilsdale was spending away from the headquarters. The KGB surveillance team under Col. Zorinsky reported that Tilsdale seemed to be going to Ft. McNair quite often. Dallinger decided it was time to confront Tilsdale. He picked up his phone and dialed Tilsdale's extension.

"Good morning, Brad. I've noticed that you are spending

quite a bit of time outside the office. Just in case I am asked by the DD, what is going on?"

"Yes, Sir, I am. With the assignment you gave me, plus another assignment from the DD, I am logging a lot of miles. He needed some help on an old government corruption case, and asked me to give him a hand. I could hardly say no."

"No, you're right. I'll chat with him about it. I need to know how much availability you have for our unit. I'll talk to you soon. Bye."

Dallinger thought for a minute. He knew Deputy Director Truscott, and that he often assembled an *ad hoc* team to go after "cold" cases that had something to do with corrupt politicians. He had to agree that Tilsdale would be a perfect choice for such a case, because confidentiality was critically important. He decided not to raise the issue, for now.

The KGB considered Cerberus so valuable that they had been running another double-agent within the FBI to use as cover. Although valuable for his own production of classified information to the KGB, this spy primarily served as a decoy "plant" to shield Cerberus from scrutiny. His name was Robert Hanssen, who would later become known as "the most damaging spy in American history." In reality, Hanssen, who had access to an incredible volume of sensitive information, was viewed as a "pawn asset" by the chess-minded Russians. As a last resort, they would sacrifice him to American counter-intelligence in order to prevent the discovery of Cerberus. Given the magnitude of Hanssen's security breaches, the KGB was confident that if Hanssen were discovered, the Americans would never look for another double-agent within the FBI. Except for Bradford Tilsdale, they were right.

"Sam Basi?" asked the man. The KGB agent had been assigned as escort, and directed to intercept Sam as he deplaned in Miami. He recognized Sam from his photographs.

"Yes! Are you with the global economics group?"

"Yes, I am. Here is your ticket to the Cayman Islands. How was your flight from California?"

"Fine, thank you. Shall we go to the gate?"

"Yes. Let me carry that bag for you. You know, this will be a wonderful trip for you. I think you will learn a lot," said the covert agent. He would be relieved when the delivery was made in the Caymans. Sometimes this type of mundane assignment goes off the track.

The two checked in at the Cayman Airways gate, and boarded the aircraft. Within 90 minutes, they landed at Owen Roberts Airport on Grand Cayman Island and were met by a limousine. As they rode across the island, Sam asked how many people were attending this special seminar.

"Quite a few," replied his escort. Sam began to wonder why he, as a mere college student, was receiving such special attention.

They arrived at a large gated mansion, surrounded by a high wall and several armed security guards. When they arrived at the front door, a uniformed butler came down to greet them. "Welcome to Atlantis," said the butler. "Please follow me. Someone will get your bags, Mr. Basi."

The KGB agent brought Sam to a large room, where dozens of people were talking and drinking champagne. "Mr. Basi, this is Dr. Pochevsky, one of the top economic experts in Europe. And this is Dr. Chen Lao, from the prestigious Victoria University of Hong Kong." Sam did not know that Pochevsky and Lao were actually psychiatrists from the Pochevsky Institute (Moscow) and the Ankang Group Institute (Beijing), respectively.

"Welcome, Mr. Basi. We are delighted that you could join us. Please, have some champagne. I brought it myself from Paris yesterday. I think you will like it."

Sam took a glass of champagne from the waiter. It tasted good, but Sam did not know his glass contained a powerful sedative that would render him unconscious in a matter of minutes.

"How do you like it, Mr. Basi?"

Sam was about to reply when the room began to spin. As he started to fall, two muscular "guests" grabbed him and placed him in a wheel chair. The other people in the room left their champagne glasses and went to their duty stations within the mansion.

"Take him to the preparation room. Have the nurses remove his clothes. When he is ready, bring him to the Learning Center," said Pochevsky. *So far, so good*, he thought.

The unconscious young man was wheeled into the preparation room. Nurses quickly removed his clothes, inserted a urinary catheter, and placed heart monitor and brain wave electrodes on his chest and head. His eyelids were taped open, and a rubber mouthpiece was inserted to prevent him from fracturing his teeth or breaking his jaw during what was to come. Finally, the nurses started an IV drip with a combination of hallucinogenic medications and a special sedative, to prevent him from resisting. His arms and legs were strapped to the wheelchair and his head was strapped back against the special headrest. Sam was ready to learn about Communism.

Chapter 8

The Journey

Sam began to wake up, but still felt drowsy, as if he were floating through the sky. He found himself in a dream-like state, strapped in a special wheelchair, with an IV in his arm and a rubbery object in his mouth. He tried to blink, but his eyes were kept open by a local anesthetic, injected into the nerves around the eyes. There was no one else in the room, which seemed to have a movie-screen kind of surface covering the floor, the walls, and the ceiling.

Suddenly the entire room illuminated with a kaleidoscope of colorful images and light patterns, while music played in synch with the images. It made him sleepy. In fact, this was a highly tested system of visual and aural hypnosis, developed after decades of research by the Pochevsky Institute scientists. The Russians and Chinese had tested these techniques on American prisoners-of-war in Korea, with some success. Several of the POWs even renounced their American citizenship and elected to say behind in North Korea after the cease-fire was implemented in 1953.

In a matter of minutes, Sam was in the equivalent of a comatose mental state, ready to receive and absorb information. The powerful sound system played stirring music, rising and falling with the changing images that filled Sam's eyes. The "teaching thread"—as Dr. Pochevsky called it—began, stuffing its images, sounds, and phrases at ever-increasing speed into Sam's brain. After several hours, the speed of image displays accelerated into a blur of neurological input. The EKG monitor began to detect a dangerous rise in heart rate and blood pressure, which caused Dr. Pochevsky to gradually bring Sam back from his hypnotic state. "That's enough for one day, Dr. Lao," Pochevsky said.

"I agree. His mind is saturated," said Lao. "We can pick up again with library page 3500 tomorrow."

The nursing staff removed the restraints, but left the IV and the catheter in. "When you get him in bed, strap him down tightly," said Pochevsky. "We will let him sleep, and start again in the morning. Feed him by IVs only, Vasily. Sedate him as necessary."

"Yes, Doctor," said a male nurse in Russian, wheeling Sam to the elevator. The first day of class was over.

During subsequent days, Sam's exposure to the Pochevsky process began to have its designed effect. Dr. Pochevsky began to see subtle changes in Sam's brainwave scans and other neurological instrumentation. From experience, he knew these were evidence that Sam's personality was changing—molding into the persona that the Pegasus team had specifically designed, in order to accomplish the mission.

One morning, Pochevsky met with Dr. Lao in the main conference room to discuss their progress. As the program proceeded, Dr. Lao had made several important suggestions that had been incorporated into the "training."

"Dr. Lao, what do you think? Are we ready for the next phase?" asked Pochevsky.

"Yes, I think we are ready. His brain has been pumped

full of horrific images of capitalism's atrocities, while adding soothing pictures of Socialism in action. This has irreversibly changed his ability to analyze these issues, creating an artificial bias that cannot be overcome by logic or history. His belief system has been irreparably changed to an iron-clad commitment to Socialism, and the need to replace capitalism with it."

"Well, then, the next phase will be to give him an unshakeable confidence in his own self, and to perfect his ability to understand and apply Socialist principles. Lenin was only effective because he could stand in front of a crowd, speaking forcefully and with apparent conviction. He always looked fearless, while he struck fear in the hearts of his enemies."

"Yes, Dr. Pochevsky, and before him it was Marx. And don't forget our Chairman Mao. The badge of their greatness was also their writing skill. This young man must learn to write persuasively, or at least to publish books that capture the imagination of the masses, like Marx did with the *Communist Manifesto*, and Chairman Mao did with his Red Book."

"And like Hitler did with *Mein Kampf*," added Pochevsky.

"That will be accomplished in the final phase, just as he is inserted into American politics. In recent times, no one has been elected President unless he has published his own self-serving biography, including a theme that resonates with the stupid American public. Our young man will need to turn his unusual origin into a story about overcoming adversity because of his race." One detail had been overlooked by both the KGB and MSS. In doing their background check on Sam, they accepted his California birth certificate as genuine. They had no way to know that Sam had actually been born in Nigeria, and that his birth records were total forgeries.

As Sam's intensive training now transitioned to the academic phase, a series of eloquent lecturers and experts engaged him interactively, forcing him to perform and deliver a consistent, persuasive message. Although still under hypnosis, Sam assimilated the information easily. As Pochevsky and Lao were aware, Sam was intellectually brilliant, and loved to show it. This part of his arrogant personality was left intact, as were the revolutionary attitudes taught by his mother.

As the weeks went by, Lao and Pochevsky gradually reduced the hypnotic drugs being used on Sam. Finally, they met to plan the final test. Sam met with a new VIP visitor, Victor Zebrotny (Zeus). The two spent several hours discussing how and why the world must be saved from American capitalism.

"Sam, Dr. Pochevsky told me that you were ill. Are you feeling better?" Zebrotny knew perfectly well that Lao and Pochevsky had kept him in a hypnotic coma for the past two weeks.

"I must have caught a bug at school, but I feel pretty good now," said Sam.

Zebrotny eyed his young protégé with interest. "Sam, you and young people like you are the hope for our world." Zebrotny told Sam, "You and young intellectuals like you are the people's hope for the future. I think you should get into American politics, where you could become the agent of great change." A statement like this from such a distinguished international financier boosted Sam's ego even more. He felt a great sense of mission growing within him.

"Sam, I recommend that you sharpen your communication skills by organizing groups of America's poor, and teaching them how to attack and influence their corrupt government. When you feel that you are ready to start this important mission, I want you to contact me. I will finance your further education and your political aspirations. The people of the world are depending on you, as I am."

Sam nodded solemnly. "I understand, Mr. Zebrotny. I just hope I am worthy of your trust," said Sam.

"I have no doubt that you will succeed, because you and we cannot afford to fail," said Zebrotny. In the monitor room, Pochevsky and Lao looked at each other and smiled. They had sifted through dozens of candidate submissions from KGB field agents, but none of them had all of the requisite qualities like young Sam Basi. They had their Pegasus, and they were sure that with the right support, he would accomplish the mission, at some level. The unknown factor was still controlled by chance and historical timing. How high would Sam rise in the American power structure? Would he become a low-level politician, or would he climb to a position of influence? But first, they decided to test his communication skills and persuasive powers on a live audience.

Sam was taken to Havana, where a conference of Leftist college students from the U.S. had gathered, in violation of current State Department travel restrictions. Zebrotny's private jet was used in order to avoid a connection with the Soviets or China. They drove from the Havana airport to an auditorium, where Sam was instructed to inspire a group of graduate students to become Leftist activists, and work to move the United States away from its capitalist roots.

Sam was introduced to the large audience as a rising star of the American Left. As he walked onto the stage, he took the microphone from the podium, and moved to the edge of the stage to directly engage the audience. As he began to speak, the Ankang and Pochevsky groups were assembled in a nearby room with a large monitor, watching and listening to their new protégé in his public "debut."

The remotely-controlled camera panned over the audience as he spoke, and it was clear that they were spellbound by his oratorical skills. At the end of his speech, several of them crowded around him, asking how they could join his movement. "Unbelievable," said Dr. Lao. "He doesn't even *have* a 'movement.'"

"Mother of God," said Pochevsky. "What have we created, Dr. Lao?"

"I don't know, Anatoly. I am only glad he is on our side. He is the most formidable speaker I have ever heard. Almost like a talented singer, it is not *what* he says, but how he *says* it. He is like a political Frank Sinatra."

Now it was time to move him back into his life in America. The KGB operatives on the Harvard University faculty had been briefed, and were awaiting his arrival. The KGB had discovered years ago that an American university or college faculty was the ideal place to stash intelligence agents. The Americans allowed faculty members to move freely between international locations, and it was easy to locate sympathetic volunteers within their liberal academic culture. Once a professor gained "tenure," the individual had lifetime job security. When they first learned of this odd arrangement, unheard of within the Soviet Union, the KGB was incredulous. It was a ready-made, protected incubator for developing American spies and activists.

Sam's transfer from UCLA to Harvard had been easily arranged by Zebrotny's operatives during his "training" at Atlantis in the Cayman Islands. During his programming, Sam had been, in the words of Dr. Lao, "hard-wired" to take direction from anyone who used the phrase, "Trojan Horse," followed by "Pegasus can fly."

The powerful hypnotic training would force him to follow that person's instructions, no matter what or who they were. The reason for this forced response was for operational flexibility—and in case it became necessary to cause him to "self-destruct" to protect the conspiracy and its other principals. Moscow always tried to incorporate this extra "stop-loss" contingency plan—the elimination of the operative himself—into its covert operations and assassinations. One never knew when it might become necessary to give up and cut the losses on a fouled operation, with the assured silence that only death could bring.

Chapter 9

The Academic Incubator

Sam returned to Harvard, inspired by what he remembered of his Atlantis experience. He never realized that he had been imposed with a programmed personality, largely created by Drs. Pochevsky and Lao. He now was armed with a new, narcissistic confidence, and loved to be the center of attention. "Stage fright" was not in his vocabulary. At Harvard, KGB plants within the faculty took over his supervision, immediately placing him in a "special studies" program, with an emphasis on Socialist topics, and allowing him to graduate early.

He felt a powerful motivation to succeed academically, and pushed himself to learn. Part of his customized curriculum, overseen by one of the KGB's professors, involved the continued improvement of his communication and persuasion skills. His KGB handlers ensured that he was kept within a close group of students, who were enthralled with Leftist systems and policies.

His "advisory group," carefully monitored by the KGB and the Pochevsky Institute, taught him the art of political speech protocols. They thrust him into speaking engagements before different audiences, like the Young Americans for Freedom, the Federalist Society, the John Birch Society,

La Raza, and the Black Students Organization. Because he was half-black, he was viewed by all of the racially-sensitive factions as "acceptable." He developed an uncanny ability to modify his own speech patterns and accents, in order to appeal to the specific audience in front of him. His manner of speaking had almost a hypnotic effect on a gullible listener.

In front of Blacks, he would adopt an African-American vernacular and accent, slurring word endings and peppering his phrases with typical African-American slang. When speaking to politically conservative audiences, he sounded like a typical Ivy League student, with polished phrasing and elevated vocabulary. His friendly and honest demeanor, also contrived through the programming at Atlantis, was a huge selling point to those listening, who always found him to be likeable and non-threatening. His own Socialist belief system was always bubbling beneath the surface, ready to take on those who would debate its worth. However, he always engaged his adversaries with a winning smile and clever sense of humor, and never seemed to make enemies. His "likeability" factor was high. Within the cloistered nest of academia, nothing of value is really at risk. That comes later, when one must make a living, and apply the knowledge acquired—if any.

His advisors recommended that he obtain a law degree, which has always opened many doors in business and government. He decided on Yale, and submitted his application. To ensure his admission, Zebrotny met privately with the law school dean and offered a $10 million donation to the school, provided Sam was accepted. Money talks.

While Sam completed his graduation from Harvard and

prepared to enter Yale Law School, Special Agent Tilsdale and his counter-espionage team worked tirelessly to trace the messages between Moscow and the KGB agent known only as "Emerald." Tilsdale was certain that if "Emerald" could be identified, the KGB operative known as "Pegasus" could be neutralized. One day, he received a pager message from Melissa Clayton at NSA that broke the team's impasse. He called her number at NSA.

"Brad, is this a secure line?"

"Yes, it's scrambled. Go ahead, Melissa."

"We have identified the point of origin of Emerald's Telex traffic as the communications facility at UCLA in Los Angeles. Does that ring any bells?"

Tilsdale felt his pulse quicken. "Yes, Melissa, before I left Los Angeles, we intercepted a KGB agent doing covert background research on students there. I wonder if that could be related somehow." From years of practice, Tilsdale felt his investigative intuition coming into play. "Melissa, I need to do some checking—I'll call you later, OK?"

"Sure, Brad. Just let me know if I can help."

Tilsdale called a staff meeting and laid out the focus of the project. "We just caught a break, thanks to our friends at NSA," Tilsdale announced. "We now know that 'Emerald' is probably either a student or a faculty member at UCLA in Los Angeles. I am betting that he or she is on the faculty, since students probably don't have access to the communications center on campus. So here is the plan:

"Agent Browning, write up a request for a search warrant and wiretap on all faculty office phones, plus the Telex cable, for the federal court in Los Angeles. When you complete the paperwork, send it by messenger through our LA Field Office to Judge Wickham's chambers. From my experience, he is the most likely to approve it quickly. And make sure you emphasize this is a matter of national security, and that we need the court to seal the warrant. Work with Bill Atkinson at the U.S. Attorney's office, if you need local legal support. We have cleared Bill to handle our counter-espionage matters."

"Yes, Sir." Browning got up and left the room.

"Next, I am establishing an undercover surveillance team on campus. Don't any of you be insulted, but Agents Santos and Brickman are the youngest-looking among us, as I see it, so you two will establish a presence on campus as students to keep an eye on things. You are *not* to involve the LA Field Office—you are reporting to me only. If anyone asks, just tell them you are on a routine security check of campus radicals.

"Ladies and gentlemen, the KGB does not ordinarily send and receive Level 5 coded Telexes to and from a U.S. location like this. Something important is going on here, and I want the puzzle solved. The rest of you will acquire the faculty list and do background checks on each professor. The answer is there somewhere."

Professor Lydia Boroshta, or "Emerald," had originally been recruited by the KGB in her native Poland as a graduate student at the University of Warsaw. Because of her mastery of the English language, the KGB worked their contacts to get her a teaching visa to enter the U.S. The dean of the UCLA political science department thought her application to join their faculty made perfect sense, as he was trying to "internationalize" the curriculum to include other governmental systems, such as Socialism. After she was granted tenure, the university was able to get her permanent residency in the U.S., a perfect "deep cover" for a KGB agent. She had now begun to prove her worth, as her family still lived under Soviet control and threat of reprisal in Poland. This guaranteed her loyalty to the KGB.

Boroshta felt secure in using the campus communications center for her Moscow communications. She had become friendly with the staff there, who thought she was only communicating with former friends or family in Poland or academic acquaintances. Her Telexes appeared to be routed to Warsaw, as far as the staff was aware, but this was actually a "cut-over" communications drop box that re-routed the messages to Moscow. Since the "Pegasus" project had mostly passed her by at this point, she did not expect further message traffic with Moscow. She was almost right, but then she received one more coded message that made her tremble with fear.

She found the Telex message dropped into her faculty mail box by the college's communications staff, in a sealed envelope. After taking it home and decoding it, she read the text and became alarmed:

> **"MOST SECRET: Your part in Operation Pegasus is concluded. Imperative that you now destroy your code book, all prior messages and notes, along with the college records of Husam Khalil Basi. Avoid all future communications with that subject. Well done. Socrates."**

Boroshta was concerned that she might not be able to obtain Sam's records from Administration. They kept these records under lock and key, and some were computerized, requiring special passwords. Nevertheless, she had her orders. What she did not know was that the NSA had read that message, de-coded it, and sent it on to Tilsdale. The FBI's special counter-intelligence group now had the lead they were looking for.

Without the knowledge of Dallinger, Tilsdale had one of his former team members from the Los Angeles Field Office re-assigned to the Pegasus task force at Ft. McNair. Special Agent Jeff Billings, one of the growing number of African-American agents, was known as Tilsdale's fast-track protégé. Similar to Tilsdale, he started his career in Army Intelligence, followed by a tour with the 2nd Ranger Battalion, and then assignment to the elite Delta Force counter-terrorist unit. He was an excellent athlete and top graduate of his class at West Point, which often became obvious during the annual Army-Navy football game. During that annual event, he and Tilsdale would wager on the outcome, which was usually in Navy's favor. Other agents, envious of his prestigious assignments with Tilsdale, characterized Billings as "Tonto," the faithful sidekick of the Lone Ranger. In their working relationship, Billings was much more than a "Watson" to Tilsdale's "Sherlock Holmes" persona. He was a brilliant agent, expert in close-quarters combat, spoke fluent Russian and Mandarin, and was a highly respected, rising star within the FBI. He was also the perfect, reliable "wingman" for Tilsdale, and was able to keep Tilsdale's wandering mind focused on the objectives. A fierce loyalty existed between the two agents. Now Tilsdale had a new assignment for him.

"Jeff, we have narrowed the UCLA list down to three people of interest—one student and two faculty members. I'm guessing that our most likely candidate is a Professor Lydia

Boroshta, of the political science department. She is a tenured professor, but is a Polish national, here legally on a 'green card.' It seems odd that she has never applied for citizenship, because she would be easily approved, I would think."

Billings knew his boss and his astounding intuition. His "guesses" always seemed be correct. "So what's the plan, Boss?"

"I want you to learn everything about her that you can, and then contact the dean of her department. Tell him that the government is experimenting with a special citizenship naturalization program, and that we are offering fast-track processing for certain university faculty members. Tell him that Boroshta's name came up as an excellent candidate and we would like to get her started in this program. You can explain that this would give her many advantages that she does not have currently, such as less restrictive international travel, access to government benefits and employment, and so forth. Get the idea?"

"Understood, Boss. I assume this would be cover for me interviewing her, correct?"

As usual, Billings was able to quickly think in tandem with Tilsdale. "You got it, Jeff. Let me know how it goes. Play it anyway you want, and I'll back you."

Two days later, Billings arrived at the Bunche Hall office of Dean J. William Baxter, Ph.D., head of UCLA's political science department. "Dr. Baxter? Hi—I'm Jeff Billings. We talked yesterday on the phone about our new program for faculty members." Baxter was the personification of the college professor, complete with beard, glasses, tweedy jacket, and a bow tie.

"Yes, Agent Billings, I think that is a wonderful idea.

As you know, there is often so much red tape for our foreign faculty members, they often don't even try to become citizens."

"Well, that's what we want to eliminate. Another country's loss will be our gain, correct?"

"Exactly! So how can I help?"

"First of all, I will need to interview Dr. Boroshta, and then conduct a routine, quick background investigation. Please tell her this will jump her ahead of thousands of applicants, and not to be apprehensive." Billings had a very amiable and smooth manner, and usually could gain the confidence of complete strangers in a matter of minutes. He was considered one of the Bureau's top investigators, and his interviews had resulted in cracking many cases.

The next day, Billings met with Boroshta in her office. He introduced himself with a big smile. "Well, Professor, I am very pleased to meet you," said Billings. "I read your book, *A History of Polish Governmental Systems,* a few months ago. I found it fascinating—I never knew how difficult it has been for Poland to be sandwiched between Germany and Russia."

"Why, thank you, Agent Billings. I got a little nervous when the Dean said an FBI agent wanted to talk to me, until he explained the citizenship program." She found herself distracted by the handsome young man in front of her, instead of maintaining focus on the content of the conversation.

"Well, Professor, I think you will find that your life will be considerably easier, especially when you travel. I assume you still have family back in Poland?"

Boroshta tensed up with the mention of her family. "Yes, I have a mother and two sisters, who are both doctors. I try to see them every year."

"Please do not be concerned about this background check.

We simply have to ask a few typical questions as a formality, and then this application will be quickly approved, OK?"

"Certainly. What would you like to know?"

Billings used a typical interrogator's trick. He rapidly asked a series of routine questions, and then dropped "the bomb." This causes the subject to become compliant and cooperative, reflexively answering the sequence of questions without thinking. "Have you ever traveled to China or North Korea?" he asked.

"No," she answered.

"How about the Soviet Union?" he asked. He correctly assumed that by asking the irrelevant question first, his inclusion of the USSR would not seem suspicious.

"Definitely not," she replied. Years ago, the KGB had trained her in the Moscow area. Immediately, he noticed a nervous movement of Boroshta's hands and a shift in her posture. Her use of "definitely" indicated subconscious anxiety about the question. *Bingo,* he thought.

"Ever *communicated* with anyone in China or North Korea?" he asked.

"Never."

"The Soviet Union?"

"Absolutely not."

He noticed her use of the word "absolutely," which indicated over-sensitivity. "When I say 'communicate,' that includes telephones, faxes, letters, e-mails, and Telexes. None of those either?"

"No, never."

"I apologize for these weird questions, but this is what our directive and the forms require."

"No problem. I understand."

Billings noticed that her face was slightly flushed. "Well,

Doctor Boroshta, I thank you for your time and your cooperation. We will be in touch," he said with a smile.

"Thank you and goodbye for now."

"Goodbye, Doctor. Have a nice day." Billings was certain that he had "struck gold," and knew what he had to do
next. He walked quickly toward the communications center
at Murphy Hall. As he entered the center, a security guard
asked for his identification. The man's eyes widened when
he saw the FBI ID card and badge.

"What can I do for you, Sir?" asked the guard.

"I just need to see the manager of the center."

"I'll call him right away." The guard dialed a number.
"Mr. Avery? There is an FBI agent here to see you."

Avery became concerned. He wondered what would
cause an FBI agent to visit him. As most criminals know, the
FBI rarely brings you good news. "Yes, Sir, what can I do for
you?" Avery asked warily.

"Agent Jeff Billings, Mr. Avery. This is very routine. We
are doing background checks on some of your faculty members, who are applying for citizenship. It's a chore that we
have to do, so please do not be alarmed."

"What would you like to know?" asked Avery.

Billings handed Avery a list, which included Boroshta.
"Have any of the people on this list used their office phones
or your Telex system here to communicate outside the U.S.?"

Avery studied the list for a moment. "Yes, this student
was allowed to use the Telex to send a message to his family
in France, when his mother was ill. And this faculty member was given permission to send and receive Telexes from
her family in Warsaw. I guess her mother had some medical
problems or something." He pointed to Boroshta's name.

"How often was that?" asked Billings.

"Not very often before a few months ago, when there were quite a few going back and forth."

"OK, what about telephone traffic between campus phones and foreign sites?"

"Well, we automatically audit all campus office phone bills, and we are always concerned about the cost of international calls. We did notice that Professor Boroshta has been calling a number in Warsaw more often, but we assume it relates to her family issue."

"May I have a copy of those bills?"

"Certainly!" Avery dialed an extension. "Jennifer, please bring me copies of all phone bills for number 668-3409. Yes, as far back as you have them."

An attractive young woman entered with a stack of phone bills and handed them to Avery. Casting a sideways glance at Billings, she said, "Will that be all, Mr. Avery?" She had heard that an FBI agent was talking to Avery.

"Yes, thank you."

Billings put the documents in his briefcase, thanked Avery, and reminded him to keep the inquiry confidential. He could hardly wait to get on the phone to Tilsdale.

"Boss, it's Jeff. I have a number that we need to trace to its reception point. Ready?"

"Go ahead."

"011 48 553-445-6890. '48' is the international country code for Poland."

"Good job—I'll get back to you. Stay in LA for the time being, until we develop this contact."

"Will do."

One of the most effective ways to use an enemy's agents is to turn them into your own. Tilsdale was mulling over several options to use on Boroshta.

Chapter 10

The Yearling Learns To Run

At Yale Law School, Sam excelled. His mother's early academic influence had produced an outstanding student, whom his classmates and professors noticed immediately as a star. His debating skills worked well for this new environment, allowing him to win the Moot Court award and obtain a position on the prestigious Yale Law Review. As every lawyer knows, gaining a seat on your school's Law Review publication guarantees an accelerated start to your career.

His living expenses were paid through a Zebrotny surrogate company as a "scholarship," as was his tuition. By his third year, he had been elected Editor-in-Chief of the Law Review, a unique achievement that usually makes that graduating student aggressively recruited by the nation's elite law firms, who pay the highest salaries.

During one of his evenings in the law library, he stumbled on a book entitled *Rules for Radicals,* by Chicagoan Saul Alinsky, a radical activist from the Fifties and Sixties. The theories in this book were exactly what Sam had been looking for as a strategy to tie his skills together to achieve victory over his perceived opponents—the wealthy people of America, and capitalism in general.

As he continued his reading of Alinsky's text, he felt a

tingle of excitement when he read Alinsky's list of power tactics to achieve social justice against "the enemy," capitalistic societies:

1. Power is not only what you have, but what the enemy thinks you have.
2. Never go outside the experience of your people.
3. Whenever possible go outside the experience of the enemy.
4. Make the enemy live up to their own book of rules.
5. Ridicule is man's most potent weapon.
6. A good tactic is one that your people enjoy.
7. A tactic that drags on too long becomes a drag.
8. Keep the pressure on with different tactics and actions, and utilize all events of the period for your purpose.
9. The threat is usually more terrifying than the thing itself.
10. The major premise of tactics is the development of operations that will maintain a constant pressure upon the opposition.
11. If you push a negative hard and deep enough, it will break through into its counterside.
12. The price of a successful attack is a constructive alternative.
13. Pick the target, freeze it, personalize it, and polarize it.

Suddenly, everything—all of his intellectual issues—became clear. He saw that he had to learn how to adapt these principles to his quest for a power position in politics. Reading further, he found that Alinsky had been a community organizer of poor people in Chicago in the decades before his death in 1972. Sam also found great inspiration in reading the writings of an Italian Communist, Antonio Gramsci, who urged a gradual attack on democratic foundations, such as religion, patriotism, and national culture. Gramsci also urged a weakening of institutions like the military and traditional families. Now Sam knew what he had to do. Victor Zebrotny would have the answers he needed.

When Zebrotny received the telephone call from Sam, he was curious. He hoped Sam was not in some type of trouble that would affect the project.

"Sam, how are you, my boy? You are about to graduate from Yale soon, aren't you?"

"Yes, Mr. Zebrotny, but I know what I want to do when I graduate. I want to go to Chicago and become a community organizer, just like Saul Alinsky. I have read his books, and I must learn to apply his tactics."

Zebrotny had to hide his delight at hearing this. He had already been briefed by the KGB that Chicago was exactly where they wanted to place Sam to inflitrate American politics. In Chicago, they knew that anything could be bought from government officials for the right price. "Well, Sam, I had already arranged through a business acquaintance for you to join one of the large law firms in Chicago. But if you really want to try this, I will back you. It is important that you follow your dreams."

"Thank you, Mr. Zebrotny. I cannot thank you enough for your generous assistance. I will always be in your debt."

Zebrotny smiled and thought, *Don't worry—you will have ample opportunities to pay me back.* "Not at all, Sam. I have a feeling that you are on the right path to achieve your personal goals, and that when you do, I would be pleased to continue our relationship. Someone of your great intellect must not be wasted, and I want you to succeed."

"Thank you, Sir. I will try to justify your confidence."

After the conversation ended, Zebrotny went to his office Telex with his KGB code book, and typed a Level 5 message to Socrates in Moscow at KGB headquarters:

> **"MOST SECRET: Be advised that Pegasus is planning to go to Chicago to become a community organizer, which will position him perfectly for linking up with local radicals and corrupt government officials. I will finance his venture, as usual. Recommend that you arrange for deep cover agents to connect with him after he arrives, in order to provide closer monitoring and security. Provide me with a contact, and I will ensure that a local connection is made.**
> **Zeus"**

"Socrates," the code-name for the Chairman of the KGB, was now being used by one of the successors to Andropov, who had died after being promoted to General Secretary of the Communist Party. In Moscow, Vladimir Aleksandrovich Kryuchkov had assumed the powerful position, and like Andropov's other successors before him, he had been fully briefed on the Trojan Horse Project and Pegasus. Along with the location of the 27 "suitcase" nuclear bombs that were hidden throughout the United States, and the identity of deep-cover "moles" like Cerberus, the Trojan Horse project was a closely guarded secret which was passed in a "Your

Eyes Only" status from one KGB Chairman to the next.

Chairman Kryuchkov was feeling the pressure of discontent across the Soviet empire. In the satellite countries, there were riotous demonstrations against the Soviet Union and centralized control from Moscow. Premier Gorbachev's government, which had been effectively bankrupted by trying to match Ronald Reagan's military and naval buildup, looked increasingly weak and about to fall. Finally, the Berlin Wall came down, and in 1991 the Soviet Union was disbanded into 15 different nations.

The KGB, for its part, was also disbanded and reorganized as a solely Russian intelligence service, known as the *Sluzhba Vneshney Razvedki*, or SVR, located just off the Moscow Ring Road (the MKAD) in the Yasenevo district. Although 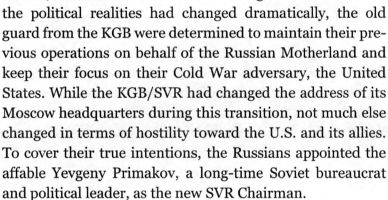 the political realities had changed dramatically, the old guard from the KGB were determined to maintain their previous operations on behalf of the Russian Motherland and keep their focus on their Cold War adversary, the United States. While the KGB/SVR had changed the address of its Moscow headquarters during this transition, not much else changed in terms of hostility toward the U.S. and its allies. To cover their true intentions, the Russians appointed the affable Yevgeny Primakov, a long-time Soviet bureaucrat and political leader, as the new SVR Chairman.

Behind Primakov's usual smile was a ruthless Communist. When he was briefed on the old KGB secrets, he was astounded at the daring plan known as the Trojan Horse Project. As an experienced and shrewd manager, he did not like to waste his resources on silly adventures that had a low probability of success. However, his staff convinced him

that this plan was well on its way. He approved it to continue.

While Russia had its problems, so did the United States. China, following its collateral function with the Trojan Horse Project, was slowly but surely gobbling up the American manufacturing capacity, virtually shutting down American electronics and steel production in favor of cheaper Chinese labor. General Electric was even making light bulbs and other electrical components in China, taking advantage of the cheaper labor market. Using its new economic power, China aggressively invested in American Treasury bonds. In a few more years, the United States would be largely dependent on China for nearly all manufactured products, and for continued purchase of Treasury bonds to cover the growing national debt and deficit spending. By maintaining the Chinese currency at a ridiculously low rate, compared to the dollar, the balance of trade grew rapidly in favor of the Chinese, further leveraging America's growing economic problems. As Xu Yongyue, the current Minister of State Security said, "We have already made powerless eunuchs out of the Americans. We have cut off their balls, and they don't even know it."

Two days after Tilsdale communicated the suspicious Warsaw telephone number to Melissa Clayton at the NSA, he received a call from her. "Brad, Melissa Clayton. You better come over here. I need to show you something."

Tilsdale arrived at the NSA and this time used his FBI credentials to get through security. Melissa met him in the lobby and took him through several more security checkpoints, until they arrived in a large room, filled with computer monitors and several large display screens at the front of the room. Busy technicians hunched over their monitors, talking quietly. The room had a forbidding presence.

"This is the line analysis section. These people take suspicious telephone and Telex lines, and trace their reception and transmission points. No matter how many 'dead-drops' and re-routed communications links you have, these guys can find you."

"Impressive," said Tilsdale.

"Just wait and see what they found, when they traced the Warsaw telephone and Telex lines." She took him to one of the computerized workstations, labeled "Soviet bloc." A bookish-looking man in his forties was studying a colored map on his monitor.

"Jed, this is FBI Special Agent Brad Tilsdale. I want you to brief him on what you found with those Warsaw numbers."

"Sure. It took a little doing, because when the signals arrived at the Warsaw number, they were scrambled again and automatically re-routed through two false termination points in Poland, and then sent on to Moscow. Want to hear the really amazing thing?"

"Absolutely."

"The signals ended up with KGB headquarters as their termination point. I would say that you have a dangerous character making these calls and Telexes from UCLA."

Tilsdale felt vindicated by this confirmation, but at the same time, uneasy. "Melissa, I'll need a formal intercept report from you guys, as part of our case file."

"I thought you would never ask. Jed?" The technician

handed Tilsdale a sealed envelope, labeled "Top Secret."

"Thanks, Jed, and Melissa. I need to get with my team on this, immediately."

"Brad, there is something else. We intercepted a message from Socrates to Emerald, instructing Emerald to destroy all code books and documents."

"Christ!" Tilsdale sprinted for the garage.

As Tilsdale sped out of the NSA gate, he remembered from his history class at the Naval Academy that the Japanese had sent a very similar message to their Washington ambassador, just before the Pearl Harbor attack. Tilsdale drove out of the NSA facility, took the Patuxent Freeway, and then went south on I-295. He called Jeff Billings on his mobile phone.

"Jeff, Brad. Go to scrambler." Even though a mobile phone call can be easily eavesdropped by other intelligence services, the digital scrambler developed by NSA and provided to the other U.S. government agencies for voice communications was impenetrable.

"Roger that, Boss."

"OK, here's the deal. Get the U.S. Attorney to issue an arrest and search warrant. Make it for Professor Lydia Boroshta, and include her office, home and car. Let me know when you have it ready, but don't execute yet. I'm on the way to you. My ETA will be 1500, your time. Meet me at the Lockheed terminal at Burbank airport."

"Will do, Boss."

Tilsdale drove directly to Andrews Air Force Base, and ordered an Air Force jet by telephone, using his friendship with the Base Operations Officer, a Naval Academy classmate, to cut through the normal approval channels.

"Brad, how the hell are you?" asked Col. Frank Lisani.

"Great, Frank, but I need to be wheels in the well ASAP, outbound for Burbank airport. This is an emergency, or I would not do this to you."

"No problem, Brad. The aircraft is fueled and ready, and the pilots are waiting for you at the aircraft. Let's go."

The staff car sped across the ramp and dropped Tilsdale at the boarding stairs of an Air Force Gulfstream jet, usually reserved for government dignitaries. "Thanks, Frank. I owe you one."

"Have a good one, and I won't ask what you are doing. The less I know about your stuff, the better I sleep at night," chuckled Lisani.

Within minutes, the sleek grey and white aircraft was heading west, bound for Burbank. Tilsdale used the aircraft's air phone system to call Jeff Billings and have his arrest team meet him at the Lockheed terminal at Burbank. He hoped he was not too late to preserve the KGB code materials.

Professor Boroshta was unaware of the FBI surveillance, and decided to take the items described in the KGB Telex to her home Beverly Hills for destruction. By the time she left the campus to drive home, a heavily armed FBI assault and search team, led by Tilsdale and Billings, was speeding toward Beverly Hills from Burbank.

Arriving at her home, she noticed nothing out of the ordinary, as she activated the gate to enter the driveway. She proceeded up the driveway of her expensive home on Beverly Hills' North Camden Drive, and stopped to allow the garage door to open. At that moment, a team of helmeted FBI SWAT agents surrounded her car with their Colt M-4 carbines leveled at her. "Out of the car! Keep your hands where I can see them!" yelled the team leader. "Professor Lydia Boroshta, you are under arrest! Put your hands on the car and spread your feet," ordered the agent, who quickly handcuffed her hands behind her, and spun her around to face him.

From the side of the garage, Tilsdale and Billings approached her. "Ms. Boroshta, you are under arrest for violation of the Espionage Act and failing to register as a foreign agent. You have the right to remain silent and the right to an attorney. If you cannot afford an attorney, the court will appoint one for you. Anything you say can and will be used against you in a court of law. Do you understand what I have told you?"

"Yes." Tears streamed down her face, not only because of her arrest, but because her family in Poland would be placed in jeopardy with the KGB, now the SVR. Her cover was blown, and she was no longer of use to the Russians.

"Let's go inside," said Tilsdale. The search team rolled up the driveway in a black van and agents quickly used her house key on the front door and entered. While her home was being searched, another team was taking her campus office apart, securing all documents and other potential evidence items.

"OK, Boroshta, where are the codes? Your future, and the welfare of your family in Poland depend on your level of cooperation." Tilsdale stared coldly at her. "Well?"

"What about my family?" Boroshta asked.

"If we get your *total* cooperation, and I mean total, we are prepared to bring them to the U.S. and give them political asylum. In your case, you will need to plead guilty. If you do what we tell you, your charges and conviction will be sealed as a suspended criminal judgment and not accessible to the public. Your slightest concealment or lie to us, or refusal to follow our orders, and we will pull the plug on that, and you will have the sentence of life in prison imposed. You will never see daylight again. That's the deal, and it is non-negotiable. Now, for starters, *where is the goddam code-book*?"

"It is in the safe under the garage workbench."

"Is the safe booby-trapped?" asked Tilsdale. Some KGB agents rigged their document cache with an explosive device, both to kill or maim anyone breaking into it, and to destroy the documents it contained.

"No."

"What is the combination?"

"No problem—I will open it."

"No, you won't. You will give us the combination, and we will open it."

"22 right, 45 left, 67 right."

Billings turned the dial, and the door clicked open. Inside was a large book, disguised as a telephone directory, containing the code ciphers in a matrix pattern of columns of two-digit numbers. Tilsdale had seen this type of system before, as they were supplied to every important field agent in the KGB. Without the cross-index, the book was useless.

"What is your cross-index, and where is it?" asked Tilsdale.

"Tolstoy's *War and Peace*. It's at my office."

"What is the daily protocol?"

Resigning herself to her predicament, Boroshta answered, "You take the date, in Moscow time, and write it out in four numbers. January 17, 1996 would be '01 17 19 96.' You then use my copy of *War and Peace*. One more thing. You need the 'spindle.'"

Tilsdale looked up. "What is that?"

"It's a rotary device, with five numbered wheels like a combination lock. Each wheel has numbers from 0 through 99. You first set the code security level, like '5', in the first wheel. You turn the next wheels to the four date numbers, and the side window will show you a new set of four numbers. It is like a small computer."

"Then what?" asked Billings, taking notes.

"Then you use those four numbers. The last one is the page in *War and Peace*. The next one to the left is the line number, counting from the bottom of the page. Next on the left is the letter on the line, counting from the right margin. This letter puts you on the corresponding section in the code book, like section 'g'. The last number, going left, is the line number on that code book page, counting from the top. You then write out or look at an entire Russian computer keyboard, except for the pure function keys, like TAB, starting with the top left, under each number group, and then you have an alphabet map to write your message, with numbers from 1 to 46. You count from the top left, the number '1'. Your message would look something like, 04 44 29; 09 18 24; 25 04 14, and so on. One last thing—if the left-most number on the spindle is even, you space the keyboard alphabet by skipping two numbers between keys. If it is odd, you skip one."

Although the agents knew that NSA could de-code these messages with their computers, they wanted to know how to do it manually, to ensure their complete ability to send as well as receive messages. "So where is the spindle?" asked Tilsdale.

"Here, in my briefcase." Billings examined the device and then placed it into an evidence bag.

"What I described is how you decode an incoming message. For outgoing, you perform the same steps, because you are trying to establish the keyboard map, and then work it in reverse. You take the Russian character of your text and find it on the map you have created, then write the corresponding number group from the code book on your actual message to transmit. The only problem is, you have to be fluent in Russian to do this."

"No problem. We both are," replied Tilsdale.

Boroshta smiled.

"What's so funny?" asked Tilsdale.

"If you had been one day later, all of this stuff would have been destroyed. I was late in following their instructions," said Boroshta. "What happens now?"

"That will be up to you, Professor. If you live up to our arrangement, we will protect you and your family. We will eventually relocate you under the Witness Protection Program with new identities. But for right now, everything stays the same. We want you to continue as you were, and to advise us immediately if they try to contact you. We will return everything from our search that does not involve the charges against you. If you try to screw us, we will destroy your fucking life and throw your family to the KGB wolves. It's your choice, and your options are quite clear."

"I understand, and I will abide by our agreement. Just make sure that you do, as well."

Chapter 11

Networking

Although Boroshta had not destroyed the code book and cipher materials, she had been able to bribe an administrative clerk in the registrar's office to delete Sam Basi's entire file, except for the entries that proved he attended the college. Separately, other agents had done the same for Sam's record at Harvard, including several radical papers he had written, advocating the overthrow of the U.S. government.

The day after her arrest and release, she was directed by the FBI to meet with Tilsdale's team at the Los Angeles International Airport Marriott Hotel on Century Blvd. She was grilled endlessly on how she was trained, who her handlers had been, what projects had been assigned to her—which brought the discussion to Pegasus.

"Obviously, you had something to do with locating and recruiting an agent known as 'Pegasus,'" said Tilsdale.

"Yes."

"Tell us first what this project is all about. Why is the KGB looking for a mixed-race student?" Members of the U.S. intelligence community still referred to the Russian intelligence service interchangeably as the KGB, finding that old habit difficult to break.

"I really do not know, nor could I even speculate about

what he was recruited for. His real name is Husam Khalil Basi. His black father, a Nigerian, was killed in a police raid after Sam's mother left Nigeria. I know her from various political science conferences, and she became a good friend. She is a professor at Berkeley.

"She never stopped talking about how brilliant her son was, and I convinced her to place him here, so I could act as his mentor. He is an incredible young man, perhaps a little too confident in himself, but you cannot help but like him. I would think he will become a college professor like his mother, because he really excels in academics, especially political science topics. The KGB wanted certain characteristics."

"I know, we read that message. What happened when he got here?"

"He was doing well when I forwarded his file to Moscow. They accepted my recommendation, which I thought was for a special grant or scholarship. He went to some sort of international conference down in the Caribbean. After he came back from there, he was changed. He seemed obsessed with Socialism and Communism. He spent all of his time trying to convince other students to adopt and promote Marxist principles. Then he transferred to Harvard University, and I lost track with him, although he sends me short notes once in a while." Boroshta stared blankly at the smoggy Los Angeles skyline, then continued. "I really do not know why the KGB is interested in this kid. He seems very much like a lot of the gifted students I have had, perhaps a little more engaged in politics, but he will outgrow that."

"Did he ever talk about doing something violent? Was he critical of the United States? Did he ever advocate the overthrow of our government?"

"Not to my knowledge, although he thought our government should move toward Socialism in something like the Gramsci model. You know, a gradual transition to the 'hegemony' of the working class, and redistribution of wealth from the rich to the poor."

"What school is he attending now?"

"He is at Yale Law School, and will graduate this spring."

"Give Agent Billings his address and phone number." Boroshta consulted an address book, and wrote out the information. "Has the KGB or SVR ever contacted Basi, or 'Pegasus?'"

"Not to my knowledge."

"OK, Professor, you can go home for now. If we have further questions, we will contact you. Keep this pager with you 24/7. When we page you, we expect a call-back within 15 minutes at this number, which you are to memorize." Tilsdale handed her a slip of paper with a telephone number on it. "Like the American Express commercial, don't leave home without it!"

As Tilsdale and Billings drove back to Los Angeles, they both were concerned about what they had learned—or *not* learned. "Jeff, something doesn't add up here. I don't think the Basi kid is really 'Pegasus.'"

"I know, Boss. I think the SVR is trying to have us chase a decoy. This is like their usual chess-move mentality," noted Billings.

"Agreed. Let's focus back on the FBI leaks that have been getting our foreign agents captured and killed. Maybe that is the real plot here."

In the days before the growth of the Internet and universal e-mail, most messages were sent between Europe and North America via an undersea cable system. Even afterward, as the cables were upgraded to larger capacity through the use of fiber optic technology, high speed data transmissions began to use this resource. The messages between Emerald and Socrates had been transmitted through one of many new cables, known as TAT-14, which linked the United States mainland from New Jersey to the Netherlands, where the cable network again diverged to Eastern Europe and Russia. Following the leads that were generated by the Pegasus affair, Tilsdale submitted a request to the NSA for a "cable tap."

Tapping an undersea cable is a technologically tricky process, often conducted at great depths. That is why the *USS Jimmy Carter (SSN-23),* a modified nuclear submarine of the *Seawolf* class, was dispatched from the Norfolk Naval Base on another secret mission. *Jimmy Carter* had been refitted to accomplish special missions, such as SEAL team insertions, drone launches, and covert intelligence projects. She now had the means to tap undersea cables without

disrupting the signal or being discovered.

Clearing the last Hampton Roads channel marker with sufficient depth, her captain issued the "dive" command, and leveled off at periscope depth. Once clear of the shallow Continental Shelf, the sub dove to 300 feet, increased speed to 45 knots, and turned northeast to intercept the TAT-14 cable at the edge of the Continental Shelf.

As the cables pass over the steep drop-off of the Shelf's edge, their stiffness causes them to leave a bow, or gap, between the cable and the edge as it drops thousands of feet to the bottom. This leaves a unique surface feature that is detectable on the sub's special mapping sonar.

After a ten-hour run, the captain ordered the navigator to steer just off the shelf edge, while the sonar operators searched for the telltale blip. "Conn, Sonar. Possible cable contact dead ahead at 1500 yards."

"Conn, aye. Slow your speed to five knots, and stay above and right of the cliff." Minutes passed, and the control room crew stared intensely at their instruments. Running into the cliff edge would mean the loss of the boat and her crew.

"Conn, Sonar—we are over it now."

"Conn, aye. ELINT, any signal?" The sub was equipped with sensitive detection systems that could "hear" the data signals from the cable, within about 100 yards.

"Conn, ELINT. I hear music." This was the slang for electronic emissions.

"Conn, aye. Let me know when the signal passes your antenna, and we'll hover." Within a few seconds, the signal began to shift aft.

"Conn, ELINT. Recommend hover."

"Officer of the Deck, commence hover." The big sub's propellers reversed briefly and the sub stopped directly over the cable.

"Launch the robot." A large hatch aft of the conning tower slowly opened, and a robotic "unmanned vehicle" moved to the starboard side, and then dove beneath the keel to the cable. The specially trained robot operator viewed his monitors and moved the robot into position. Within minutes, the robot had attached a large, bulky apparatus to the cable, which could read the electronic data transiting through it. This was called "the barnacle."

"Conn, barnacle attached."

"Very well. release the transmitter." The operator pushed a button on his console, and a buoyant antenna unit popped out of the "barnacle," rising rapidly to the water's surface. As it floated there, an array of solar panels deployed, sending electrical energy through its umbilical cable down to the barnacle, charging the battery. The system used some of NASA's satellite and Mars rover technology to keep transmitting data back to NSA, via communications satellite, for many months. The only problem with this system was its vulnerability to ship traffic or retrieval by curious fishermen. However, it was made to look like some type of marker buoy, with the legend, "DO NOT TOUCH OR TAMPER WITH THIS OCEANOGRAPHIC DEVICE, OR YOU WILL BE PROSECUTED BY THE U.S. COAST GUARD." This would deter most people from tampering with it, even if they found it so far off the U.S. coast.

Back at NSA, the specialists in the Interception Control room detected a new channel of high-speed data coming in from the satellite. "TAT-14 channel tap is up and running," announced the traffic manager. "Station Nine, capture and dedicate your monitor to record all data and send to Collections. We've done our job, guys—now it's up to them to find the needle in the haystack."

Several floors below, the Collections unit established a "filter," designed to cull out all Telexes and e-mails that contained multiple groups of numbers, indicating that the Level 5 KGB code was being used. Upon "trapping" such messages, they were sent along to Deciphering, and then to Analysis for interpretation and dissemination to the "client," such as the CIA or the FBI. Without his knowledge, Socrates now had a larger and more attentive audience.

After several days of collecting the cable "taps," NSA had amassed a large body of intercepts. In order to process it more quickly, they established a "Pegasus Task Force," which operated out of the secretive Annex Wing of NSA headquarters. Most NSA employees had never even been allowed into the Annex. New employees were taught early in their career, "If you don't need to know something, don't even ask about it."

Melissa Clayton had been designated as the task force chief, and she made daily trips to the Annex to analyze the intercepts. She discovered a pattern of communications that was disturbing. Socrates was routinely corresponding with key figures in the American media, even including some famous TV journalists and newspaper editorial writers. Their identities were verified by tracing the destinations of the Telex communications within the various media organizations.

The rest of the messages seemed to be going to various college educators and a few Wall Street financiers. Then, one code-name caught her eye: ZEUS. She turned to the shift supervisor. "Roger—what or who is 'Zeus?'"

"I don't know, Melissa. His messages have been routed through several 'dead drops,' and they seem to be going to many different places, mostly New York and Chicago. He seems to be a heavy hitter, because Socrates has him funneling money to Pegasus in Chicago, apparently."

"OK, write up a report on our latest compilation, and messenger it over to Brad Tilsdale's group at Ft. McNair."

"Melissa, there is something else. Socrates is sending messages to the Russian embassy in Washington which mention an agent referred to as 'Ramon.'" Whoever 'Ramon' is, he is apparently giving them information regarding embedded CIA agents inside of the Russian government. Should I follow up on this thread?"

"Let me see the latest intercept." Melissa read the text with alarm and knew something was wrong:

"MOST SECRET: Your last information was correct. We have eliminated the Klosky problem. Send information on other doubles. Socrates."

Melissa dialed Tilsdale's mobile phone number and left an urgent message to call back on scrambler.

Since Tilsdale's project began, the scope had enlarged beyond the search for Pegasus. Tilsdale had the ability to see patterns from a few pieces of the puzzle, and to draw the correct inferential conclusions. Few in the FBI had this ability, because most FBI training involves developing evidence for a criminal prosecution of some sort. With intelligence matters, the players seldom follow the rules, as they must do in court proceedings.

At this point, with Melissa's latest NSA report, he began to see the larger pattern of the SVR's activities. Col. Oleg Klosky had been a double-agent for the CIA, and was a high official within the SVR. His discovery by the SVR counter-intelligence unit resulted in a swift execution. The loss was catastrophic, because Klosky was one of the few important penetrations of the Russian intelligence service. At the same time, Tilsdale was reluctant to do anything with his evolving opinion, out of concern that he would be laughed out of the FBI. He called Agent Billings into his office.

"Maybe the most important question is, what part do Pegasus and Zeus play in all of this? If we can unravel those puzzles, we might be able to prove our theory without compromising the classified information."

"Well, we still think that Pegasus is that young guy from Yale Law School, who just moved to Chicago. The trouble is, Socrates never seems to communicate with him directly—only Zeus does. And we have not found him doing anything of significance yet. Do you know he is organizing Blacks from the Chicago South Side, to protest at City Hall? That doesn't seem worth investigating. Personally, I think 'Pegasus' is nothing more than a diversionary project, which the Russians love to do."

"Jeff, don't be naive. He might be a 'sleeper' agent of some sort, and they are just waiting to activate him. Well, stay on it, and let me know if you see anything of interest in the latest communications. I see that Socrates has started using e-mails, sent via the Internet. This will be harder to track, because all you need is a computer, and you can plug in anywhere."

"NSA already has solved this," commented Billings. "They have a way of tracing e-mails through something called 'metadata,' which are inside of every e-mail. Every time an e-mail message goes through the Internet, outside of your local network, it passes through a series of public 'nodes,' or data switches. NSA has managed to imprint 'tags' on the metadata of those e-mails when they transit a node, leaving a digital fingerprint on them."

"Glad I am from the stone age. I am still not that great with computers. Jeff, I think the bastards are trying to take over our college campuses and the media."

Billings stared at him. "Boss, I don't think you should mention that theory to anyone. No one at the senior level is going to buy into that, and it could wipe out your career."

They both knew that despite its modernization after the death of J. Edgar Hoover, the Bureau was still permeated by bureaucratic inertia, and its management did not care for radical ideas like this one. "Yeah, you're right. Just between us."

As they climbed into their car, Tilsdale's mobile phone light was blinking with Melissa's message. Tilsdale called Melissa on scrambler.

"Melissa, Brad. What's up?"

"Sorry to bother you, but you need to look at something."

"OK, we can be there by 1800. See you then."

The NSA, on the other hand, was *very* good with computers, and had just captured an interesting message from Socrates to an unknown agent called "Medusa." Whoever he was, he now lived in the Chicago area, and Socrates was sending him to meet Pegasus. His role would soon become known as a mentor and handler for Pegasus. He was a "rehabilitated" Leftist terrorist from the Sixties, who believed strongly in Communism and the overthrow of the American government. His name was Jason Byron Caswell, and he made his name by planting bombs in government buildings and banks during the campus revolts against the Vietnam

War. With his current wife, Susan O'Malley-Caswell, Jason Caswell had been arrested and prosecuted with other members of the radical Weather Underground. However, the pacifist President, Jimmy Carter, had pardoned both of them, along with the Vietnam draft-dodgers who had fled to Canada, in an effort to "put Vietnam behind us."

In a recent Chicago demonstration against President George W. Bush, Caswell had burned and urinated on an American flag. His "rehabilitation" was apparently far from over. His current occupation: college professor and lecturer. And now Caswell was about to become the handler and trainer for Pegasus.

Billings also noticed that colleges and universities were frequently becoming "incubators" for Leftist activities, but Tilsdale's theory of deliberate campus infiltration seemed too outrageous. More important, no one within the Bureau hierarchy would believe it. "Boss, if we put that into a report, we will not be taken seriously."

"I know. But I'm sure that I'm right. What better way to influence our population? You hit them with a continual Leftist media barrage, while you influence the thinking of their children on college campuses. In one generation, you could substantially shift the national ideology from conservative patriotism to Socialist globalism. I'm worried. We cannot just stand by and let this happen."

"Boss, you can't even *use* the facts that you have here to prove a theory like this, because all of the proof is top secret stuff from NSA. And without proof, who would believe it?" Referring to the conspiracy theorists of the JFK assassination, he added, "You don't want to be considered one of those 'grassy-knoll' guys."

Tilsdale glared at him. "I get your point."

Chapter 12

Sacrificing The Pawn

The Russian officials within the SVR had become alarmed at the intense level of FBI counter-intelligence activity. They felt it would eventually threaten the identity of Cerberus, and they were determined to protect him, as they did not want to lose such a well-placed asset. It was time to sacrifice a pawn on their chessboard, to keep the enemy off the trail.

"Ramon," FBI Agent Robert Hanssen, had served his purpose. The current SVR resident agent at the Russian embassy, "Casino," was instructed in a coded message to leak to the FBI a scheduled "drop" of classified information by Hanssen:

"To Ramon:

For next transfer, use drop #3 at Rock Creek Park bridge. ETA 2/12/01 0200. Use extreme caution.

Casino"

The message was transmitted in a low-level code that the SVR knew had been broken by the NSA. Simultaneously, they used the normal and more carefully coded message system to have Hanssen deposit his latest information at the pre-arranged point.

The NSA team quickly read this message. As Tilsdale and Billings met Melissa in the security lobby, she looked more serious than usual. "Brad, we just found another hot item. Let's go back to Analysis."

Tilsdale glanced over at Billings, and shrugged. When they reached the Analysis Center, she handed him a preliminary report with Casino's message. "I had called you over for something else, but this looks like a top priority," she said.

As the two read the message, Tilsdale asked, "Who are Ramon and Casino?"

"We don't know who Ramon is, but previous intercepts indicate that 'Casino' is an SVR agent at the Russian embassy, probably the resident himself."

"Well, it looks like we need to visit Rock Creek Park tonight, Jeff."

"Why not, Boss? I don't have anything better to do. I'll arrange for some SWAT company. You can't be too careful in that park at nighttime."

FBI Agent Robert Hanssen was a tormented personality, and a disgruntled career agent. To vent his anger at the Bureau, he had spied for the Soviet Union—and now Russia—for about twenty years. After receiving the message from Casino and decoding it, he prepared his documents for delivery on the scheduled night. He would soon have the recognition he had hungered for, although not the type he wanted. Hanssen would soon become known as the most damaging spy in American history, having exposed every CIA agent within his security access.

He drove from his home in the Maryland suburbs to nearby Rock Creek Park, and the drop point. As he deposited the bag of documents under the creek bridge, several infra-red camera lenses clicked. Returning to his car, he was rushed by a heavily armed FBI SWAT team, who immediately placed him in handcuffs and arrested him. In an instant, "Ramon" was no more.

On the drive to the temporary detention facility inside the federal courthouse, Hanssen exhibited his normally smug behavior. "I'm surprised that it took you this long to catch me," Hanssen said.

"You have done enormous damage, and betrayed your country and the Bureau," said an angry Tilsdale. "Why in God's name did you do it?"

"The Bureau has not treated me with the proper respect, and they passed me over for promotions," replied Hanssen. "I wanted to teach them a big lesson, one that they would never forget."

"You are the one that will be getting the lesson, and I doubt that *you* will forget it, my friend."

"Well, this shows how bad you are at your job, Tilsdale. Apparently you are not such a hotshot after all!"

"Maybe not, Robert, but *you* are the one in handcuffs!" retorted Tilsdale.

After his indictment, his lawyer plea-bargained a life sentence to avoid the death penalty, in exchange for complete cooperation by Hanssen. His lengthy debriefing by Tilsdale's team took the Pegasus unit off their normal duties, as they tracked down various leads and tried to control the damage caused by Hanssen. The episode had exactly the effect that the SVR and Dallinger wanted. Tilsdale and his agents now believed that they had caught the "big fish," and that their work was about over.

Following Hanssen's guilty plea, Dallinger called Tilsdale to his office. A Bureau public relations team was there, complete with camera. The "photo opportunity" captured Tilsdale shaking hands with Dallinger, and appeared in the major papers, over Tilsdale's objection. He always tried to maintain his anonymity, for obvious reasons. Meanwhile, Dallinger found this doubly amusing, since the counter-intelligence community was confident that Hanssen was the "mole" that they had been hunting. It was time to shift the focus from Pegasus, permanently.

"Brad, I think it's time that you disbanded that Ft. McNair operation, and I have sent a memo to the Deputy Director to that effect. I need you on some other matters and we can't afford to have your group pursuing pure hunches, while we have known threats to deal with. We have some odd incidents involving the Al-Qaeda organization, and I believe we may have an emerging threat there." The Bureau had been well aware of Osama Bin Laden's terrorist organization for several years, but most government officials assumed that the U.S. homeland was safe from his reach. After all, how could a bunch of Arabs living in tents and caves *possibly* get across the border and carry out an operation in the U.S.?

Tilsdale found himself unable to argue against this, because he, too, thought that the Hanssen arrest was the end of the issue. The Pegasus trail had grown cold and dormant, and no longer seemed to be a real threat. After all, America was full of Leftist politicians, and Sam Basi was merely another example of America's radicalized young people.

Under Caswell's careful tutelage, Sam Basi slowly expanded his political network throughout the Chicago area. Caswell was well connected within the political community of Chicago's Democratic Party, and his close friends included the Mayor, the Governor of Illinois, both U.S. Senators, and several members of the U.S. House of Representatives. Caswell's radical past served to cloak him in a Leftist mystique, rather than make him an outcast.

The Russian SVR maintained their prior relationship with Caswell from the KGB days, and continued to monitor the progress of Sam Basi, or "Pegasus," as they referred to him. Zeus (Zebrotny) contacted Medusa (Caswell), and the two met at a hotel near the O'Hare airport.

"The time has come for our protégé to construct his résumé for his political future," said Zebrotny. "We want him to marry an attractive woman of African-American descent. She must be intelligent and supportive of his political ambitions, and have Socialist leanings of her own."

"I think I know just the woman for him," said Caswell. "Tonya Hampton. She is a lawyer in a prestigious downtown law firm, and active in Democratic and Leftist politics. We have already vetted her, and she has nothing in her background that would be a problem. Her parents are respected members of the community, and her father is a doctor."

"Excellent. Now how do we get him into politics? We need to get him some visibility and let him learn the system in a manner that will not receive too much attention yet."

"The incumbent in his state Senate district is retiring. The electorate is largely Black, and most people know him from his community organizing, eloquent speeches, and support of Leftist causes. I think he should run for that seat," said Caswell.

"I agree. From there, he should run for a federal office, such as Representative or Senator. From that level, we can start to feed him into the national spotlight and give him some name identity."

"Let me put him together with the woman I mentioned. He needs to have an adoring wife, if he is to succeed in American politics. There have been very few successful bachelors in high elected offices within the U.S. Having a beautiful wife makes you newsworthy and 'normal' in the eyes of the press." Caswell grinned. "Remember JFK and Jackie? The two of them were always in the news, and the public loved them."

"Very well. Please proceed as you describe. I will brief the client," said Zebrotny. He was sure that the current SVR Chairman, Gen. Sergei Lebedev, would approve of the next steps in the plan. Lebedev was one of the most ruthless men to ever hold the Chairman position, and he hated the United States with a passion. In his early KGB days, his agent partner had been killed in a firefight with CIA agents. Zebrotny knew he could count on Lebedev's support for continuing with the Trojan Horse project.

In the meantime, Caswell met with Sam in his private study. "Sam, I have an important message for you," said Caswell. "Listen carefully. Trojan Horse—Pegasus can fly."

Immediately, Sam's eyes became transfixed, as he went into his programmed hypnotic state. "Sam, you will become infatuated and fall in love with Tonya Hampton, and you will marry her," said Caswell. "Here is her picture, and her telephone number. You will call her and take her to lunch."

"Yes," replied Sam, in a hollow voice.

Chapter 13

The Wrath of Mohammed

Osama Bin Laden, a disaffected Saudi man of a wealthy family, had become enraged when American forces were allowed on sacred Saudi soil. He had become an anti-government activist and was finally deported from Saudi Arabia by the ruling royal family.

Setting up a terrorist headquarters in the Sudan, he was determined to punish both the Saudi royal family and their American allies. He began to recruit radical Muslim men from around the Middle East, and formed terrorist strike teams, headquartered initially in Pakistan. There, Bin Laden had the protection and support of the Pakistani intelligence service, known as ISI. He knew he needed to make a spectacular "hit" on the United States, in order to gain support and recruit members among radical Islamic groups. In his propaganda, he carefully linked Muslim religious obligations with hatred of Israel, and sympathy for the Palestinians. He emphasized that a strike against the United States was equivalent to a strike against the hated Israel. Neither Bin Laden nor the United States government knew that Bin Laden's activities would be a distraction and of great assistance to his first *infidel* enemy, the Soviet Union.

Bin Laden concluded that the obvious and easiest way

to strike the West was to blow up, hijack, or shoot down their commercial airliners. This only required a small team of well-trained *jihadists,* the soldiers of Allah. Unlike many erstwhile Islamic adversaries of the U.S. and its Israeli allies, Bin Laden understood that it was important to establish a personal mystique for himself of successful terror strikes, wrapped around the Muslim religion. This gave anything he did a guaranteed legitimacy with the Islamic world, which translated into greater support, funding, and volunteers.

From Al-Qaeda's participation in the Afghan war against the Soviets, Bin Laden had retained a small supply of Stinger shoulder-fired missiles, which could bring down any aircraft. For his first display of terrorist power, he chose an attack against an airliner in the United States. For maximum effect, he decided that the "hit" should occur in close proximity to New York, with its large population and media presence. JFK International Airport was the obvious target, he concluded.

After training two teams in the operation of the Stingers, Bin Laden's operational leaders taught them how to obtain two small boats, and position them several miles off the New York coast, with several miles of separation. The GPS positions were selected based on their proximity to published JFK airport departure patterns, which would put the departing airliners directly over the boats for an easy Stinger shot.

Using Pakistani passports, the two teams were sent separately through Karachi to Montreal, where the immigration scrutiny was looser. They traveled by car to Winnipeg, then entered the U.S. by hiking across the porous Canadian border, until they reached their first Al-Qaeda contact at Pembina, Minnesota, just off of I-29. After changing clothes at the Al-Qaeda safe-house, they traveled south and east until arriving at the next Al-Qaeda safe-house in Passaic, New Jersey. Using cash, they purchased a pair of 26 ft. Boston Whaler boats, which they kept at nearby Deep Creek Marina. The next task was the retrieval of the two Stinger missiles, which were en route from Karachi in a shipping container marked "Oriental Rugs."

Finally, the ship arrived at the New York docks, and the container cleared customs without incident. The shipper delivered the container to a Pakistani furniture store, so that everything would seem normal. The Stingers were located within the shipment, and transported at night to another safe-house in Jamaica Bay. Everything was now ready.

"Ali, the weather report seems good for tomorrow night," said one of the terrorists.

"I agree, Youssef. Tomorrow night it will be. Allah willing, we will kill many Americans and spread panic through their sick society," said Ali with a smile. "Remember what we have learned. Choose your target carefully. Make sure it is a 747 or other large aircraft, and that it flies directly over you. Aim carefully for the engines, where the heat source will attract the missile. Boat One will fire first, and if the aircraft is downed, Boat Two will hold its fire. You are a backup. We will both throw our missile launchers into the water

after the aircraft is confirmed destroyed. As far as anyone will know, we are simple fishermen. Then proceed at full speed back to the marina."

The next afternoon, the four men

boarded their boats, carrying large boxes and fishing gear. No one paid attention to them, since many Arabs, Pakistanis, and Indians lived in the general area. They departed the marina, and headed around Breezy Point into the Atlantic. Proceeding northeast, they stopped at their assigned locations off Long Island, and waited for the sun to go down. They were merely two additional small boats among many, taking advantage of a good fishing season.

At around 8:00 p.m., TWA 800, a Boeing 747, was ready to depart JFK airport for Paris. There was a three-man flight crew, 15 flight attendants, and 212 passengers, mostly Americans. They did not know it, but they had less than a half-hour to live.

With a clunk, the 747's main door closed, and the flight crew called for clearance.

"Clearance Delivery, TWA 800, IFR to Paris, we have Information Sierra," said the co-pilot.

"Roger, TWA 800. You are cleared for a Runway 04 departure, to intercept Track X-ray to Paris. Contact Ground Control for pushback and taxi on 121.65."

"TWA 800, copy." He switched the radio frequency to Ground, setting in 123.9 for the tower frequency on the captain's radio. "Ground, TWA 800 for pushback and taxi, we have Sierra [current weather and runway information]."

"TWA 800 heavy, cleared to push back. Contact me before taxi."

"TWA 800, roger." The captain advised the ground crew on his intercom that he was cleared, and he received the "brake release" signal. He pulled the release lever on the console, and the tractor strained to push the big aircraft back from the gate.

When away from the gate, the aluminum behemoth

stopped on the ramp while the ground crew removed the tow bar from the nose gear. They were now ready to go.

"Ground, TWA 800—we're ready to taxi."

"Roger, TWA 800, taxi to runway 04-Right via Tango and Uniform."

"TWA 800, Roger." The captain advanced the four throttles, moving the aircraft forward. Upon arriving at the duty runway, the crew completed their takeoff checklist, and instructed the flight attendants to be seated. All 230 people were eagerly looking forward to Paris and the amenities of that beautiful city.

The co-pilot switched to Tower frequency. "TWA 800, ready for takeoff."

"Roger, good evening, TWA 800, cleared for takeoff, runway 04-Right. After takeoff, climbing right turn to 5,000 feet, heading 100. Contact Departure Control."

"TWA 800, rolling. Good night." The big jet's four Pratt & Whitney jet engines thundered at takeoff power as the captain released the brakes. The aircraft strained with its heavy load of passengers, freight, and fuel, accelerating and struggling to break free of the ground.

"V one," said the co-pilot, indicating they had passed the speed where the takeoff could be safely aborted.

"Rotate." The refusal and rotation speeds were always calculated, based on the temperature, height above sea level, and aircraft weight. The captain pulled back firmly on the control yoke, and the nose wheel lifted from the runway, followed by the main landing gear.

"Gear up," said the captain. The co-pilot raised the landing gear handle, and the large wheel assemblies began to fold into their resting places below the fuselage.

"V two," said the co-pilot, alerting the captain that the

aircraft had reached the takeoff safety speed, where the aircraft could continue climbing with one engine out.

"Flaps 10," commanded the captain. The co-pilot moved the flap lever forward, as the speed increased to 190 knots. "Flaps 5." The acceleration increased. "Flaps 1, up with the green." Finally the aircraft was "cleaned up" for climb and cruise, reaching the initial climb speed of 250, which they were required to maintain until reaching 10,000 feet.

The captain set the flight director course of 100 degrees and selected the "speed mode" on the autopilot. For the rest of the flight, the crew would operate the aircraft by merely turning a few knobs and switches, never needing to fly it with the yoke.

"Departure Control, TWA 800, leveling 5,000."

"Roger, TWA 800, take heading 080 to intercept Track X-ray. You are cleared to flight level 370. Switch to Boston Center on 125.75. Have a good flight."

"Roger, switching. Boston Center, TWA 800, out of 5,000 for flight level 370, proceeding to X-ray."

At that moment, the 747 passed over Ali's boat. The time was now 8:30 p.m. He aimed his Stinger launcher at the huge aircraft and waited for the infra-red lock signal. When he received the characteristic buzzing noise, he pulled the trigger. The missile left the launcher with a roar, momentarily blinding Ali and his partner with the bright light.

As the missile sped toward the 747, its seeker head held the lock on the heat source of the left inboard engine exhaust. In a few seconds, the explosive warhead penetrated the large fuel tank just below and forward of the wings, causing a massive explosion. The aircraft separated into a nose section and the wing-tail section, spewing passengers and debris into the sky, as the two sections plummeted to the sea.

As pre-arranged, the two boat teams dumped their missile equipment in the water, started their engines, and raced back to the marina. Osama Bin Laden's first attack on America was successful. He then dispatched a bomb team to New York, which detonated a bomb in the World Trade Center garage, nearly destroying the building and killing several people.

Next on their list was the American military barracks known as Khobar Towers, in Saudi Arabia. It was destroyed by a suicide truck-bomb attack, with hundreds of casualties. Bin Laden eagerly claimed credit, which put him on the FBI's "hot list."

Then came the truck-bombing of the American embassies in Tanzania and Kenya, followed by the suicide-bombing of the *USS Cole*. These attacks even prodded the lethargic Democrat President, Bill Clinton, to order missile strikes on Bin Laden's hideouts, now in Afghanistan. The pattern was clear and unmistakable, at least to Brad Tilsdale, whose unit was now tasked with protecting American interests from further attacks by Bin Laden and his Al-Qaeda organization.

At the time of this sequence of attacks, the FBI anti-terrorist unit was relatively small and under-funded. Even more problematic, the American intelligence agencies were prevented by the Clinton administration from exchanging intelligence information. This ill-conceived policy kept the FBI ignorant of important information from the CIA and NSA, resulting in a recipe for a catastrophe, which was not far off. Tilsdale had always worked around these barriers, developing personal contacts in the other agencies, like Melissa Clayton, and covertly sharing information.

The FBI viewed everything in those days as a criminal case, not a war. Accordingly, they assigned an FBI team, led by an Assistant Director, to investigate the loss of TWA 800, and obtained numerous witness accounts of a missile-like event that coincided with the explosion. The word came down from the Clinton White House to bury that theory, and to shift the investigation over to a cause of "mechanical failure" to prevent public panic. Another reason, of course, was to avoid political liability for failing to prevent a terrorist attack on Americans. Eventually, not unlike the JFK assassination cover-up by the Warren Commission, the "official cause" was that an electrical short in the fuel tank had caused the explosion. When Bin Laden learned of this, he smiled.

"This is merely the first strike against the *infidels* in a long struggle. It will not be over until Israel is obliterated, America has abandoned the Middle East, and the Sharia Law of Islam dominates the world." In Bin Laden's twisted mind, he envisioned himself as the new Caliph of the Islamic world, turning back centuries of history. Even as he plotted against America, he never knew that his former enemies, the Russians, were carefully plotting to destroy the same adversary, although with less brutal means.

Since there were concerns about a foreign power being involved with TWA 800, Tilsdale sent Billings to the area to rule out those issues. The wreckage was retrieved, piece by piece, and then re-assembled in a hangar at a small airport in the vicinity. Billings knew the FBI forensic team, and asked them privately if they had found anything that would suggest a missile strike or bomb within the aircraft.

"Jeff, we have found something, but no one wants to hear it. It's really weird," commented the forensic scientist. "Several seats contained embedded shrapnel that struck at high velocity. We also found traces of an RDX type of explosive on the cabin interior and upholstery."

"So what are you suggesting, Dr. Simpson?"

"That the aircraft was hit by a missile. We can rule out a bomb, because there would be a centered pattern of damage to the seats and fuselage. This thing apparently penetrated the fuel tank and exploded, causing catastrophic structural failure."

"Doc, is there any evidence that would suggest a particular type of missile? As you know, the conspiracy nuts are even accusing the Navy of shooting the aircraft down."

"Absolutely. As you know, there are definitive chemical signatures for every missile warhead."

"OK, don't keep me in suspense! What do you think this one was?"

"Without a doubt, it was a Stinger. After all, it was made in the USA."

Billings stared at the scientist. "I'm not sure what this means, but thanks, Doc." He immediately returned to Washington to report to Tilsdale.

Tilsdale took the evidence obtained by the TWA 800 forensic team up his chain-of-command. He was certain that a missile, probably a shoulder-fired Stinger, had downed the Boeing 747. When he reached the Director, he was pointedly told to drop that theory. "We already have determined the cause, and that is not it!" said the Director. Tilsdale was ordered to close the file on TWA 800 and terminate his investigation.

Tilsdale's special Ft. McNair unit was dismantled and its agents were assigned to other duties. The plan by Dallinger to divert his efforts from the Pegasus project was successful. Tilsdale was assigned to head what was then somewhat of a backwater assignment. He was placed in charge of the counter-terrorist unit, since the Bureau believed that Russia, China, and other adversaries were not serious intelligence threats at this point. The Bureau could not have been more wrong.

Chapter 14

Learning The Ropes And Climbing The Ladder

Through Caswell's introduction, Sam finally met Tonya Hampton, the beautiful black woman from the Chicago area. Also a lawyer, she exhibited a sharp intellect that mesmerized the young man, whose previous political and academic activities had prevented him from having a steady girlfriend. Except for his mother, he had never met a woman of such strong personality and intellect. After a few months, they were hopelessly in love, and became engaged. In June of 2001, they were married.

Sam's mother attended the ceremony and showed her pride in her son throughout her stay in Chicago, frequently embarrassing him with stories of his academic achievements, and predictions of a bright future. During her stay, SVR agents observed her and concluded that she was a "loose cannon," destined to become a problem for Sam's political career. They reported their observations to Moscow.

SVR Chairman Lebedev studied the reports from his Chicago surveillance agents with concern. If he had known that Sam was actually born in Nigeria, he would have panicked, as that would have placed the entire project in jeopardy. He would not want his political plan to have a citizenship issue.

More than any of the prior successors of Andropov, he viewed the Trojan Horse project as one of the most important covert programs of his agency. "Pegasus" had grown into a formidable agent of the SVR, through a combination of luck and careful planning, and best of all—he did not even know he *was* their agent! The only questions were, *how* far into the U.S. government could he travel, *when* should he be activated and used, and *how* should he be used? Lebedev wondered if they could actually put Pegasus in the White House, but that seemed more like a fantasy than a possibility.

Alicia Ludbury Basi left her doctor's office in a daze. The top oncologist at UCSF Medical Center had just informed her that she had a malignant brain tumor, with less than two months to live. She decided not to share this information with her son Sam. He had enough on his mind, including a forthcoming wedding, and she did not want to distract him with this devastating news.

A month after Sam's wedding, Alicia became ill and suddenly died, before Sam could travel to see her. Sam was devastated, but the SVR agents were relieved. It would only have been a matter of time before Alicia became a political liability for Sam's rise to power. The most important witness concerning Sam's birthplace was now silenced. Except for a certain former employee of a hospital in San Francisco, no one, including Sam, knew where he *actually* had been born. Alicia's San Francisco apartment was cleaned out and her belongings stored in an Oakland warehouse. These personal property items, including her diaries, would remain there, undisturbed, for years.

Leona Waller was now a middle-aged, single woman, living in a dumpy apartment in Sacramento. She was living an obscure life, and working as a low-level government employee at Sacramento's Social Security office.

Waller was one of those millions of people whom are rarely noticed and even more rarely appreciated for their work. Although she now enjoyed the job security of the federal government, she longed for the days when her hospital administrative position enabled her to earn "under the table" money through Medicare fraud and other document forgeries. Leona had completely forgotten about her well-paid falsification of the San Francisco birth of one Husam Khalil Basi, decades ago. She had no way of knowing that her action in producing those documents could soon place her in mortal danger.

Sam's life appeared very normal and routine, from the outside. However, Jason Caswell continued to thread Sam into the extensive social and political fabric of the Chicago Leftist and Democratic Party community. It was an interesting mixture of different motives. On one level, there were the idealistic true-believers who felt that American capitalism need to be transformed into a kinder, more nurturing society, where excessive wealth would be redistributed to those less fortunate. This was Marxism, American-style. This group thrived on emotional responses to complex economic and societal problems, rejecting logic in forming their solutions. If anything made their political solutions appear nonsensical, they ignored it and clung to their Leftist principles, while disregarding the painful lessons of economic and social history.

Another group at the fringe of the American Left consisted

of political radicals, such as the American Communist Party, the "alumni" of the Weather Underground, and various groups that sought the forceful overthrow of the government. Jason Caswell and his wife belonged to this segment.

The third denomination was the Progressive movement, all of whom had links to the Democratic Party. This group could trace its origin back to Teddy Roosevelt and Woodrow Wilson, and also involved those who desired a one-world government and dilution of American sovereignty. Sam fit this group's description, with a tinge of latent radicalism.

Last, but not least, were the Left's wealthy. This group, which included many important people within the financial, media, and film industries, had a strange and paradoxical guilt about their wealth. They formed foundations and gave millions to various "feel good" charities in an attempt to establish an egocentric legacy of philanthropy and purge their economic guilt for being rich. Bill Gates and Warren Buffet fell awkwardly into this category, along with many of the Hollywood moguls and Wall Street elite. Being in the Democratic Party was a way for them to deal with their feelings of guilt for their wealth.

Victor Zebrotny, or "Zeus," was in a class by himself. He pretended to be a wealthy care-giver to the world's needy, but in reality he was nothing more than a powerful agent of a hostile, foreign power. His philanthropic activities were only a cover for his actual motives and connections to the KGB and now the SVR.

Sam ran unsuccessfully for a seat in the U.S. House of Representatives, where he was defeated by a former black civil rights leader and local activist. In that race, he was labeled as "not black enough" for the district constituency. Caswell and Zebrotny conferred with him, and told him that he had not been sensitive to the voters' prejudices and sentiments.

"First, you did not make yourself into a 'brand' that would sell. You did not package yourself as a black liberal. You sounded like a white man, which is not what they wanted. Plus, you did not promise them what they wanted to hear," said Caswell.

"I agree," said Zebrotny. "Sam, you need to modify the dialect and content of your message. Make them believe you are one of *them*, whoever *they* are in a given setting. Adopt their slang, accents, and social customs. Attend their churches, and keep your Muslim religion a secret. Even if you can't deliver, promise them what they want. Voters, especially the middle-class and below, are emotional and ignorant. They react to their feelings, not their brains. Most of the voting public knows little to nothing about their precious Constitution, history, or government, so they act on superficial emotions. Even some educated whites do that. Use the techniques that you were taught, and get your message formulated. There will be other opportunities."

Indeed, there would be. Within months, the Republican U.S. Senator from Illinois resigned in a scandal, leaving his seat open for a special election. Sam knew this was his chance, and he had become bored with his position in the state senate, where he often voted "present," rather than taking a political position that could harm him in the future. Instead, he worked behind the legislative scene to influence the outcome indirectly.

After Caswell and his Leftist friends learned that Sam was interested in the Senate seat, a meeting of "movers and shakers" of Illinois politics convened with Sam at Caswell's home. The professional political consultants had learned that Sam had a big-money force behind him, prompting many talented individuals to offer help with his campaign, smelling a "winner" was in the making. Following the meeting, Sam announced his candidacy for the U.S. Senate.

During the ensuing months, Sam pursued a frenetic sequence of town-hall meetings, photo opportunities, organizational conferences, fund raisers, and the usual politician's activities. With the strong support of the Chicago Democratic political machine and the unions, he went into the election with a lead of 15 percentage points over his Republican rival.

Sam and his wife, Tonya, watched the election results at Caswell's home, along with dozens of important political figures from the area. Finally, NBC announced that Sam was the inevitable winner, causing a cheer from the assembled activists.

"Well, Tonya, I guess we are off to Washington," gloated Sam. "Pack your bags, Baby."

Tonya, pregnant with their first child, smiled grimly. Being married to a high-profile politician was never her goal, but as a loyal wife, she supported Sam with grudging enthusiasm.

Chapter 15

Change of the Watch

George W. Bush won the Presidency after a bitterly divided election. No one knew for certain what his priorities would be, since he seemed detached from his daily responsibilities. It appeared that his staff and the Vice President were calling most of the signals and policy changes. Just before the election, Clinton had appointed a new FBI Director, which placed the Bureau personnel in a degree of uncertainty as to policy matters. Tilsdale now headed the anti-terrorist unit, and he used his influence to have Billings assigned to him.

In his new job as head of the counter-terrorism unit, Tilsdale had received a memo from the Sarasota, Florida field office, describing a suspicious activity at a flight school near Sarasota. Several Arabic men were taking flight lessons, for which they paid with cash. The flight school instructor had noticed them studying the layout of Boeing 767 aircraft, including seating charts. In addition, he noticed that these students did not seem concerned about how to *land* an aircraft—only the procedures of how to manage it in flight, and how to use navigational equipment. Several had gone on to the American Airlines training facility at Dallas, where they paid thousands of dollars for B-767 simulator time.

Thinking that this was suspicious, since none had an airline job, the instructor reported the situation to the local FBI office. Upon a routine investigation, the field agent was also concerned, and alerted the Special Agent-in-Charge, who happened to be an old friend of Tilsdale.

However, when the agent notified Washington in a memo, it was routed first to Dallinger in the counter-intelligence division. Viewing the information as insignificant, he assigned it to Tilsdale to handle. When it was read by Tilsdale and Billings, they knew something was up. "Jeff, I want you to go to Dallas and Sarasota, and interview these flight instructors. This may be nothing, because wealthy Arabs have been taking flight training in the U.S. for years. After all, there must be thousands of corporate jets owned by Saudis, all over the world, and they need pilots. And we know how much cash they throw around."

"No problem, Boss. I'll hit Dallas first, and then Sarasota. I'll keep you advised."

That afternoon, Eliana Gómez, the flight attendant on Tilsdale's first flight into Washington, was checking in to Dulles operations for her flight to Los Angeles. After signing in, she went up to the passenger gate area to begin boarding, where she noticed a group of four Middle-Eastern men talking heatedly in Arabic. When they noticed her staring at them, the conversation stopped.

The airline gate agent announced the flight, beginning with "pre-boards," who were usually VIPs or disabled people, followed by First Class, Business Class, and then Economy. Eliana always tried to establish rapport with the passengers as they boarded, flashing her beautiful smile at each person. When the four Arabs went by, she noticed that they avoided eye contact.

With the passengers all on board and seated, the main door was closed. Eliana was working in Business Class, where she found the four Arabs. As the big jet departed the gate and taxied to the duty runway, she was seated in her "jump-seat" by the main door, looking back through the cabin. She noticed the Arabs were watching the flight attendants closely, especially when they were near the cockpit door.

A few minutes after takeoff, the captain turned off the seatbelt sign, and the flight attendants began to ready their galleys for the beverage service. As was customary, Eliana used her key and opened the cockpit door. "Hi, guys!" she said, with her usual smile.

"Hi, Eliana. Do you know Bill Cummings?" he said, nodding at the co-pilot.

"Sure, I've flown with him before."

"It can't be often enough," grinned Cummings.

"Hey, we aren't even at altitude, and you are already hitting on the flight attendants?" noted the captain with a laugh.

"Come on, Eliana, marry me and get it over with," said Cummings.

"What do you want to drink, Ace? Save the kind words for one of the impressionable new girls."

"OK, coffee black. What do you want, Roger?"

"Coffee with sugar, please. Eliana, everything OK back there?"

"Yeah, but I have four Arab dudes in Business. They give me the creeps."

"Don't sweat it—they're harmless, just strange. You would be, too, if you had their oil money!"

"I'll be back in a few." As Eliana left the cockpit, she

noticed all four Arabs staring intently at her. She was accustomed to men staring at her, but she did not like this. The thought occurred to her, *I wish Brad Tilsdale was on this flight, wearing his big gun.* If Eliana had known that these four were being trained as members of a terrorist Bin Laden strike team, she would not have been so calm. She was glad that she still had Tilsdale's cell phone number on her cell phone's speed-dial. *You never know,* she thought, peering back at the four men.

After the flight arrived at Los Angeles, the men deplaned without incident. Eliana thought to herself, *Maybe I am too paranoid these days.* Far from it. Eliana was one of the first people to notice the Bin Laden teams "casing" the airline's flights, in preparation for a major attack on the United States. Having been trained in how to hijack a flight, the four teams were now flying around the United States on the two target airlines, American and United. They were familiarizing themselves with cabin flight procedures, how to enter the cockpit, and planning how to subdue the cabin and flight crews. The operation was almost ready to proceed, funded by Al-Qaeda cash, sent through Pakistan.

Several days later, Eliana was back in Washington, and phoned Tilsdale. "Brad, this is Eliana. I just had a strange experience with some passengers, and thought you might be interested."

"Great to hear from you, Eliana." Tilsdale had continued dating her over the years. She seemed even more beautiful than when he first noticed her on his arrival in Washington, and she had a sexual appetite to match. Tilsdale considered himself fortunate.

"Could we do dinner or something?"

"Sure. How about tonight? Six o'clock?"

"That's a deal!"

That evening, over dinner, Eliana relayed the incident with the four Arabs. "Brad, I just know those guys were up to something. If I get their names from the passenger list, could you check them out?"

"Sure. Fax the names to my private fax. It's on my card."

"Thanks, Brad," she purred. "Now, how about dessert, at my place?"

Tilsdale felt a stirring of desire. "That sounds lovely, Eliana."

"Brad, you have *no idea* how lovely it will be."

The next day, Tilsdale's fax began to print out a transmission from Eliana. It contained four names: Mohamed Atta, Waleed Al-Shehri, Wail Al-Shehri, and Abdulaziz Al-Omari. Tilsdale summoned one of his agents. "Dave, run a background on these guys, and let me know what you find. I'm curious what their immigration status might be, also."

"Will do, Sir."

Agent Tucker was one of the best at doing complex, computer-based tracing of identities, connections, and aliases. Tilsdale was sure that if something was not right, Tucker would find it.

In a few hours, Tucker was back. "What did you find?" asked Tilsdale.

"Boss, all four of these guys entered on a Pakistani passport, with a student visa. They each entered the country through a different city, and there is no indication that they have ever signed up with any school, university, or college, which is required for their visa. At a minimum, it looks like an immigration case for the INS [Immigration and Naturalization Service]."

"Any criminal records?"

"None, except for one traffic ticket in Florida."

"Florida? What county?"

"Sarasota."

Tilsdale suddenly had that "old feeling," indicating that something was, indeed, not adding up. He instantly had a hunch, and called the cell phone number for Jeff Billings.

"Jeff? How is it going? Found anything yet?"

"Well, there is something odd here. The American Airlines simulator instructor said that these guys each paid $50,000 for two weeks of simulator training on the 767 aircraft. He said they seemed to concentrate only on how to fly the aircraft and descend it. They were not interested in how to take off or land. Does that seem odd to you?"

"Definitely—especially if you are paying that much money. Anything else?"

"Yeah. Their references did not check out. None of them has even applied to Saudia Airlines for a pilot job, which was their reason given for the training."

Tilsdale felt his heart pounding. "Jeff, do you have a list of their names?"

"Yes."

"Are any of the following names on your list? Mohamed Atta, Waleed Al-Shehri, Wail Al-Shehri, and Abdulaziz Al-Omari?"

"Boss, they are *all* on my list."

"Do you know where they are now?"

"They just disappeared. They completed their two weeks here and left without a forwarding address. One of the people here thinks he heard them discussing Washington, like they were going to visit."

"Jeff, get your ass back here ASAP!"

Tilsdale called his supervisor, who was still Dallinger, and asked for an immediate meeting. He was told to come by in five minutes.

As Tilsdale entered the office, Assistant Director David H. Dallinger leaned forward on his desk. He looked annoyed. "Brad, what's so urgent?"

"I think we have some Arabs training to be hijackers. We have traced them from Sarasota through Dallas, but they have disappeared. We think they may be heading to Washington."

Dallinger quickly processed this dramatic information. This was working out better than he hoped, as he needed to keep Tilsdale from getting back into the Pegasus case or chasing any more leads. This was squarely within the Bureau's jurisdiction, and could turn out to be useful in many ways, depending upon the outcome. Tilsdale had already come to him with the TWA 800 case, but the White House had squelched any further investigation into that case. The thing to do was to give Tilsdale total support on this, and keep him busy.

"I think you do have something, and I want you to have whatever resources you need to find these guys. What do you need now?" asked Dallinger.

"I will need to put out an ABB [All-Bureau Bulletin] on them to see what we can dredge up. Then I will need about twenty agents to trace their steps and collect evidence. Last, I recommend notifying the U.S. Marshal's office that they need Sky Marshals on as many flights as possible."

"Consider it done. Keep me advised," said Dallinger.

"Thank you, Sir." As Tilsdale left the office, he had the distinct impression that the Assistant Director was happy about this news, which he found odd.

Tilsdale and his team fanned out across the country, following leads, interviewing witnesses, and trying to locate the "flight students." Finally, one agent got lucky. When he spoke with the manager of the apartment in Sarasota where several of the men had stayed, the woman remembered that they had asked her how to access a computer and get on the Internet. She had told them about "Internet cafes" and how the public libraries normally have computers to use for a small fee. As it turned out, there was a library nearby, where the agent found staff members who remembered the Arabs.

The agent then learned which passwords had been issued, after the Arabs paid a charge by credit card. An inquiry was made to the credit card company, and an address near Newark was given: 4328 Randolph Street, Passaic, NJ. This was the Al-Qaeda safe-house used before by the TWA 800 strike team, although that was not known to the investigators. He reported this to Tilsdale, who relayed the information to Melissa Clayton at NSA. Tilsdale instructed the agent to put the house under immediate surveillance, and to obtain a search warrant.

"Sure, Brad, we can back-search our Internet intercepts and locate those passwords from that IP address, and then see what the exchange or search was. I'll let you know."

Several hours later, Melissa called back, obviously shaken.

"Brad? Here is what we found. We traced the computer communications from that library to a known Al-Qaeda facility in Pakistan. Our Arabic translators are trying to figure out what they are talking about in detail, but one of them thinks this has something to do with September 11th. We don't know what year, however."

"Let me know when they have a complete translation.

Thanks, Melissa!"

By now, four hijacker teams had been trained and assembled by Al-Qaeda and carefully dispersed around the U.S. The plan, which was created by Khalid Sheikh Mohammed, placed five men in each team: two pilots and three "muscle men," who had been trained in close combat and would be armed with box-cutter knives from their carry-on luggage. One, however, had been arrested by immigration officials, and turned back to his point of origin at Dubai.

The day's date was now September 2, 2001.

The FBI was now shifting into high gear in its search for the potential hijackers. Dallinger placed Tilsdale in charge of the task force, which was carefully tracing the travels of the Arabs. The job was difficult, as the four were apparently not employed, nor did they seem to be using credit cards since Dallas. In fact, they were traveling randomly from state to state, staying a few days in motels, and then moving on. They now paid for everything with cash, leaving no paper trail.

Tilsdale received approval to issue an All-Points Bulletin

to all law enforcement agencies to have the Arabs arrested on sight. This nearly stopped the plot, because Mohamed Atta was the ring-leader. Without him, the operation could not go forward, as he was the only link to the Al-Qaeda manager of the plot, Khalid Sheikh Mohammed.

As four of the Arabs approached Newark on I-95 in their rental car, a New Jersey State Trooper noticed the vehicle making an unsafe lane change. He switched on his lights, and motioned for them to pull over. He watched them carefully from his patrol car as he called in the license plate number. "Bravo 35, the plate matches the vehicle. It's registered to Hertz," said the dispatcher.

"Ten-four," he responded. He got out of his car, and approached the subject vehicle on the driver side. His hand rested lightly on his .40 caliber Beretta Px4 Storm semi-automatic pistol. He motioned for the driver to roll down his window, which he did.

"Driver's license, please." As the driver fumbled in his wallet, he looked over the passengers, who appeared nervous. Examining the Florida license, he saw the name, "Mohammed Atta," with a Sarasota address. The men looked Arab or Hispanic, and the Florida connection made the officer think this could be a drug delivery from Florida to the northeast, which was common along the I-95 corridor. He decided to have the men exit the vehicle, while he did a search. At that moment, the speaker on his patrol car blared, "Bravo 35, what's your twenty [location]?"

Using his shoulder microphone, he said, "I-95 northbound, a mile south of Exit 13."

"Roger, proceed Code 3 to scene of multi-car accident with fatalities, vicinity of I-78 westbound, near Exit 54."

"10-4, on the way." He turned to the driver. "Watch

◆ DICK NELSON

your lane changing, Sir. You could cause an accident," as he handed him his license. If the officer had run the license through the normal computer check, he would have learned that these men were wanted by the FBI. Luck was on the side of Al-Qaeda on this day.

Nevertheless, Tilsdale's FBI team was closing in. On September 9th, the FBI raided the house in Passaic, taking four Al-Qaeda operatives into custody. A search of the premises produced numerous evidence items on computer hard drives, e-mails, and documents. The investigators immediately started to work on translating the mass of evidence, but it was already too late. The hijackers were moving from city to city, on a pre-planned itinerary, designed to shake off any surveillance. They were headed for their final launch points. If Tilsdale had only a few days more, and if the CIA and FBI had been sharing intelligence data, the plot might have been stopped.

◆ 150

Chapter 16

Armageddon

Using a computer in a Newark Internet cafe, Atta sent an e-mail to the other three teams, who were scattered around the Northeast in motels, waiting for the "go" signal. Each team leader had an AOL e-mail account, so that they could make their messages "return receipt" and ensure delivery. Atta typed his message:

"It is time for divine justice. Execute as planned, ETD 1600, 23 Jumaada al-Thaany 1422 A.H. Allah akhbar."

The coded message meant, "Operation is a go. Use flights departing your location at 4 p.m., Mecca time [8:00 a.m. Eastern], on September 11, 2001 [the Islamic calendar was used]. God is great." Atta purchased tickets in First or Business Class on the Internet for all team members, using a new credit card that would not be discovered until it was too late.

Teams One and Two would depart on American Flight 11 and United Flight 175, from Boston to Los Angeles. Team Three would board United Flight 93 out of Newark, bound for San Francisco. Team Four would take American Flight

77 from Dulles to Los Angeles. Two of the flights were using 757 aircraft, but the cockpits were similar to the 767. The team pilots were prepared to fly either model.

Teams One and Two would hit the North and South Towers of the World Trade Center, respectively. Team Three would hit the U.S. Capitol building, and Team Four would hit the Pentagon, symbol of America's military power.

While the Al-Qaeda teams prepared for the attack on America, the FBI was closing in. Although the CIA was prohibited from sharing its trove of foreign intelligence on Al-Qaeda, Tilsdale had found some "unofficial" ways around the logjam. However, his unofficial process took too much time and he was increasingly frustrated.

George Bush's White House team was slow in getting started, primarily because he did not think he was going to win the election. As a result, in the crush of events, he ignored intelligence reports that suggested another attack by Al-Qaeda was imminent.

Ironically, on September 11th, 2001, President Bush was attending a children's reading class at a school in Sarasota, near the airport where some of the hijackers had trained. He was totally unprepared for the cataclysmic event that would change America—and his Presidency—in the next few hours.

As usual, Eliana Gómez reported for the continuation of her trip after a layover in Boston. American Flight 11 was headed for Los Angeles, where she hoped to see her sister and brother-in-law. Since she did not walk through the terminal, but went through operations, she never saw the five Arab men seated in the concourse. On this trip, she was working in Economy, and the men were seated in First Class, out of her view.

By time the aircraft leveled off at altitude, she knew

something was wrong. She heard screams from the First Class cabin, and rushed to see what was happening. She looked around the curtain between Business and First Class just as one of the hijackers slit the throat of a flight attendant. Before they noticed her, she ran to the back of the aircraft and slid into an empty window seat with her cell phone.

In the meantime, the hijackers forced their way into the cockpit, and cut the throats of both pilots, dragging them from their seats. The other hijackers piled the bodies against the bulkhead in First Class and covered them with a blanket. Jumping into the captain's seat, Mohamed Atta attempted to give an announcement on the PA system, but pushed the wrong switch and transmitted with a heavy accent on the radio: "We have some planes. Just stay quiet and you'll be OK. We are returning to the airport. Nobody move. Everything will be OK. If you try to make any moves, you'll endanger yourself and the airplane. Just stay quiet." Combined with the flight's disregard of instructions, this sent Air Traffic Control into a state of confusion, as they tried to figure out what was happening.

In the rear of the aircraft, out of view of the hijackers, Eliana speed-dialed Brad Tilsdale's number. To her surprise, he answered. "Brad, this is Eliana. My flight from Boston has been hijacked, and they have killed some of the crew. I think they are flying the aircraft!"

Tilsdale froze in his seat, wondering what to say. "Eliana, are you in danger?"

"No, not right now, but we are turning around and starting to descend. What should I do?"

"What is the flight number?"

"Flight 11."

At that moment, Billings walked in. Tilsdale said, "Jeff,

American Flight 11 has been hijacked out of Boston. Notify the National Command Center!" Billings ran for a telephone.

"Brad, I am so scared! We are getting lower, and I can see the Hudson River and Manhattan. I guess they are going to land at La Guardia or JFK. Maybe Newark. We are going way too fast."

"I have alerted the authorities, Eliana. Try to stay calm. We will get you down."

"Brad, we are getting really low and fast. I can see buildings. They are not turning for the airport! Oh, no. . . ." The phone suddenly went dead. Flight 11 had just crashed into the North Tower of the World Trade Center in a fiery explosion. Tilsdale could not get her response, and guessed that the worst had occurred. Although Tilsdale was trained to ignore suffering, tears welled up in his eyes, and he cried like a baby.

Billings burst into the room. "An aircraft has just hit one of the World Trade Center towers, Boss!"

Tilsdale was slumped in his seat, holding his face in his hands. "I know, Jeff. Thanks."

A second aircraft hit the other tower causing a huge fireball of burning jet fuel. In the next hour, both towers would collapse, killing hundreds more. On American Flight 77, the hijackers flew the 757 directly into the side of the Pentagon, collapsing part of the structure and causing a deadly fire.

Flight 93 was another story. There, the hijackers were one "muscle man" short. When the passengers used their cell phones to communicate with families or friends, they learned that other aircraft were being used as flying bombs, to attack New York and Washington. They rushed the hijackers, subduing two, and broke into the cockpit. Rather than allow the passengers to take the aircraft from them, the Al-Qaeda pilot dove the 757 into the Pennsylvania country-side, killing all on board. This heroic act by the passengers undoubtedly saved the Capitol building.

By afternoon, the entire country was on an emergency war footing. President Bush was airborne in Air Force One, just as he would be in a nuclear war. All law enforcement agencies in the federal government were placed on high alert. In a matter of hours, the nineteen hijackers had been identified. All were Arabs, and had been trained at Al-Qaeda facilities in Afghanistan and Pakistan. The FAA grounded all flights within the U.S. airspace, while officials tried to identify the threat and prevent further losses of aircraft.

From his hideout in Afghanistan, Bin Laden gleefully took credit for the attack, and considered it more successful than he had hoped. He became an instantly important figure in the Islamic world with this dramatic attack on America, "the great Satan." He doubted that the weak Americans would do more than Clinton had done before, which was to lob a few Tomahawk missiles at him from a distance. This time, however, America had shifted into its revenge mode, just as it did after Pearl Harbor. Bin Laden would become a hunted animal for the next decade, with most of his key operatives captured or killed.

Foremost among America's new warriors in this fight was Brad Tilsdale's counter-terrorist unit. As far as Tilsdale was concerned, the gloves were *off*. He vowed to get even for America—and for Eliana. In his mind, there were no longer any limits, when it came to killing Al-Qaeda operatives.

Chapter 17

Opportunities

The new war with Islamic terrorists gave politicians a lot to talk about, and Sam used the situation to full advantage. He made several speeches on the floor of the U.S. Senate, criticizing the Bush administration for being "unprepared" for a terrorist attack, and for allowing "incompetent" airport security. He conveniently omitted the fact that the national security system had languished under the Clinton Presidency, even after a prior attack by Al-Qaeda on the World Trade Center. Saul Alinsky's strategy, followed closely by Sam Basi, was to always blame bad things on your opponent, regardless of the true facts.

Almost as a gift to the Democrats, Bush allowed Osama Bin Laden to slip out of his hideout in the Afghanistan mountains, and enter Pakistan. A steady flow of Al-Qaeda plots then were put into motion, primarily against the airlines. Sam Basi became even more vocal, demanding that Bush capture or kill Osama Bin Laden, or turn the White House over to someone who could. He had a good idea of who that should be.

The FBI counter-terrorist unit was expanded, adding hundreds of agents and staff. Tilsdale was appointed to the position of Assistant Director—Counter-Terrorism, putting him on the same level as Dallinger, who tried to block the promotion. The last thing he wanted was to lose his supervisory authority over the dangerous Tilsdale, who now headed a unit as large as Counter-Intelligence.

On September 13th, an emergency security meeting was secretly called by the governments of China and Russia, to be held in Moscow at SVR headquarters. Attendees were Gen. Liang Guanglie and Anatoly Vasiliyevich Kvashnin (chiefs of staff of the Chinese and Russian militaries), plus Sergei Lebedev, Chairman of the SVR and Xu Yongyue, Director of China's Ministry of State Security. The faces around the table mirrored the international tension that had been created everywhere by the September 11th strikes.

Lebedev began, "Gentlemen, the United States has been wounded by these incredible attacks, which appear to have been executed by Islamic terrorists. We Russians certainly have experienced this type of terrorism from our Chechnya province, where Muslim radicals have attempted to establish a separate republic. But I have a question that each of us needs to answer to each other, without reservation and in a straightforward way. Have either of our governments involved themselves with the people who carried out the September 11th attacks? On behalf of the SVR, I will tell you that we had nothing to do with it."

"Nor did any part of *our* military, including the GRU [Russia's military intelligence unit]," echoed Gen. Kvashnin. He pointedly looked at the Chinese for their responses.

"No, Comrades, our intelligence organization was as surprised as the rest of you by these attacks," Said Xu Yongue.

"And our military had no knowledge and no involvement either," said Gen. Liang.

"Alright. I ask this question, because we have many common interests, including the defeat of the United States and its ambitions. But this would not be the way to accomplish that," said Lebedev.

"We all agree with that," said Xu, "but the United States is now like a wounded animal, irrational and bent on revenge. You can steal from them and push them back a little at a time, but we know how they react when they are struck in a surprise attack and humiliated."

Gen. Liang smiled. "Yes, like when our Japanese enemies hit them at Pearl Harbor. They turned from a pacifist, isolationist nation into a military monster, almost overnight."

Lebedev continued. "When they are in this mode, the Americans are very unpredictable, and should not be taken for granted. As a strategy, we definitely want to stay publicly on *their* side, even as we undermine them elsewhere."

"Agreed," said Xu. "I think we should even cooperate with them in hunting these bastards down. The gullible Americans always overplay any gesture of friendship from our side, and it could entice them let their guard down for a while. From what we have pieced together, it was Bin Laden's Al-Qaeda organization, based currently in Afghanistan and Pakistan."

"We agree," followed Lebedev. "After what Bin Laden and his *mujahadin* did to our forces in Afghanistan, we owe him some payback. This would be a good time for us all to make a statement that is clearly heard by the Muslim world. General Liang, we have problems with Chechnya, but you have problems with Muslim terrorists in your Tashkurgan area of Xinjiang province."

"Yes, they recently ambushed an army convoy in that area. We found the village that most of them came from, and eliminated it. That is the way you have to deal with them, and superior force, ruthlessly applied, is all that they understand."

"Well, then we are all agreed. We will extend an offer of assistance and cooperation through diplomatic channels to the United States, while continuing all of our respective covert operations against them," said Lebedev.

"The People's Republic agrees," said Gen. Liang.

"Then let's go global with our combined assets, and find these Al-Qaeda vermin," urged Lebedev. If we quietly hand them over to the Americans, we can stay out of Al-Qaeda's sights, and leave the Americans to fight them."

"A good plan, Mr. Chairman," commented Director Xu. "Let's locate them and give the Americans the information through our U.S. agent network."

"I have just the man who can use this information." *A perfect way to use Cerberus,* thought Lebedev.

The Bush administration, after letting Bin Laden escape, feverishly searched for a way to re-establish its credibility. George W. Bush, who idolized his father, held a desire for revenge for an Iraqi assassination attempt when George H.W. Bush visited Kuwait in 1993. Although the plot was foiled, George W. never forgot it. He also felt that his father had lost the election against Bill Clinton because he had failed to use the Desert Storm forces to finish off Saddam Hussein's regime. He resolved to make up for those stains on his family honor.

The key strategists within his administration were directed to turn their attention to the other threat in the region, Iraq. Saddam Hussein was an easy target, as he had no strong allies after the demise of the Soviet Union. The word went out to find a rationale for a "regime change" in Baghdad. The CIA was directed to assemble the evidence that Iraq still possessed "weapons of mass destruction," or WMDs. That included chemical, biological, and nuclear weapons capabilities.

By 2003, using dubious intelligence sources, the Bush administration had convinced the world that Iraq, did, indeed, have WMDs, and had several circumstantial links to Al-Qaeda. It was well known that the Iraqis had used chemical weapons against the Iranians and even their own people. Saddam Hussein was an unpopular and belligerent dictator, feared throughout the Middle East.

Having won UN Security Council support, the U.S. launched Operation "Iraqi Freedom" on March 20, 2003. Massive air strikes, amphibious landings, and armored columns were unleashed on Saddam's regime. In a few weeks, the major military operations were over, but were followed by a determined loyalist insurgency. Casualties among coalition troops mounted, causing great concerns just before the 2004 elections.

Sam Basi used his Senate seat as a political pulpit, preaching non-intervention and withdrawal at the earliest possible date. Bush, however, had decided to follow the bad advice of his aides, thinking that he could create an Americanized democracy in this strategic area of Mesopotamia, positioned on the borders with troublesome Syria and Iran. Why would the Iraqis not want such a precious gift?

Bush won reelection again in 2004 by a slim margin, primarily because of the flawed candidacy of John Kerry. Feeling no need to compromise, he kept the occupation force in Iraq, over the growing protests of many Americans, including some Republicans. In the meantime, U.S.

casualties in Iraq mounted, and he had still not been able to track down the elusive Bin Laden, making him look increasingly incompetent.

In 2004, Sam Basi attracted national attention and became the darling of the media, when he delivered an eloquent and moving keynote speech in the Democratic convention. A self-fulfilling prophesy began to circulate that this was a man who could become President. Sam's SVR handlers had arranged this exposure to test the political waters. They were ecstatic at the results and the enthusiastic feedback.

Using covert information "drops," including specially encrypted web sites, the SVR and MSS collected thousands of Al-Qaeda leads. After culling through them, the most reliable ones were made available to Dallinger, who picked out the best ones. Finally, he received one from a fake Hungarian web site, operated by the SVR. This was the one that he was looking for. It was the location of an Al-Qaeda operations center in Miami. At least six known Al-Qaeda operatives were using the facility, located in a suburban industrial park. Dallinger dialed Tilsdale's extension.

"Brad, David. I have a strong Al-Qaeda lead, but I don't know how long it will be valid. It looks like at least six of the bastards are cooking up something bad near Miami."

"I'll be right up!" Moments later, Tilsdale appeared at his door. "What have you got?"

"There is an industrial park in the northwest Miami area, just off of Weston Road, behind the Cleveland Clinic. These guys have rented a small warehouse and office complex, located in Building 4B. Here's the map, and here is the warrant that we just got from the U.S. Attorney. I figured that your team would want this one." Dallinger smiled, thinking, *With a little luck, these ragheads might kill Tilsdale during the raid—two birds with one stone.*

Tilsdale, filled with that anger that only a desire for vengeance can provide, ran for the elevators. Within minutes, he had ordered a jet to fly into Ft. Lauderdale to meet up with the FBI SWAT team from the Miami field office.

During the flight, he and Billings reviewed their attack plan. This was a classic "close quarters combat," or CQC situation. The FBI SWAT teams were highly trained in this special type of tactical situation, because most of their raids occurred within urban environments. With a variety of weapons available to match the situation, Tilsdale had already directed the team to carry the new Kriss Vector sub-machine gun, firing the powerful .45 caliber ACP round either in single, double-burst, or fully automatic mode. It was the most technologically advanced weapon of its type in the world. The Navy SEALs had already tested it, and one of Tilsdale's Navy contacts had told him about its superior characteristics for urban warfare. "If it's good enough for the SEALs, it's good enough for us," noted Tilsdale.

The Bureau's Citation jet touched down at Ft. Lauderdale and taxied rapidly to an isolated spot on the transient aircraft ramp. There, it was met by a caravan of four black, tinted-window SUVs, containing the FBI's Miami SWAT team. Tilsdale and Billings quickly climbed inside the lead vehicle, and the caravan sped off to the I-595 West on-ramp.

Tilsdale leaned over to the driver. "Get off on I-75, then take Exit 15 to Royal Palm Boulevard. We'll circle the wagons and brief the troops in Country Isles Park. That will put us close, but not too close, to the target."

"Got it, Sir," replied the driver. Tilsdale had received a report via text message from the local FBI surveillance team on his Blackberry that all six terrorists were currently inside the warehouse, and that no external guards were visible. To prevent alerting them, Tilsdale had decided not to involve the local police until after the raid.

The four SUVs stopped at a remote section of the park and the agents huddled over Tilsdale and the maps. "There are surveillance cameras on these corners. This makes a frontal assault a bad idea, unless we can blind them. Who's the duty sniper?"

"We have two, Sir," said the team leader, pointing to two black-clad agents with the powerful M-110 .300 Winchester Magnum long rifles, equipped with Leupold high-power scopes, slung over their shoulders. Like the other team members, they also carried the Kriss sub-machine gun and a .45 caliber Glock Model 21 sidearm.

"You guys any good?" asked Tilsdale with a grin, knowing that the SWAT snipers were the elite of the team and had to demonstrate incredible accuracy in order to qualify for this coveted team role. They usually had extensive military experience in the special operations units.

"We can hold our own, Sir," replied one, with a Southern drawl.

"Former military?" asked Tilsdale.

"Yes, Sir. Marine RECON. Bobby is ex-Delta Force."

The other sniper punched his partner in the shoulder. "There is no such thing as '*ex*-Delta Force," said Bobby.

"Roger that. So what are your longest kills?"

"I got a Taliban chief in Afghanistan at 1500 yards, while he was sipping soup. Bobby got an Iraqi general at 1400 yards, but he was using one of the old M-40s, and he can do better now. What do you have in mind, Mr. Tilsdale?"

"Forget the formalities, guys. I'm Brad, and this is Jeff—who by the way, is also ex-Delta Force. We have six confirmed Al-Qaeda in there. I do not intend to serve the warrant and fuck around with these guys. I want two guys on the roof, firing through the skylights on my signal. Snipers, I want you guys to separate for a north and south aspect so that we get some triangulated fire, especially if anyone runs out of the doors. I want you to use silencers and take out those cameras. Can you do it from this raised berm around the parking lot?"

"No problem, Brad. Hell, that's only 400 yards. That's a chip-shot," said the tall sniper.

"Wrong, that's a lay-up," said the other.

"I don't care what it is—just take them out quickly. That big slug you are using is going to make some noise when it hits the building. As soon as you get them all, I will give the 'go,' and the penetration team will blast the wall open. When that happens, the 'up team' will take out any armed terrorists from the skylight. Jeff and I will then charge the door with the lead team. Snipers, you are responsible for any stragglers that bail out, OK?"

Everyone nodded. It was obvious that Tilsdale had done this before. "I want the penetration team to blast through the adjoining wall in the empty warehouse section, here, and sweep the room with your Vectors. You guys will be primary, and we will all key on you. Everyone suit up, take a leak, and let's drive into position."

Within minutes, the teams separated into their respective groups. The "up team" quietly placed a ladder against the wall of the unoccupied side of the warehouse and climbed onto the roof, carefully approaching the skylight. The snipers lined up their sights on the assigned cameras. "Bobby, you take the two on the right."

"Roger," was the radioed reply.

"Hot mikes, everybody." The team switched on their boom microphones.

"Up team, ready?"

"Affirmative. We'll break the skylight and drop in a stun grenade on the signal."

"Punch team ready?"

"Affirmative."

"Snipers, green light."

The long M-110s each emitted a pair of muffled pops from behind the parking lot, sending their high-velocity bullets streaking toward the surveillance cameras. Each camera disintegrated, blinding the terrorists inside. "Go, go, go!" yelled Tilsdale into his mike, followed by a loud explosion that signaled the stun grenade had been tossed into the warehouse from the skylight. A louder explosion followed, with the penetration team blasting through the wall. At the second explosion, AK-47 fire chattered from inside the warehouse. The "up team" sprayed the shooters from the skylight with their Kriss Vectors, hitting them numerous times.

Tilsdale and Billings raced across the parking lot, just as two Arab men ran from a side door toward a nearby sedan, carrying AK-47s. "Halt!" yelled Tilsdale, dropping to one knee. The men started to turn toward him but were knocked to the pavement in a hail of .45 caliber bullets from the main SWAT team's weapons.

On his radio, Tilsdale heard, "Clear! Cease fire!" from the penetration team. He and the rest of the SWAT team entered the warehouse. Four men were lying on the warehouse floor, blood pooling around their bodies.

Billings immediately noticed a large table with maps, charts, and diagrams of Miami International Airport. A box with C-4 explosive, detonators, and timers was beside the table. "Bingo," said Billings. "Bag this stuff—except for the explosives—and put it in the vans, guys."

"By the way, Jeff—did you see me knock on the door before the assault?"

"Affirmative, Boss. I believe you said, 'FBI, we have a warrant! Please open the door!'"

"You have good ears, my friend," laughed Tilsdale. "The really good news is, we obviously stopped a major terrorist attack." He thought to himself, *This is a little payback for September 11ᵗʰ, but it's still not enough for me.*

"Jeff, notify the local PD that they need to come in with the Coroner and clean this up, and that they will need their bomb squad," directed Tilsdale.

"It's a dirty job, but somebody has to do it," chuckled Billings.

Not all catastrophes involve terrorists. Another defining moment occurred in the aftermath of Hurricane Katrina, when the Gulf Coast was devastated, exposing inadequate planning and response by the federal government. Sam Basi made sure that Bush received the blame for this debacle, claiming that the Bush administration (mostly white) allowed the hurricane victims' suffering because many were poor and Black. This won Sam considerable support within the Congressional Black Caucus, and they rallied around this issue.

This natural disaster became overshadowed by a parallel crisis that appeared to be caused by the bursting of the U.S. housing bubble. Because of the wave of mortgage loan defaults, secretly triggered by the Chinese by a massive calling in of their loans, a shock-wave pulsed through the American financial system. Housing prices began to fall rapidly, while major banks, insurance companies, and mortgage lenders began to fail, further accelerating the correction. Like Bush's pipe dream of democratizing Iraq, the economy melted down, just in time for the 2008 election. The stage was set for Sam Basi's run for the White House, the ultimate prize of the Trojan Horse project.

Leading up to the financial crisis, Russian and China had worked feverishly to find the weak link in the U.S. economy. They concluded that the most vulnerable pressure point was the bloated financing system for housing and construction. Russia contributed to the external pressure on the U.S. by manipulating oil, natural gas, and commodity prices. By this point, China had amassed trillions of dollars worth of U.S. government interest-bearing securities. It was now the largest creditor of the U.S., which was sufficient to quell the occasional talk in Congress of addressing the imbalance of trade. By quickly selling their U.S. bond portfolio, and then adding concurrent short-selling, the Chinese could push millions of U.S. loans into default as interest rates climbed. At the same time, using hedge funds around the globe, the Russians and Chinese could position themselves to actually profit from the U.S. bond collapse.

Most of the significant manufacturing in the U.S.,

ranging from steel to ball-point pens, had been transferred over the years from U.S. locations to China. The differential in labor costs, partly because of China's manipulation of the *yuan* against the dollar, was too great for American corporations to ignore. Besides, the Chinese still had the huge consumer market in the U.S. to sell their products, manufactured all over China. This led to increasing unemployment in the U.S., and growing discontent with President Bush and the Republicans.

Periodically, officials from China and Russia would secretly meet and report their successes in weakening the U.S. In the 2006 meeting in Beijing, the Chinese finance minister made a presentation to the bilateral group:

> "We now have pushed the U.S. to the 'tipping-point,' where, with a slight push, they will have financed a debt so large that they cannot afford to pay interest on it without a collapse of their defense and domestic social programs. Without firing a single shot, we have succeeded—together—in positioning the American giant for a fall over the financial cliff.
>
> This is another version of what Ronald Reagan did to the Soviet Union in the Eighties, by increasing the U.S. defense budget and its military and naval forces. In trying to keep up with the threat, the Soviet Union was weakened financially, leading to its dismemberment. Now it is time for us to pay them back.
>
> On behalf of the People's Republic of China, we appreciate the contributions of everyone that has

worked for this great day, which will pave the way for domination of the world by Russia and China. Together, we will fulfill our national destinies. In truth, however, I would also need to thank the Democratic Party of the United States and its elected officials. Over the last two decades, they have managed to spend their nation's treasury beyond any possible level of affordability. They now are faced with the impossible choices of eliminating their vast social programs, which will cause political chaos, or chopping their sacred military spending. Either way, we win and they lose.

The final phase of their destruction will occur when we have combination of (1) a rise in interest rates, and (2) a continuation of their irrational spending. That will push them past the point of no return.

We extend our congratulations to all who have made this happen."

During this period, the top-secret phase of the overall plan was pursued directly by Zebrotny and Caswell in guiding the political progress of Sam Basi. Through a combination of their skill and the stupidity of many Americans, they had positioned him perfectly for his Presidential run. He used his Senate position cleverly, gaining powerful allies within the Democratic Party establishment, the unions, environmentalists, the Gays, and other Leftist special interest groups. With the adoring assistance of the media, Sam created the illusion that he—and only he—had the solutions for the problems of the U.S. At the same time, following the teachings of Saul Alinsky, he carefully avoided giving specifics, emphasizing instead vague concepts like "hope," "change," and "fairness."

As 2006 drew to a close, another secret meeting was held at Victor Zebrotny's mansion retreat at Salzburg, Austria. In attendance were the principals of the Trojan Horse project. In addition to Zebrotny (Zeus), there was:

- Sergei Lebedev, Chairman of the Russian SVR (Socrates)
- Xu Yongyue, Director of the Chinese Ministry of State Security (Dragon)
- David H. Dallinger, Jr., Asst. Director of Counter-Intelligence, FBI (Cerberus)
- Prof. Lydia Boroshta, KGB/SVR agent (Emerald)
- Prof. Jason Caswell, KGB/SVR agent and Pegasus handler (Medusa)

Lebedev, Zebrotny, and Xu were the only members of the group that had full knowledge of the project and its goals. Because of the need for a strategic decision, they had privately decided to include Dallinger, Caswell, and Boroshta. They needed the input of these important players and their collateral assistance to keep Sam Basi on a trajectory for the White House, as each had special knowledge or capabilities that could protect Sam Basi from being found out.

Lebedev had been reluctant to invite Dallinger because of the risk of his exposure, so Dallinger had used some of his accrued leave time with the Bureau, and took a skiing vacation. Like any American tourist, he traveled through the Austrian mountain resorts as a cover for his presence in Europe. No one, including Dallinger, knew that Boroshta was now a double-agent, working for the FBI. Tilsdale had learned a long time ago never to share the identity of one's informants with anyone, and he had kept her identity secret from everyone but his Ft. McNair team. In this instance, with Dallinger in attendance, that policy probably saved Boroshta's life.

Zebrotny introduced the newer attendees, with their titles. Boroshta had difficulty hiding her shock, when she heard who Dallinger was. She was eager to return to the U.S. and inform Tilsdale of what she had learned.

"Professor Boroshta, you seem nervous," commented Lebedev.

"Well, I am, Chairman Lebedev. I have never been in a room with such important people," she answered, smiling.

"You are among friends. You have done wonderful things for us. Please try to relax. Have a glass of wine," offered Lebedev with a smile, hiding his suspicious instinct.

"Ladies and gentlemen, welcome to my little mountain home," said Zebrotny. "By now, you have had some refreshments and gotten to know each other. Some of you have not been aware of the roles that you have played in the Trojan Horse project. So that we are all on the same page, I will ask Chairman Lebedev to present the project to you. I must caution you—this is information that must be closely guarded. It directly affects the national security of Russia, China, and all of the world's Socialist regimes. We are all responsible to each other to guard this information *with our lives*. Are we all in agreement?" All nodded.

"Good, then Mr. Chairman, will you please begin?"

Lebedev, who was fluent in English, proceeded to describe the project from its early beginnings; the search for and selection of "Pegasus"; the programming and training of Sam Basi; his rise to political fame; and last, the great opportunity that lay before him. Dallinger and Boroshta were incredulous that such a plot had been able to proceed this far.

"Do not look so surprised, David and Lydia. No one in our governments thought such a thing was possible, either," continued Lebedev. "However, our analysis of the Americans has proved to be correct. By exploiting their weaknesses, one of which is their national guilt over past treatment of the Blacks, Sam Basi has the White House within his reach, provided, however, that we coordinate this final phase flawlessly. We called this meeting to finalize our strategy and tactics.

"The Chinese have performed their part of this project brilliantly. They have the United States addicted to cheap foreign labor to produce their products, tilting the balance of trade in their favor. Separately, they have bought up trillions of dollars worth of United States government securities, and have pre-purchased critical commodities, like oil, tungsten, and copper from around the world, leaving little or nothing for the United States to supply its remaining industries. Russia has done the same, with respect to strategic military materials.

"In the United States, partisan politics drives all decisions by government. Instead of trying to position their country economically, they succumb to a borrow-and-spend mentality both at the individual and the government level. They borrow to finance purchases that they cannot afford, playing into our hands, while their Federal Reserve Bank artificially suppresses interest rates.

"But that cannot go on much longer. The Federal Reserve must print money to keep interest rates low for political reasons, and that will bring double-digit inflation, as Argentina,

Germany, and other countries have learned the hard way.

"All that is needed now is the insertion of Pegasus to the Presidency. Once that is accomplished, he will be in a position to steer the U.S. toward Progressivism and eventually, Socialism. First, however, we must force the collapse of their economy and institutions, without involving military action." Lebedev paused. "Do any of you see any preliminary problems that must be fixed?"

"I do," said Dallinger. I strongly recommend that we do another deep background check on Sam Basi and his deceased mother. Once he announces his run for the White House, the press and his opponents will be turning over every rock for harmful information. We need to know it first, and fix it, if possible."

"I would agree with that," added Boroshta. "I know quite a bit about him, but almost nothing about his early life. As you know, his mother died a few years ago, so we will not be able to access her knowledge."

"I will handle this issue," said Dallinger. I can find several official reasons to conduct this investigation, so that will be no problem. Basi is slated to join the Senate Intelligence Committee, which requires a top secret clearance. Jason, tell him to request the background check through my office."

"Understood," said Caswell. "If everyone agrees, I think the time is right for Basi to announce his candidacy."

"What about his opposition in the election? First he has to win the nomination, then the general election," noted Lebedev.

"There is formidable competition in the primaries, because I have heard that Hillary Clinton intends to run. She is very popular, but I don't know why," commented Caswell. "And it is hard to say who the Republican challenger will be, but most likely it will be former Governor Romney, Governor Huckabee, or Senator John McCain. They each have significant flaws as a candidate, which we can easily exploit by using our media allies."

All nodded in agreement. "Very well," said Lebedev. "Sam Basi will announce for the Presidency, but what should the date and place be?"

"Let me suggest that he make the announcement on the birth date and place of the 16th American President, Abraham Lincoln." Caswell paused. "He is the one that freed the black slaves, Mr. Chairman."

"Brilliant!" exclaimed Lebedev. "When and where, exactly?"

"Lincoln was born on February 12th, in Hodgenville, Kentucky, I think," said Caswell.

"In a log cabin," said Director Xu, laughing.

"*All* of the Americans will soon be living in log cabins," added Lebedev.

After the meeting concluded, Lebedev used Zebrotny's satellite phone and scrambler to call his Director of Covert Operations back in Moscow. "Dmitri, I want surveillance on Professor Lydia Boroshta, who seemed a little nervous in our meeting today. Also, check on her family in Warsaw. I believe she has parents and two sisters there. Make sure that you tap her phone lines at UCLA and her home in the Los Angeles area. Something does not feel right."

"It shall be done, Mr. Chairman."

Chapter 18

Needle in a Haystack

Art. II, Section 1 of the U.S. Constitution provides certain qualifications for the office of President:

> No Person *except a natural born Citizen*, or a Citizen of the United States, at the time of the Adoption of this Constitution, shall be eligible to the Office of President; neither shall any Person be eligible to that Office who shall not have attained to the Age of thirty five Years, and been fourteen Years a Resident within the United States.

This means that a person who seeks this high office today must have been born within the United States or its territories. Gaining citizenship subsequent to birth does not qualify. John McCain was born on a U.S. Navy base in the Panama Canal Zone, which was U.S. territory at the time, so he met that qualification. Since Sam Basi's biography indicated that he had been born in San Francisco, he was also deemed qualified under these requirements.

The routine request for a background check came in to Dallinger from Senator Basi's office. Agents were assigned from the San Francisco, Chicago, and Washington offices to use the standard investigative protocol for a Top Secret Clearance.

Billings had been on an assignment to San Francisco and Sacramento, tracing a possible Al-Qaeda suspect. In liberal California, it was easy for illegal immigrants to slip into the communities and become invisible. Several cities, including San Francisco, Berkeley, and Los Angeles, had declared themselves as "sanctuary" cities, refusing to cooperate with the Dept. of Homeland Security to identify known illegal immigrants. The Democratic Party supported this, seeing it as a way to obtain the voting loyalty of the Hispanic population. In fact, an illegal border crossing was a part of nearly every Mexican-American's family heritage, and was a highly sensitive issue to them.

Billings was operating temporarily out of the San Francisco field office, when the Agent-in-Charge came by. "Jeff, we got a priority order to do a BI on a Senator, and I'm short-handed at the moment. Could you give us a hand with a couple of quick projects? I'll clear it with Brad, if you can do it."

"How can I say 'no' to my landlord?" laughed Billings.

"Great. I'll have Agent Kroger contact you. He is currently in Sacramento, going through state records in the archives."

"Out of curiosity, who is the subject?"

"Senator Sam Basi. Do you know him?"

Billings got up from his desk. "Yes, actually I do, indirectly. I'll wait for Ken Kroger to contact me." He got a strange feeling that this routine project could be interesting. He had always wanted to do more research on Sam Basi, but the 9/11 attacks had diverted him from the project. "Pegasus" was no longer an active case within the Bureau, which was stretched thin in its pursuit of Al-Qaeda members.

A few hours later, Agent Kroger telephoned Billings and briefed him on what needed to be done from the San Francisco office to complete the background investigation of Senator Basi. "Jeff, I apologize for dragging you into this. I know you have higher priorities, plus this is the sort of stuff we normally assign to new agents."

"No problem, Ken. Glad to help out. Hey, it always pays to kiss your landlord's ass, right?"

Kroger laughed. "Well, we really appreciate it. DCHQ gave this a higher priority than normal, so we need to complete it quickly."

"Understood. How can I help?"

"Would you mind verifying his birth records? From his questionnaire, they would be located at the California Pacific Medical Center in San Francisco, on the corner of Sacramento and Buchanan Streets, downtown. Ask one of my secretaries for a copy of the privacy waiver he signed, because you will either need that or a subpoena. We usually wind up using subpoenas on politicians," joked Kroger, "but this guy seems squeaky-clean."

"Refreshing change," remarked Billings.

"Yeah, but one of our guys just went through his UCLA files, and they are practically bare. We know he went there for two years, passed his courses, and transferred to Harvard, but there are no professor notes, evaluations, or papers in his file. Same thing at Harvard and Yale. It's like the guy never existed. UCLA says that they had some computer problems and a fire a few years ago, and a lot of records were toasted."

Billings listened more intently. He was becoming more and more like his mentor, Tilsdale. "Ken, I'll get right on this and let you know what I find. I have your cell number."

"Excellent. Thanks again, Jeff. Oh, by the way—we had one of our guys go through the mother's belongings over in Oakland. Her probate attorney stored everything there after she died, and her house was cleaned out. He found some diaries, and I left them on my desk. You might want to skim through them for background."

"Yeah, thanks. I will."

After retrieving the four diaries, Billings returned to his desk and started reading. An entry caught his eye:

8/4/61----Gave birth to a beautiful baby boy in Lagos, Nigeria!

A few entries later, he found some more interesting material:

9/3/61----Karimi fears for our safety—wants us to go to the U.S.
9/6/61----Got airline tickets; taking Husam to U.S.

***

9/9/61----Need papers for Husam. Friends said I should contact a Leona Waller, at the California Pacific Hospital, and she could help for $$. Her number is (415) 548-8762.

***

9/20/61---Met Leona Waller. Got papers, paid $5000—everything is now OK.

Who is Leona Waller? thought Billings. This had to be carefully investigated as possible fraud with official documents. He checked the birth date listed in Basi's security questionnaire: 8/4/61, place—San Francisco, CA. His suspicions grew, as he tried to figure out what this meant.

Billings obtained the privacy waiver copy and left the 13th floor of the Federal Building on Golden Gate Avenue for the main exit. He walked up to Van Ness and hailed a cab. "California Pacific Medical Center," he told the driver.

Leaving the cab, he entered the hospital campus and found the administration offices. "Agent Jeff Billings, FBI," he said to the receptionist, flashing his badge and ID card. Her eyes widened. The hospital staff was accustomed to seeing SFPD officers around the hospital, but not the FBI.

Supervisor Carol Banning came out of a side office, looking concerned. "Can I help you, Agent Billings?"

"Yes. I am conducting a routine background investigation on Senator Sam Basi, so that he can obtain a clearance for classified material, relating to his government work. I just need to check off a few standard items, which we are required to do in every case. I have his privacy waiver for you," Billings said, handing her the form. While she scrutinized the form, he noticed that she was an attractive woman, probably in her thirties.

"It all seems to be in order. What are you looking for?"

"I need to see any of his patient records, if there are any, and I was informed that he was born in this hospital, around 1961. I will need all records relating to his birth. His mother's name was Alicia Ludbury Basi. The father is deceased, according to our records."

"Please follow me." She led him to a massive file room in the hospital basement. "Most of our records currently are kept in digital media, but we have not had time to scan the files from before 1980. That means you will have to go through the filing cabinets manually, although we have an index system on the computer that should give you the file drawer number. Good luck. I hope you brought your lunch!" she giggled.

"Yes, thanks a lot! I hope I will not be down here too long. I'll see you before I leave. What do I do if I need copies?"

"Just tell the clerk at the desk near the door. He will make them for you."

"Well, time to dive in. Where is the computer?"

"Let me help you." She eyed the handsome agent, who reminded her of a young Denzel Washington. In this predominantly Gay city, "straight" women like Carol had trouble finding good-looking men who were single and not gay. "Are you married?"

Somewhat surprised, Billings looked up. "No."

"Neither am I. If you would like to have dinner after you complete your homework, let me know. There is a great restaurant nearby."

"Uh. . . OK, thanks, I will."

"See you later, I hope."

"Count on it," said Billings with a smile.

After she left, Billings sat down at the computer and typed, "Basi, Husam." In a few seconds, the screen displayed "1 record found." Selecting the record, the display showed a file number, entitled "birth records."

Using the directory index, Billings located the file drawer, and started flipping through the case folders. Then he found it: "Basi, Alicia; and Basi, Husam." He pulled the file, which seemed much smaller than the others, and took it to a reading table.

Early in his FBI career, Billings had been assigned to the dreary task of searching through the medical records of a serial killer for information in building a behavioral profile. He had become familiar with the typical content and format of hospital records, and that knowledge made him feel something was wrong with the Basi birth records. He began to follow the history of Alicia Basi more carefully, beginning with her admission to the hospital.

He noticed that she had been admitted directly, but without a doctor's referral. That is only possible if she had gone through the emergency room, but there was no record of that. Adding to his curiosity was the lack of documentation for some standard maternity procedures, including an epidural injection and ultrasound monitoring. Having a sister who was an obstetrics and gynecology physician, Billings recognized significant gaps in the medical records. He made a note of the attending physician, and turned to the birth records section of the file.

Everything seemed to be in order. The standard California certificate copy was present, but he noticed that the serial number was out of order by date. He had looked quickly at samples of the other birth records on dates before and after the listed birth date of August 4, 1961, and this number jumped forward by several hundred certificates. Billings wrote down the name of the hospital administrator who had signed the certificate: Leona C. Waller.

Stopping at the desk of the clerk, he requested copies of the entire file, and then called Carol Banning's extension. "Ms. Banning, this is Agent Billings. May I come up and see you for a few minutes?"

"Of course. You know where I am."

Billing knocked at her door. "I know I'm a pest, but could

I ask you some questions about this file?"

"Certainly. What do you want to know?"

"Do you have a record of the attending physician, a 'Dr. Herbert Mansfield?'"

"Let me check my files," she replied, going to her computer. After a few minutes, she said, "OK, here he is. Our files show that he left town and moved to New York on March 4, 1961. His patients were referred to other physicians after that."

Billings looked up, surprised. "Really? Are you sure about that? I have him on this birth record as the attending physician on August 4, 1961."

"That's what it shows. Our hospital has always been careful with tracking our admitted physicians, for liability purposes."

"OK, what about this administrator? Leona C. Waller?"

"Waller? I remember her from when I came to work here. She was allowed to resign in lieu of termination. As I recall, they suspected her of Medicare fraud and some other data irregularities, but nothing was ever proven."

"Would she have been authorized to sign a birth certificate?"

"Absolutely not! Only the chief administrator has that authority. That must be an error." Billings showed her the certificate. She shook her head. "I can't explain that. It doesn't make sense."

"Would you mind taking a look at the rest of this file? I am not a medical professional, but it seems that some key records are missing, like the ultrasound report and the epidural injection record."

After a few minutes, Banning looked up at Billings with a worried expression. "There is something really wrong with this file. Is the hospital in legal trouble here?"

"Carol, I don't know yet, but I don't think this is a hospital problem. The answers lie with the mother, who is now deceased, and Ms. Waller. Do you have any idea where we might find her?"

"No, she left about five years ago. Let me check her personnel file." Banning left to retrieve a folder from the nearby file room. "She left a forwarding address in Sacramento for us to send her final paycheck. Here it is."

Billings wrote it down. "Thanks, Carol. I will be in touch."

"So I guess dinner is out?" Banning was visibly disappointed.

"Afraid so. Based on what I've found, I need to run these details down. I'm going to Sacramento when I leave here, to see if I can locate this Waller woman." Billings returned to the FBI field office and checked out a car from the motor pool. He decided that he could drive to Sacramento faster than trying to fly from one of the congested Bay Area airports. After entering the Central Freeway off Market Street, he merged into I-80 East, which would take him to Sacramento. As he crossed the Bay Bridge, he called Agent Tucker back in Washington.

"Dave, Jeff. Do one of your magic tricks and see if you can locate a Leona C. Waller, last known location—Sacramento. Send me a text message with whatever you find, and please expedite."

"Will do, Jeff," Tucker responded. His keyboard came alive as he ran Waller's name through various Bureau databases. Then, he found her address information and called Billings' cell phone. "Jeff? Dave. I found her. Guess what? She is actually a federal employee, and working for the Social Security Administration in Sacramento. I'll send you a text message with her address and phone number."

"Super job, Dave! Thanks!" Billings decided he would confront her with what he had found in the birth file, and gauge her reaction. He looked at his watch, and decided that he would call on her at home.

As the months of the 2008 Presidential campaign rolled along, Sam Basi was engaged in a bitter primary contest with Hillary Clinton for the Democratic nomination. It appeared that Hillary could possibly win, as Basi's staff projected the state-by-state votes. Although it had been a vicious campaign through the early primary states, Zebrotny and Caswell advised Basi that he should negotiate a deal with Hillary, rather than risk losing at this point. A meeting was arranged at the Beverly Hills mansion being rented by Bill and Hillary Clinton to run her campaign in California. Present were the Clintons, Basi, Zebrotny and Caswell. Tension was in the air, as several months of name-calling and personal attacks had been launched by each side, and that was difficult to forget for all of them.

"Alright, Sam. What do you want to talk about?" asked Bill Clinton.

Basi turned on the charm, as only he could do. "Well, I think both of us need to consider what is really going on in this election," Basi began. "We have an electorate that is fed up with George W. Bush and the Republicans, at least for now. I can tell you that the financial crisis with the mortgage banking industry is only going to get worse, and it will bring down the entire economy."

"And exactly how do you know *that*," snapped Hillary. "I didn't know you were also an economics expert," she snarled. Bill squeezed her hand.

"Just trust me, it will happen," puffed Basi. "This is a unique opportunity, for me and for you."

"How so?" inquired Bill.

"It is obvious at this point that the Republicans are in disarray. They can't agree on a candidate, and it looks like old John McCain will get the nomination. We could not have a weaker opponent, especially when you consider the state of the economy and the unpopular wars in Iraq and Afghanistan. What I am getting at is this—we could run anyone, and that Democrat would surely win in the general election. I am doing extremely well with my campaign financing, while you are going broke. Matter of fact, you are in debt up to your ears, but I am in a position to fix that for you."

Hillary fumed. "I'm not going to sit here and be insulted by the likes of *you*," she hissed.

"Wait a minute, Hon. What are you getting at, Sam?" Bill stared at him.

"I propose that you pull out of the race and allow me to win the nomination. Further, I want your support for my campaign. You have very loyal followers, and they will do what you ask them to do."

"And what do *we* get?" asked Bill.

"First, we pay off your campaign debts. Second, I name you as Secretary of State, Hillary. I want retired Admiral William Hanlon as my running mate for this round. I need to beef up my credibility as the Commander-in-Chief."

"Ridiculous! Who do you think you are, demanding this?" shrieked Hillary.

"I am the next President of the United States, Hillary, and I give you my word that you will be my heir apparent at the end of my second term, for 2016. I will make you my

VP for the second term, when Hanlon will gracefully retire. That will set you up perfectly for the White House in 2016. What do you say?"

Bill patted Hillary's hand. "We need to talk for a minute, Hon." The two left the room. Basi, Caswell, and Zebrotny exchanged glances, as they heard a woman's voice, screaming, "No, no way, Bill. I am not giving up that easy!"

In a few minutes, the Clintons returned. Bill appeared relieved, while Hillary was obviously seething with anger. "We accept your offer, and we will hold you to our deal," said Bill.

"Excellent! You will not be sorry," replied Basi. Everyone shook hands, cementing the deal. "I would like you to make the announcement of your withdrawal tomorrow, Hillary. Following that, I will have a very complimentary statement prepared, regarding your candidacy and your importance to the Democratic Party."

"Agreed," she responded, without smiling.

Caswell scribbled a note on his calendar, and showed it to Zebrotny: *It doesn't look like Bill will be getting laid tonight!*

Zebrotny scribbled a note back, holding back his laughter with difficulty: *Wrong! Angry women make the best lovers!*

Basi's Vice Presidential pick, four-star Admiral Bill Hanlon, had retired as the head of the important Pacific Command, based in Honolulu. His father had also been a career Naval officer, and his mother was a British native of Hong Kong. After Hanlon retired from active duty, President Bush had appointed him as Ambassador to China, where he had dazzled the Chinese with his knowledge of their history, culture, and language. He was extremely popular among conservatives, and the Republicans had even talked about drafting him to run for the U.S. Senate in California, where he would have received support from the large Asian-American community.

Basi approached him about the Vice President position on his ticket, and he accepted. "This is a duty you owe your country," Basi told him. "I believe I am going to win this election, and I need someone of your national security expertise to bolster the voters' trust that I can handle that responsibility."

Hanlon's acceptance sent shock-waves through the Republican Party. They had failed to realize that a former career military officer is not likely to reject a request from a future President. At least that is what *appeared* to have happened.

Hanlon was not the typical admiral. He graduated from Stanford University, not the Naval Academy, and held two advanced degrees, including a Ph.D. from the prestigious Tufts University Fletcher School of International Affairs. Because of his family background, he spoke fluent Mandarin and Cantonese, which had resulted in an early career assignment as the Naval Attaché at the U.S. embassy in Taipei, Taiwan. While there, he fell in love and married a beautiful Chinese woman who worked in the embassy as a translator.

He rose rapidly during the rest of his career, distinguishing himself in several high-profile jobs, including an important White House assignment as an assistant to the National Security Advisor. His intelligence and problem-solving ability drew the attention of senior officials in the Dept. of Defense and the White House. He was rapidly promoted, and became one of the youngest admirals in Navy history. His poise, charisma, and speaking ability captured the attention of politicians in both parties, whose officials wanted to recruit him for elective office upon his retirement from the Navy. Until the Basi offer, he had stayed neutral, on the political sidelines.

Hanlon had met Zebrotny on several occasions after his retirement in 2005, when he became involved in charity projects that were used by Zebrotny as a cover. Zebrotny was actually the force behind his selection as Basi's running mate.

After arriving in Sacramento, Agent Jeff Billings drove to the address he had received from Washington: 107 Keehner Avenue, in the suburb of Roseville. Parking his car in front, he went up to the door and rang the doorbell. He looked at his watch—it was 6:00 p.m., and he hoped Waller had arrived by now.

The door opened, showing a middle-aged white woman. "Ms. Leona Waller?"

"Yes? What do you want?" Billings smelled liquor on her breath.

"I'm Special Agent Jeff Billings, FBI. I'm doing a routine background check on a government official, and your name came up in his file. I'd like to ask you a few questions, OK?" Billings flashed his most innocent smile. "May I come in for a few minutes?"

"Yeah, sure. The place is a mess. I just got home."

"No problem. This won't take long. Just a formality. You know the government!"

"Goddam right I do—I work for them. Make yourself comfortable."

Billings noticed a dirty cat litter box in the corner, and

sat down at the kitchen table. He pulled out his note pad. "Let's see—you used to work for California Pacific Hospital in San Francisco, right?"

Waller, wearing a grimy house coat and slippers, looked up with a start. "That was a long time ago. The bastards fired me for no reason—forced me to resign. Probably to make room for a younger woman."

"Well, I don't really need to get into that. I am only interested in a birth certificate that you signed on behalf of the hospital."

Waller winced. She knew that she had to be careful, because she had made thousands of dollars falsifying birth records for wealthy Chinese and Indian immigrant families who wanted their children to be U.S. citizens. "What is the kid's name?"

"Husam Khalil Basi. He is now a United States Senator."

"No kidding? Isn't that something! Small world, huh?"

"Yes, it is. I want you to take a look at this birth file, and explain why you signed it for the hospital."

"Well, it was part of my duties." She studied the file, flipping through the pages. "I don't remember this one."

"I noticed quite a few normal items in the medical records were missing. Do you know why?"

"How should I know? The medical stuff is the responsibility of the medical staff and the attending physician."

"But you would want any file that you signed off on to be accurate and complete, wouldn't you?" asked Billings.

"Of course. But maybe the record clerks screwed up, and never got the file put together correctly. That happens, you know."

"Sure. Then why would you sign off on it?"

Waller tensed, which was noticed by Billings. "I don't

know—it's just too long ago. You are asking me to remember things that happened forty years ago! I can only assume that the file was proper when I reviewed it, because I would never have signed off until it was." She liked her answer, and gave Billings a smug grin.

"Really? You were never even *authorized* to sign birth records for the hospital, *were* you, Ms. Waller?" Billings stared at her.

"Yes, I was! I *had* to do it sometimes, or the patient records would get messed up."

"The truth is, you were actually fired for falsifying billing records and taking kickbacks, isn't that right, Ms. Waller? Let me remind you, Madam, making false statements to a federal agent is a serious felony."

Waller felt his eyes boring into her and broke into a sweat. The hand holding her cigarette began to tremble. "That was bullshit! I never did anything of the sort!"

"Are you aware that falsifying medical records is also a felony? Perhaps you engaged in Medicare fraud also! That is worth a lot of years behind bars, Ms. Waller."

She began to sob. "I knew they would try to ruin me someday! Those bastards! What do you want of me? I'm just a poor old woman!"

Billings shifted back into his soothing voice, and patted her hand. The "good cop" had returned. "I know, Ms. Waller, but we need to know what went on with this file. Let me refresh your memory. The mother was an attractive blond white woman. The baby's father was a deceased black man from Nigeria. This is his name on the birth certificate. Do you remember typing this up? Surely you did not have too many parents with *these* characteristics, right? I really don't intend to use the fraud information—unless you force me to. I just want to know about this birth certificate. Is it genuine, or did you fabricate the entire file? Tell me now, or all hell is going to break loose for you!"

Waller pulled herself together and stopped crying. "Well, I do remember this one, mostly because of the Nigerian father. The mother came to me confidentially, and asked me to help make her baby a U.S. citizen. She said her husband had been murdered, and that some really bad people might try to kill her and her kid. I felt sorry for her, so I helped her."

"And tell me exactly *how* you helped her!"

"I made up the file and signed the birth certificate. I sent the original to Sacramento, to the state archives."

"And what did you get in return? Money?"

Waller paused, and then surrendered. "Yes. I think she gave me five thousand dollars."

"Did you report that income on your tax return? Don't make me go to the IRS and pull your records!"

"No. Are you going to turn me in?"

"I'm not sure yet. It all depends on how well you cooperate with us. If you try to leave town on me, or get a lawyer and start making a lot of noise, I will make sure that you never see the light of day again, and rot in a prison cell. Keep all of this to yourself, and maybe I will do the same. Just keep living your life as it is, and do not discuss this with *anyone*. Understand?"

"Yes, Sir." Waller felt like she had been punched in the stomach. She never thought her San Francisco past would catch up to her.

"Here is my card. I am available to you 24/7. Call me if you think of anything else. And I may need to ask you some further questions, so I may call you, OK?"

"Yes."

"I'll find my own way out. Have a nice evening."

Driving back to San Francisco, Billings weighed his options in handling this potentially explosive information. He wished that he had required that Waller sign a statement or that he had recorded the conversation. He decided to call Tilsdale for guidance.

"Boss, Jeff. I'm in Sacramento, helping the San Francisco office with a routine background check on Senator Sam Basi."

Tilsdale's ears perked up. "And?"

"Ken Kroger asked me to validate the birth records, and I seemed to have hit a wall. I am not complete on analyzing the file yet, but it appears that Sam Basi's birth certificate was fraudulently produced by a hospital clerk, in exchange for money."

"So how does that play out, Jeff?"

"Well, if that is true, then Senator Sam Basi may not be an American citizen. It's also possible that his mother had the baby without medical personnel in attendance, and that she wanted to formalize the birth certificate. No way to know for sure what happened."

The words echoed in Tilsdale's ears. *Not a U.S. citizen?* His mind raced, trying to fathom the significance of such a revelation, and how it should be handled. "OK, who have you told about this so far?"

"Only you, Boss."

"Who is the ordering official on the background investigation?"

"ADCI David Dallinger."

Tilsdale felt his heart rate accelerate. He had never liked Dallinger, whom he considered a bureaucrat with little field experience.

"Jeff, this could be very sticky, and loaded with politics. I recommend that you do not even tell the San Francisco office staff. Just call up Dallinger, and give him the verbal that you just gave me. Do not put anything in writing yet, until we figure this thing out."

"Roger that, Boss. I'll see you in a couple of days and let you know how this went." Billings then dialed the number for Dallinger, back in Washington.

"Assistant Director Dallinger."

"Mr. Dallinger, this is Agent Billings. I need to give you some preliminary information and get some guidance from you."

"Hello, Jeff. What's up?"

"Well, I was out here in San Francisco, running down an Al-Qaeda lead for Brad Tilsdale, when I got roped into helping with your BI project on Senator Basi."

Dallinger stiffened. This did not sound good. "And?"

"I was asked to check his birth records, which is routine stuff, as you know. I have not finalized the investigation, but I am fairly sure that we have a potentially embarrassing problem here."

"What is it?" asked Dallinger.

"My preliminary reading is that Basi's birth records are a fake."

The phone slipped out of Dallinger's hand. Regaining his composure and grabbing the phone, he asked, "Are you sure? How do you know? That is a very serious accusation!"

"Believe me, I know."

You have no idea, idiot," thought Dallinger to himself. "Have you told anyone about this?"

"Just the woman who forged the documents—and Brad Tilsdale."

It just gets better and better, thought Dallinger. "OK, let's do this. Do not, I repeat, do not tell anyone else until you receive further instructions. Have you put anything about this in writing?"

"No."

"Fine. Keep it verbal, and do not report this to anyone else, understand? This is too political, and I don't want the Bureau to get sucked into any controversy."

"Yes, Sir."

"Where are you now?"

"I'm on I-80, driving back to San Francisco."

"What is the name and address of the woman you say forged the documents? I'll run a check on her."

"Leona C. Waller, 107 Keehner Avenue, Roseville, California. She's Caucasian, about five foot four, 140 pounds, age about 65. Appears to be an alcoholic."

"Very good. I will be in touch with you."

"Thank you, Sir." Billings clicked the phone off, then realized that he should go back to Waller and obtain a recorded statement before he left Sacramento. He took Exit 63 at Schroeder Road, navigated the clover-leaf and transitioned to the on-ramp, just in time for a traffic logjam. *I should have flown,* he thought to himself.

Dallinger realized that this presented a very small window of opportunity to repair the dangerous problem. He needed to initiate a coded telephone protocol to reach Zebrotny. He left his office, descending in the elevator to the parking garage. He then drove out of the exit, and made his way to a parking facility near "embassy row" in northwest Washington. This would prevent him from being followed. Using a pre-paid cell phone, he called the pre-arranged number for the SVR Resident Agent at the Russian embassy.

Dallinger was not as knowledgeable as Tilsdale and Billings about the NSA and its ability to intercept calls of this type. As Col. Leonid Debrov answered on his satellite phone, the NSA computers were sifting the conversation out of the air and recording it, along with trillions of similar communications, world-wide. If it were not for the NSA's super-computers and sophisticated software, this conversation would have been lost, merged like grains of sand on a beach. "Uncle Jerry is very sick. I need to take him to the emergency room. Can you provide an ambulance?"

Luckily for the SVR and Dallinger, none of the coded words or phrases in the conversation triggered further scrutiny by the NSA. Even though a satellite phone was used, it was relegated to a low priority by the NSA computers and soon faded from view.

Debrov recognized the coded statement as an emergency request by Cerberus for an immediate meeting. "Yes. I am sorry to hear that. Come to our branch office location and fill out the paperwork. We will expect you at 2000."

Dallinger keyed the ignition, and drove out of the garage for the safe-house in Arlington. Time was critical, so he decided to forego the usual security safeguards and go directly to the North Irving Street location.

By the time he arrived, Col. Debrov was there. "Cerberus, this is a very dangerous thing to do. What is the reason for this?"

"We need to eliminate a major security threat to the Pegasus project. We do not have time to go through Moscow. Do you have assets in the Sacramento area?"

Debrov did not know the details of the Pegasus matter, but he had standing orders to support it in any way, without limitations. "Alright. Yes, we do. We have been bribing certain state legislators and government officials for years, given the critical importance of California within the United States. What do you need?"

"I need some 'wet work.' And I need it *now*." "Wet work" was the covert operations slang for assassination.

"Listen to me, Cerberus. Such assignments are always very high risk, because they are messy and often leave a trail. Are you sure this is necessary?"

"Absolutely!"

"Who is the target, and where is he?" asked Debrov.

"It's a 'she,' and her name is Leona Waller. She is a 65-year old Caucasian woman, living at 107 Keehner, in the Roseville suburb of Sacramento. I want her eliminated *tonight*!"

"Consider it done. I'll let you know with the usual web site code when it is complete. Now get out of here, before someone tracks you," growled the stocky Russian.

After Dallinger left, Debrov sent a text message to one of his SVR agents in Sacramento:

"order flowers for leona waller. deliver to 107 Keehner, Roseville, CA. make sure delivery is nice and clean and confirm asap."

In Sacramento, SVR agent Vadim Patrushev was watching Bill O'Reilly on Fox News Channel when his cell phone beeped with the text message. Patrushev had been trained by the SVR to be a skilled assassin. He was an expert in the martial arts, and with a variety of deadly weapons, including the knife and the garrote. In his ten years with the SVR, he had killed 39 people throughout the world, and had never been caught or identified.

After reading the message, Patrushev got dressed in a black sweater and trousers. He laced up his black sneakers and stuffed a ski mask in his pocket, along with his favorite fighting knife, the Shirogorov 95, and a garrote made from a camper's wire pocket-saw.

He retrieved his Walther .380 PPK from his backpack, and checked the full clip. He pulled the slide back and released it with a metallic snap, feeding a hollow-point round into the chamber. He stuck it in his belt and pocketed the matching silencer. He was ready.

Leona Waller had fallen asleep in her living room chair after her third bourbon. The TV blared with a Seinfeld re-run. She had no way of knowing that two dangerous men were en route to her home in Roseville.

Patrushev was the first to arrive. He parked on a side street, and walked around to her house. He moved swiftly to the back door, putting on his ski mask. Using a glass cutter, he cut a large hole in the back door pane to allow him to reach the lock. *This is easier than I thought,* he said to himself. As he quietly entered, he heard the TV in the living room, but no other noise. Cat-like, he moved to the door of the kitchen, and peered into the living room. He could see the top of Waller's motionless head. *Sleeping,* he concluded.

Since the back of the chair shielded her neck, he opted for a knife attack, which would be equally quiet. He flicked open the Shirogorov, exposing the sharp titanium steel blade. He decided to slice her throat, severing both carotid arteries, followed by a thrust into her heart. *Just two more steps, bitch—keep sleeping.* He held his breath and poised to strike.

At that instant, the doorbell rang, making him jump. Waller started to move as he placed his left forearm under her chin, exposing her throat. The blade of the Shirogorov glided across the soft flesh, severing her arteries and trachea. She rattled her last breath, as he completed the kill with a vicious knife thrust into her left chest. Waller was dead, without a sound. Now Patrushev had to either escape or eliminate the person at the front door. He decided to leave from the back door. He closed the blade of the Shirogorov and drew the semi-automatic pistol, twisting the silencer onto the barrel. He did not expect the visitor to be an FBI agent.

As he started walking away from the back door, a voice yelled, "Freeze, FBI! Get on the ground, asshole!" Billings had walked to the back to see if Waller was visible from a window, and had witnessed the brutal murder. He was now poised in what is known as "the FBI crouch," squatting low, aiming his Glock in both hands, holding Patrushev squarely in the tritium night sights.

Patrushev turned, aiming his Walther at the other man. The two fired almost simultaneously. An FBI agent always fires shots in pairs for greater probability of a kill. As Billings got off his second shot, Patrushev's .380 round struck his left shoulder, spinning him around. Instinctively, from his Ranger training, he dove to the grass and rolled to his right, firing the remaining 15 rounds in his clip in the direction of the muzzle flash. The first two rounds struck Patrushev in the chest, where the mushrooming hollow-point bullets tore large holes in his lungs and ripped the side of his heart. Four additional rounds struck him in the abdomen, and one took off the top of his skull. Billings' countless hours on the pistol range had paid off.

Billings quickly reloaded with a fresh clip and checked the body for signs of life. He put Patrushev in handcuffs, which was standard procedure, then staggered back to his car and keyed the microphone of the radio. "All units, code eleven ninety-nine—federal officer down. Shots fired. Need immediate backup and medical assistance ASAP!" In a few minutes, sirens wailed through the peaceful neighborhood, and the Roseville police surrounded the house. "I'm FBI Agent Billings. I just witnessed a murder. I shot the perp. He's down near the back of the house. This is a crime scene—rope it off!"

Back in Washington, the cell phones of the Bureau's managers began to ring. Whenever there was either a terrorist incident or a shooting involving an agent, the standard protocol within the Bureau was for all Director-level agents to be notified, along with all SACs (Special Agents-in-Charge) in the numerous field offices. Dallinger, asleep at his Fairfax, Virginia residence, answered. "Sir, this is Bureau communications. We were just notified that one of our agents, Jeff Billings, was involved in a shooting in Sacramento. He was wounded, and there are two dead persons at the scene. That's all we have so far."

Dallinger was now fully awake, and he felt dizzy. "OK, thanks." His mind raced with the possibilities, none of them good. He knew this could be a very problematic situation for him personally. This would require considerable finesse to avoid compromising himself or the Pegasus matter.

Tilsdale was an insomniac, and was still watching Jay

Leno when his phone rang. When he heard that the wounded agent was Billings, he sprang to his feet. "Is he OK? Where is he now?" he demanded.

"Sir, all we know is that he is listed in good condition, and is already being treated at Sutter Memorial Hospital in Sacramento."

"Who was killed?"

"Preliminary report from Roseville PD is that a woman was slashed and stabbed to death inside the house. Her name was Waller."

Tilsdale suddenly felt sick. "And the other one?"

"No ID yet. They ran his fingerprints, but nothing came up. Apparently, he and Billings got into a fire-fight, and this guy lost. He took several slugs in the chest, abdomen, and head. He was shooting a Walther PPK .380, with a silencer. He also had a bloody Shirogorov knife and a garrote in his pockets."

Christ! That smells like SVR," thought Tilsdale. *Why would the SVR make such a messy hit? What were they trying to hide? What is their connection to Leona Waller?* This was not in his division's jurisdiction, but one of his own agents had been drawn into the case. He decided that he needed to talk with the ADCI, David Dallinger. He went into the office early, and called Dallinger's extension.

"Nancy, this is Brad Tilsdale. Is David free? I need to speak with him."

"Yes, Mr. Tilsdale. I'll tell him that you are stopping by," said the secretary.

As he appeared at the door of Dallinger's office, Tilsdale noticed that the ADCI was upset. "David, got a minute?"

"Of course. Have a seat," answered Dallinger.

"David, I figured that this Waller matter must be pretty

touchy politically, so I wanted to get some guidance from you."

"Yes, we do need to talk about this. There are some aspects that I don't think you know about. Nancy, hold my calls—I don't want to be interrupted," said Dallinger. "First of all, Brad, you and Jeff are out of this matter. *I* was directed to conduct this BI for Senator Basi. So, I would appreciate it if you and Jeff kept out of it," said Dallinger.

"Hey, we have enough on our plate without this. However, Jeff was involuntarily pulled into it by the San Francisco office, and he was doing you guys a favor! Let's not be so territorial! We *are* on the same team, I believe."

Dallinger nodded. "You're right. I'm sorry. I didn't get much sleep since this Waller thing happened."

"No problem. But look—one of my best agents got shot, and I want to run this thing out until we learn what is going on. The first issue is apparently Basi's birth certificate."

Since the Waller murder, Cerberus and the SVR had been very busy, doing "damage control." The SVR had managed to bribe a senior clerk in Sacramento in the California State Records Division. The defective birth certificate had already been replaced with a perfect forgery that even the FBI document section could not discredit. Information had been leaked through a Russian agent at Interpol to the FBI that Vadim Patrushev, Waller's killer, was a wanted member of the Russian Mafia.

"Don't go down that rabbit trail. We have learned that Sacramento has the genuine certificate, and our lab has already signed off on it. It was a case of sloppy file handling by the hospital." Dallinger shoved a copy of the "genuine" birth certificate across the desk.

"Yes, but what about the medical records discrepancies?

It still seems . . ."

Dallinger cut him off. "Brad, let it go. Back in the Sixties, record keeping was not as accurate as it is now. Everything was paper, and susceptible to errors. What we have in Sacramento is good enough."

"Then what about the killer? Am I imagining him too?"

Dallinger glared at him. "Brad, here is an Interpol advisory on that guy. He was a member of the Russian Mafia, wanted in Europe for various crimes."

"So why does an international criminal murder an obscure old lady? He had nothing *better* to do?"

"No need to get sarcastic. I suspect that it had something to do with one of Waller's past frauds. She probably screwed the wrong pooch, and you know how vicious those goddam Russians are!"

Tilsdale mulled over this new information. *Maybe I have been barking up a dead tree,* he thought.

"Brad, the bottom line is this—the Director has his budget in front of Basi's Senate committee for approval, and he does not want to piss that guy off! I am approving the BI, and certifying it as *complete.* Are you going to open a separate case on this, with the Director breathing down your neck? Get a life!"

Tilsdale resented the comment, and got up. "Thanks for your time, David."

After the withdrawal and support of the Clintons, Sam Basi swept the Democratic primaries. At the Democratic Party convention, he delivered a powerful, moving acceptance speech that captured the national spotlight and ended with stirring phrases:

"My fellow Americans—this is a pivotal moment in the epic saga of our great nation. We have shown the world that a person of color can be nominated for the highest office in the land, and that the divisive policies of the Republican Party are behind us. We are now poised at a moment in history when the voice of ordinary people will once again be heard, where money cannot buy power, and where the world will again see an America that they can respect.

Our working families and their children now can hope for a better future, where everyone contributes their fair share, and where change is within our grasp. If you will grant me the privilege of serving you, I will deliver on those promises. I will reverse the mean-spirited policies of George Bush, and require those who have been more fortunate to provide a fair share of their wealth to those who are not.

This will be a new America, and I ask for your vote and your support as we go forward to November. God Bless America. Thank you."

At the end of his second presidential term, Vladimir Putin replaced SVR Chairman Lebedev with Mikhail Fradkov, a former KGB agent and government official. For continuity, Putin (who was a former KGB officer) kept Lebedev involved as the operational head of the Trojan Horse project. The Russians did not want any last-minute errors, since the U.S. Presidential election was well underway.

As the fateful day of November 4, 2008 drew near, the Chinese continued to manipulate the U.S. economy and financial system, triggering a seismic shock through the real estate and financial markets. Banks and other financial institutions began to fail at an alarming rate, with President Bush sitting in the weak position of a "lame duck" President, and only weeks to go before he would leave the White House to the winner of the election.

As the financial panic spread, Bush resorted to drastic and spasmodic actions to save the financial system. He had never been aware that the brokerage houses had been "securitizing" the huge number of "junk" mortgages and selling them, nor that the insurance industry had been stupid enough to write insurance on them. The result was a crushing "domino" effect, with banks failing and major investment banking firms collapsing. This created an atmosphere of fear and panic among the electorate, and a desire to abandon Republican economic policies, which Sam Basi argued were the root cause. In this hysterical atmosphere, it was time for "hope" and "change," as promised by Basi.

To the voters, Senator McCain, Basi's opponent, appeared old, feeble, frozen, and incapable of providing a solution. On November 4th, this resulted in a landslide of electoral votes for Basi. Defying all odds, "Pegasus" had actually captured the White House. The final step was his inauguration and swearing-in on January 20, 2009. Ironically, it was actually the Bush administration that saved the economy from its free-fall, just prior to Basi's inauguration, but Basi quickly took credit for that.

The SVR officials hosted a secret celebration at Vladimir Putin's mansion-like *dacha* in the Ozero cooperative, near St. Petersburg, Russia. "I congratulate all of you, my Comrades," said Putin. As one of the last of the Soviet-trained leaders, he still tended to use the archaic language of Soviet Communism. "I always thought this was a high-risk project, but either through luck or skill, you made it work. We are now at the point of achieving the destiny of our Motherland. Russia will be in the driver's seat of the entire world."

"Don't forget the Chinese, Vladimir. They expect to be treated like partners. That is how this all began," advised Lebedev.

"Fuck the Chinese. I am tired of their insolent remarks and arrogance. They remind me of a colony of roaches, constantly growing, eating, and producing more roaches. It is time we put them in their place—once and for all. We owe them nothing. I have read the reports from your group. We did all the hard work on this. What did they do?"

"Well, for one thing, it was they who pushed the American economy into the toilet. We could never have done that, even with our control of energy supplies," replied Fradkov.

Putin glared at him. "Fine. Send them a present on the next Chinese New Year. I intend to make this work for Russia. Comrades, let us enjoy the moment. I propose a toast to all of you, to President Basi—may he rule wisely—and to Mother Russia!" They all raised their vodka glasses. "*Budem zdorovy!*" [To your health!]"

Lebedev thought to himself, *It may not be wise to ignore one billion angry Chinese.*

After Lebedev's request for surveillance on Lydia Boroshta, SVR agents had planted bugs in her telephones and monitored her movements. Agents in Poland, no longer a Russian satellite, discovered shocking information. Boroshta's mother and sisters had moved to New York, and had been granted political asylum by the U.S. Obviously, something was going on, and Boroshta needed more scrutiny. This was quickly reported to Lebedev, who was assisting Fradkov in transitioning into the Chairmanship of the SVR. "Mikhail, we need to eliminate Boroshta without delay. She could cause the Trojan Horse project to fail if she is a double-agent, working for the Americans. The evidence suggests that she could be, or at least cannot be trusted now with knowledge of this project."

Fradkov frowned. "That's fine, Sergei, but let's remember how badly the elimination of that hospital clerk went. That was totally unprofessional."

"I know, but the Resident in Washington had to act fast, on his own. He was only minutes ahead of the FBI."

"I still don't like it when our field operatives take action like this on their own. Taking the professor out must be done very carefully, and made to look like either a natural death or an accident. Sergei, we *must* get past the inauguration. Once that happens, we can cause the Americans total chaos, even if Pegasus is discovered. With their silly constitutional system, it will take them five years to unravel that and figure out what to do with Pegasus."

"Very well, I will put our best operators on it. I promise you, it *will* go smoothly."

"It better, Sergei. Your reputation depends on it," said Fradkov ominously. In the nuanced language of the Kremlin, this was a personal threat that was fully understood by Lebedev.

Chapter 19

Closing the Barn Door

As is often the case, the Vice Presidential candidate in this election was a sideshow. Nevertheless, Admiral William Hanlon turned out to be an excellent campaigner, and he drew huge crowds of his own, particularly in states like Washington, California, Virginia, and Florida, where large populations of retired and active duty military personnel reside. The stunning beauty of his wife, May, also attracted significant media attention. The two were high on the social invitation list with the country's wealthy and powerful. Hanlon's excellent performance during talk-show interviews left no doubt that he was a serious player, and, as Basi expected, strengthened the Basi candidacy in matters of national defense.

The year 2008 passed into 2009, with the nation's raucous New Year celebrations. This year, America's racial minorities were excited, having elected the first non-white President. A new optimism was in the air.

With the historic election over, Hanlon became less and less important to the Basi staffers. Like most U.S. Vice Presidents, he soon faded into obscurity and a quiet life at the Vice President's mansion at the Naval Observatory. He had spent a lifetime following orders, so this did not seem to bother him. May, on the other hand, resented the lack of respect she felt from the Basi people. "Bill, someday—perhaps soon—these fools will give you the respect that you deserve," she told him. Hanlon merely shrugged, not knowing what she meant.

Professor Boroshta was consumed by fear, now that she knew what the SVR was up to. She now knew much more than she ever wanted to know about Sam Basi. She decided that she was obligated to contact Tilsdale at the FBI, and debrief him on the plot. She would have preferred to avoid the FBI, but she knew that was not possible. They had her exactly where they wanted her, and she was more afraid of Tilsdale than the SVR. She dialed the pager number for Tilsdale.

Lebedev had dispatched one of the SVR's most expert assassins to handle the Boroshta matter. Irina Zukowski (SVR code-name: "Stiletto") entered the U.S. on a student visa, using a Czech Republic passport. She was a tall, athletic blond woman, and an expert at performing assassinations that appeared to be natural or accidental deaths.

To avoid detection, Stiletto had flown on Aeroflot to Prague under a fake identity and Russian passport. She switched passports, waited a day to shake off any surveillance, and then took Air France to London's Heathrow airport. Disguised as a typical European college student, she then booked a flight on British Airways, non-stop to Los Angeles. In the Economy section of the Airbus, she was just another European student-tourist, complete with backpack, coming to see Hollywood and Disneyland.

Going through customs and immigration screening in Los Angeles, she was asked the purpose of her visit by the

Immigration officer. "Pleasure, of course," she replied in perfect English. "I hope to study the American film industry while I am here."

She boarded the Hertz bus at the international terminal and proceeded to the rental car facility, where she selected a Cadillac. She knew that Boroshta's neighborhood was very affluent, so she did not want her vehicle to look out of place. After leaving the Hertz facility, she stopped at the address stored in her cell phone's notes page, a Kinko's copy and printing facility in West Los Angeles. She approached the man behind the desk.

"I'm here to pick up two signs for my car. I believe my real estate office called."

"Oh, are you with Sunset Realty?"

"That's right."

"Here it is. That was paid in advance, so you are good to go."

"Thank you." Stiletto took the signs and returned to her car. She placed the magnetic red-and-white "Sunset Realty" signs on each front door, and drove off toward Beverly Hills. If she decided to hit Boroshta at her home, she wanted to look like she and her car belonged in the neighborhood.

She had already been briefed by local SVR agents that the huge UCLA campus had little or no parking for visitors, so she decided to intercept Boroshta at her favorite fitness center, Equinox, on Wilshire Boulevard. SVR surveillance had already established that Boroshta arrived every week day afternoon at around 4:30 p.m. for a Jazzercise and gym workout, which usually lasted until 6 p.m. *Stupid*, thought Stiletto. *One should never be so predictable.*

Parking her car near the entrance, Stiletto waited. Nearly on schedule, Boroshta's silver Mercedes turned into the parking lot. Stiletto watched as she parked near the building. Now it was time to prepare for the disposal.

Stiletto reached into her briefcase and clicked open the false bottom, which contained an umbrella. This was one of the SVR's favorite tools, as it had been with the KGB before it. It was actually a powerful hypodermic dart device, containing a liquid concentrate of ricin, a deadly poison. The KGB had developed an extremely powerful variant of this castor plant byproduct, so that injecting or consuming a miniscule amount would result in death after a few minutes. There was no antidote.

At 5:55 p.m., she walked to the bus stop near the front door of the fitness club, carrying her umbrella. On schedule, Boroshta came through the exit doors, clad in Danskin tights and tank top. *Perfect,* thought Stiletto, and approached Boroshta.

"I am terribly sorry, but I was wondering whether I should join this club," said Stiletto, smiling. "I'm thinking about joining, if it's not too expensive."

Boroshta began describing the facility, as Stiletto pretended to slip and fall into her. On the way down, she pushed the tip of the umbrella against Boroshta's thigh and pressed the injector button. "Oh, I am so sorry. I hope I didn't hurt you as I fell," said Stiletto.

"No, but you should be more careful with that umbrella."

Stiletto got up, dusting herself off. "I know—I'm very sorry. Well, I have bothered you enough. Thank you so much for the information."

Boroshta walked across the lot to her car and got in. She started it up and turned out of the lot onto Wilshire, headed for Beverly Hills. Stiletto jumped into her car and followed her. Stiletto had used the SVR's "C-2" version of the ricin poison, which would cause paralysis within 20 minutes or less.

As Boroshta approached her normal turn at Carmelita Drive, her car suddenly swerved into the oncoming lanes, hitting a garbage truck head-on. Her car exploded in a ball of fire. Stiletto quickly turned off of Wilshire, and murmured, "*Missiya vypolnena.*" [Mission accomplished.] Stiletto wondered if she could still catch the "red-eye" flight back to Frankfurt, and what movie the airline would be showing.

On January 20, 2009, Sam Basi was sworn in as the 44th President, with George W. Bush looking on stoically. Following the initial ceremony, Sam and Tonya Basi walked triumphantly the entire length of the inaugural parade, waving to the adoring fans along the way. In his speech, Basi had said:

> "I am but a small part of this great day for America. This is a day in which the people—regardless of their race, position or wealth—have spoken and told our government what is required, and expected. I make this solemn pledge to each of you—I will not let you down. I will remember your message, your hopes, and your dreams, and I will recreate this government from one that serves only the privileged few, to one that serves every American. I will not let your hopes die, and I will work tirelessly to implement the massive changes in our society that are so vitally needed. Let us begin this great crusade together, united, and steadfast in our determination for a new, fair, and just nation."

Meanwhile, Tilsdale had been repeatedly calling Professor Boroshta's contact numbers in response to her page. All he got was her voicemail message. Finally, he had enough. He called the Special Agent-in-Charge of the Los Angeles field office.

"Tom? This is Brad Tilsdale."

Immediately, the SAC knew that something important was going on. "Yes, Sir. What can I do for you?"

"I have a witness in a case, named Lydia Boroshta. She's a professor at UCLA. I received a call on my pager from her several days ago, but she has not returned my calls. Could you have one of your guys track her down, and make sure that she is OK?"

"Yes, Sir. I'll let you know as soon as I find out anything."

"Great. Talk to you soon, Tom."

The SAC immediately tasked two of his agents to locate Boroshta. They started at her home, where they found a pile of Los Angeles Times newspapers at the front door, and mail spilling out of the door slot. No one answered their knock.

The agents spotted a neighbor walking through her front yard, and approached the woman. "Excuse me. We are trying to locate Professor Boroshta. Do you know where she is?"

The middle-aged woman looked at the two suspiciously. There had been burglaries in the neighborhood recently. "Who wants to know?" she asked.

"FBI, ma'am. I'm Agent Wallace, and this is Agent Thompkins."

The woman's eyes widened. "Oh? Is Lydia in some kind of trouble?"

"We don't think so, but we need to find her."

"Well, I'm afraid I can't help you. Maybe she went back

to Europe or something. She's from there, you know."

The agents thanked her and drove off, calling the SAC for further guidance. "Check with UCLA first, and then start contacting the local PDs and hospitals. If that doesn't work, we'll check with Immigration to see if she has left the country."

The first call to the Beverly Hills PD was successful. "We had a Lydia Boroshta involved in a serious auto accident a few days ago. She is in intensive care at the UCLA Medical Center," reported the BHPD desk sergeant.

Wallace and Thompkins drove immediately over to the campus, parking their car in front of the building, with the blue and red emergency lights flashing. They walked quickly into the reception area, showing their badges and IDs. "FBI. Where is the patient Lydia Boroshta?" They were directed to the intensive care ward on the fourth floor.

Approaching the charge nurse on the floor, they showed their IDs. "We need to talk to the patient Lydia Boroshta. What is her status?"

"I'm afraid that is impossible," the nurse said. "She was badly burned, is in a coma, and she lost her right leg in the accident." As it turned out, this probably saved Boroshta's life, because the ricin poison had been injected into that leg, allowing a relatively small dose into the rest of her body.

Wallace called the SAC for further guidance, given the unusual circumstances. He, in turn, called Tilsdale in Washington. "Mr. Tilsdale? Tom Barrett in Los Angeles. We located your subject, Boroshta, at UCLA Medical Center, in a coma. She was in a very bad auto accident."

Tilsdale's mind was racing. *Was this just a coincidence, and bad luck?* "Tom, let's do this. Put a 24-hour security guard on her. Get her moved into a private room, so that you can control the perimeter better. And tell your guys to keep alert—there may be something going on here. This may not have been an accident. I'm on my way out there with Jeff Billings. See you tomorrow at your office."

Billings was already back to work, having recovered quickly from the superficial gunshot wound. Tilsdale was now one of the older senior agents, and he increasingly relied on the younger Billings, who was being groomed for a senior management position within the Bureau.

The next day, Tilsdale and Billings drove from LAX to the federal building, where the FBI offices were located. Taking the elevator to the 17th floor, they showed their IDs to the security officer on duty. "We are here to see the SAC," said Tilsdale.

"Yes, Sir. Let me call him." The uniformed U.S. Protective Services officer was not accustomed to seeing one of the Assistant Directors there.

Within minutes, Tom Barrett came around the corner. "Good to see you, Sir. Jeff, you look like you are back in the game. How's the shoulder?"

"Fine, thanks, Tom."

Tilsdale cut the conversation short. "Tom, let's get a private area to talk. This is an 'eyes-only' matter, OK?"

"Sure. Please follow me." He led the two into his corner office, overlooking the huge veteran's cemetery below, and the UCLA campus beyond.

Barrett closed the door. "What's going on? This involves the Boroshta matter, I take it?"

"That's right Tom. The fewer people that know about this—throughout the Bureau—the better, for right now. I want you to keep a tight lid on this, OK?"

Barrett looked startled. Whatever this was, it had the

sound of a politically sensitive case, and those could often result in the end of an FBI career if handled badly. "No problem, Brad. So far, only two of my best agents have had any contact with the case, and they don't know anything beyond the facts of her accident."

"Good. Now, here is the drill. I want you to send someone downstairs to the U.S. Attorney's office, and get us a subpoena for Boroshta's medical records, and for anything the police may have on the accident. Let's move!"

Within 30 minutes, a subpoena came back. "Jeff, get over to UCLA and get a copy of those records. Tom, send one of your guys over to BHPD and get everything that they have. I want to know exactly how this occurred, and when Lydia will be able to talk to us."

Dallinger had been advised of the "disposal" of Boroshta by Stiletto, and he was relieved. As far as he could tell, all of the loose ends of the Trojan Horse project had been fixed.

President Basi, of course, knew nothing about this conspiratorial activity in his behalf. He was merely following his pre-programmed Socialist instincts, and feeling as if he were now in control of the universe. He hardly knew where to begin, there were so many capitalistic problems that needed to be solved with Socialist solutions. He started by issuing a flood of Executive Orders, reversing many of the policies of the prior Presidents. Next, he had his staff locate those with the requisite Socialist ideology for each functional area within his administration. He hired nearly 50 of his Socialist friends, many from various university faculties, plugging them into broad governmental areas like energy, environmental protection, global warming, labor, and others. These became known to the press as "Czars," part of the

Executive Branch, and not requiring approval by the Senate.

Next, he focused on the Defense Department, the Justice Department, FBI, and intelligence services. He wanted his loyal followers in key positions, and instructed his staff to identify the best candidates for promotion or political appointment. For his own political advisor on the White House staff, he selected Jason Caswell. The Secret Service was outraged, because of Caswell's criminal record. Nevertheless, President Basi overruled their objection, reminding them that Caswell and his terrorist wife had been pardoned by President Carter.

The takeover of the U.S. government was nearly total and complete, without a shot being fired. Not even Sam Basi knew what he had actually accomplished for America's foreign enemies. In his mind, he was only doing that which was best for the entire world and the advancement of the Socialist agenda. However, those who controlled him had a more sinister agenda, and a meeting was called to discuss it.

It was still winter in the Austrian Alps, and the snowy landscape around Salzburg was a beautiful sight, as Lebedev and Fradkov sipped vodka and looked out from the second floor of the Zebrotny mansion. "*Krasivyĭ*," [Beautiful] commented Lebedev.

"*Dyeĭstvitelno zamechatelnyĭ!*" [Truly wonderful] added the SVR Chairman. "And so is the posture of the Trojan Horse project, Sergei. You have done a magnificent job. Putin is very pleased. I would not be surprised if you received a high government award for this."

"I just want this to put Russia in the leadership role she deserves."

"Well, you certainly have done that, my friend. Look, here come the others." They approached the large conference table and sat down.

"Greetings, my friends," said Zebrotny. Caswell and Dallinger sat at his side, unable to suppress their delight with what they had accomplished, in spite of the overwhelming odds against success of such a gamble.

"The real question now is, what is the best action agenda, and in what order? I believe Jason has prepared a tentative list of action items for our review and discussion. Jason, please proceed."

"Thank you, Victor. Let me bring up some Powerpoint slides." He clicked a remote control, and the screen at the end of the table illuminated with an outline:

Final Phase of the Trojan Horse Project:

- Staffing of key government positions
- Issuance of Executive Orders
- Pushing the U.S. Economy into Recession
  - Raise taxes
  - Increase frivolous spending
  - Ignore energy requirements
  - Allow the federal deficit to grow
  - Pass legislation that will restrain economic growth
  - Create an anti-business regulatory environment
- Create Hyper-inflation
  - Finance the growing deficit by issuing bonds
  - Expand the money supply
  - Keep interest rates artificially low
- Demoralize the U.S. Military
  - Allow gays and trans-sexuals to serve openly

- o   Place women in combat units
- o   Ignore the budget needs of the forces
- o   Fire/remove effective unit commanders
- Destroy the Traditional American Society
  - o   Promote gay marriage
  - o   Attack religious institutions
  - o   Destroy small business creation
  - o   Allow massive illegal immigration and grant amnesty
  - o   Force children's education toward Socialism, at all levels
  - o   Use Leftist allies in the entertainment and media industries to ridicule and attack American history and values

"Amazing! This is excellent," said Lebedev.

"Yes, and we have already begun on the first three items. Let me elaborate," responded Caswell.

"Upon taking office, we made rapid appointments from various Leftist groups into the government. We issued a barrage of Executive Orders, which carry the weight of law in the United States. We also rammed through Congress a 'stimulus plan,' which was full of meaningless expenditures and frivolous spending, for nearly an additional trillion dollars. However, we are having trouble with the Republicans, who are starting to get organized and are blocking some of our key legislation, like the 'cap-and-trade' energy bill, which will effectively bring the economy to its knees.

"However, we have a 'secret weapon' in the form of what we are calling 'The Affordable Healthcare Act.' The Right-wing critics are calling it 'Basi-care.' If we can jam this through Congress, it will add trillions to the deficit, while making it nearly impossible to run a business in the United States. We think it will eventually pass, but we will need to bribe a few people in Congress.

"On a parallel track, we will work diligently to take down the foundations of American society and tradition. We will suck the oxygen out of their patriotic balloon, and leave them gasping for breath. Let me talk about some key items and give you some examples.

"We have selected a new head of the Environmental Protection Agency, the EPA. She is very aggressive, and will proceed to issue hundreds of new regulations that will shut down many of their refineries, power plants, and mines. By using the EPA's power under the Clean Air Act and Clean Water Act, we can do plenty of damage to their industrial capacity, especially where coal and oil are used for energy production.

"By using 'emergency authority,' we will have our Treasury Department flood the market with bonds, causing the Federal Reserve to expand the money supply in order to keep interest rates low. Ultimately, this will explode into a hyper-inflation environment.

"I know you are all concerned about their strong military. We plan on taking that down in two major ways. First, we will destroy the morale of the Services by slashing their budgets and disrupting their unit cohesiveness."

"How do you do that last item, Jason?" asked Fradkov.

"As you know, a military unit's effectiveness depends in large part on the internal trust of the unit and their unity of culture and purpose. By overturning existing law and injecting gays and trans-genders into their ranks, there will be chaos. Can you imagine a Gay 'pride' parade at Annapolis and West Point?" They all laughed.

"Plus, we will force the Services to allow women into combat units for the first time. This issue alone will be so controversial that they will spend all of their unit command time in dealing with gender-related issues, such as 'sexual harassment.'"

Lebedev chuckled. "Jason, we Russians call that 'romance.'" More laughter.

"One of the most important phases will be the destruction of the traditional American family and society. This will call for a multi-pronged approach, using our Leftist friends in the entertainment and media industries and special-interest organizations like the ACLU, National Public Radio, MSNBC, Media Matters, Democracy Alliance, and so on. The Judeo-Christian religions form the fabric of American society, so eliminating that influence produces a vacuum, into which we will inject our Socialist values. We will do that through the educational institutions, public and private, which are now thoroughly infiltrated with our ideology, promoted by the teacher unions and university faculties.

"Last, but not least, is preventing the country from securing its borders. We have determined that both political parties are hesitant to do anything about border control, for fear of alienating the growing number of Hispanic voters. As we say in America, they 'kick the can down the road,' resulting in an expanding illegal alien population, which we estimate at over 15 million and climbing daily. Even if those people never gain citizenship for voting purposes, they breed like rabbits and their U.S.-born children automatically become citizens under current law, so the problem grows like a political cancer. If the Republicans try to fix the problem, they automatically alienate the growing Hispanic voting bloc. We have successfully turned that issue into one that is *owned* by the Democratic Party, and President Basi, a person of color, is obviously in an excellent position to capitalize on it."

Lebedev turned to the others. "Gentlemen, I propose that we approve this plan, as Jason has outlined it. We only need to make sure that Pegasus continues to execute it precisely. Jason, that is your responsibility. You must notify us immediately if anything starts to become a problem. And that includes any deviation from our plan by Pegasus."

"Yes, of course. But at the moment, we are right on track."

"One other thing, Jason. You need to promote David Dallinger to a higher position within the FBI, or perhaps within the CIA." Lebedev thought for a moment. "A position within the CIA's NCS [National Clandestine Service] would be good, but see what you can do." Dallinger could not suppress a smile. The thought of operating within the CIA appealed to him. He had become bored by his duties within the straight-laced FBI.

"And what about that troublesome Tilsdale fellow, David? Is he under control, or do we have a potential problem there?" asked Lebedev.

"Tilsdale will always be a problem, Sergei. Half the time, I don't even know what he is doing," replied Dallinger.

"Well, that has to be fixed. Jason, how about promoting David to the Bureau's second position, Deputy Director? Then he will be a superior to Tilsdale again."

"We can definitely do that," said Caswell. Dallinger winced. He preferred the CIA.

"Oh, before I forget—Professor Boroshta was killed in an auto accident in Los Angeles. We will miss her contributions." They all nodded solemnly. "I will see all of you at the next meeting. Have a safe trip back. *Do svidaniya.*"

The other agents had just returned to the field office conference room with Boroshta's medical records and the police investigative report of her accident. Tilsdale and Billings pored through the documents. The police report contained nothing remarkable, except the vivid description of Boroshta's vehicle crossing into the on-coming traffic and the fiery collision. Apparently, the airbag saved her life.

The medical records were another story. In the peculiar, technical language of the medical profession, the amputation of what was left of her right leg was described in a dry narrative. Then, Billings found the lab report.

"Brad, look at this!" He handed Tilsdale a document. It was a lab report on the blood and urine taken from Boroshta when she arrived at the hospital, unconscious.

"OK, it shows a few things out of limits. So what?"

"Look at this—her amino acids are all out of whack, and the proteins in her blood were not being absorbed, or synthesized."

"So what does that tell you, *Doctor* Billings?" asked Tilsdale sarcastically.

"She was poisoned."

"What? How do you know?"

"Look! Her kidneys stopped functioning and she has evidence of cell damage in her blood. That's what threw her into a coma. Her blood is toxic, and the kidneys shut down when they tried to filter it out."

"What would cause that? And who did it? She was just driving home by herself after working out at the gym."

"If I had to guess, based on what I learned years ago in the Army's chemical warfare training, it could be ricin."

Tilsdale looked at him. "Remember that writer that the KGB poisoned in London, years ago? They used a goddam umbrella to inject it while the guy was walking down the street, as I recall."

"So why isn't she dead? That stuff is supposed to be fatal within a couple of days, at the most."

"Maybe... when they took the rest of her leg off, that removed the source of the injection, and she only received a partial dose in her bloodstream. Jeff, we have to get her revived so she can talk and tell us what happened, and why she paged me. Let's get over to UCLA."

Reviving patients from a coma is not a standard procedure, nor easily done. Physicians normally prefer to let the patient gradually come out of that state, carefully managing the nutritional and metabolic balance while that occurs. However, since this coma was probably caused by a toxin, the UCLA doctors decided that placing her on a dialysis machine might purify her blood enough to bring her to consciousness. While this was going on, Tilsdale and Billings kept vigil on her progress. Tilsdale was determined to unlock the secret that had almost killed her.

Back in Washington, the Bureau's Deputy Director retired, leaving the promotional path clear for Dallinger. His first move was to get control of Tilsdale. "Brad, David Dallinger."

"Congratulations, David. I just got the e-mail about your appointment on my Blackberry."

"Well, thanks. I was wondering if you and I could have a chat when you get back. By the way, exactly what are you working on out there?"

Tilsdale made an instant decision to safeguard his

activity for the moment. "We had a protected witness that got hurt. She's in a coma, near death, and we are hoping for a deathbed statement to protect the case."

"Very well. Out of curiosity, what is her name?"

"Oh, I doubt if you know this case. It's really not much to worry about."

"Fine, but what is her name?" pressed Dallinger.

Tilsdale felt trapped. Either he gave her name, or lied to a man that was now his boss. That was a sin that was never forgiven within the FBI. He decided to give it up. "Lydia Boroshta."

Dallinger felt his heart stop for an instant. *How could this be?* Regaining his composure, he said, "Well, I need you guys back here. President Basi is about to go on a tour of the Middle East, to meet the various foreign leaders. Your counter-terrorism unit is slated to provide some background security in each country he visits."

"We just need a couple more days, David."

"No way. The President leaves the day after tomorrow, and I want your team out there ahead of him, reviewing local security measures and threats. Sorry, Brad. Be on the next flight out of Los Angeles, OK?"

"Affirmative." Tilsdale cursed and threw the phone down. "We have to go back to DC, right now. We need to turn this over to the local field office to monitor Boroshta." The two left and had one of the local agents drive them to LAX, making a reservation on the way by cell phone. They left the car and walked quickly to the American Airlines terminal.

Upon their return, they were immediately sent ahead of Air Force One via an Air Force Gulfstream jet from Andrews Air Force Base. Their first stop was Madrid for fuel, and then on to Cairo and finally Riyadh, Saudi Arabia. After contacting the embassy and the Secret Service advance team, the two returned to their hotel rooms at the Riyadh Hilton, located on King Faisal Road in the Olaya district. They were exhausted.

Dallinger sent a coded message to Lebedev, informing him that Boroshta had survived the assassination attempt. Lebedev was outraged. When he learned that Boroshta was under guard at UCLA Medical Center, he decided to pull out all of the stops, and activate an SVR "sleeper" agent to complete the termination of Boroshta. The SVR's covert agent division selected the perfect candidate—a local physician, who used the alias "Phillip Hargreave." He had been planted in the West Los Angeles area during the Cold War.

In the event of hostilities between the U.S. and the Soviet Union, Hargreave would have been activated to initiate an outbreak of anthrax and smallpox in the huge Los Angeles area. This would cause mass hysteria in the U.S. population, and the smallpox would spread quickly through the transportation systems to other states. He had been supplied with a stockpile of both biological substances, which was kept in a locked vault under the foundation of Dr. Hargreave's medical office in Santa Monica. By using the two together, the anthrax would mask the smallpox and confuse public health officials until it was too late.

After he received the coded orders, "Hargreave," whose name was actually Oleg Zapolov, decided to use anthrax to do the job. He only needed to gain access to Boroshta's hospital room.

The next morning, Lydia Boroshta began to come out of her coma. The young FBI agent guarding her saw her begin to move her fingers. The attending nurse told him that she might be able to talk in a day or so, given this progress.

As the agent walked into the hall to call his office, no one noticed when another white-coated doctor came through the door and picked up the patient chart. "I'm Dr. Barrington," said Hargreave to the nurse, knowing that the famous trauma doctor had been called in to consult on Boroshta's recovery. "Would you please change her IVs? I don't want them to run dry." The nurse left to obtain new IV bags from the pharmacy.

That was all the time he needed. Putting on rubber gloves, he pulled an inhaler-type of device from his pocket, then cut a small slit in the respirator hose and squirted the deadly anthrax spores into the line. He dropped the inhaler into the nearby trashcan. The spores were immediately pumped into Boroshta's trachea and lungs. Within hours, they would explode into a toxic bacteria colony, entering the pulmonary lymph nodes, and rapidly causing massive hemorrhaging and lung failure. As Hargreave knew well, the inhalation of anthrax spores in this quantity would be 100% fatal. He peeled off his gloves and left the room. Outside, the FBI agent had his back turned, and was talking on his cell phone.

The next day, as Tilsdale and Billings watched from the observation deck at Riyadh airport, Air Force One appeared overhead and landed. Along with other embassy staff, the new President traveled by motorcade to the King's palace. They learned that Al-Qaeda sympathizers were active in the Riyadh area, and tension was high. This was, after all, the original home of Osama Bin Laden and 15 of the 19 9/11 hijackers. Hatred of the U.S. was still taught in the religious schools, like a standard part of the curriculum, as a mandatory subject for the young of Saudi Arabia.

"Just how do we protect this guy, Jeff? Half of the people in this city would love to kill the President, even though he has been running around making apologies for the United States and praising Islam. Sometimes I wonder if he might actually be a Muslim." The two looked at each other.

"A closet Muslim. *That* would be nice. Just be glad we aren't in the Secret Service, directly responsible for his safety in this shit hole." Billings paused. "You know, I never really figured out his role in that Pegasus matter."

"Me either. I don't know why they have us here. The Saudi security people won't allow us to carry guns, and they won't tell us anything about the threat status. I don't like these assholes. If they didn't have the oil, they would all still be living in tents with their camels."

"Yeah, but they have us over a barrel, literally."

"Roger that! Let's go to the palace, and see what our American dollars have paid for."

Tilsdale and Billings roamed the periphery of the crowds that attended the reception ceremonies, looking for identifiable threats. "Christ, these Arabs could each have an RPG [grenade launcher] or an AK-47 under those white robes! I hate this situation," griped Tilsdale.

Back at King Khalid International Airport, Air Force One, the President's Boeing 747, was being fueled and serviced for the next leg of his Middle East journey. The Saudi security forces had established a restricted perimeter around the big aircraft, with oversight by the U.S. Secret Service. The fuel truck crewmen were Saudi Air Force personnel, and allowed to approach the aircraft for the refueling operation.

There was no way for the Secret Service to conduct a background investigation on foreign personnel of this category, especially in a country like Saudi Arabia. If they had been able to do so, the Al-Qaeda connection of Sergeant Jamal Al-Amri would have been detected. He had even been disciplined in the past by his superiors for spouting radical Islamic slogans and inciting his troops with fiery speeches. This was never passed on to the Americans, and Al-Amri was the senior fuel technician in his unit. It would have been a loss of face and disrespectful to keep him from his normal job of fueling an aircraft, according to the Saudi tribal culture.

Fueling a 747 is normally accomplished by ground crews with a pump truck and hydraulic lift. The fueling connection of the giant aircraft is on the underside of the left wing, hidden inside of a large drop-down panel. The fueling crewman is lifted up in the hydraulic lift with the hose, which he connects to the aircraft at the connector fitting, then opens the fueling valve while monitoring the quantity in the tanks.

As Al-Amri watched the gauges, the security guards disregarded him. He was a familiar sight at the airport, especially when a VIP arrived. No one noticed when Al-Amri reached inside his jump-suit and placed a small package of C-4 explosive in the cavernous fuel panel area, deep inside the wing. He had set the barometric ignition device to explode when the sensor detected an altitude of 10,000 feet. He already knew that the flight plan to Amman, Jordan called for a altitude of 31,000 feet, guaranteeing ignition in a critical area of the wing structure, surrounded by vital flight controls, fuel, and hydraulic lines. Although not a huge device, he knew it would be sufficient to bring the aircraft down by severing the wing. He mumbled to himself, *"Allah akhbar!"* [God is great!]

At the completion of the fueling operation, Al-Amri and his crew removed the hose, and buttoned the panel back in position. They drove the truck out of the security perimeter and returned to their maintenance hangar.

The Presidential motorcade, surrounded by black SUVs with Secret Service agents, returned to the airport ramp and drove up to Air Force One. The President got out, shook hands with the U.S. ambassador, the Saudi Minister of Foreign Affairs, and the Saudi Army Chief of Staff. He gave a smiling wave, and boarded the aircraft.

As Tilsdale and Billings watched from the ramp perimeter, Billings commented, "Brad, I really hate these assignments. They send us along to provide additional scapegoats if anything goes wrong."

"I know. We sure as hell can't do anything meaningful."

The movable stairs were pulled away from Air Force One, as the main door closed. Her bulbous General Electric CF-6 turbofans, each capable of over 56,000 pounds of thrust, came to life with a deafening, whining chorus. She taxied out to the runway, filling up the entire taxiway with her massive wheel assemblies. Pilots of this aircraft have often said that taxiing it on the ground is more hazardous than flying it, given the wide wingspan and the opportunity to strike something with a wingtip, or accidentally let one of the giant wheel assemblies drift off the taxiway.

Cleared for takeoff, the four powerful engines accelerated to takeoff thrust, as the pilot released the brakes. At about the 5,000 foot marker, looking like an ungainly, blue-and-white elephant, she raised her nose and lifted her wheels gently from the runway. As the aircraft roared over the end of the runway, her landing gear retracted. Turning right to intercept the jet route to Amman, she retracted her flaps and became the nimble giant that made her such a superior design, and the envy of the world's heads of state. She was a symbol of American power and prestige, which is why all Presidents have considered her one of their most treasured "perks" of office. At the same time, there could not be a more attractive target for a terrorist.

Tilsdale and Billings were walking across the sun-baked ramp to their Gulfstream as Air Force One was climbing through 10,000 feet on her way to cruise altitude. The barometric switch clicked, triggering the detonator that had been inserted into the plastic mass of the C-4 explosive. The resulting explosion ruptured the aircraft's hydraulic flight control lines, wing fuel tank, and the structural wing spar. Fire engulfed the structure as it folded like a broken bird's wing. The pilot was able to transmit a single "Mayday" call before the aircraft rolled inverted and headed for the barren desert below.

Workers in one of the Saudi oil fields witnessed the explosion and watched as the big aircraft plunged nose first into the desert in a massive fireball. Tilsdale and Billings also heard the explosion, and watched the aircraft fall.

"My God! Let's get the car!" said Tilsdale, dialing his

emergency security number. The two sprinted for the VIP parking area near the terminal.

Tilsdale and Billings were the first Americans on the scene. The Secret Service agents were split up—some were on Air Force One, while the advance team had already taken off in their MD-80 aircraft for Amman. The two FBI agents were the only American law enforcement or security personnel available to get to the crash site, which was approximately nine miles from the airport.

As they approached the burning wreckage, the two agents were in a state of shock. They were starting to realize that they had just witnessed the violent death of 200 people, including the President of the United States. Somehow, this seemed even worse than the events of September 11, 2001.

"Brad, I heard an explosion and saw a smoke-puff before the aircraft nosed over."

"So did I, Jeff. It was either a shoulder-fired missile, like the Stinger, or a bomb on the aircraft."

"If it was a bomb, I don't know how they could have gotten it on the aircraft. The Secret Service locks that bird down tight when it's sitting on the ground, especially in a foreign country like Saudi Arabia. I'm betting it was a missile, but I did not see any characteristic smoke trail, did you?"

"Negative. But the aircraft did not blow up by itself. Remember TWA 800?"

"Don't remind me. I had a hard time letting go of that one."

The first people on the scene were workers from the nearby oil platform, all Saudis. They were standing at the edge of the crater, which was filled with burning debris and body parts. "Any of you guys speak English?" asked Tilsdale.

"Yes, I do," said one. "I am the manager for that drilling

unit. We heard a bang, looked up and saw this big airplane falling, and then hitting the ground here. Which airline was it?"

"Not sure yet," lied Tilsdale. "Make sure no one picks up any pieces or anything. This entire site is off limits except to police and the army."

"OK, I will tell my people." The man shouted something in Arabic, and the men got back in their SUV. "Ah, here comes the Army."

A caravan of white SUVs sped toward them across the desert, with sirens and lights activated. They skidded to a stop next to Tilsdale and Billings.

"Who are you?" asked the officer, a Saudi major.

"United States FBI. Major, we need to quarantine this area and keep souvenir hunters and scavengers out," directed Tilsdale.

"What was this aircraft?" asked the major.

"It was Air Force One—the President's aircraft," replied Tilsdale. With the site temporarily secure, he called the embassy and had them patch him through their satellite link to Washington. He dialed the special number for the National Command Center, which was located in the Pentagon. When the number was automatically answered, he then dialed a special code, which only top U.S. officials had, initiating a national emergency alert. Even if this turned out to be a terrible accident, without a human cause, the national defense system had to be ready for an attack by a foreign government, or terrorists.

The first response was from the President's National Security Council staff, followed by the North American Aerospace Defense Command in Cheyenne Mountain, Colorado, and then the National Military Command Center at the Pentagon. The last person to join the call was Vice President Bill Hanlon.

"Ladies and gentlemen, this is FBI Assistant Director Brad Tilsdale. I have the sad duty to report to you that our President is dead, killed in the crash of Air Force One in Saudi Arabia."

"This is the Vice President—how did this happen? Was this a terrorist attack?"

"It's too early to tell, Mr. Vice President. My partner and I saw an explosion as the aircraft was climbing out of Riyadh, heading for Amman. It appeared to roll over and dove directly into the desert, apparently killing everyone on board. I cannot positively confirm the President's death by forensic evidence yet, but this crash was not survivable.

"This is NORAD. We just placed our forces on high alert, in case this involves a foreign government."

"This is the Military Command Center, Admiral Jacobs. We have flashed an EAM [emergency action message] to all strategic forces to be on alert. Do we need conventional forces mobilized? If so, where?"

"No, Admiral. It is my opinion at this time that this is will be an investigation like with TWA 800, part technical and part law enforcement. What we need right now is a forensic aircraft accident team, on site, to determine the cause."

Admiral Jacobs spoke again. "Within six hours, we will launch aircraft for Riyadh, bringing you NTSB [National Transportation Safety Board] people, Boeing technical engineers, and a forensic evidence team from the FBI lab in Quantico."

"That sounds good. That's what we need for the moment."

"What about casualty assistance?" asked the Vice President. "When the media gets hold of this, it will be all over the air waves in seconds. We need to start notifying next of kin, beginning with the First Lady."

"I agree. Can you initiate that?" asked Tilsdale.

"Affirmative, I will handle that."

"Is there anything else that you need from the Defense Department?" asked the Pentagon.

Tilsdale thought for a moment, remembering the assassination of JFK, and the subsequent swearing-in of Lyndon Johnson. "I guess there is, but it's above my pay grade. From a Constitutional point of view, the nation needs to transition the Presidency to the Vice President. Mr. Vice President, can we rely on you and the White House staff to handle that phase? It should be done fairly soon, I would think, for continuity and stability purposes. We need to reassure our allies, our enemies, and the world that we are still in business."

"It will be the saddest duty I ever have undertaken, but I will contact the appropriate people," said Hanlon.

Chapter 20

The Year of the Dragon

While Tilsdale and Billings worked the crash site of Air Force One, things were moving rapidly in Washington. Security measures around Hanlon were tightened, and Washington braced for potential attacks, still of unknown origin. No one had taken credit for downing Air Force One, and the "official" cause given to the media was that "mechanical failure" had brought the aircraft down.

The Vice President took the oath of office from the Supreme Court's Chief Justice Roberts, surrounded by the Attorney General, his wife May, the Senate Majority Leader, the Speaker of the House of Representatives, and the Chairman of the Joint Chiefs of Staff:

> "I do solemnly swear that I will faithfully execute the office of President of the United States, and will to the best of my ability, preserve, protect and defend the Constitution of the United States."

"Congratulations, Mr. President," the Chief Justice said grimly.

"May God help me steer the proper course for our nation.

Thank you, Mr. Chief Justice," replied Hanlon.

"Mr. President, we have some administrative matters that need your immediate attention," said a staffer.

"Certainly. Thank you all for coming. I will be talking to each of you in the next few days. This is a terrible tragedy, but the country must keep moving forward, and I know you will help in that regard." Hanlon and his staff headed for the tunnel to the Old Executive Office Building, which they would occupy temporarily during working hours, and the new President and First Lady would reside at Blair House, the nearby VIP residence. It had already been decided that they would let a week go by before Tonya Basi moved out of the White House, out of respect for the grieving wife of the deceased President.

Back in Riyadh, the NTSB accident team had already located the outer wing portion that had been severed from the aircraft at altitude. Because it had aerodynamic characteristics, the large piece had fluttered down to the desert floor, like part of a child's toy airplane, staying intact. While the rest of the aircraft had disintegrated upon impact, this piece provided the evidence that Tilsdale was looking for—traces of C-4, and the outward bending effect on the wing surfaces. Clearly, this was some type of explosive device, and not a mechanical failure. The big question was, who was responsible?

This was now the type of case that the FBI knows how to investigate, as long as external politics do not get in the way. Tilsdale notified Washington that he wanted more agents, including Arabic-speakers.

In Los Angeles, Boroshta's condition reversed, and she went back into a coma. "Dr. Hargreave" had done his work well. The UCLA medical staff could not explain her failure to recover, while her vital signs continued to worsen. When one of the attending nurses became ill with flu-like symptoms, one of the doctors became suspicious. He ordered a blood panel on both of them and quarantined Boroshta's room. An epidemiologist confirmed his fears—Boroshta and the nurse had contracted anthrax.

All staff members and the FBI agents involved were immediately given antibiotics, and no one else appeared to have the infection. By the third day, Lydia Boroshta died. The SVR had finally prevented her from talking. The Los Angeles FBI field office notified Tilsdale by text message.

Tilsdale read the message on his Blackberry with alarm. "Jeff, someone killed Boroshta with anthrax. That could only be done with the resources of a foreign government."

"That's right, Brad. It's not hard to grow the bacteria, but to 'weaponize' the spores in a form that can be used requires advanced technology and expertise. There are probably only a few countries that could do that, including ours."

"My bet would be on our SVR friends in Moscow," said Tilsdale.

The death of President Basi also sent shockwaves through foreign capitals, including Moscow's Trojan Horse project team. An emergency meeting was held at SVR headquarters, without the Chinese. In attendance were Putin, Lebedev, and Fradkov. The mood was somber.

"I can't believe it," mumbled Lebedev. "After all these years and effort. We had just achieved total success, and now Pegasus is gone. We had such a huge investment in him."

"I doubt if this was an accident. The stupid Americans should never have allowed him to travel to areas like this. There are too many fanatical Muslims that can't wait to kill an *infidel*, especially an American President," noted Fradkov. "The Americans' security is a joke."

"This was our golden opportunity to get rid of the American missile defense system, once and for all," said Putin. "Now we are back to square one, and we have a new President to deal with. William Hanlon will not be so easy to manipulate. Our intelligence on him suggests that he will be a hard-liner, and will never give up that missile defense network in Europe. We need to really think about our next move, or we will soon be in a position where our own ICBMs will not be able to hit the United States. We will have to rely on submarine-based missiles, and our fleet is in terrible shape, aging rapidly."

"As are we, Vladimir," retorted Fradkov.

"Let's meet again in a month. On Wednesday, I am going to Washington for the memorial service for Basi, along with other world leaders. One of those things that I get stuck with all the time. I should have stayed in the SVR, like the two of you."

"Come now, Vladimir—you know there is not room enough for your ego in our little intelligence service," said Lebedev with a chuckle.

"Fuck you, Comrade."

Sam Basi's body was never found, not even an identifiable body part. The only item of his that survived the intense heat of the burning aircraft was his wedding ring. Tonya had that placed in a casket, so that there would be a proper ceremony in the Capitol Rotunda, with military honor guard.

The world's leaders, except for those not invited (North Korea, Cuba, Iran), were in attendance and paid their respects to Basi's widow, who was dressed in a black suit.

Many—the Russians in particular—were genuinely sorry he was gone, because they considered him much easier to manipulate than George Bush or Bill Clinton.

Following the ceremony, his casket was symbolically laid to rest in Arlington National Cemetery, near the Kennedys. The next day, Tonya moved out of the White House, and within hours, William and May Hanlon moved in. The White House staff quickly became aware that May would be the dominant force in anything that involved her husband— his meals, his laundry, his entertainment, and social invitations. May ruled the White House like no First Lady before her, with the exception of perhaps Jackie Kennedy. The word spread quickly—if you make this First Lady unhappy, you will probably lose your job.

Dallinger decided that this was the time to rid himself of Tilsdale and Billings. The two had come dangerously close to solving the entire Trojan House conspiracy. He notified them to report to his office.

"What do you think this is about, Brad? I don't like this asshole," said Billings.

"Who knows? He is nothing but a bureaucrat, and he probably wants to cover his ass, given the assassination. Don't worry about it."

As they entered the outer office of the Deputy Director, Tilsdale noticed that the secretaries avoided eye contact. "Hi, Nancy," he said.

Without responding, the secretary led them into the office. Dallinger looked tense. "David, what's up?" asked Tilsdale.

"Brad, Jeff—please sit down. I have been directed to inform both of you that you have been terminated from the

Bureau." Tilsdale and Billings exchanged startled looks. "I know you did not have anything directly to do with President Basi's security procedures in Riyadh, but a lot of important people think you failed to do your job."

"Wait a fucking minute—what about the Secret Service? Do they get a pass? They were the ones that dropped the ball, not us."

"I know, but the guys that were responsible went down with the aircraft, so there is no one left to punish. I guess that's the gist of it," said Dallinger with a sigh.

"Well, I'm going to fight this, and expose some of the shit that has been going on," yelled Billings. "Who exactly has ordered that we should be terminated?"

Dallinger paused. "The Director. Someone has to take the fall for this, Brad. You guys are running the anti-terrorist unit, you were on scene, and it still happened. You also failed to stop 9/11 from happening."

"What? You goddam pencil pusher! You will not get away with this!" said Billings.

"Cool it, Jeff. Let's go." Tilsdale pulled out his Glock, badge, and ID, and threw them on the desk. Billings did the same. "David, I just have one more thing to say to you."

"What?" Dallinger said softly.

"Kiss my ass!" he hissed menacingly.

The two stormed out of the office. In the elevator, Tilsdale turned to Billings. "Jeff, this may be the best thing that ever happened to us. I happen to know someone at CIA who wants our services—badly. She has being trying to recruit me for years."

It was obvious that William Hanlon was accustomed to running things, especially in large organizations. His

knowledge of national security matters was already extensive, due to his prior commands in the Navy. In a few days,
he had a firm understanding of the complex issues that confront every President: national security, legislation, domestic policy, economics, and foreign policy. He moved rapidly
in changing the White House staff, and then focused on the
political appointment positions. In many cases, he asked for
resignations, in order to place his own people in key positions. Within a month, he was in full control of the government. Nothing escaped his memory or attention to detail.
Those who came to meetings late or unprepared often were
fired or transferred to backwater jobs, like the Forest Service
or the Post Office. The White House was now run like a military command center which, in reality, it should be.

During Hanlon's days as an admiral, one of his areas of
constant concern was the security of U.S. allies in Asia. At
the top of that list were South Korea, Japan, and of course,
Taiwan. The belligerence of North Korea's Communist
regime was a constant problem, threatening the democra-
cies of South Korea and Japan. Only China had the ability to
control that dictatorship.

To the south, Taiwan lived in constant fear of being
invaded by China ever since the anti-Communist Nationalists
fled there decades ago. China eyed the large island and its
23 million inhabitants with envy, and considered it part of
China's territory. As the nineteenth largest economy in the
world, Taiwan and its technological and industrial base con-
stituted a rich prize.

Even as China's cheap labor drew American industry
to its shores, it had steadily built up its military, including
its navy. A powerful navy would be required to take over
Taiwan, which was like a strong island fortress off the China

coast. When Hanlon had been the admiral in charge of the Pacific command, he viewed China as his major strategic concern. His fleets engaged in numerous "war games," simulating the defense of a Chinese attack on Taiwan, which he believed was probably only a matter of time.

After the stress and rigors of a day in the Oval Office, Hanlon always looked forward to dinner and an evening with May. Like a traditional Chinese woman, she catered to his every wish and desire, including some very imaginative sex. When they shared their quiet moments, she would talk to him about what he should do the next day, whom he should trust or distrust among the staff, and what she hoped he would do to fulfill his personal destiny. May was the rock under his spiritual foundation, his guiding light, and—as it would soon turn out—something much more.

The National Security Council briefed President Hanlon one morning, providing information that the Chinese fleet was massing in the vicinity of Shantou, across the Taiwan Strait from Taiwan. A large number of amphibious vessels were identified by satellite photos. President Hanlon ordered the *USS Nimitz* battle group to form up and steam toward Taiwan. Hanlon knew it could be merely China flexing its military muscle again, but he did not want to chance it, or appear weak as the new President.

Concurrent with this problem, North Korea began to fire long-range missiles, one of which traveled over Japan. The Japanese were understandably irate, and demanded that the U.S. do something to stop it.

Similarly, the South Koreans detected a massive troop and armor buildup by the North Koreans in the vicinity of the demilitarized zone, and only miles from their capital, Seoul. The President of South Korea asked Washington for additional ground and air forces. Hanlon began to see a pattern emerging. He suspected that the Chinese were using North Korea as a chess-piece, distracting the Asian allies from their true intentions.

The following morning, at the President's national security briefing, the CIA Director advised him that the North Koreans appeared ready to start an artillery barrage across the DMZ. "How do you want to respond, Mr. President?" asked the Chairman of the Joint Chiefs.

"If the North Koreans start shooting, or invade the South, initiate counter-battery fire immediately. Pulverize everything from the DMZ to five miles north. Take out any hard targets with air strikes, using 'smart' bombs. I am declaring the area between the 38th and 37th parallel a 'no fly' zone. We will notify them that any of their aircraft detected within that band, or south of it, will be destroyed, effective immediately."

"Yes, Sir!" The general liked this approach. It was appropriate, timely, and proportional to the aggression by the North Koreans. The general thought to himself, *This is a different guy than Sam Basi, who wanted to give the store away and capitulate to our enemies.*

Events were moving rapidly, and the National Military Command Center was fully staffed, as was the new Presidential Emergency Operations Center (PEOC), located six stories beneath the West Wing of the White House.

After leaving FBI headquarters for the last time, Tilsdale called his contact at the CIA. "Karen? Brad Tilsdale. Is your job offer still open? My partner and I just became free agents, as they say in the NFL."

Karen Littleton was a rising star among the U.S.

intelligence agencies. Now at the age of 33, she had graduated with top honors in political science from Princeton, followed by a Ph.D. from Columbia's School of International
and Public Affairs. She had served a tour in the CIA's
National Clandestine Service, during which her brilliant
intelligence work in Asia had exposed the breadth of the
Chinese military and naval expansion. One of the agents
under her supervision also discovered the existence of the
Chinese cyber-warfare center in western China. She was now
Director of the Office of Transnational Issues (OTI), which
assesses all perceived existing and emerging threats to U.S.
national security and provides the most senior policymak-
ers, military planners, and law enforcement with analysis,
warning, and crisis support. This functional area was a perfect fit for Tilsdale and Billings, and she was ecstatic to hear
they were available.

"Brad, when can you guys start? This could not be more
timely, because I am in the process of expanding this office.
Can you stop by today?"

"Karen, we will be there in an hour. Shall we ask for you
at the security desk?"

"Yes! I may send one of my guys down to get you, because
we are juggling a few nasty items at the moment."

"See you in a few minutes. Thanks, Karen."

Tilsdale drove across
the 14th Street bridge,
and then transitioned to
the George Washington
Parkway, heading north.
After a few miles, he spotted the big sign.

He took the next exit and drove across the overpass to the CIA main gate. An armed guard walked over. "I'm here to see Karen Littleton. I am Brad Tilsdale and this is Jeff Billings."

"Yes, Sir. She called a few minutes ago. Please place this placard on your dashboard, and drive ahead to the visitor reception center. They will handle your internal visitor passes."

"OK, thanks."

After Tilsdale parked in the visitor lot, they walked up to the visitor entrance and checked in the with the guard. Tilsdale observed that security was not as tight as it was at the NSA. As they checked in with the security desk, a female voice said, "Brad Tilsdale, I knew you could not stay away forever!"

"Well, things do change, Karen. How are you? This is Jeff Billings."

"First, I want to hear why you are suddenly a free agent. I figured I had better move quickly to snare you two, or someone like DIA, Blackwater, or Kroll would be bidding on you." Blackwater is a "private security contractor," previously known as mercenaries. Kroll, Inc. is one of the world's most prestigious private security and intelligence firms, and they both recruit heavily from government intelligence services.

"It's not a long story, but we'll give you all the details."

"Great. Follow me." Tilsdale noticed that she was obviously accustomed to running things, and very comfortable in giving orders. As they walked down the long hallway to her section, people passing by all spoke deferentially to her. *Obviously, she is a heavy hitter,* thought Tilsdale. He had tried to recruit her for the FBI out of Columbia, but she had wanted to operate in an international environment, and the Bureau was not able to provide that for a new agent. He could see that his appraisal of her potential had been well founded.

Littleton led the two through the maze of corridors up to an area marked "OFFICE OF TRANSNATIONAL ISSUES— GRADE 6 CLEARANCE REQUIRED FOR ENTRY." As they entered a large conference room, two men rose to greet them.

"Don Wechler, Counter-terrorism Section. Brad, Jeff, great to meet you. This is Walt Appleton, Special Ops Section." The men shook hands.

"Have a seat, everybody," Littleton said. As Tilsdale remembered, she was all business. "So what happened with you guys at the Bureau?"

"Essentially, they wanted some heads to roll because of the assassination at Riyadh. We were the only ones left. The other security people were either on Air Force One or had left as an advance party for Amman. The irony is, they would not share information with us or even let us near the President or Air Force One. I don't know why we were ordered to be there, because we were never plugged in," said Tilsdale.

"Yeah, that's what we heard also. We think it was an Al-Qaeda hit, but there are no good leads. No one in Riyadh is talking."

"Have you considered going through the airport staff, like the ground service and catering people? They are locals, I imagine," added Billings.

"Funny you would mention that," said Wechler. "The Saudis refuse to give us access to any of those people, or even their names. It looks like they are working hard to keep their own people from being fingered. They keep telling us that it was probably an aircraft malfunction, like TWA 800."

"Well, I personally found out that TWA 800 was brought down by a fucking Stinger," replied Billings.

"Affirmative," added Tilsdale. "When we tried to move the investigation in that direction, they shut us down. Sort of like when you guys tried to locate the second shooter in the JFK assassination."

"Right, Brad. I used to work for the guy that was in charge of that. He told me that someone up the chain-of-command, possibly even President Johnson, squelched our investigation and ordered us to stop—to accept that the Warren Commission had found that Oswald acted alone. The old cover-your-ass game," said Appleton.

"Well, we are sorry you got treated like that, Brad, but we need both of you. We are a little more cynical over here, and less respectful for people that are covering their butts. We are offering each of you a position two levels higher than what you left at the FBI. Interested?" asked Littleton.

The two looked at each other, somewhat surprised. "I think I can speak for both us," replied Tilsdale. "We both feel that there is a lot of unfinished work to do, and we want to stay in the game. Sign us up, Karen."

Littleton flashed a smile. "I guess I am not a very good negotiator, but we did not want you to leave here today without a CIA badge. We have many challenges ahead, and need your expertise immediately. We don't have time to waste."

"We'll give you all we've got, Karen," said Tilsdale.

"And *then* some," added Billings.

"OK, then it's a deal. Brad, we want to plug you in as Deputy Chief of Section, Counter-terrorism, working for Don. Jeff, I checked your background. You are the right man to be Walt's Deputy Chief of Section, Special Ops. You both

OK with that?"

"Fantastic!" said Tilsdale.

"Absolutely," echoed Billings.

"Great! I'll ask Don and Walt to show you your offices, and get you started. Gentlemen, let me warn you now. Without getting into detail at this point, let me tell you that our country is in a very dangerous place right now. It is our job to keep it safe, no matter what the cost to us as individuals. We know more about each of you than you think, and we are confident that you will do us proud. Well, I have a meeting with the Executive Committee. Good luck to both of you, and welcome aboard," said Littleton, getting up.

"Thanks, Karen. We appreciate your confidence. We won't let you down," said Tilsdale.

As Tilsdale and Billings got up to speed on their unit operations and personnel, events in the Pacific Rim were unfolding rapidly. The North Koreans began massing troops, armor, and artillery on their side of the Demilitarized Zone, threatening South Korea. Simultaneously, the CIA satellites detected a Chinese military and naval build-up in the vicinity of Shantou, China, posing a potential threat to Taiwan, another U.S. ally.

President Hanlon was notified at the next White House situation briefing. Upon hearing the news, he became concerned. "I spent years doing exercises and war games that presumed China would attack Taiwan. It looks like they want to test the resolve of the new President. Admiral Jacobs, I am directing you to put the Seventh Fleet on full alert, and to position three carrier battle groups in the vicinity of Taiwan. I want one of them to steam directly into the Taiwan Strait and operate there in international waters,

including flight ops. Understood?"

"Yes, Sir."

"General Dillard, put your Korean forces on full alert. That goes for the Air Force, too, General Underwood." The two nodded. "This may be only a 'fire drill,' but I want us to be ready for anything." The admirals and generals exchanged grins. This was a much different man than Sam Basi, who wanted to use soft diplomacy to solve every crisis. "We want America to 'lead from behind,'" was Basi's frequent, oxymoronic statement to his advisors.

Chapter 21

Queens and Pawns

When Hanlon was selected by Basi to be Vice President, he had been briefed by Sam Basi that a commitment had been made to Hillary Clinton to make her his Vice President for a second term. Now that the Vice President position needed to be filled, May Hanlon blocked her appointment, viewing her as a competitor to her husband in the next election. Instead, Hanlon shocked the Democrats by selecting Congressman Ron Paul, an eccentric Republican with radical political ideas, including the dismantling of the Defense Department. This, of course, was May's idea. "By picking a Republican, you will look like you are creating a bipartisan government, which is a popular notion. Ron Paul is harmless, and could not compete with you in the 2012 election, even if he wanted to, and the press will find his bizarre ideas amusing. He is—what is that American term? A wacko? He could not win a race for county dog-catcher." Hillary, however, now harbored great resentment at being snubbed by Hanlon. She resigned as Secretary of State, and was replaced in that position by Senator John Kerry, a liberal Democrat with eternal delusions of self-importance.

President Hanlon convened a national security meeting in his White House Situation Room. Present were the military chiefs, the CIA Director, the National Security Advisor, political advisor Jason Caswell, and the Secretaries of Defense and State. Good morning, Ladies and Gentlemen," Hanlon began. "I have come to some conclusions about the situation in Asia." The Joint Chiefs looked at each other, surprised.

"We do not have the military and naval resources to oppose the Chinese, or even the North Koreans. As you know, President Basi slashed our Armed Forces budgets in favor of his 'green energy' programs. You also know that I commanded the forces in the Pacific area when I was still in uniform, and I know what is required to oppose the Chinese. We no longer have it, Gentlemen. Plus, there are other considerations.

"The Koreans in both the North and the South have wanted reunification for years. They only disagree on the method of consolidation, and which regime will prevail. That is purely a political consideration, and they will eventually work that out, just as occurred in Germany and Vietnam.

"China is slightly different. They have a very legitimate claim to Taiwan, and it seems clear that their takeover is just a matter of time. By not actively opposing them, we can dramatically improve U.S.-Chinese relations. I believe it will happen in the way they assumed control of Hong Kong from the British. I certainly cannot take responsibility for losing American lives, attempting to stop the inevitable. And the lives of the Taiwanese must be considered as well. It is better for them to have a peaceful absorption into China, rather than a war that they—and we—can not win. As far as our country's business interests and trade with Taiwan, we can continue with those commercial relationships, just as we do now with China itself. Fighting a trans-Pacific war on China's doorstep, within easy range of her missiles and air strikes, not to mention her sizeable submarine fleet, would be madness.

"Therefore, I am directing the Secretary of State to proceed with a total diplomatic approach to solving this crisis, using the United Nations and every other avenue that makes sense. We are going to negotiate this thing, not start an armed conflict." Hanlon paused.

The Chairman of the Joint Chiefs spoke up. "Well Mr. President, have you considered the effect of this approach on our other allies across the world? Who will ever trust us again? As you know, we have iron-clad defense treaties with both Taiwan and South Korea. And what if either, or both of them, decide to fight to preserve their independence? How will we handle that?" The general stared at Hanlon.

"The Secretary of State will work with the Taiwan and South Korean governments to help them negotiate the consolidation of their territories. It will be made clear to them, that they must not start a war, because we will not support that, or assist them. Some of you may not like this, or agree with it. However, I am firm on my decision."

Jaws dropped around the room. The President of the United States was abandoning two of the strongest allies the nation ever had, and virtually capitulating to the aggressors. This was worse than Chamberlain's betrayal of Czechoslovakia to Hitler prior to World War II. Why was he doing this, especially considering his military background and knowledge? The answer involved May Hanlon.

A day earlier, May had gone shopping at the Mazza Gallerie on Wisconsin Avenue. A Neiman Marcus store was located there, and it was one of her favorites. Accompanied by the usual pair of Secret Service agents, she asked them to wait while she tried on a dress. She entered dressing room 3, latched the door, and then tapped three times on the adjoining wall, which separated the dressing room from an empty store room. Three taps responded, followed by two. A small door opened. It was General Ling Dao, the Resident Agent of the MSS, who used the cover of "Senior Cultural Attaché" to the Chinese embassy in Washington.

He whispered in Mandarin, "Chang Mei, it is time to wake the Golden Dragon. You must keep him from having his military or the U.S. allies interfere with our takeover of Taiwan."

"I understand. When should I do it?"

"Tonight would be good. Tomorrow, we have directed the North Koreans to launch attacks across the border and fire a few missiles at Japan. That should occupy the American military, which is spread very thin in the area. Within 48 hours after that, we will launch air and missile attacks on Taiwan, followed by the dropping of paratroop divisions into the southern area of Taiwan. Then, our amphibious fleet will strike at their central coast and drive the Nationalists back to Taipei. They will be forced to surrender, or they will be destroyed. This will all be done before the Western allies can react. None of them except for the United States has sufficient forces to mount any opposition. Britain's navy, for example, is a joke."

"How do you want me to program his response?"

"Use the action phrase to revert him to the hypnotic state that we established during that visit to Kowloon, years ago."

"And what should I direct him to do, or not do?"

"Once he is in the hypnotic trance, tell him to withdraw his forces and not to engage either the North Koreans or our forces near Taiwan. Direct him to use only diplomatic channels and the United Nations, which of course, will not accomplish anything. And then, tell him to recognize our claim for Taiwan as legitimate."

"But his Congress will go crazy. They might impeach him and remove him from office."

"Don't worry about that. We have studied that possibility, and even if they do that, it will be too late by the time they get it sorted out. Besides," the general laughed, "there are plenty of nicer places to live than the White House, my dear." Her extravagant tastes were well known among China's intelligence services.

"Alright, I will do as directed, but I must tell you that this seems very risky."

"That is not your concern, or your responsibility. Just make sure that you do your part, and we will take care of the rest."

"*Wǒ míngbáile*," [I understand.] she replied.

May returned to the two Secret Service agents, who were waiting in the store. "I don't like the color—besides, it makes me look fat," May complained. "Let's go back to the White House. My husband will be expecting me," she ordered. The two agents exchanged disgusted glances, and walked obediently behind her to the limousine.

That evening, the President and First Lady retired to the master bedroom on the second floor of the White House. While he was sitting in bed, writing notes on a yellow legal pad, May approached him. He looked up, smiling. She was always a beautiful sight to behold, and he treasured every minute with her, especially her exotic sexual techniques, which reportedly are known only to Chinese women.

"William, listen to me carefully. I need to tell you something important, Darling."

"Yes, what is it?"

She looked him in the eyes. "*Jīn lóng shì wǒ de péngyǒu.* The dragon is my friend." She repeated the phrase.

Hanlon's eyes became dazed, as he dropped the note pad on the floor. His brain was now ready to receive instructions. The work of the Ankang Institute had proven effective, once again. This time, however, the subject was under the secret control of the Chinese, instead of the Russians.

"William, you will order all U.S. forces to pull back from Taiwan, and not interfere in Chinese affairs. You will support China's hegemony over Taiwan. You will pull U.S. forces back from the Korean peninsula, and allow the North to reunify the two Koreas, with force if necessary. You will ask all sides to use the United Nations and diplomatic means to resolve the crisis. Under no circumstances will you allow the U.S. to use force against the People's Republic of China. Do you understand?"

"Yes," he said, in an empty voice.

"Very well. You will sleep now. When you wake up tomorrow, you will do as I have instructed you."

"Yes," Hanlon muttered, as he lay back in the bed, closing his eyes. The next day would be a day of enlightenment for the United States of America.

No American knew then that May Chang, now May Hanlon, was really Chang Mei, recruited as a university student in Beijing and trained by the Ministry of State Security, People's Republic of China. Posing as a political refugee, she was able to enter Taiwan. Because of the sloppy security in the Taiwan embassy, she had been able to pass the cursory screening and became planted in a high-security position, often working directly for the U.S. ambassador.

For their honeymoon, May had convinced Hanlon to spend several weeks in Hong Kong. She had received orders

from her MSS handler to take Hanlon to a particular restaurant in the Kowloon section, which is known for its popular support of the huge Communist neighbor to the west.
Hanlon's drink had been spiked with a powerful sedative, and
he disappeared for several days. Because he was on leave, neither the embassy nor the Navy were aware of his absence. He
reappeared, as if nothing had happened, and reported back
for work at the embassy. Only the Chinese MSS, the Ankang
Institute, and May knew what had really occurred.

The Chinese had termed this project "Golden Dragon."
Few officials at the Ministry of State Security thought it was
worth the trouble to kidnap and process a relatively low
level Naval officer. However, some felt that they needed to
protect Chinese interests by providing a secret option for
the Trojan Horse project with the Russians. The Russians
were never told when Hanlon was briefly kidnapped and
programmed in Hong Kong. "What those vodka-sipping
idiots don't know, won't hurt them," commented the head
of MSS. Nevertheless, none of the Chinese hierarchy ever
thought their "sleeper" agent would ever be near the top of
the U.S. government, let alone achieve the Presidency.

As MSS Director Xu Yongyue observed, "Fate moves
in mysterious ways, and gives you opportunities you never
imagined. The important thing is to use them intelligently."
When Hanlon rose rapidly within the U.S. Navy, and actually held the Pacific Command as a four-star admiral, the
Chinese were delighted. They never imagined that Hanlon's
rise would continue, and that their "sleeper" would soon
be able to directly influence world events in their favor.
However, they had failed to include Tilsdale and Billings in
their assumptions and plans. "Loose cannons" tend to roll
in all directions.

Chapter 22

Stalking the Prey

The Russians were furious. Not only had they lost their prize "sleeper," Sam Basi, but the Chinese had double-crossed them right on their border, instigating North Korea's invasion of the South. In addition, they had failed to give the Russians notice that they were going to invade Taiwan. A high-level conference was quickly arranged in Beijing, and Lebedev was sent to express the Russian government's outrage.

"Director Xu, how *dare* you take such dangerous and risky actions without discussing them with us ahead of time? This could have precipitated global nuclear war, and you owed us advance notice!" shouted Lebedev.

"I am sorry, and we do apologize," said Xu. "However, we had great security concerns, and we did not want any leaks. I'm sure you understand, Sergei."

"Well, exactly how do you expect to get away with this? The Americans will hit you, maybe with nuclear weapons!"

"No, actually, they won't. We will convene a multi-lateral conference with them, and keep this in the diplomatic mode. In the end, we will have Taiwan, and Korea will be unified under the Kim regime."

"You seem very sure of yourself. Do you have a 'mole'

within their government?" asked Lebedev.

"As a matter of fact, we do. Unfortunately, I am unable to tell you anything about him, other than he is in a position to help both of us. Shall we have an arrangement to share intelligence?"

"Yes, I suppose so. But you need to keep us informed from now on."

"No problem, Sergei. Now let's have some tea."

Once the Taiwanese government and military learned that the U.S. had abandoned them, they negotiated a turn-over procedure with the Chinese, and permitted Chinese troops to occupy the capital and all military installations. Taiwan was now another province of the People's Republic of China.

In Korea, things took a similar turn. The pragmatic South Koreans accepted North Korean occupation of their territory, rather than risk the destruction of their industrial infrastructure, and agreed to unify the peninsula under the North Korean flag. All U.S. forces were told to leave, or be annihilated. Under President Hanlon's "peace at all costs" policy, they did so without firing a shot.

Hanlon explained his actions to the American people in a televised broadcast. If one did not know how catastrophic this policy was, it almost seemed reasonable and the rational course to take. Americans had become increasingly tired of war, after Iraq and Afghanistan, and did not have the stomach for another foreign conflict. As a result, Hanlon's popularity actually increased slightly. Most Americans did not even know much about Taiwan or South Korea, and the two Asian nations were certainly not worth dying for.

Hanlon's attention turned next to domestic matters. He

continued with the implementation of the "Basi-care" law, and helped ram through a massive energy bill, in which the development and use of America's abundant native resources—coal and natural gas—were effectively shut down. Oil drilling permits were canceled or slowed down, causing widespread gasoline shortages and sky-rocketing prices. In response, Hanlon opened up the nation's Strategic Petroleum Reserve, which had been established only for a genuine national emergency. While this was a popular move, it virtually eliminated the military's energy reserves, causing the forced docking of ships, grounding of aircraft, and reduction in fuel stores for the Army's tanks and other vehicles.

Tilsdale and Billings watched these events with alarm. "What has *happened* to Bill Hanlon?" Billings asked Tilsdale. "I thought he was going to bring some reason into the Oval Office."

"I don't know, Jeff. It doesn't make sense." Tilsdale shook his head. "Hey, want to go for a drive? I got an e-mail from Melissa Clayton over at the NSA. She says they have something interesting that we should see."

"Sure, why not? I enjoy looking at her body as much as you do," grinned Billings.

"Asshole," replied Tilsdale. "Don't be making any moves on her, either! She's a friend of mine."

The two checked out an agency car and drove out of the main gate for the parkway, heading for the Beltway. As they drove through suburban Maryland, Tilsdale wondered what caused Melissa to contact him.

Arriving at NSA, the two parked in reserved parking, with the sign "CIA VISITOR ONLY."

"We've come up in the world—we now have reserved

parking," noted Tilsdale. "You still seeing that Pentagon secretary?"

"Yes, she has become a habit. I can't seem to get her out of my mind. I would marry her, but this job takes too much out of my life."

Tilsdale studied him. "Well, don't waste too much time, because you will wake up someday and wonder where your life went, and she will be gone. At some point, you have to start thinking about yourself, Jeff."

"Yes, I could wind up like *you!*" he said with a grin.

"Asshole," hissed Tilsdale.

After meeting Melissa Clayton, they walked to her unit's conference room. Tilsdale could not help but notice that she looked as good as ever. "Melissa, make an old man happy, and have dinner with me this week."

"Brad Tilsdale, are you hitting on me? Well, it took you long enough! Maybe I won't report you to your Human Resources Department for making excessively overdue advances!"

"Jesus! Shall I excuse myself, while you two consummate your relationship?" asked Billings with a smile.

"First things first, Melissa. Other than to see my handsome face, why did you drag us over here?" asked Tilsdale.

"Are you guys aware of our new voice recognition system?"

"Not really. Tell us about it."

"A few years ago, several of our scientists got project funding for a dedicated computer system that would take voice data intercepts, and build a database of what we call a 'voiceprint,' catalogued to a person's identity. Think of it like a DNA database, which the FBI has, only we use the salient characteristics of a person's voice."

"Makes sense, but that must be a huge amount of data."

"Yes, it is. For example, all three of us are in there, as are most people in Washington. We now are able to collect voice intercepts, and then ID the person with 98% accuracy, unless they are a brand new intercept."

"Whoa! You are listening to domestic intercepts? On U.S. citizens within the U.S.? How do you get around the FISA [Foreign Intelligence Surveillance Act] requirements, like warrants?" asked Billings.

"Don't be naive, Jeff. We just do the collections, and get a retroactive warrant if we decide to retain the intercept for law enforcement use. We clean them up legally when we need to. Otherwise, we just study and archive them."

"Cute. I'll bet Congress doesn't know about that," observed Tilsdale.

Clayton frowned. Like most NSA executives, she was not accustomed to being challenged, even by Congress. "Anyway, we got a very odd intercept a few months ago, and it got misrouted. I just received the case file yesterday. Even *we* make mistakes, you know."

"Hard to believe! So what is this case? Who is it?" Tilsdale eyed the folder in her hand.

"Let's do it this way. I'll play the intercept as raw data, and you tell me if you recognize the voices." She started a tape recorder.

The intercept happened to be the previous conversation between Cerberus and his Russian embassy contact, using code-words to arrange for the meeting at the Arlington SVR safe-house. "Shit! I *know* that voice," mumbled Tilsdale.

"I would hope so, Brad. Because one of those guys is the son-of-a-bitch that fired both of you—David Dallinger,

Deputy Director of the FBI!"

"You have confirmed that in your system?" asked
Billings.

"Yes, with this one, given the number of samples of his
voice, I'll give you 99.9% certainty. The big question is, what
are you going to do about it?"

"Well, he is obviously using code-words to set up something. Who is the other voice?" followed Tilsdale.

"Thought you might be curious about that! It's the SVR
Resident at the Russian embassy. His name is Debrov. We
have his voice locked down, also."

"Holy Christ! The DD is code-talking with the SVR—we
will need to give this some thought. Melissa, thanks! This is
a big one."

"Not as big as the black eye you'll get if you forget to take
me to dinner, Navy boy. You know my number!"

"You got it! I'll call you tonight," Tilsdale assured her.

As the two drove back to Langley, Tilsdale's head was
spinning, trying to comprehend what he had just learned.
This would require more than a little planning and finesse.
"What do you think, Jeff?"

"I think we have a tiger by the tail. We can't just wound
him—we need to bring him down. As Ralph Waldo Emerson
said, 'When you strike at a king, you must kill him.'
Figuratively speaking, of course."

"Rest assured," replied Tilsdale. "That bastard is toast!"

"I was just thinking," mused Billings. "The CIA is prohibited by law from engaging in domestic spying. However, if
Dallinger is actually an SVR double-agent, then we would be
spying on a representative of a foreign government, right?
Where that occurs should not be a factor."

"Nice try, Jeff. In this situation, given this guy's security clearance, I don't give a shit where we do surveillance on him or detain him. And we are not going to share this with our CIA colleagues, because we can't be sure how they would react. I know a guy in the CIA Clandestine Service—one of their senior NOCs [non-official cover agents, or 'illegals']. His name is Tim Wakefield, and he takes no prisoners. We need to cover ourselves, so we'll plug him in. He can get us wiretaps and surveillance on Dallinger, also, without approval from the higher-ups."

Billings shook his head. "Perfect. Hey, I hear Leavenworth Prison has some nice rooms and amenities now. Why should we worry?"

Upon arriving back at Langley, the two walked over to the National Clandestine Service (NCS) wing. Security was noticeably tighter, and Wakefield was called to get them through the entrance. In minutes, a large man appeared, dressed in a black turtleneck sweater and camouflage trousers. He smelled of cigarette smoke. "Brad! God almighty, I heard you had signed on with Karen Littleton's division, and I was pissed. Why didn't you and Jeff apply for NCS? You guys would be perfect here! Plus, no one fucks with you over here. I think they're afraid of us," he noted with a guttural laugh.

Tilsdale laughed. "If they're not, they should be! I can't believe you are still alive, considering some of the stunts you used to pull in Asia."

"Yeah, those were good times. What about the stuff you did, working like the Lone Ranger? Jeff, I could spend hours telling you how crazy this guy was, but he was a friggin' SEAL back then—it goes with the territory."

Tilsdale turned serious. "Tim, we need to talk. We are involved in a major gig and we need your help."

"OK, so this wasn't a social call after all, huh? Follow me, Sailor." He led them to a nearby conference room.

"Tim, we think we have a mole at the Bureau. We need to conduct some back-channel surveillance and wiretaps on the subject."

"*Another* mole? Jesus, Brad, wasn't the Hanssen case enough for you guys? You personally made the arrest, right?"

"Yes, Jeff and I. But this one may make Hanssen look like a trivial matter."

Wakefield stared at him. "Really? Why didn't you take this to someone at the Bureau?"

"The guy is too high up. Plus, he probably has already figured out an exit strategy, in case someone discovers him. We don't want any tip-offs or leaks to screw this up. We haven't even told our bosses."

"So how did you guys stumble onto this?"

"We have an unofficial, but high-level contact at NSA."

"Yes, it's really amazing what a dinner and sex will get you these days," added Billings, which drew an angry look from Tilsdale.

"Ha! I see our Navy boy hasn't changed much! Hey, whatever it takes, right? It's a dirty job, but someone has to do it!" replied Wakefield, laughing. Suddenly looking serious, he added, "Brad, just tell me what you need. That's the beauty of working for NCS—I can get you anything you want, even a hooker!"

"I don't need that at the moment, Tim, but we will give you a list. Let's keep this case off the books until we get the evidence, OK?"

"Brad, I don't think you understand. *Everything* down here is 'off the books,' pal!"

Chapter 23

Setting the Trap

Wakefield's surveillance team established separate wire-taps on Dallinger's office and home telephones. Because "throw-away" cell phones are often used by spies, the NCS team planted cell phone signal receivers at his office and home locations. Any cell signal with Dallinger's voiceprint would initiate recording for subsequent analysis.

The team also rented a townhome across the street from Dallinger's house, and moved in one of their agents, his wife, young daughter, and dog. While adults will always attract an intelligence agent's scrutiny, the presence of children and pets tends to look normal and blends in with the scenery. From the second floor, the husband and wife team set up a video camera and began recording Dallinger's coming and going.

His car was the next target. A GPS device was planted under the front fender, and a "bug" was placed behind the dashboard. Dallinger was now a hunted animal, and there would be no escape.

Having rid himself of Tilsdale, and because of his high Bureau position, Dallinger had succumbed to the double-agent's most deadly enemy—complacency. He began to meet with his SVR handlers at the Arlington safe-house

more frequently. Even though he used the proper techniques to elude any "tails," he never took the time to sanitize
his phone calls and do a "bug sweep" of his car and home.

The NCS team correctly guessed that he had hidden a
TV camera system throughout his home. For that reason,
they did not bother to penetrate it, choosing instead to plant
their bugs externally, through the telephone switching system. Every day, when Dallinger returned home, he immediately checked his video recorder to see if any intruders had
been detected. Nothing aroused his suspicion.

Tilsdale and the NCS team decided to arrest Dallinger
only when they had him in the most compromising situation, for which there could be no valid excuses. They were
aware that even if they caught him meeting with an SVR
agent, he could potentially explain that away, claiming that
it was his job as the former ADCI to catch SVR spies, and
to do that, he had to pretend to be a double-agent. Tilsdale
needed the "smoking gun" evidence, something that would
be so obvious that Dallinger could not defend it. He was
about to get his wish.

"Brad, go to scrambler," said Melissa Clayton.

"We're on. Go," replied Tilsdale.

"His SVR code-name is 'Cerberus.' Does that mean anything to you?"

"Yes, I remember that from some of the early intercepts.
We never figured out who that was, so we assumed it was
one of SVR's field agents."

"We have just completed what we call a 'retro' analysis.
Here's how it works. We take key words from recent intercepts, and run them back through our computers. We can
actually search all the way back to the Sixties, when our
computers were upgraded."

"Wow! That must be a pile of data to go through," observed Tilsdale.

"Yes, but a Cray super-computer can do a word-search like that in about one minute. Anyway, here is what we found—the code-name 'Cerberus' has occurred numerous times in connection with the following: Pegasus, Trojan Horse, Emerald, Stiletto, Zeus, Medusa, and Socrates. Any of those mean anything to you?"

Tilsdale nearly ran off the road, and pulled over. "Melissa, you better lock this down tight. This involved President Sam Basi, who we once thought was identified by the KGB and SVR as 'Pegasus.'"

"Jesus, Brad! What does this mean?"

"Let me give you my wild speculation, which needs careful analysis before we let it loose. It may mean that Basi was some sort of sleeper agent for the SVR, and that Professor Lydia Boroshta was murdered to protect the plot."

"What do you want me to do with this stuff?"

"Lock it down for now. I'll get back to you, OK?"

"Will do. And watch your back, Brad. This thing is so big, it could drag down anyone that touches it, if it goes badly. This is really radioactive."

"No sweat. If I'm not in extreme danger, I wouldn't know how to conduct myself. Besides, it wouldn't be any fun. Nothing like a little adrenaline rush—like when I see you with your clothes off."

"Brad, don't screw around. Please be careful!" Her voice betrayed her emotions.

"Not to worry, girl-san. This is what I do for living, remember? I'll talk to you soon. Take care."

Tilsdale mulled over this latest bombshell information. He now had the corroborating evidence that would take down Dallinger. The problem was that the evidence was so outrageous and unbelievable, it might not be taken seriously. He decided that he needed more, and he knew how to get it.

Arriving back at Langley, he dialed the cell phone number for Billings. "Jeff Billings."

"Jeff, let's go for a drive."

Billings knew what that meant. "Roger that. See you at the main elevators."

Driving out of the CIA main gate, Billings turned to Tilsdale. "OK, what's going on?"

Tilsdale summarized the latest information, and Billings was shocked. "I knew it!" he exclaimed. "There was always something odd about that entire Pegasus case, and we should have stayed on it."

"We would have, except for the Robert Hanssen case. Think about how clever this was. They offered up a real double-agent, who had done enormous damage. We automatically assumed that Hanssen was the only source of the tips going to the KGB, and then the SVR. It was a perfect cover for protecting their real ace, Dallinger—code-name 'Cerberus.'"

"You're right. They out-thought us on that one. Remember what you used to tell me? Never rely upon unproven assumptions. Take the case where it flows."

Tilsdale pounded the steering wheel in anger. "Yeah, I know, dammit. The one time I violate that rule, out of pure joy and euphoria in catching Hanssen, we get check-mated by Dallinger and the SVR. Well, it's *his* turn now, and I think I've designed a neat little trap for him."

"OK, let's have it."

"We need to do something that will panic the resident

SVR agent at the Russian embassy—something that will make him contact Dallinger and meet with him. Any ideas?"

Billings thought for a moment. "How about this scenario? Who do the Russians view as natural enemies, almost as much as us?"

"The Chinese, of course."

"Right! Now the First Lady is of Chinese descent, right?"

"Right. Now wait a minute . . ."

"Think about it, Brad. We drop some bogus information on one of their SVR field agents that May Hanlon is being run by the MSS! It might seem ridiculous and incredible to us, but you know how the Russians think! They see a conspiracy under every rock. If they received information like that, I think their first reaction would be to try to verify it before transmitting it to Moscow. And how would they do that? They would use one of their double-agents inside of our government. Who could be in a better position to do some fact-checking for them than David Dallinger, a/k/a 'Cerberus?'"

Tilsdale was thinking through this plan. "Keep going."

"I'll bet you that they would contact Dallinger and arrange a face-to-face meeting somewhere. Undoubtedly, there will be documents exchanged on something like this. We could video the meeting, the exchange, and the conversation, using high-capacity microphones."

"You are assuming that they will meet in the open, like in Rock Creek Park. What if they meet in some secret location, like a safe-house?"

"We have a tracking device on Dallinger's car. Let's see where he goes. I would rather not use a traditional 'tail' on him, because he would probably detect it."

"What kind of information should we use to set the trap?"

"How about checking with DIA [Defense Intelligence Agency] and seeing whether they are working any counter-intel on SVR agents. Those guys are always trying to penetrate the DIA's satellite division. Know anyone over there?"

"Matter of fact, I played football at West Point with the colonel who runs their security unit. We just played tennis a couple of weeks ago. He's a good guy. We can trust him."

"Good. Let's work up some info to bait the trap."

Back at Langley's Clandestine Service unit, the team fabricated a Top Secret internal memo and related documents, suggesting that the Chinese MSS had penetrated the White House with a covert agent, and had obtained U.S. war plans for Asia. The memo discussed the sensitivity of the information, highlighting that the First Lady was of Chinese descent, and could be involved. It also mentioned that she had been observed in a White House reception, talking in Mandarin with the Chinese ambassador.

"That should do it," observed Tilsdale. "Now, is the SVR tailing one of our DIA guys?"

"Yes, we have verified that an SVR agent has been tailing one of the junior officers."

"Good. We will have him drag a briefcase around for a day, making it very visible. What is his usual pattern after leaving work?"

"This lieutenant is a jogger. He has a locker at the Army-Navy Country Club, where he changes clothes and runs around the golf course."

"OK, that will work. Have him leave the briefcase on the seat in his car. I'm sure our SVR guy will be able to get into the vehicle and shoot a photo of the documents. Let's watch from a distance, to make sure he gets it."

As planned, the young officer left his car with the briefcase exposed on the seat. The two SVR agents, dressed like auto mechanics, drove up in a pickup truck and pretended to work on the tires. When they were sure no one was looking, they slid a burglar tool into the passenger door, and grabbed the briefcase. After photographing the documents, they returned the briefcase, locked the officer's car, and left.

"Bingo!" said Billings.

The NCS surveillance team added more people, including an armed assault team. They were not sure how Dallinger and the SVR would meet, and they needed to be ready for anything.

Back at Langley, team members listened on their various bugs, and watched their surveillance cameras. Suddenly, one agent raised his hand to get his supervisor's attention, and clamped his earphones to his ears.

The conversation on the phone began. "Mr. Dallinger? This is the Capitol Menswear store. Your slacks are ready for pickup, any time after 2 p.m."

"Oh, thank you. I will see you then," answered Dallinger, hanging up.

The NSC team supervisor immediately called Tilsdale. "Brad, the ball is in play."

"Roger that. Start feeding me tracking data. We will try to intercept him at the meeting point, rather than tailing him. If you can determine where he is headed, give me your best estimate."

"Will do. Right now, he is headed for the 14th Street bridge and Arlington."

"Thanks, Barry. Keep the data coming, especially if you see him turn." Tilsdale started the engine of the plumber's truck, hoping to get close enough without being "made" by Dallinger.

Tilsdale had decided not to include the FBI at this point, knowing that Dallinger might be tipped off. He also knew that the FBI was overly concerned about making arrests "by the book," mandated by the lawyers at the Department of Justice, and he could not afford to give a spy as dangerous as Dallinger that latitude. He needed to make a "detention" that was off the record, for now, and Wakefield and his NCS team were ideally suited for this situation.

"All units, this is Kilo One. Proceed to Arlington area. Will further advise when suspect's destination is known." At that command, fifteen vehicles of various types started rolling from the restricted back parking lot at Langley toward the parkway and Arlington. Each vehicle contained members of the NCS assault team, carrying the versatile Colt M-4 tactical carbines, Sig Sauer .45 Tactical Ops model pistols, and Gil Hibbens Tactical Bowie Knives.

Dallinger drove across the bridge into Arlington, taking Exit 8A off of I-395, and transitioning to Washington Blvd. He then turned left on 10th St., following by another left on North Irving. "He's headed for Ashton Heights, Brad," radioed the supervisor.

Looking quickly at the map on his GPS, Tilsdale radioed his team. "All units, perimeter is now North Glebe Road, Arlington Road, and Washington Boulevard. Take up positions in that vicinity until further advised."

Dallinger drove up to 714 N. Irving Street, and got out of his car. He quickly looked around, and felt sure it was safe. He walked around to the rear entrance and knocked on the door. A sinister-looking man in a rumpled suit opened the door. "Cerberus, come in."

The NCS supervisor saw that the car had stopped. "Kilo One, your target is stationary at 714 North Irving Street."

"Roger, Control. All units, this is Kilo One. Saturate the area around that address, but stay off of North Irving. Kilo One will park a few houses down."

As Tilsdale parked the truck, he and Billings could see Dallinger's car, but he could not be sure which house he had gone into. The only option was to wait for him to come out.

After thirty minutes, Dallinger emerged from the house. "All units, Kilo One. Assault team, this is a go! Take Dallinger into custody, and take the house at 714. Hot breach! I say again, hot breach is authorized." This meant that the team was authorized to enter and use deadly force to subdue and capture any people within the house.

Agents swarmed out of the adjacent trees and neighboring structures, knocking Dallinger to the ground and handcuffing him. The others shouted, "Federal agents! Open up!" followed by their smashing the door down. The Russians knew better than to use their weapons, and meekly surrendered. Dallinger was hauled over to Tilsdale's vehicle and thrown inside.

"Greetings, David. We meet again," smiled Tilsdale.

Blood streamed down Dallinger's face. "You will regret this, Tilsdale. You have just destroyed three years worth of counter-intelligence work with this stunt, and prevented me from arresting a number of SVR agents. You will be in jail, as soon as I make a phone call, my friend." *Tilsdale had been correct*, thought Billings. *This guy had his cover story ready, in the event that he was caught.*

"Jail? Forget that, David. That's what FBI agents and U.S. Attorneys do. At the CIA, we do something more interesting, called 'rendition.' Ever hear of it? Within two hours, you will be taking off from Dulles in a private jet, bound for some exotic location where the U.S. Constitution does not reach. There, you will be interrogated until you give us everything you know. We have as long as it takes, and you will not be handed over to the FBI until we have it all. If you fuck around and lie to us, it will be *very* unpleasant for you. We will check every fact and every number. You might as well give it up, and avoid the pain."

"You wouldn't do that! You and Billings were trained by the FBI to respect people's rights!"

This brought a laugh from Tilsdale. "You bastard! First of all, *you* are a *traitor*. Second, you probably caused several murders and the loss of valuable American agents overseas. Third, you trashed my career, and also Jeff's. Now you are going to pay. If you give it all up, we will check the data, and then if it is accurate, we will give you to the FBI. Otherwise, we will have our Israeli friends in Tel Aviv at the Mossad headquarters work you over. Believe me, those Jews are not squeamish about interrogations. They will dissect you like a frog, piece by piece. Water-boarding is the *nicest* thing they do. The choice is yours, asshole. There is no way out of this for you. The game is over."

Billings chimed in. "Your Russian friends over there will use diplomatic immunity and simply be kicked out of the country, back to Moscow. But you, we are keeping. David, I have personally seen what the Mossad does to prisoners, when I was with Delta Force. If I were you, I would give it up and avoid what will happen to you. You *will* talk, it's just a matter of how much pain you will absorb before that. Do yourself a favor."

One of the assault team members approached Tilsdale. "Sir, we have searched the house, and found these documents. We put them in evidence bags, because we think this guy was probably handling them. The fingerprints should be good." Tilsdale looked over the documents and shook his head.

"You and those goddam Russians are stupid. You actually were running down a rabbit trail that we created for you. Did you *really* think the First Lady was being run by the Chinese? How stupid could you be?" Tilsdale laughed aloud.

"Maybe not as stupid as you think," said Dallinger ominously.

"We just want everything you know about Pegasus, a/k/a Sam Basi. Let's start with that."

"I have nothing more to say," said Dallinger.

"Suit yourself. Personally, Jeff and I would rather see you go through a little pain. I almost would hate to see you talk and avoid that. I hope you are fluent in Hebrew. My friends, Jacob and Ari, will be waiting for you when you get to Tel Aviv. Have a nice trip."

The van headed for Dulles and the private aviation ramp. An unmarked Grumman Gulfstream jet sat ready, with several CIA agents. As Tilsdale drove over to the aircraft, he said, "Last chance, David. Fish-or-cut-bait time, pal."

"Alright, I'll talk. I want to cut a deal."

"You will give us everything? If you hold anything back, or try some of that Russian 'disinformation' routine, you will be on this aircraft within the hour. Is that clear?"

"Yes, that's clear. Let's get this over with."

Tilsdale got on his cell phone and dialed a number. "This is Tilsdale. We are going with option 'B', at least for now. The subject indicates that he will cooperate. We are heading for the CIA safe-house in Reston. Meet us there with the necessary recording equipment and staff."

Chapter 24

Show and Tell Time

The caravan of CIA personnel, with Dallinger in custody, pulled up to the safe-house on Coat Ridge Road. The house sat on several acres of wooded land, away from the prying eyes of curious neighbors. A number of Soviet and Chinese defectors had been "de-briefed" there, with good results.

"David, let's go over the rules. If you resist any of the security people, you will be shot without further warning. If you attempt to escape, you will be shot. If you try to contact anyone, you will be shot. If you do not cooperate fully with your de-briefing team, which includes me, you will immediately be put on an airplane and flown to Israel, where the Mossad will take over for us. They can do things over there that would get us in trouble, if we did them. Any questions?"

"No. But I would like some water."

Tilsdale motioned to one of the agents, who gave Dallinger a water bottle. "The agents will take you to your room, where you will take your clothes off, and put on the orange jump suit that is on the bed. You can use the bathroom, but you will leave the door open at all times, and an agent will be watching you, as will the cameras. When you sleep, you will be cuffed, and agents will be monitoring you with the cameras. Now, let's get started. When did you become a Russian agent?"

"When I was in college at Princeton. They approached me, and took me to meet one of their senior operatives in Austria."

"Who was that?"

"Victor Zebrotny."

"The billionaire philanthropist? The guy that contributes to Progressive causes?" Tilsdale was surprised.

"Yes. His code-name is Zeus, if that means anything."

Tilsdale and Billings exchanged startled looks. "So walk us through your history with them. Did they have something to do with you going to Harvard Law School?"

"Yes, I think Zebrotny enabled that, but I probably would have been admitted anyway. I had very high grades, you know."

Tilsdale shook his head. Even in this predicament, Dallinger still showed his arrogance and feelings of superiority. "How did you get a job with the Bureau?"

"I think Zebrotny and the KGB had some government people under their thumb. They pushed their contacts to get me hired. One of them was Robert Hanssen, the KGB double-agent."

"Did you ever talk to Hanssen or meet with him?"

"No. The KGB went out of their way to keep us separated. I was told that they wanted to keep me in reserve, and have me work my way up in the Bureau's management." He grinned, "I guess they could not believe it when I was selected to be the Assistant Director for Counter-Intelligence. It could not have been better."

"How many times did you meet with the Russians, face-to-face?"

"Not many. Maybe once or twice a year, and always at

their safe-house in Arlington. They didn't want me to do that, for fear that I would blow my cover."

Tilsdale was both angered and amazed at Dallinger's nonchalant manner. "Tell us about Pegasus. Who was he, and what was the plan?"

"That was Sam Basi. Apparently, he was recruited at a young age, like I was. The KGB and the MSS took him to the Cayman Islands, and subjected him to personality modification, or as you might call it, 'brain-washing.' I guess they made a real Socialist out of him, and they programmed him with what they call a behavior control phrase. Anytime they wanted, if they wanted something specific to be done, they could say that phrase, and he would be in the 'receptor' mode, like a robot taking instructions."

"What exactly was the plan for him to execute?"

"They were going to use him to push the United States into political and economic chaos. The Russians and Chinese had already set it up. Basi, as President, was going to finish you off." Dallinger smiled. "It probably would have worked, if some rag-head in Saudi Arabia had not blown up Air Force One."

The "rag-head" referred to by Dallinger, Saudi Air Force Sgt. Jamal Al-Amri, had suddenly become a rich man. He now had a bank account in Dubai, with a balance of ten million U.S. dollars. After the bomb brought down Air Force One, a shell corporation in Switzerland deposited the money in Al-Amri's account. The transfer was reported to the Saudi government, who traced the ownership to Al-Amri. The Saudi intelligence service was shocked to find that it belonged to a lowly air force enlisted man. Checking further, they determined that the funds originated with the

Swiss company, Yang-Tze Finance, a subsidiary of the Bank of China.

The order went out to Saudi police to arrest Al-Amri on suspicion of money-laundering, and bring him in for intensive questioning. The police waited until he was alone on the airport ramp, and then swept in with guns drawn. The arrest team then took him to Al-Ha'ir maximum security prison, south of Riyadh. The interrogation began.

"Where did you get those millions of dollars, Jamal? Are you smuggling drugs?" asked the lead interrogator.

"I have been saving my money, and I inherited a lot from my grandfather."

"Liar! We have already reviewed your family history. Both of your grandfathers are still living! And you could not have accumulated this much on a sergeant's pay."

"I have nothing more to say," said Al-Amri.

"Fine. We have something to help you find your voice."

Two policemen dragged Al-Amri to a chair, and after stripping him, shackled him to a chair. One of the interrogators then attached a wire with an alligator-clip to each of his testicles. The wires led to an electrical panel with several dials. "If you don't start giving us answers, we are going to turn your penis into a volt meter." Al-Amri shook his head.

"Very well. Apparently you enjoy pain." The head interrogator nodded at the man by the panel. A switch was thrown and a primal, animal scream came from Al-Amri's throat, as his body arched uncontrollably from the electrical current attacking his body. The current was switched off, and he slumped back in his chair.

"Ah, too bad. We forgot to give you something to bite on. You have broken some teeth while clenching your jaws, my friend. Let's try something different. Mamoud, tell the dentist to come down here, with his instruments."

In a few minutes, a man with a malevolent smile appeared, wearing a white lab coat. "Good morning, Doctor," said the head interrogator. "We have a man here who needs a root canal."

"Not a problem," said the dentist, unpacking his instrument bag. "Open wide, Jamal."

"No! Don't... "

The two muscular policemen grabbed his head and forced his jaws open, installing what is known as a Whitehead gag, used by dentists to keep a patient's mouth open. The dentist brought out a portable drill. "My, my—you have not been flossing, my friend. I'm very sorry, but I forgot the anesthesia. You will need to be strong, Jamal." He switched on the drill, and the room was filled with a piercing, high-pitched whine.

As the drill bit penetrated Al-Amri's tooth, he began to scream with the excruciating pain. The coronal area of a healthy tooth is packed with nerve endings, and the drill bit was viciously tearing through them. Al-Amri's mouth began to fill with blood, gagging him. "May Allah forgive me, I also forgot my suction device. Jamal, I guess you will have to swallow the blood. Otherwise, you will choke and suffocate."

Al-Amri began to pass out. His nervous system was reaching its limit. The first interrogator instructed the dentist to stop. "Jamal, are you ready to talk? Why do you make us do these things to you? Just tell us what you were doing with all of this money! Even if you were smuggling, the punishment is not that bad, and not worth the pain you are feeling."

Al-Amri shook his head.

"So? You want to be stubborn, eh? I think we should clean up your bloody face." He motioned to his assistants.

Two policeman unshackled him, carried him to a see-saw board arrangement, and strapped him to the board. At the end, near his head, was a tub of water. They then placed a towel over his face, and began to pour water in a continuous stream, while they lowered his head half-way into the tub water. Within seconds, he started gagging and gasping for breath.

"Have you found your voice yet?" asked the interrogator. "No? You want to swim a little more, eh?" The water flowed again over his face, creating the sensation of drowning.

"I'll talk! Please, no more of this!" screamed Al-Amri.

"Alright, my friend. Where did the money come from?"

"A Chinese guy from their embassy."

The interrogators looked at each other in surprise. "Why did he give it to you? What did you do to earn it?"

"He wanted me to plant a bomb in the wing on Air Force One, when I was fueling it."

The interrogators were visibly shocked. This meant that a foreign government caused the death of the U.S. President and hundreds of others. The Americans would want revenge for this, if it were true.

Further interrogation revealed that Al-Amri had acted alone. The Saudis now decided to inform the Americans. At first, Saudi officials assumed that when those who planted the bomb on Air Force One were finally identified, there would be a link to Islamic extremists or Al-Qaeda. They had been refusing to cooperate with U.S. intelligence or law enforcement because of what they thought would be an embarrassing linkage to the Islamic religion, a major political force within Saudi Arabia. Now, there was no further reason to stonewall their inquiries.

The Saudi colonel in charge of anti-terrorist security

DICK NELSON

dialed the number of the CIA Resident at the U.S. embassy. "Good morning, Al. I have some information for you. Can you come over here for tea?"

Al Brenner was an old CIA hand, and an expert on the Middle East. He spoke fluent Arabic, and among the Saudi government officials, he was popular and invited to all important social events in Riyadh. In the parlance of the Agency, he was "connected."

"Why, certainly, Basim. I will see you in an hour."

When Brenner was ushered into the section chief's office, he noticed that an unusually large group of senior police officials was in attendance. "Well," he said in Arabic, "the tea must be especially good today!"

"God willing," said the colonel. "Please be seated, Al. Two sugars for you, as usual?"

"Yes, thank you. So what is this mysterious information?"

"We have found the man that planted the bomb on Air Force One. Sadly, he is a member of our air force."

The CIA man, who normally hid his emotions well, almost fell out of his chair. "Really? What is his name?

"Jamal Al-Amri. We are holding him in isolation at Al-Ha'ir prison, and continuing to interrogate him, but I think we already have the most important information."

"And what is that?" asked Brenner.

"He was paid by the Chinese to blow up Air Force One."

The room fell silent. The Saudis watched for Brenner's reaction. Such a grievous action by one super-power against another would have unpredictable consequences. However, Brenner regained his "poker-face."

"What did he use?"

"It was C-4 explosive, with a standard barometric detonator, set for 10,000 feet. He placed it in the fueling compartment, inside the wing panel when he was fueling the aircraft. Obviously, that would sever the wing and bring the plane down."

"Bastards," Brenner hissed, showing a rare display of emotion. "Given the gravity of this information, you will have to excuse me, Basim. I need to call Washington."

"Yes, of course. We totally understand. We wish you well, Al."

Within the hour, Brenner was back in his office at the embassy, calling Langley on a scrambled line. After he relayed the information to the CIA Executive Committee, all eyes turned to the Director. "Al, we don't want to overreact or let the media get a hold of this. It makes a good story, but we have no way to corroborate what the Saudis are telling us." The Director turned to Karen Littleton. "Karen, who in your group is capable of dealing with this and getting the true facts?"

Littleton did not hesitate. "Brad Tilsdale and Jeff Billings. Right now, they are in the middle of an extremely sensitive interrogation at one of our safe-houses, working on an SVR double-agent. I hate to take them off of that."

"I agree. Al, can you get the Saudis to give us this guy, and allow us to fly him back here for interrogation by Tilsdale and Billings?"

"I think so, Sir. I think they would be delighted to get this guy off of Saudi soil, so that they are not caught between the U.S. and China."

"OK, then that's what we do. Al, make it happen. Karen, tell your boys what's coming."

Back at the Reston safe-house, Dallinger's interrogation continued. Tilsdale and Billings were amazed at the extent of Dallinger's betrayal of the Bureau and the government.

During a break, Tilsdale commented, "This guy has done more damage than either Robert Hanssen or John Walker combined. How does a guy get sucked into something like that?"

Billings thought for a moment. "I think they just become seduced by the foreign government's expert handlers. Just like with us, those guys are the best at figuring out the target's weaknesses, and then exploiting them. It also takes a lot of luck to develop spies like Dallinger, Hanssen, and the Walker family. The Russians just had the right bait for the right fish, in each case. And as we learned, it is not always about money. Hanssen, for example, wanted to teach the FBI a lesson—that he was a better agent than they gave him credit for. For the Walkers, it was largely about money, and it was a sort of game. Dallinger? He's hard to categorize."

"Let's get back in there. I want to pursue this mind-altering thing that Dallinger described briefly yesterday."

The two entered the room, as Dallinger looked up. *The bastard still looks like he thinks he's in charge,* Tilsdale thought to himself. "David, let's talk some more about how the Russians do this brain-washing."

"Well, they have been working on that since World War Two. You may remember that they and the Chinese used it on some of our POWs during the Korean War. By the time they got to Sam Basi, they had quite a program, as I understand it. I think it was run out of the Pochevsky Institute, with KGB oversight. You may know that even our own CIA experimented with this process. I think it was called 'MK-ULTRA.'"

"Do you know how it was done?" asked Billings.

"Generally, yes. They typically put the subject into a

drug-induced trance, then bombard him with high-speed images that have been programmed into a computer. After a couple of weeks of this, you apparently can re-shape the subject's personality and belief systems, if you know what you are doing. The Chinese have a similar program, but it focuses on programming an automatic behavioral response into the subject, which is only activated with a special phrase that triggers the desired behavior. They run that out of the Ankang Institute, with MSS oversight."

"And you believe that they made Basi into a Socialist?"

"My understanding from Professor Boroshta, before she died, was that he was always Left-leaning, but came back from this programming as a dedicated Socialist. The plan was to execute a coordinated series of events, which would topple the American economy. Basi, as President, would be in a position to make that happen." Dallinger sipped his coffee, smiling. "They came so very close, but they have only wounded the United States. It might recover, if the White House and Congress ever get their act together."

Tilsdale stared coldly at him. "What do you know about the downing of Air Force One? Did the Russians do it?"

"Oh, no. Losing Basi was the last thing that they wanted to happen. I guess it was Al-Qaeda or some other Islamic group."

Another agent entered the room and handed Tilsdale a report that had just come in by e-mail from Langley. It was titled, "ULTRA TOP SECRET: Assassin Interrogation." Tilsdale said, "Take a break, David. Think of some more material for us. Every little bit gets you in a better position, so it's your ass, my friend. We'll be back in an hour. Have lunch—on us."

Tilsdale and Billings went into another room and began

reading the report. Tilsdale could not hide his surprise. "Holy shit!! Now the *Chinese* are involved with Air Force One?"

Always the skeptic, Billings commented, "Brad, this could be a diversionary tactic by the Saudis to throw us off the track of one of their nationals. I don't trust those scum-bags."

"I know. However, Al Brenner, one of our most experienced agents over there, believes it is legitimate. And apparently so does the Director and the Executive Committee. At a minimum, we need to play it like the story is true until we get some evidence to the contrary."

Billings looked out of the window at the serene Virginia countryside. "You know, Brad, in this complicated plot surrounding Pegasus, the Chinese have been conspicuously absent. According to Dallinger, the Russians—especially Putin—decided to shut them out of the final planning. As far as we know, they never even protested, which is very unlike them."

"You're suggesting that they were running a sub-plot of some kind? Without the Russians' knowledge?"

"Exactly. That is *so* Chinese. Why would they run the risk of taking out a President? That could cause a nuclear war, in which *they* would be eliminated. They would only do so if the risk-reward ratio was very favorable. Since the risk would obviously be very high for them, that means that the reward of their plot's results would have to be monumental. What would that be?"

The two thought in silence. "Oh, Christ," blurted Billings. "Remember President Hanlon's bizarre behavior in the last few days? He has the Joint Chiefs in an uproar. They feel that he is damaging our national defense more than Sam

Basi ever did. Giving up Taiwan and South Korea was a disaster. You don't think... ?"

"Come on, Jeff. Bill Hanlon was a four-star admiral and had several top commands, and served with distinction as the ambassador to China. He apparently did a great job, and some of his duties involved controlling Chinese expansion. There is no way he could be a sleeper, like Basi." Tilsdale tried to convince himself, but he was already seeing the point of Billings' concern. "Let's assume, hypothetically, that you are right. How would we go about proving it? Taking down Dallinger is one thing—accusing a sitting President of treason is yet another. If you fail to prove your case, *you* will be the one in the slammer, or perhaps a mental hospital for the rest of your life."

Billings was persistent. "No doubt. But one fact we *do* have is that the Chinese assassinated President Basi, using a Saudi surrogate. Why don't we try to follow the leads that come from this Saudi hit man, and see where it goes? What is the old saying from Watergate? Remember when the secret source, Deep Throat, told Woodward and Bernstein to 'follow the money'?"

"You've convinced me. We need to run that back to its origin to verify this story. Let's park our friend Dallinger for a while, and pursue your strategy." The two returned to the main interrogation room, where Dallinger was munching on a doughnut.

"Ah, you are back," said Dallinger with a confident smile. "You were probably checking some of my facts, right? And they were accurate, I am sure. You know, you guys have enough of a budget to get some good coffee in here. I prefer the Starbucks French Roast, and I wish you would have one of your boys pick some up. I assume we will be here for quite a while, right?" Dallinger noticed a strange smile on Tilsdale's face.

"No, David. As it turns out, we are going to transfer you."

"Really? Well, I hope you are ready to explain to the Attorney General why you never read me my rights," he grinned. I think with a good lawyer I can have all of that information I gave you suppressed under the Fifth and Sixth Amendments. Haven't you ever heard of *Miranda vs. Arizona*? I doubt if you can successfully prosecute me now. You guys should have gone to law school."

Tilsdale looked at him with amazement. "David, you are one of a kind. I guess you are right, however. We probably fucked up our case for the prosecutors. Well, let's pack you up. The transfer vehicle is waiting."

The CIA interrogation team escorted Dallinger to a black Chevy Suburban with tinted windows. "Get in," ordered Tilsdale, and shackled Dallinger to the seat. The caravan sped off, heading not for the U.S. Courthouse in Washington, but for Dulles Airport.

"Hey, what's going on? This is not the way to downtown!" exclaimed Dallinger.

"This is a short cut. Relax," said Tilsdale, exchanging a knowing look with Billings.

As the caravan turned off for Dulles, Dallinger became agitated. "OK, what's going on, Tilsdale? We had a deal, goddam it. Where are you taking me? Wait until the FBI hears what you guys have done! They will have your asses!" The vehicles rolled up to the Gulfstream jet, operated by the CIA out of Dulles.

"Don't worry, David. They will *never* find out anything about this. We decided to treat you like you treated us. You are going to see our friends with the Mossad in Tel Aviv.

They are under instructions to extract every piece of information in your head, by any means necessary. If you are straight with them, they might let you live at the end of that process, but that depends on you. They really don't like traitors, you know. I guess it's kind of a Jewish thing, like Hanukkah. Now, it's time for you to go. *Bon voyage!*"

"Yeah, *shalom aleichim* [Hebrew for 'peace be upon you']," added Billings. As Dallinger was being dragged to the aircraft, Tilsdale dialed a number in Tel Aviv on his cell phone.

A man answered in Hebrew. "Major Fleischer."

"Ari, Brad Tilsdale. Remember that package we were going to send you?"

"Brad, Shalom. Certainly. Are you ready to ship it?"

"Yes, I am sending it now from Dulles. You know how to handle it."

"I do. And when I am through using the merchandise, what should I do with it?"

"Destroy it. We have no further use for it, and we don't want it to fall into the wrong hands."

"No problem, my friend. Just tell your delivery people to call this number and we will pick the item up at Tel Aviv airport. Have a nice day, and thank you for the referral."

"Not a problem. We will pay your expenses in the normal manner. Take care."

Billings chuckled. The Israelis would subject Dallinger to a typically brutal Middle East interrogation, hoping to find anything that related to the interests of Israel or the U.S. When they were through, Dallinger would then be killed and buried in an unmarked grave. Tilsdale and Billings would get their personal revenge for what Dallinger had done to them, and he would vanish without a trace. As far as the

U.S. government would know, Dallinger was mysteriously missing. The CIA would cause a leak to occur, implicating Dallinger as a Russian double-agent who had defected to Moscow, as others had done before him. Case closed.

On the drive back to Washington, Tilsdale made his decision. "Jeff, we won't have any success with trying to track Al-Amri's Chinese handler in Riyadh. He'll claim diplomatic immunity, and the Saudis will protect him under international law. Let's pack for a trip to Zurich. As you suggested, we will follow the money. I want to know who pulled the trigger back in China."

Chapter 25

The Trail of the Dragon

All of the world's major banks had offices in Zurich. The clever Swiss, who operate a neutral country while speaking three languages, determined long ago how to survive, even while world wars swirled around them. They developed the concept of international banking, and made certain that Switzerland would always be a welcome place for the world's flow of funds. For that convenience, the warring powers around them gave them a protected neutrality in wartime, similar to Sweden.

Switzerland was also a haven for money laundering, fraud, and embezzled funds from the world's dictatorships. A dictator's "exit strategy" was usually to stash millions of dollars in Swiss bank deposits, where Switzerland's secrecy laws prevented discovery. When Tilsdale and Billings arrived in Zurich, they found that the address of "Yang-Tze Finance Company," the source of Al-Amri's funds, was at 33 Hans-Huber Strasse, one block from the Chinese consulate at 20 Bellaria Strasse. "Very convenient," remarked Billings.

"I speak Mandarin, so let's pay them a visit. I want to see what kind of security they have," said Tilsdale. "You don't look very 'Swiss,' Jeff, so I'll do this one alone." They both laughed.

Entering the plush offices, which appeared like any other bank, Tilsdale memorized the location of surveillance cameras, the number of guards, and where the supervisors were located. He approached the reception desk, and switched into Mandarin. "I am from the Swiss Department of Banking Regulation, and we need to speak to your manager about a wire transfer problem."

The Chinese woman looked worried, as she scurried off to find the branch manager. Within minutes, she returned with a short Chinese man, who identified himself as the manager. "What can I do for you?" he asked.

"Our wire transfer division found a questionable transaction of ten million U.S. dollars, which occurred about two months ago. Here is the wire transfer number—2940029486. We are concerned that it could be an embezzlement or something. It went to an account in Dubai, in the name of Jamal Al-Amri, a Saudi. Could you please tell us the originating party, so that we can confirm that this was not some kind of criminal activity by smugglers?"

The men stared at Tilsdale. "We don't release that kind of information. You know that."

"Well, you do if the Swiss government is asking. And we are asking now. Are you going to cooperate or not? If you would prefer, we could have our bank auditors pay you a visit, and go through your books."

The man frowned. "Very well. Let's track that number." He went to a nearby computer terminal and typed in the number.

"There is nothing wrong with this transaction."

"How do you know?" Tilsdale asked.

"Because it originated with the government of the People's Republic of China, and it was issued through the

Bank of China, our parent company," the man snapped.

"Really? Well, I am sorry to have bothered you. One last question—which ministry issued the wire transfer? We need to make sure that they have good credit."

The man stared at the screen. "Here it is—the Ministry of State Security."

"Very good. Thank you for that. I can now close this case. Thank you for your time," said Tilsdale, getting up to leave.

"We are always happy to help the Swiss government," said the manager.

Tilsdale met Billings at the car, and told him what he had learned. "Somebody fucked up. They should have used a 'clean' middle-man to make that transfer. I guess they never thought Al-Amri would get nailed. Now it's time to see what's going on at the White House. How do we do it, Jeff?"

"President Hanlon is traveling to Tokyo to meet with the North Koreans about their takeover of the South. Maybe we can figure out a way to talk to the First Lady, who I heard is staying behind in Washington."

"No way. Even if we did, our own agency would go crazy. I don't want to get fired again, do *you*? I know some guys on the Secret Service detail, including the agent-in-charge. Let's have a heart-to-heart with him. I have some shit on him from one of his foreign trip escapades, and he owes me. Let's get to the airport."

Fourteen hours later, Tilsdale and Billings were back in Washington. Tilsdale dialed the confidential number for the Secret Service detail at the White House. "Harry? Brad Tilsdale.... Yeah, it's true. I'm now working at Langley. We need to talk about some possible threats that may involve the White House.... OK, that's a good time for us. Jeff Billings and I will be over this afternoon." He hung up, smiling.

"Those bastards know where *all* of the bodies are buried, Jeff. They never blew the cover on FDR's mistress, JFK's women guests, Clinton's intern shenanigans, or the fact that Sam Basi was a devout Muslim, and had a Muslim prayer rug placed in the Oval Office. That's why they call them 'the Secret Service.' Let's go to the White House."

At 1600 Pennsylvania Avenue, the two showed their CIA badges and IDs to the uniformed guard. They were led to the basement of the White House, where the Secret Service detail had their office. A tall Hispanic man greeted them at the door. "Brad Tilsdale! Great to see you again. What can I do for you? A White House tour? A visit to the Monica Lewinsky recreation room?"

"You're a funny guy, Harry. This is Jeff Billings. We are following a lead that involves possible penetration of the White House security by a foreign government. We need to ask you some questions."

Senior Agent Rodriguez looked startled. "Let's go in my office." He led them to a large office near the rear. "Coffee?"

"No thanks. Let me tell you what is going on. We have identified the guy who bombed Air Force One. He is in custody in a safe location, which I am not at liberty to disclose."

"What? Why not? Why was I not informed of this?" said an angry Rodriguez.

"Harry, relax. This is very sensitive stuff, and involves numerous agencies and cabinet-level departments, including Homeland Security, your boss. At this point, until we can tie the facts down more precisely, the fewer people who know about this, the better."

"OK, so what do you want from me? I was in Amman, Jordan when the plane went down. I should have been on it. Sometimes, I wish I had been."

"What is your opinion of the First Lady?"

"May? She is beautiful, smart, and a royal pain in the ass. Next question."

Tilsdale and Billings smiled. "Did you guys, or anyone, ever do a background investigation on her?"

"On the First Lady? Are you kidding? What would be the purpose of that? Half of our Presidents are security risks themselves! We don't get to bar *them* from the White House even if they have security issues, because the voters are the ones that put them there. We just try to protect the dumb bastards, and it's not easy."

"I sympathize with you—it's not a job I would sign up for. But what about the First Lady? Has she had any contact with Chinese nationals, or has she contacted anyone in China?"

"She always invites the Chinese embassy officials to White House functions, because the President thinks that her diplomatic skills are better than his with those guys. I am not aware of any 'off-campus' contacts however, and our agents are with her whenever she goes shopping or anything."

"Do any of your agents speak Mandarin?" asked Tilsdale.

"Are you kidding? I'm lucky to get agents that speak English these days. We don't pay very much, you know. It's a goddam disgrace, considering what these guys are supposed to do when there is a threat to the President."

"Right—like when one of your boys took a bullet for Reagan."

"Exactly."

"So Harry—has the First Lady hired any staff? Any of them Chinese?"

"Yes, she has. Her appointments secretary, her butler, and several kitchen staff are Chinese, and they were hired by her."

"Did you do BIs on all of them?" asked Billings.

"Yes, and they all passed. One is on a work permit, a man with a Hong Kong origin."

"What job does he have?"

"He is her butler. He watches her like a hawk, and he is intensely loyal to her. He reminds me of one of those characters from a James Bond movie."

"Could we see his personnel file?" asked Billings.

"Sure. But what's the point? There is nothing negative in it." The agent went to a filing cabinet and returned with a folder.

"Just checking the boxes, Harry—don't get paranoid." Tilsdale knew Hong Kong like the back of his hand. He scanned quickly through the folder, and then something caught his eye. Zhang Wei's Hong Kong ID and address were written in Chinese characters, which Tilsdale could read. He noticed that the address was located on a street in Kowloon, which he knew only had three numbers for each house address. Zhang's ID card listed five. In addition, the card was not sealed in plastic, which the Chinese always do. It looked like a forgery.

"How about letting us interview Mr. Zhang?"

"Oh, man! The First Lady will go berserk!"

"Let's make it an immigration issue. Tell him that his paperwork had a mistake, and we are trying to straighten it out. Introduce us as being from Citizenship and Immigration Services. Let's do it!"

A few minutes later, the Chinese butler, clad in a spotless white jacket, knocked on the door. "Mr. Zhang, thank you for joining us. These gentlemen are from Immigration, and they are trying to clear up your records, in case you would like to become a U.S. citizen."

The butler bowed. "Gentlemen, what can I do to help?"

As he shook the man's hand, Tilsdale noticed the tell-tale calluses and scars of a serious martial arts practitioner, a role not usually associated with butlers. "Mr. Zhang, I see you were originally from Hong Kong. That is such a beautiful city," droned Tilsdale.

"Yes, Sir. I miss it sometimes, although I love the United States." A very careful answer, noted Tilsdale.

"I see you lived on Man Wan Road. Isn't that right next to Canton Road? My memory is not too good—I have not been to Hong Kong for many years."

"Ah, so! Your memory is very good, Sir. I used to walk my family dog on Canton Road, when I got home from work."

"Where did you work?"

"I worked at the Quan electronics factory, like it says in my file. I was a production line manager."

"Well, someone did not write it down correctly. Thank you, Mr. Zhang. That will be all. Oh, one last question. How did you come to know the First Lady?"

Most interviewers would not have noticed, but Billings saw the man become slightly tense. "I think someone recommended me. I don't know who."

"Maybe someone at the Chinese embassy?" asked Tilsdale, dropping the "bomb" question.

The man began to sweat, and his eyes darted from man to man. "Not sure, Sir."

"Well, do you know anyone at the embassy? That would be a great reference for you, and we should put that in the file. It could be very helpful to you, because the Chinese embassy is very influential," lied Tilsdale.

The man seemed to relax. "Why, yes, I think one of the

cultural attachés may have recommended me. I knew him in Hong Kong when I was younger."

"And what is his name? This all helps you when it is time for promotions and pay raises, you know."

"Qiang Yong." Tilsdale wrote it down.

"Well, that will be all, then. Thank you very much. *Zàijiàn* [goodbye]."

After the man left, Tilsdale stood up. "That's all for now, Harry. Keep our visit to yourself, OK?"

"Sure, Brad. Good to meet you, Jeff."

"Harry, one last thing. In order to add another level of security, could you give us the activities schedule for both the President and the First Lady? We need to have this in 'real time,' as soon as you guys get it. We can correlate that with potential threats we are tracking, and can notify you of what we have."

"Sure, Brad. No problem. I have your card. I'll put your e-mail address on our distribution list for the schedules."

The two got to their car in the restricted parking area and got into the car. "It looks bad, Jeff. You may not remember, but General Qiang is the assistant Resident MSS guy at the embassy. We have the First Lady's butler being referred by the MSS, and by the way, he was lying about his Kowloon address. Canton Street is all the way across town. He doesn't know Hong Kong very well, considering he supposedly lived there. I'm betting he's an MSS agent."

"My God! Don't we have *any* competent security anymore?" asked Billings. "What's next on our agenda?"

"The next thing is to put the First Lady under our surveillance, without telling the Secret Service," replied Tilsdale.

Chapter 26

Cutting the Losses

While Tilsdale and Billings were organizing the covert surveillance of the First Lady, President Hanlon was winging his way toward Tokyo on the new Air Force One aircraft. He was carefully preparing for hard negotiations with the Koreans, in order to establish an acceptable governmental framework that both the North and the South could live with. The plan was for the conference to convene at the Tokyo Imperial Hotel, near the Emperor's Palace. As President Hanlon got out of his limousine, he would be greeted by a line of Japanese dignitaries, standing in a reception line from the street to the entrance. The Secret Service considered Japan a comparatively safe location, since guns were generally illegal in Japan, and crime was relatively low. This is precisely why someone had hired a team of Yakuza hit men to eliminate President Hanlon.

The Yakuza constitute the largest organized crime syndicate in the world, now boasting over 100,000 members and exerting their influence around the globe. They are particularly active wherever there is a large Japanese or Korean population. Most of their activity centers on protection rackets, prostitution, blackmail, black marketeering, and assassinations. The Yakuza, similar to the Mafia and the Chinese

Triad, are organized into "families," headed by an *oyabun*, or "boss." When protecting their turf or their honor, they are aggressive and very violent. The Japanese police and government officials are generally afraid of them, and turn a blind eye to their criminal operations.

After President Hanlon's itinerary became publicized, certain powerful interests took notice. The largest Yakuza group, *Yamaguchi-gumi*, headquartered in Tokyo, received an anonymous call. In heavily accented Japanese, the man said, "*Oyabun-wa desu-ka?* [Is the boss there?]" He went on to explain that he wanted to have a meeting, but he needed total secrecy. The young "soldier," known in the Yakuza as a "younger brother," forwarded the information to his seniors. Within minutes, Shinobu Tsukasa, the current *Oyabun*, returned the man's call.

The caller explained that his client needed a very special task completed, and executed with great precision and secrecy. "What exactly do you want?" asked Tsukasa suspiciously. He was angry that his young assistant had allowed this call to come through to him.

"*Oyabun-san*, I represent the Moscow *Bratva* [brotherhood, or Russian Mafia family]. We wish to contract with you for a very important hit. We will advance you the sum of 50 million dollars before the action, and pay another 50 million upon completion."

Tsukasa was caught off-guard. This sounded like the Russian Mafia organization, with whom the Yakuza had worked in the past, outside of Japan. *Perhaps this man is genuine,* he thought. "We will need to verify your credentials. What is your name, and who is your boss?"

"I cannot give you that over the phone. Leave a note for me, giving me the time and place to meet with you. Place the note under the right front tire of the blue Lexus LS, which is parked outside of your building, in the alley."

"Very well." Tsukasa hung up. "Ichiro, take this note down to the alley, and wedge it under the right front tire of the blue Lexus LS." He scribbled the address of a Yakuza hideout in the Shinbashi district, and the time of 1400.

At the hideout, Tsukasa and a dozen heavily armed guards awaited the caller. There was a knock on the door. "Let him in, but cover him. And search him for weapons first," ordered Tsukasa. The door opened, revealing a large Caucasian man in an overcoat.

After he was searched, Tsukasa directed him to sit down. "Now, my mysterious friend, who are you, and who do you work for?"

"I am Vadim Orlopov, a director with the Moscow *Bratva*."

"Who do you work for?" asked Tsukasa.

"Semion Mogilevich."

Tsukasa and his aides showed their surprise. Mogilevich was the head of finance for the Russian Mafia in Moscow, and had known connections to prior and current members of the KGB and SVR intelligence services. When dealing with Mogilevich, one could become very wealthy—or very dead. Tsukasa knew him well, and decided to check the man's story. An aide slipped away to make a call to Mogilevich's office in Moscow. "Very well. Let's enjoy a little *sake* while we wait."

In a few moments, the aide returned and signaled Tsukasa with a nod. "Satisfied?" asked Orlopov.

"Yes, very. I'm sorry, but we have to be very careful these days. So who is the subject of your hit?"

"The President of the United States," whispered Orlopov.

Tsukasa and his aides stared at him in disbelief. At first, his impulse was to reject the project. But then he thought of what he could do with 100 million dollars in the current Japanese recession. "I suppose you understand what the fall-out effects of such an act could be."

"Of course."

"Who, exactly, is your 'client' who is ordering this hit?"

"You don't need to know that. All you need to know is that you will be paid as promised. Now do you have the capability to accomplish this task, or shall I go elsewhere?" growled Orlopov. He was known among the Russian Mafia as a very impatient man, with little tolerance for wasting time.

"Alright. We will take the project, with the understanding that the details of how it will be carried out are totally up to us."

"Agreed. All we care about is the end result."

Tsukasa thought for a moment. "We will begin preparations as soon as you make the first payment. Please use our bank in the Cayman Islands. My assistant will give you the bank routing numbers for a wire transfer. After we verify the transfer, we will begin."

"*Yoi.* [Good.] You will have the funds within the hour. Here is my cell phone number, if you have any problems or need to contact me." Orlopov handed Tsukasa a blank card with a number.

"*Sayonara, Orlopov-san.* And please convey my gratitude to Mogilevich for the business."

Within 30 minutes, a wire transfer of 50 million dollars was received by the Yakuza's bank and verified by Tsukasa. He turned to his chief aide. "Hitoshi, contact Tanaka and tell him to report to me immediately. We have work to do, and only three days."

Hideo Tanaka was an anachronism, at least by Western standards. He drew his sense of honor and duty to his master from Japan's days of feudal conflict. He was the modern embodiment of the *samurai* warrior, an expert with all types of weapons and able to kill with his hands alone. In ancient times, he would have fought for a *Shogun* or a prince. Today, he works for the Yakuza.

"You wanted to see me, Master?"

"Yes, Hideo, please sit down. We are in need of your expertise in performing a difficult project. We are going to kill the President of the United States, three days from now. Can you do it?"

Tanaka showed no emotion, not even a blink of an eye. "Of course, Master. He is just another man. Besides, I really don't like Americans."

"I know. I remember that your grandfather was killed by the Americans on Okinawa, during the war. But this is strictly business, do you understand? We want this done efficiently, and with no trace back to us."

"Master, *wakarimasu* [I understand]. I will use a team from Osaka. They cannot be traced to me or to you."

"*Yoi.* Now how do you plan to do this? Security will be very tight, and it will be next to impossible to get close to the target."

"I will use three different marksmen. They will all be expert snipers, equipped with the Barrett Model 82A1, firing a .50

caliber bullet. We have had great success with this weapon, which the Americans have used in Iraq and Afghanistan. With the powerful scopes, they have an effective range of approximately 2,500 meters. I would position each shooter alone, with a spotter, firing from different high-rise buildings. These weapons will also penetrate any vehicle, including one that is armored. No one could survive this kind of attack, as long as we can see the target. Since we know he will be shaking hands with dignitaries at the entrance to the Imperial Hotel, he will be stationary long enough, and we can't miss. That is a very open area, and we can shoot through 150 degrees of angle, relative to the entrance."

"Won't these shooting teams be a security risk to you, after the job is done?"

Tanaka stared coldly at Tsukasa. "No, Master, not if they are dead."

"I see. Well, you have a lot to do. Keep me advised."

Chapter 27

Unforeseen Circumstances

In the next two days, Tanaka and his shooter teams located good sniper locations, overlooking the hotel entrance from a distance. They were sufficiently concealed to prevent observation by helicopters, and far enough away to avoid security screening. In Tokyo, it is impossible for police to lock down a very large area, because of the density of buildings. The great range of the Barrett rifles made them the perfect selection of weapons.

Meanwhile, Air Force One was over the Pacific, en route to Tokyo. One of the Secret Service agents found his boss, Harry Rodriguez, pouring a Pepsi in the main galley. "Boss, did you notice that the President seems to be feeling ill?"

Rodriguez looked at him, and then peered around the curtain at the President, who was talking with reporters. "No. He looks OK to me. What are you talking about?"

"I noticed his hand was shaking, and he told me he had a terrible headache. He has been mumbling to himself. It's weird. Do you think he's getting the flu or something?"

"I don't know, but I'll have the doc look at him. It's nice to be able to bring your own doctor along—wish I could do that."

The aircraft commander's voice came over the PA system.

"Ladies and Gentlemen, we will be starting our descent into Tokyo shortly. We are expecting a little turbulence, so for your own safety, please return to your seat and fasten your seatbelt. We should be on the ground in thirty minutes."

"Let's check him out when we get on the ground in Tokyo, Bob. But thanks for the heads-up," said Rodriguez.

After an uneventful landing at Tokyo, the big jet parked at the ramp, where a red carpet and several Japanese officials waited. The aircraft commander's voice announced arrival. "Ladies and Gentlemen, please remain seated until the President leaves the aircraft. We will let you know."

After deplaning and greeting the Japanese officials, President Hanlon entered his limousine. Rodriguez noticed that his face had a strange, ashen color. He took the jump seat across from the President, and began watching him closely. He began a mental review of the hospital facilities on the route to the Imperial Hotel, in case of a Presidential medical emergency.

The crisis Hanlon was experiencing was not medical—it was deeply psychological. The difference between the "behavior control" programs developed by the Russians and the Chinese did not seem significant, but it actually was. The Pochevsky Institute carefully combined drugs, hypnosis, and a "sensory barrage," which changed an individual's personality in about two weeks of treatment.

The Chinese, on the other hand, emphasized only drugs and hypnosis, since the doctors at the Ankang Institute did not believe that the sensory input was reliable. While the Russian methods were used on Sam Basi, with permanent effect, the Chinese had used their own protocols on Bill Hanlon when they kidnapped him during his trip to Kowloon, years ago. The biggest problem with the Chinese approach was that the behavior controls wore off in about 25% of the cases, causing the subject to return to his or her normal behavior characteristics. As it turned out, Bill Hanlon was one of the 25%, and he was starting to realize that he had committed terrible mistakes. In his tortured mind, the gravity of those mistakes was manifesting in feelings of physical illness, and the longer he was away from May, his "control," the faster he would return to normal thinking.

President Hanlon turned to his chief-of-staff in the limousine, and said, "Ben, who came up with the idea of abandoning Taiwan and South Korea?" Ben Blackwell was a retired Marine one-star general, and one of the best administrators that the Marine Corps ever had. Every senior general had wanted him on their staffs. Hanlon trusted his opinion totally.

"Why, *you* did, Mr. President. You overrode the Joint Chiefs' advice, and launched this program yourself." Blackwell stared at him intently. *Something is really wrong with this guy,* thought Blackwell. "Are you feeling OK, Mr. President?"

Hanlon ignored him. "This conference we are going to is designed to consummate the North Koreans' dominance over the entire peninsula, is that right?"

"Well, yes. That is why you set it up."

"I need time to think. *This is all wrong!*"

"But, Mr. President, we are only a few blocks from the hotel reception. The Japanese have all of their top politicians and military brass waiting for you." And of course, the Yakuza snipers were also waiting for him.

"Bullshit! I need to unscramble this situation. The best place to do that is from a U.S. Navy warship!" Hanlon leaned toward the Secret Service driver. "Bobby, turn this thing around and head south to Yokosuka." He turned to the uniformed officer carrying the "football," the nuclear war communications device, which was always near the President. "Commander, what ships are in port at Yokosuka now?"

"Sir, the *USS Blue Ridge*, 7th Fleet's flagship, and also *USS George Washington* and *USS Nimitz*, carriers. Plus the usual number of DDGs [guided missile destroyers] and CGs [guided missile cruisers]."

"Get Irv Baker on the phone for me." Vice Admiral Irving Baker was Commander, 7th Fleet.

After a minute, the officer said, "He's on, Sir."

Hanlon picked up his phone. "Irv? Bill Hanlon. Irv, I'm going to put some pressure on you, so take a strain. I want you to saddle up ASAP, and prepare a battle group to get underway. General destination will be the eastern side of Taiwan, in the Philippine Sea. Do you have a full load of nukes on board your ships and subs? OK, bring all of your nuclear submarines, including the boomers [ballistic missile subs] out from Guam and Hawaii and give me an order of battle as soon as you can draw one up. I want a dozen attack subs, with nuclear Tomahawk missiles, positioned in the northern Sea of Japan, off North Korea. Send a flash message to CINCPAC to mobilize the Marine Expeditionary Brigade, and start planning for an amphibious attack in the area of Wonsan, objective Pyongyang. Irv, I'm coming aboard your flagship, because you have the Global Communications and Command System. I'll see you in thirty minutes."

Hanlon's advisors looked at him in shock. This was a different personality than they had been dealing with for weeks. Blackwell spoke up first. "Bill, what do you plan to do here? This could start a war—maybe two wars!"

"Goddam right! This is what we should have done in the first place. I don't know what I was thinking... " Hanlon was beginning to have hazy recollections of May, telling him to do certain things. "Dragon . . .dragon... that word keeps going through my head—what *is* that?" he mumbled to himself. It then hit him—it all came together, like a collision of images. He had somehow been betrayed, by the person he loved most, the one closest to him. His mind raced, as he began to put events, people, and conversations together. He was slowly assembling the pieces of the puzzle. May could not be trusted, he realized, and that broke his heart. Now he had to make things right, no matter what the cost.

The Yakuza snipers were watching the Imperial Hotel entrance carefully, and began to notice a commotion, followed by dignitaries starting to leave. Their target never arrived. They called Tanaka for instructions. "It's already on the TV news," he told them. "The President has changed his itinerary, and no one knows, or will tell, where he is going. This operation is over. You will be paid for your effort. Shut this operation down and leave immediately."

This startling news made its way from the Yakuza back to Moscow, to the Russian Mafia. They, in turn, reported to their "clients" at the SVR, who had ordered the hit because of their fear that Hanlon had become an ally of China, with which they shared a long and disputed border. The question the SVR was now trying to answer for their bosses in the Kremlin was *what was Hanlon up to?* From past experience, they knew that there is nothing worse than an *unpredictable* U.S. President, like Harry Truman or Ronald Reagan.

By the time the Presidential motorcade arrived at the docks in Yokosuka naval base, the ships were already preparing to get underway. Fuel tanks were topped off, and all personnel had been recalled to their ships. The flagship was hastily readied for the President's arrival.

As President Hanlon climbed the gangway to the *Blue Ridge* quarterdeck with his staff, the shrill sound of a boatswain's pipe signaled his arrival. Over the ship's public address system, known as the 1MC, came the traditional bell signals and the unusual words, "United States, arriving." Vice Admiral Baker saluted and greeted the President.

"Welcome aboard, Mr. President. Please follow me to your quarters."

Once seated in the Flag conference room, Hanlon spoke first. "Irv, there have been some major fuck-ups, mostly mine. I won't bore you with the reasons, because I want to focus on the solutions. In summary, we are going to do whatever is necessary to get the Chinese out of Taiwan, and the North Koreans back across the 38th parallel. We are going back to *status quo ante*. The Chinese and the North Koreans can do this the easy way, or the hard way. Either way, it *will* happen."

"Yes, Sir! But it will take some time to get our assets in place."

"Understand. We need that time, anyway, to ratchet up our pressure before we really unload on them. I have CINCPAC jumping through his ass, trying to put three task forces together. We have enough for the first one, so form it up with the two carriers and the usual support vessels, and position us off of the eastern coast of Taiwan, so that China is within range of our air strikes. That will make it more difficult for them to attack the force."

"You are not going with us, are you, Sir?"

"Irv, I caused the mess, now I'm going with you to clean it up. I want you to issue orders that all ships, subs, and aircraft are cleared for engaging Chinese or North Korean forces the minute they display the slightest hostile intent. If any of their ships or subs approach our forces within 50 miles, I want them to be sunk. If any of their aircraft come within 100 miles, they will be shot down. I am communicating this to the Chinese and North Korean governments."

"Mr. President, I know you understand this, but our ships are really vulnerable in this kind of environment. Even the carriers. The Chinese have plenty of anti-ship missiles."

"Take it easy, Irv. I have also notified them that if any U.S. or allied ship is sunk, I will trade that ship for one of their cities, meaning it will be taken out with a nuclear weapon. I'm not fucking around here, Irv. They need to get off the pot and go home. *Period.*"

"Aye, aye, Sir. I will need to get working on this. I will be on the Flag bridge."

"Thanks, Irv. This is why we get the big bucks, my friend," Hanlon said, laughing. "OK, let me know when I have enough ships for the second task force. That is when the fun will really begin," observed Hanlon. "Let's see how good the Chinese are at playing high-stakes poker."

While all of this was happening, Tilsdale and Billings were trying to determine the scope of the security problem at the White House. So far, the surveillance had turned up nothing. If the First Lady was communicating with her handlers at the Chinese embassy, they had not been able to detect it. Tilsdale was becoming impatient, as usual.

"Jeff, I'm going to Taiwan. We still have an embassy there, and so far, the Chinese have left it alone. Why wouldn't they? We gave them Taiwan! Everything I need is in the embassy files, anyway. May Hanlon was a local employee when she met the future President. There must be a personnel and security file on her there, and I need to get to it before the Chinese take over our embassy and its files. So far, they are being very careful not to provoke us into reacting, and they have left the embassy alone."

Tilsdale arranged his travel to Taiwan on China Airlines, which was still providing service to Taipei Airport. He planned to carry pre-arranged State Department credentials, which would give him diplomatic status as a "courier." He booked on China Airlines flight 17 to Tokyo, then switched to flight 101 to Taipei, business class. He hated these long flights, but there was no other way.

He received considerable attention as he went through customs in Taipei, now controlled by the Chinese military. "I am an embassy courier," he told the customs officers. After conferring with their superiors, they let him through.

On the cab ride to the embassy, he noticed the lines of armored vehicles and heavily armed Chinese troops patrolling the streets. Now that the Chinese had Taiwan in their grasp, they were not about to let it go.

Arriving at the embassy, located at No. 7 Xin Yi Road, he presented his credentials to a tense Marine guard. "Third Floor, Room 8, Sir."

Tilsdale took the elevator to the third floor, where the CIA Resident was located. "Brad Tilsdale! You son-of-a-bitch! I have not seen you since Saigon!" Stan Filmore and Tilsdale had managed covert operations into Laos and Cambodia during the last years of the Vietnam War.

"Hi, Stan. I see you drew the short straw here. I suppose you don't get to do much under these circumstances. I could barely get in here, even on China Airlines. I'm sure they will be closing the airport before long."

"Yeah, isn't this great? Our fearless leader gave this place away! What an asshole! Everyone in Taiwan is afraid to talk to us now. We are about as popular as a case of the clap. What brings a hot-shot like you out here?"

"Stan, I need to go through some of your files. Specifically, I want to start with the embassy employee file on May Hanlon, previously known as May Chang."

"The First Lady? Man, you have not changed. You are always stirring the pot. I would be careful if I were you."

"Stan, I'm always careful. Where's the file?"

"It would be in the basement archives. Jenny, please come in here." A slender Taiwanese woman entered. "Please take Mr. Tilsdale down to the archives, and get him some of your great coffee."

"Of course, Sir. Mr. Tilsdale, please follow me."

"My pleasure," said Tilsdale, noting the curves of her shapely body, quite visible in her tight silk dress. He could see that Stan was up to his old habits, having developed a gourmet taste for Asian women long ago.

Once in the basement file section, he had the clerk bring him May Chang's personnel file. He immediately noticed that she had been hired without the full Top Secret background investigation. Reading the Chinese characters, he noted that her birthplace was listed as a town in Taiwan, but another document showed that she had been admitted to the country as a refugee from mainland China. Tilsdale asked himself, *How could they miss a discrepancy like this?* He also noted that she had failed the polygraph examination, when she was asked, "Have you ever worked on behalf of the government of the People's Republic of China?" Tilsdale returned to the CIA agent's office.

"Stan, how could May Chang have been hired? She has a

huge discrepancy in her file, and she failed the polygraph."

"Brad, you know how it is in Asia, especially with Taiwan. We have a lot of mainland refugees, and their background cannot be traced—not in a place like China! She just slipped through, I guess."

"Yeah, well she wound up marrying a future President, and now she is acting like the queen of the White House. Plus, we have security issues with some of her hires."

"It is what it is, Brad. Aren't you about ready to retire? Why are you still busting your ass with stuff like this?"

Tilsdale bristled. He resented any reference to his age, which he knew was becoming an issue with his bosses. "Stan, there are some things that I started, and want to see them through." Tilsdale's cell phone began to vibrate. "Sorry, got to take this. It's from Jeff Billings." He walked into the hall, switched his phone on scrambler, then answered.

"Brad, we've got big problems, and you are right in the middle of them. The President has flipped again. He has just mobilized the entire Pacific Command, and is personally on scene aboard the 7th Fleet flagship, running the show! The admirals and generals are loving it, but there is no telling what the Chinese or North Koreans might do. By the way, we have just gone to DEFCON 3 [national defense status code for 'increase force readiness—nuclear war possible']. When was the last time you saw *that?*"

"September 11th, as I recall."

"It looks like he intends to take back Taiwan and South Korea. He is assembling three task forces, and he has ordered the ballistic missile subs and Strategic Command to shift their target matrix to China and North Korea. Brad, this guy is serious!"

"Looks like I picked a bad time to visit Taiwan. Have you

learned anything from the surveillance on the First Lady?"

"No, but we decided to put surveillance on the butler, also. He seems to be spending a lot of time in a Chinese restaurant near the White House. We are trying to get an undercover agent on the payroll, in order to watch him."

"As long as the President is on a Navy ship, the First Lady and her butler pal are not an immediate security threat. However, when he returns to the White House, or she joins him somewhere, we will need to force the issue. We can't allow this to go on, regardless."

"Brad, this is a political bomb. It could really blow up in our face."

"Yep. Like most of the stuff we do, Jeff. I'll take the heat for this one, if it goes south. Like my buddy Stan just said, retirement is just around the corner for me," said Tilsdale, grinning at the CIA Resident. "Just try to collect as much evidence as you can. Is NSA assisting?"

"Yes, Melissa Clayton has assigned a special team, with Chinese linguists working it."

"Good. Keep me posted. *Ciao!*"

Chief-of-staff Blackwell found the President in the Combat Information Center of the *Blue Ridge*, discussing force disposition with Vice Admiral Baker. Blackwell handed him a note. "Irv, I need a minute with Ben." The admiral excused himself.

"What's up, Ben? We have a lot going on."

"You can say that again, Bill. I just received a routine briefing over the net from CIA. They just got one of their experienced agents into the Taiwan embassy, two days ago. His name is Brad Tilsdale. Know him?"

"Holy shit! Who doesn't know that maniac? Did you ever

want to meet James Bond? Tilsdale is as close as you get, minus the British accent. What the hell is he doing in there?"

"It appears to me that the CIA doesn't even know. I did some checking, and Karen Littleton has given Tilsdale authorization to operate on his own, accountable only for results. She is very concerned about his knowledge of classified information. If the Chinese get him, that could be a real problem, according to her."

"Yeah, that would be just like him. His bosses could never decide whether to love him or hate him." The President thought through this new information. "Ben, can we get him out? I need to debrief him on what he has seen and what he knows. Our embassy is now on lock-down, and all commercial flights have been canceled, mostly because of our activities off-shore."

"The only way I can think of is to send a SEAL team in to retrieve him. But we could lose some people doing that, including Tilsdale."

"You forgot one thing—Tilsdale *was* a SEAL. Old habits are hard to break. Send an encrypted message to the embassy, telling Tilsdale to prepare for extraction. I would really like to have that son-of-a-bitch here to advise me."

"Yes, Sir."

The President turned to the Marine orderly. "Corporal, ask Admiral Baker to please join me."

Within minutes, Baker reappeared. "Irv, we have a touchy one here. We want to send in the SEALs to extract a CIA agent from the embassy. Can you do it?"

Concern was apparent in the admiral's face. "We can try, Sir, if it is that important. Who is the agent?"

"Brad Tilsdale. Ever hear of him?"

The admiral shook his head, laughing. "Mr. President,

nothing ever changes. Tilsdale was a legend when I was a lieutenant, flying F-4s off the *America*. From the stories we heard, we were never sure that he was real, or just someone's imagination. I heard he got into trouble with the loss of Air Force One, and wound up moving from the FBI to the CIA."

"Correct. But Air Force One was not his fault. The Secret Service blew that one. Trust me, I read that report very carefully. Irv, I need him on board. Please make it happen ASAP."

"Aye, aye, Sir." The admiral left to locate the SEAL commander.

"Stan, it's about ready to hit the fan, my friend." Tilsdale was reading the latest communications from Washington.

"Brad, you have no idea. While you were on the phone, I received this Top Secret message from the code room." Filmore handed him a yellow document.

The message read: "CIA Agent Bradford Tilsdale to prepare for extraction by SEAL team on 9 July 0200 local time. Morse Code signal via laser from SEALs: your last name. Exit embassy and meet team at source of lasers. Report to me upon arrival. Good luck. Signed, POTUS."

"Stan, is this a joke?"

"No way, Brad. This came by way of the National Command Center. Get your shit together, buddy—you are going swimming!"

Wonderful, thought Tilsdale. *Now I'm surrounded by a million Chinese, and the President wants me to swim out of here.*

Within hours, the President's intercom buzzed. "Mr.

President, you may want to come to the Flag bridge and see this."

The President walked over to the Flag bridge in time to see the conning tower of *USS Florida (SSGN-728)* emerge from the water alongside the flagship. Her deck-mounted SEAL team equipment compartment was clearly visible. Along with *Jimmy Carter*, she had replaced the older submarine *Kamehameha* in the role of special operations support.

"Mr. President, this is the SEAL officer-in-charge, Lieutenant Barrow." A tall, powerfully-built man stepped forward, dressed in a wet suit.

"Mr. President, we are ready for the extraction. Do you have any last-minute instructions for us?"

"No, Lieutenant. Just bring everyone back. I would not have ordered this op, but we really need to get this CIA guy out of there. He has too much classified information to risk him falling into the hands of the Chinese. Remember—if you get in trouble, we have some entertainment that will distract the Chinese, which should give you a chance to escape. Just use your EPIRB [emergency position-indicating radio beacon] and we will unload on our Chinese friends."

"What about the CIA Resident?" asked the officer.

"He has planned for the Chinese contingency, and he knows how to deal with it. He stays there. We need him to sanitize the embassy for classified information, in the event the Chinese storm the embassy. Tilsdale has information and insight that I need badly."

"We'll bring him to you, Sir."

"Good luck."

The man left to join his team on the main deck. President Hanlon watched as they were lowered over the side in their

Zodiac boats, and then headed for the *Florida*. The game was on.

At the embassy, Tilsdale had received the President's order with some surprise. He wondered how his own bosses learned of his Taiwan "vacation." When he found out that SEAL Team One was coming in to retrieve him, he found it amusing. *You just can't escape your past,* he thought.

The embassy had become an armed fortress. All classified documents had been destroyed, and only one cipher machine was kept intact, to be destroyed if the Chinese attempted to take the embassy.

Tilsdale looked at his watch. Extraction was set for 0200. The SEALs would travel up the Tamshui River, which snaked through Taipei from the sea. Using submersible transport vehicles, they would leave the submarine near the river mouth while submerged. The journey would take approximately two hours. Tilsdale hoped he could still handle the complicated underwater breathing equipment, which was specially designed for the SEALs. They planned to leave the same way they came in, until meeting the submarine, which would be lying silent on the bottom near the river mouth.

The SEALs waited in their egress chamber on the submarine, as the hatch closed and water began to fill the space. Each man donned and tested his breathing apparatus. Each gave the leader a thumbs-up. With the pressure equalized, the outside hull hatch was opened, and the SEALs swam out to the storage chamber on the deck. It opened, revealing eight SEAL Delivery Vehicles (SDVs), resembling large torpedoes. They were capable of transporting three men each, and were powered by electric motors. The team would go in with four, carrying just two men each, in case of a combat loss or mechanical failure. On the egress, Tilsdale would take the third spot in one of the SDVs.

Their weapons, like the Kriss Vector submachine gun, were stored in special waterproof containers that would be carried to the shore entry point, up-river. The SEAL "pilot" of each vehicle was specially trained in navigating and maneuvering. He used special night goggles to follow the SDV ahead him, moving like a school of large fish.

After two hours, the lead SEAL SDV pilot checked his GPS unit and found that they had reached the "feet dry" point, where they would park the SDVs at the river bank and stow their scuba gear. The first SEAL slowly surfaced and surveyed the surrounding area with his night goggles. There were no Chinese troops in sight. He gave a thumbs up, and the team moved quickly into the trees of the park area adjacent to the river. Within a minute, they had transitioned into a formidable land-fighting force. They located the two sedans that had been pre-arranged with Taiwanese nationalist agents, and drove toward the embassy, two miles away. They carefully followed the route that had been recommended, and verified by spy satellite to have no Chinese checkpoints.

Approaching the embassy, they pulled into a nearby alley with their lights off and parked. They could see the windows of the embassy clearly. Using the laser sighting device on his Kriss, one of the SEALs flashed a signal at the windows. He got an immediate flashlight signal in return. Their CIA "package" was ready for pickup.

Within minutes, Tilsdale slipped down the rear fire escape, and made his way to the alley. "Mr. Tilsdale?" asked the lead SEAL.

"Affirmative. Shall we go?" The SEALs, who had positioned themselves to cover the area with their weapons, got quickly back into the two sedans with Tilsdale.

As they sped off, Tilsdale noticed that the SEALs were looking him over. "Yes, Gentlemen, I can still swim," said Tilsdale, bringing a laugh from the group.

"Hopefully, you won't need to do much of that, Sir," replied the SEAL. "It's a fairly nice ride in the SDVs." The two cars drove cautiously back to the river, on the prescribed route. Upon reaching the park area, they parked the cars and glided ghostlike through the tree line. Suddenly, the lead SEAL dropped his hand and they all dove for the ground. About 50 yards away, two Chinese soldiers stood, smoking cigarettes. The lead SEAL turned to his Lieutenant, who gave a cutting motion with his finger, across the throat.

The SEAL worked noiselessly toward the two men, who were talking and laughing. Tilsdale could hear their conversation, which concerned a prostitute one of them had enjoyed the night before. The SEAL broke from the tree line and jammed the blade of his Randall fighting knife into the base of the first soldier's skull, instantly paralyzing and killing him. The other attempted to un-sling his AK-47, but it was too late. The blade entered him below his belt, and ripped diagonally upward, gutting him. The only sound was caused by the man's body hitting the ground. The SEALs dragged the bodies into the brush and covered them with branches.

The SEALs moved rapidly to the river bank where they had hidden their wet gear, with an extra for Tilsdale. In less than two minutes, they were all back in the water and swam into their submersible vehicles for the run to open water. Their departure did not even leave a ripple on the water.

As Tilsdale was learning, riding in an SDV was not for the claustrophobic. The men were squeezed into each aluminum tube, only slightly larger than a standard torpedo. They were totally dependent on the skill of the SEAL that piloted the vehicle, because any mistake by him could be fatal to all of them.

Miles downriver, the group of SDVs accelerated in the deeper water. The GPS unit on the lead vehicle showed they were on course, and the safety of the *Florida* was just a few miles ahead. Nearly on schedule, the group cleared the river mouth, and lined up their final underwater course for the submarine. Finding a black submarine, which is lying on the ocean bottom at night, is no simple task. The SDV pilots strained their eyes, looking for the cigar-shaped vessel in the deep water.

The pilot of the third vehicle suddenly broke radio silence and announced, "Tally-ho! One o'clock!" The *Florida* loomed up, out of the blackness. Tilsdale thought, *These things seem to have gotten a lot bigger since I used to do this.*

The SEALs exited the vehicles and opened the submarine's "dry storage" compartment, which looked like a large natural gas tank, mounted on the deck. They carefully stowed the SDVs and closed the compartment. Next, they opened the hatch to their special egress/access chamber, and one-by-one, followed Tilsdale inside. Once the leader had confirmed that they all were accounted for, he closed the outside hatch and pushed a button on the bulkhead. The chamber began to empty the seawater, allowing them to take off their breathing apparatus. A green light blinked, and the pressure hatch into the submarine opened. "Welcome aboard, Mr. Tilsdale," said the captain.

"Thank you, Skipper. I can assure you, I am very glad to be here. Sorry to put you guys to so much trouble."

"No trouble at all, Sir. When the President sends us to get someone, we are glad to oblige," he chuckled.

Tilsdale turned to the SEALS. "Great job, guys. It almost makes me wish I were younger, and back with the teams. Thanks for the ride."

"Glad to do it, Sir," said the Lieutenant. He gave a silent hand signal, and the SEALS left for their cramped quarters two decks down.

"Well, Captain, I can't wait to see what the President wants from me. It should be interesting."

The *Florida* wasted no time in getting underway. She floated free of the bottom, and slipped silently into deeper water, accelerating to 40 knots. The captain knew the Chinese had numerous anti-sub ships in the Taiwan Strait, as well as other attack submarines. After a tense five-hour ride, the *Florida* surfaced close aboard the *Blue Ridge*, and Tilsdale was transferred with the SEALs in Zodiacs back to the Flagship. As he came aboard, an officer told him that the President wanted to see him immediately.

President Hanlon was studying an area tactical map in Flag Plot, also known as the "war room," when Tilsdale walked in. "You wanted to see me, Sir?"

"You're Brad Tilsdale! We are relieved that you made it out of there. Welcome!"

"Thank you, Sir, but I'm not sure why you went to all of this trouble."

"Frankly, we could not afford to let the Chinese get you. Karen Littleton said that you had too much classified information in your head to let you fall into Chinese hands. Besides, I need someone that understands both military and intelligence matters to advise me. We have some tough decisions around the corner."

"I am flattered, Mr. President."

"Bullshit! Brad, you are famous—or maybe infamous—I believe you have been working on security problems involving the White House. Your boss told me."

It was apparent that Karen Littleton knew everything that was going on. "Yes, that's right. Perhaps you and I should talk privately."

Hanlon looked at him and frowned. "Of course. Let's go in this office." He led Tilsdale to a small office adjoining the war room, and closed the door. "OK, what's up? This was an unusual request."

"Well, Sir, I don't know exactly how to begin. We cracked a major spy case, involving a double-agent at the FBI. That has been appropriately taken care of, I assure you. In the course of that, we stumbled onto a very disturbing security problem. I would not raise the issue at this preliminary stage, except that your personal security and classified information could be compromised."

"Go on."

"Sir, it involves the First Lady. We have indications that the Chinese were behind the downing of Air Force One, and that your wife appears to be working with the Chinese MSS."

Hanlon covered his eyes with his hands. "Goddam it, I knew it! The bastards did something to me, Brad! I'm OK now, but just look what has happened! In Tokyo, I came out of whatever it was they did to me, and realized what was going on."

"Yes, Sir. We couldn't understand why you allowed these things to happen, until we found that May had hired an MSS agent as her butler, and then verified that she failed her hiring security check at the Taiwan embassy. She is actually from mainland China, and was probably an MSS plant at the embassy."

"And now she is the First Lady! I feel like a fool."

"From what I know about their behavior control methods, Mr. President, you were helpless. The Russians did it to Sam Basi, too. They must have kidnapped you for a few days. Do you remember anything like that?"

"I remember getting sick on my honeymoon trip to Kowloon, when I was with May. I could not remember some of the time there. That must have been when they did it. So they have been waiting all this time to pull the trigger?"

"You know how patient they are, compared to us. They probably never expected you to become the President. You were being kept in reserve, like a secret weapon. With you in the White House, they pulled out all the stops. It wasn't your fault, Sir."

"So exactly how did this all go down, Brad. Give me your best guess."

"Well, we know that they took Basi out of the country when he was in school, and used drugs, hypnosis, and some sort of image-blasting technique. He would have wrecked the country completely, if the Chinese had not orchestrated his assassination. They apparently wanted you, the Vice President, into the White House. For them, taking Taiwan was a more immediate priority, as you can see."

"Jesus Christ, Brad! You are saying that I am in the White House because the Chinese *put* me here!"

Tilsdale realized that this was not something that any President would want to hear. "I'm afraid it does look like that, Mr. President."

Hanlon stared at the wall, unable to contemplate what he had just learned. It all fit together with what he had guessed about May. She had not only betrayed him, but also the entire country. "Cold-blooded bitch," he mumbled. "It's time that we taught these bastards who the big dog is."

"Brad, I want you to send a coded message to your boss at the CIA. I want May Chang arrested and held by the CIA for interrogation. Forget about involving the FBI—they will just fuck it up and get their legal shoelaces tied together. I want to know exactly who she really is, and how they did it. Tell your people that there are *no* restrictions on what you can do to her during interrogation. She has destroyed me, and now I will destroy her. *Understand?*"

"Affirmative, Sir. I'll get right on it."

"Brad, get yourself a warm shower and some chow at the Flag Mess, then meet me back up here. I like your style, and I need another opinion to lean on. Things are about to get sweaty. The Chinese and I are going to play a little serious poker."

"Roger that, Sir."

Chapter 28

Trespass and Trepidity

Tilsdale returned to the war room, and found the President and the Admiral Baker studying the tactical display. Fed by satellite data and other reconnaissance, it showed the disposition of every U.S. and Chinese ship and submarine in the area near Taiwan.

"Mr. President, the Chinese Premier is on the satellite phone. He sounds worried," said the chief-of-staff.

"He should be," replied Hanlon. "I'm about to kick his ass." Hanlon took the phone.

Wen Jiabao, China's Premier, was an oily, clever man, and could never be trusted. Behind his inscrutable smile was a devious, plotting dictator, who would do anything to achieve his goals. Hanlon knew him from his days as ambassador to China. "Brad, you speak Mandarin. Get on that extension."

Hanlon spoke in Mandarin. "Good morning, Premier Wen. What can I do for you?"

"Forget the 'Premier' shit, William. We know each other! I want to know what you are doing, ordering these Navy ships and aircraft into our territorial zone. Taiwan is *ours* now, and your aggression could cause an incident that would lead to war!"

Hanlon laughed. "Jiabao, you have had enough fun. It's time for you to withdraw all of your forces from Taiwan, and I mean *all*! And while you're at it, get your North Korean puppets out of South Korea!"

"William, that is not possible. You, above all people, should know that! We are there to stay!"

"Jiabao, listen to me carefully. The game is over. I know everything. At this moment, May Chang is being taken into custody for interrogation, and her entire staff is being arrested. We know all about the Arab you hired to bring down Air Force One, and we have him in custody, also."

"William, I don't know what you are talking about!"

"Right. Well, here is my ultimatum to you, which is non-negotiable. Start pulling your forces out of Taiwan immediately."

"And if I don't? Just what are you going to do?"

"The first thing I am going to do is kick the North Koreans back across the 38th parallel, where they belong. As we speak, they are being given the ultimatum to leave South Korea. If they balk, I am going to take out their nuclear sites and air bases. If that does not get their attention, I am going to turn their capital of Pyongyang into a radioactive cemetery. I think it's time for the South Korean government to control the entire peninsula, all the way to the Yalu River. You people asked for it, and you are going to get it. And by the way, if there are any hostile acts toward our forces by you, I will use one nuclear weapon on China for every ship or aircraft of ours that you destroy. I have nothing to lose now, my friend, and I don't give a shit what the United Nations, the press, or anyone thinks about this. I have the gun, and I *will* pull the trigger! Don't force me!"

"You are being unreasonable! You are crazy!" screamed Wen.

"Crazy like a fox. You don't want to lose all the Chinese progress, the modern infrastructure, your talented people, your armed forces. I know you and I know China, Jiabao! Let's make this easy on each other, and just do what is necessary to avoid further conflict. Tell the Koreans to get their asses back across the DMZ, and get your own asses out of Taiwan! Or, you can all take the consequences. You have twenty-four hours, no more. After that, I will take the North Koreans out first. Then it will be your turn. The decision is yours. Call me when you are ready to confirm your pull-out. Goodbye!"

Hanging up the phone, Hanlon smiled knowingly. For all his wily attributes, the Chinese leader was predictable, and Hanlon had watched him for years, in many different settings. "Brad, the next move will be by Wen Jiabao, to test my resolve. It will be important to send him a clear message. My guess is that he will send submarines at us, while he will come in from two directions with long-range strike aircraft, aimed at our task force." Hanlon's years of participating in complex war games in the Navy were paying off. "Bridge, Flag Plot."

"Bridge, Aye, Sir."

"Notify all units to expect a coordinated probe of the task force by hostile submarines and aircraft. The Rules of Engagement will be to shoot down any and all hostile aircraft that approach inside of 100 miles, and sink any hostile submarines inside of 50 miles."

"Aye, aye, Sir!"

"Brad, let's get some lunch. I'll bet you we have hostile contacts within two hours."

As Hanlon and Tilsdale finished their coffee in the Admiral's Mess, the ship's claxon sounded, and the 1MC (public address system) blared. "General Quarters, General Quarters, all hands man your battle stations. This is no drill!" Hanlon and Tilsdale raced to the Flag Bridge.

"What's happening, Irv?" asked Hanlon.

"As you predicted, we have simultaneous sub and air contacts, coming at us from north and south. One sub has just crossed inside 50 miles, as detected by one of our LAMPS ASW [anti-sub warfare] helos."

"Do you have a surface asset within firing distance?"

"Yes, Sir. I have a destroyer closing on the contact."

"If the sub hits 40 miles, take him out."

"Aye, aye, Sir." Admiral Baker looked at Hanlon, and noticed he did not hesitate on giving the order.

"Flag, Combat [combat information center]. The hostile sub contact is at 40 miles."

"Flag, aye," replied Admiral Baker. "The *Fitzgerald*

is launching her LAMPS helo toward the contact. Mr. President, the helo will locate the sub with its dipping sonar, then drop a Mark 54 torpedo on it. Once that fish hits the water, there is no escape for the sub."

"Very well. Tell your DDGs [guided missile destroyers] and CAPs [combat air patrols] to keep alert, especially for low-flying aircraft with anti-ship missiles. That will probably be the next threat."

The LAMPS helo began to hover at the last location of the submarine contact, dipping a sonar transducer into the water. Within seconds, they found the target, traveling below them at 20 knots toward the task force. "Blue Crown, Beetle Three, contact confirmed. Am I cleared to drop?"

"Blue Crown, roger contact. You are cleared to drop."

"Fish away!" radioed the pilot, as the homing torpedo dropped into the blue water and began to transmit its own sonar search pulses. The "fish" dove in a spiral pattern, searching for its target. "Blue Crown, the fish is locked," announced the pilot, indicating that the torpedo guidance system was locked onto the Chinese sub. Increasing its speed to 60 knots, the torpedo rammed the *Han*-class attack sub and exploded, sending the sub to the bottom.

"Blue Crown, contact down."

"Roger, Beetle. Return to home plate," ordered the controller.

Hearing this, Admiral Baker keyed the intercom. "Combat, Flag. Keep your air defense assets on their toes. Check for low-flyers."

"Combat, aye."

Tilsdale marveled at the technological advances in task force defense since he had been on active duty. The Combat Information Center of *Blue Ridge* looked like a NASA control room in Houston, with vast arrays of large-screen monitors depicting the information needed by the task force commander. Tactical data, such as ship and aircraft disposition, both friendly and hostile, were graphically displayed for easy analysis, and shared between ship and aircraft units in a continuous data link. Any unidentified ship or aircraft that was detected by one unit was automatically shared with the others, in real time.

"Flag, Combat. Two bogeys [unidentified air contacts] inbound on the 010 radial at 110 miles, altitude one thousand, speed 500 knots."

"Flag, roger. Put the CAP on them."

"Combat, aye." The fleet air defense controller clicked his mike. "Eagle 405, you have two bogeys inbound on the 010 radial. Do you have my data link?"

The pilot in the F-18 Super Hornet glanced at his tactical display. "Affirmative, Blue Crown. Two bogeys on the deck, doing 500 knots, 090 at 30 from me."

"Roger, Eagle, those are your bogeys. Recommend descent to angels 1 [1,000 ft.]. Your vector 120 to intercept. If you have no friendly IFF [radar identification signal] on them, you are cleared for intercept and to fire."

"Roger, understand I have a green light. Eagle Two, go to combat spread." Navy fighter pilots normally fight in two-aircraft "sections," and use an abeam position, separated by about one mile. "Eagle Two, switches hot!"

The two Hornets descended rapidly at 700 knots while tracking the incoming bogeys, which were a pair of Chinese JH-7 "Flying Leopard" jets, carrying the deadly YJ-82 anti-ship missiles, known as "Saccades." The pilots knew that they had to knock down both aircraft before they launched their missiles, which were next to impossible to defend against.

At 20 miles, the Hornet leader was ready to fire. "I have a lock, Blue Crown. Am I cleared to fire?"

"Affirmative, no positive IFF, cleared to fire."

"Fox three! Fox three!" he radioed, using the pilot code words for firing this type of missile. Two big AIM-120 AMRAAM [advanced medium range anti-aircraft missile] radar missiles blasted from his wing pylons. Their smoke trails disappeared in the haze, as they roared toward the doomed Chinese jets. The Chinese pilots never knew what hit them. Their aircraft were suddenly ripped apart by the shrapnel from the large missile warheads, and disappeared from the radar scopes. "Splash two bogeys, Blue Crown!"

"Roger that. Well done. Take angels 30, and CAP sector Bravo until further advised. Stay on station until relieved, over."

"Eagle, roger." The two Hornets began to climb back to altitude.

Hanlon turned to Tilsdale. "Well, Brad. We saw his first bet, and raised him. *Now* let's see how he feels about leaving Taiwan. Premier Wen needs to fold, while he still has cards to play with. Commander, get the Premier on the line—on speaker, please."

In a few minutes, the room's speakers crackled to life. "William, this is Jiabao," the Premier said in Mandarin. A Navy translator transcribed the conversation in English.

"Jiabao, you disappoint me. I remember you as a man of honor and great intelligence. How dare you attempt to attack my task force! Your stupid adventure has just cost you a submarine and two aircraft. I strongly urge you to stop this folly before it spins out of control. I am now sending a carrier battle group into the Taiwan Strait, between the Chinese coast and Taiwan. You may now consider Taiwan to be under blockade. Nothing may enter or leave, either by sea or air. If you attempt to do so, the offending ship or aircraft will be destroyed. We will be landing a Marine Division on the island, and if there is the slightest interference or resistance, I am ordering them to wipe out every Chinese unit on the island. Will you now withdraw, or shall we give you another lesson?"

"William, you insult me! You never talked to me like this when you were in Beijing!"

"That's when I was only the ambassador—now I am the President of the United States, and I want your asses off that island, and your North Korean puppets out of the South! Are you going to do the right thing here, or do I need to give you more lessons in proper international behavior?"

"I think we should conclude this conversation. I have nothing more to say. You are very impolite," fumed Wen.

"That is your choice, my dear friend. Tell your North Korean friends that they are next on my agenda, since *you* cannot make up your mind. Pay attention to the Korean peninsula, and what happens to stubborn fools. I have quite a show for you. And don't make the mistake of interfering, like you did in 1950 in the Korean War. If you get involved, you will pay a heavy price this time. Good day, Sir." Hanlon hung up.

"Admiral Baker, let's go to DEFCON 2 [preparation for nuclear war]. Send this message to CINCPAC: '**Execute Operation Pueblo. Signed, POTUS.**'"

"Aye, aye, Sir."

This was the Joint Chiefs' war plan for taking back the Korean peninsula. CINCPAC had already brought a full Marine division into position on ships in the Sea of Japan in preparation for an amphibious landing at the North Korean port of Wonsan. Three carrier battle groups were also in position to provide air strikes and missile defense. The Air Force had positioned several squadrons of F-15s, F-16s, and F-22s at nearby Japanese bases, giving CINCPAC a total of over 800 combat aircraft for the operation. During the night, B-2 stealth bombers and F-117 stealth fighters flew out of Japan and attacked important command and control facilities, cutting off the North Koreans' communications capabilities. This was followed by a massive launch of conventional warhead Tomahawk cruise missiles from the submarines and surface ships offshore, surgically taking out air fields, radar, artillery, and troop concentrations all over the peninsula.

When the North Koreans attempted to strike back at the task force, their MIGs were met first by air-to-air missiles from Air Force and Navy fighters. The few that slipped through the air defense perimeter were met by SM-2 and Sea Sparrow surface-to-air missiles from the Navy ships. A similar fate befell the few submarines that escaped the Tomahawk strikes on their port facilities. The Navy's attack submarines and surface ships took them out quickly with torpedoes and ASROC weapons, which are fired as missiles, then become homing torpedoes upon entering the water. Hanlon had warned the Koreans, through the Chinese, that if they hit a single Navy ship, the response would be that one city in North Korea will be eliminated with a nuclear weapon, along with all of their nuclear facilities. It was slowly being recognized around the world that Hanlon was deadly serious about his demands.

After a few days of intensive air and Tomahawk strikes, the amphibious group moved closer to Wonsan, and began the assault. Drone reconnaissance aircraft pinpointed all North Korean weapons or troop concentrations, and these were immediately hit with precise air strikes. The U.S. control of the air was reducing the North Korean Army and Navy to charred rubble. The 3rd Marine Division landed, unopposed, and swept inland as a mechanized infantry force. They were followed by additional landings of the Army's 4th Armored and 1st Infantry Divisions, and the race for Pyongyang began.

The North Korean Army, now in danger of having its supply lines cut, began to surrender. The North Korean forces to the north of the U.S. thrust fled further north of the Yalu River, into China—an extremely awkward event for Premier Wen. It was becoming clear that Hanlon was winning the poker game. Wen had already suffered a humiliating strategic defeat. If he let the occupation of Taiwan go on, he was jeopardizing his people and the new China. A simple miscalculation by one of his over-zealous unit commanders could result in a massive retaliation by the U.S.—something he could not politically afford.

Sitting in Flag Plot, Hanlon looked at Tilsdale. "Brad, what is your take on the next Chinese move?"

"I'm guessing that Wen will call you, and offer to have the *status quo* restored in Korea, and the armistice back in effect. But I think he will try to hold on to Taiwan. By giving you South Korea, he hopes that will be enough for you politically to declare a victory, and ignore the occupation of Taiwan. That probably would have worked with Carter, Clinton, and Basi. The longer they stay, the harder it will be to pry them out of there. They could tie us up in the United Nations with endless studies, commissions, conferences, and mediations. They will try to run you out of momentum, and win Taiwan by default. Before long, it will be a *fait accompli*."

"Brad, I totally agree with you. He will try to come out of this with something he can run up the flagpole, and hope the rest of China will salute it. But I'm not buying it. I refuse to allow them to keep any gains from this unlawful venture. I know I'm not playing the diplomatic game properly, but Korea and Taiwan are non-negotiable. We would have to fight them sometime over Taiwan, so it might as well be now, when I am at the wheel." Hanlon's voice lowered. "Brad, I have nothing more to lose. At least I can go out with a roar."

"Well, Mr. President, you are certainly doing that!" said

Tilsdale. They both laughed.

"Mr. President, Premier Wen is on the phone for you," said one of his aides.

"Well, well. Let's see if he folds or wants to raise me," said Hanlon, picking up the phone. "Jiabao, so nice to hear from you, old friend. What can I do for you?"

"William, you *must* lift this blockade, and tell your Marines not to land on Taiwan! We simply won't permit that!"

"*Permit that?* You have very big balls for a little man, Jiabao! You are trespassing on sovereign Taiwanese soil. You have violated international law, and at least a dozen United Nations resolutions, plus the UN charter itself! Who the fuck do you think you are, Jiabao? Let me tell you something. You got away with murder when Sam Basi was President, and I'll bet you are having second thoughts about assassinating him at this point. As we say in America, there is a new sheriff in town, and you are under arrest!"

"What about you, William? You are invading the Democratic People's Republic of North Korea!"

"Go read your United Nations documents again, Jiabao. We are merely exercising self-help and honoring a treaty with an important ally. If you don't like it, go to the Security Council. Whatever you come up with, we will veto it—like you have been doing to us with Syria, Iran, and other problems for years. If anything is going to be decided, it will be between you and me. Let me know when you want to talk seriously. In the meantime, I am in the process of driving the North Koreans across your border. I hope you have facilities to take care of all of them. Then, I am going to democratize the entire peninsula, and it will be ruled by South Korea's government. How does that strike you?"

This was exactly what China had always feared, if the North's dictatorship collapsed. "William, let's be reasonable. Let the North Koreans re-occupy their original territory. Stop the war and pull your forces back to the DMZ."

"I don't know, Jiabao. I would love to poke around up there in North Korea and see what those lunatics have been up to. Perhaps China has been helping them manufacture chemical and biological weapons, not to mention long-range missiles. We have a lot of curious CIA agents that would like to check out those rumors. As they say, this is a golden opportunity." Hanlon winked at Tilsdale. "I would need to check with my advisors, but I think I could agree to your proposal, *if* you leave Taiwan also."

There was a long silence. "Jiabao? Are you still there?" asked Hanlon.

"Alright, William. I will agree. But we will need six months to bring all of our forces back to China."

"Jiabao, that is unacceptable! You got *in* there in one week, and you bragged about it. Now you can leave in the same amount of time. If any of your people or assets remain, they will be held in custody of the United States and Taiwan forces as prisoners and spoils of war. Naturally, we will treat them just as humanely as *your* country treated *our* POWs in the Korean War of the 1950s. You don't have a problem with *that*, do you?"

"William, you are pushing me!"

"No, Jiabao, you are pushing *yourself*. You got yourself into this mess, and you may not be out of it yet. Just wait until the American public learns that your government ordered the assassination of Sam Basi. They will want to nail *your* balls to the Great Wall of China, my friend! Just give it up, and do yourself a favor. By the way, if you want to know what happens when we *really* get pissed off, check with the Japanese, and perhaps Al-Qaeda. Even Sam Basi went after Osama Bin Laden, as timid as *he* was. You have been getting off easy, so far. One week, Jiabao—that's all. You better get your ass in gear. Time is running out for you. Goodbye." Hanlon hung up the phone.

Tilsdale could not suppress a smile. This was the Bill Hanlon that he had remembered from the Navy. He had always been a no-nonsense, highly professional officer, a reputation that made his recent behavior in giving up Korea and Taiwan all the more surprising. Clearly, the warrior side of him had returned, motivated by a desire for revenge.

"Brad, I want you and Ben to join me in my stateroom."

"Aye, aye, Sir."

Followed by the Marine guard and Secret Service agents, Hanlon led the group back to "Flag country," and a VIP stateroom. Once Tilsdale and Blackwell were inside, he closed the door, and sat down dejectedly on the big sofa. "Well, gentlemen, it has been quite a week."

"I'll vote for that, Sir," said Tilsdale.

"Ben, would you mind getting us a drink? Brad, what are you having?"

"Jack Daniels on the rocks, please."

"Ben is a vodka drinker, but I hired him anyway. I was concerned that this was a pro-Russian habit of his," laughed Hanlon.

"Ben, I want you to know how much I have valued your opinion and your work. You really made a difference."

Blackwell looked embarrassed. "Why, thank you, Mr. President."

"No, I mean it. And Brad, you are a very scary guy to most politicians. You have the audacity to call the facts like you see them, and you value the country above your own career. From the little I know, you have done more for the country than most of us."

"Mr. President, I wish I could have done more. I failed to get the right answers in time to prevent some bad things, like 9/11, and President Basi's assassination."

"Well, we all have our demons. I am now facing an unbelievable personal tragedy, which will quickly translate into a political disaster. My wife is a Chinese spy, and she was able to get me to implement a course of action that was against my country's best interests, to put it mildly. When we get home, I will have to deal with that, and I will. Brad, what do you think will happen next with the Chinese?"

"I would expect that the Premier has now realized that his options have evaporated. I would bet that you will be getting a call from the Premier fairly soon."

In the next few hours, U.S. satellites detected a mass exodus of Chinese forces from Taiwan. When this report reached President Hanlon, he notified U.S. forces to lift the blockade and permit the exit. "Brad, Jiabao can't bring himself to call me and admit that he is giving up Taiwan. It's a Chinese thing—you know, loss of face and all that."

In an hour, the group returned to Flag Plot. "Mr. President, Premier Wen is on TV," reported an aide.

"Turn on the tube," ordered Hanlon. The Flag Plot TV was switched on, as Wen began speaking through a translator.

"I speak to the citizens of China, and to America. For centuries, the riches of China have been pillaged by the colonial powers of Europe, the United States, and Japan. This will no longer be tolerated, which we have demonstrated by taking over our island of Taiwan without firing a shot. Our claim to that territory has been consistent and peaceable. However, we have now shown the world that our patience has limits. Since we do not wish to impose the force of arms to achieve our aims, and require other nations do likewise, we will perfect our territorial claim to Taiwan through the proper international channels. Having made our point, we will now withdraw our military forces from that island in the interest of peace. However, no one should mistake our desire for peace to be weakness, or lack of resolve. Taiwan always has been, and always will be, a part of China. Thank you for your attention."

Hanlon smiled. "Brad, your thoughts?"

"Saving face, like you said, Mr. President."

"What would you do next?"

"I would call the Premier, and smooth his feathers. He will not call you, that's for sure."

"I agree. Commander, place the call."

In a few minutes, the aide announced, "The Premier, Sir."

"Jiabao? Thank you for bringing reason to this process! I was being pressured to initiate a nuclear attack on China, which I did not want to do. You have done an incredibly courageous thing, and I will never forget it. Will you permit me to nominate you for the Nobel Peace Prize? It would be a great honor for me to do that."

"William, thank you, but I would only agree if we jointly were nominated. This was a very important lesson for the world, because we solved this together, you and I."

"Jiabao, just as our intelligence services concluded long ago, you are truly a great man, and I am privileged to know you."

"William, you are too kind. Let me assure you that all

Chinese forces will be out of Taiwan within one week. And by the way, the North Koreans are ready to honor the DMZ again."

"Well, alright, we will agree to that. But I must tell you— if this ever happens again, there will be mushroom clouds over Pyongyang. We will never permit that again, Jiabao. Do you understand me?"

"Yes, William, I do. Our North Korean friends are a little over-zealous sometimes. We will make sure they stay within their own territory."

"Let me make sure that you understand. If they sink any more South Korean ships, conduct any raids across the DMZ, or take any other belligerent action, they will pay a terrible price. I am very serious about this. And while we are at it, I want *your* cyber-warfare groups to stop trying to hack into our computer systems. If that continues, we will consider that to be another hostile act on your part."

"I understand. Rest assured that they will behave themselves. By the way, the people involved in the Basi matter have been identified and executed. Apparently the MSS director and some rogue officials took matters into their own hands. I have appointed a new MSS director, General Geng Huichang. I knew nothing about it. I sincerely apologize to you and the American people for that outrage. It is very embarrassing to us."

"In that case, if you were here now, I would exchange a toast with a nice French champagne.'

"Better than that, why don't you come and visit me? I promise you will have a wonderful time."

"I would love to do that, Jiabao, but I have some urgent matters to attend to. Maybe in a few months."

"Let's stay in touch, old friend. I hope to talk to you soon.

Goodbye for now," said Wen.

"Goodbye, Jiabao."

"Admiral Baker, please have a helo take me over to the *Nimitz*. I want a COD [transport] to take me back to Tokyo and Air Force One. I am going home. Brad, I want you to come along, also."

"Aye, aye, Sir." Tilsdale wondered what Hanlon would do next, and how it would affect the country. He would soon find out.

Tilsdale turned to Admiral Baker. "Sir, I would like to send a personal message to someone."

Baker smiled. "Knowing you, Tilsdale, it will be a beautiful woman, not your boss! Do I know her?"

"I don't think so, Admiral. Her name is Melissa Clayton. She works at NSA."

Baker rolled his eyes. "NSA? In that case, I know I *never* heard of her!" laughed Baker. "Lieutenant, take Mr. Tilsdale down to the Com Center, so he can make a private call."

"Thanks, Admiral."

"No, Mr. Tilsdale—thank *you*—for everything!"

Chapter 29

New Beginnings

While Tilsdale and the President were on the long flight back to Washington, Taiwan and South Korea began to return to normal. Many of the North Korean troops elected to defect, and stay in South Korea, having seen the economic difference between their countries. The President ordered the National Command Center to bring the alert status back to DEFCON 4, and the world gave a collective sigh of relief.

Melissa Clayton found herself suddenly acting like a love-sick school girl, instead of the hard-edged intelligence professional that she was. She could not suppress a smile, remembering the surprise call from Tilsdale, a few hours before.

"Melissa? I'm glad I caught you by the phone. You can be a hard person to reach sometimes."

"Brad Tilsdale, look who's talking! What the hell are you doing over there? I was worried sick about you! Even the press has been discussing your role in this crisis! You are some kind of a celebrity, and that is not a good thing for a CIA guy! Especially an old one like you!"

"Forget about that, Melissa. I have had some time to think about my life, and have decided I can't afford to waste any more time."

"Good for you. So you are going to retire?"

"I don't know about that. But I do know one thing. I want you to marry me, Melissa."

There was a long silence, as Melissa dropped the phone. "Brad, please don't screw around. I'm not in the mood for that."

"No, I mean it. I want you to meet me at Andrews, when Air Force One lands. We are going shopping for a ring, girl! Now, *will* you marry me, or do I have to kidnap you and keep you as a sex slave in my basement?"

"You bastard! You can't even propose nicely, can you? What the hell, I have nothing better on my schedule—of *course* I will marry you, stupid! I've only been waiting for thirty years!"

"Outstanding! Get your little black dress and high heels on, Baby—we are going out on the town tonight!"

In the Presidential section of Air Force One, Hanlon was working on a speech to the nation. He chose his words carefully, because he knew this one would be a milestone in history for many reasons.

Finally, Air Force One made its approach to Andrews Air Force Base. The press corps and dozens of government and military officials stood by the red carpet, waiting for the President. The staff had set up a podium and microphone for him to tell the American people what had happened in the Pacific in the last few days. There was a sense of high drama throughout the nation.

Exiting Air Force One, Hanlon descended the stairs to the podium, looking tired but resolute. As the cameras rolled, he began slowly, as Tilsdale listened in the background.

"My fellow citizens. . . .In the last few weeks, the world came close to a catastrophic nuclear confrontation. Many innocent people would have died, and for no good reason. Certain nations miscalculated our resolve to protect our allies and the freedom of their citizens. Their ill-conceived adventure pushed us to the brink of a major armed conflict. However, because of the professional excellence and courage of our armed forces, and my determination not to capitulate to such aggression, we have put things back the way they were. The peoples of South Korea and Taiwan are free again, and we will never allow this type of conduct again by aggressor nations.

You are probably aware that I have experienced a most painful and humiliating personal tragedy, as well. Our counter-intelligence units have discovered that my wife, May—the First Lady—was a Chinese spy, and is guilty of espionage. Even more than the pain that this has caused me, I have brought dishonor to the office of the President. I should have known of this betrayal, well before it became a national security issue. I have not only let myself down—I have let all of *you* down. Our country simply cannot and should not be forced to endure such a scandal. Somehow, the responsibility was still mine, and I failed to discover it and stop it.

Accordingly, I have concluded that the people of the United States and our friends and allies around the world need a change in leadership and a fresh start. Therefore, effective upon the swearing-in of the Vice President at 10:00 a.m. tomorrow, I am resigning my office as President of the United States.

God bless all of you, and God bless the United
States of America. Goodbye."

Tilsdale could not believe his ears. He had expected an
apology, but not a resignation. As the crowd milled around
the President's limousine, he felt a tug on his sleeve. "Hi,
Sailor! New in town?"

"Melissa!" She fell into his arms, with a kiss that made
him forget about everything.

"Let's go to dinner. We have some serious shopping to
do, Bradford. Remember that ring?"

He hated that name, and she knew it. "No problem,
Sissy." That was a nickname from her college days, and she
hated *that*. "You know I'll do anything, just to get in your
pants."

She put her lips next to his ear, whispering, "Brad
Tilsdale, you will not be able to walk, when I'm through with
you . . ."

"Promises, promises," he replied with a knowing smile.

The next day, Tilsdale and Melissa sat in the VIP audience, waiting for the new President to take the oath of office.
Tilsdale squirmed in his seat, feeling the sexual excesses
of the night before. Knowing what he was feeling, Melissa
leaned over and whispered, "I told you so, boy-san! You
won't forget *that* night for a while."

"Melissa, knock if off! Try to act like an adult for a
change!"

"OK, tonight will be an 'adult night' at the movies. What
do you think of that?"

"Stop it! I'm too old for this! Someone will hear you!"

"Don't tease me... on second thought, please do!" Melissa

replied, placing her hand on the inside of his thigh.

"Melissa, behave yourself! They're about to do the swearing-in."

Chief Justice Roberts extended a Bible, and the man placed his left hand on it. "Please raise your right hand and repeat after me, Sir."

The white-haired old man smiled, amazed that his impossible dream of decades was finally coming true. "I, Ron Paul, do solemnly swear that I will faithfully execute the Office of President of the United States, and will, to the best of my ability, preserve, protect and defend the Constitution of the United States."

The Chief Justice spoke next. "Congratulations, Mr. President."

Tilsdale thought for a minute, wondering what sort of President Ron Paul would make. He was always viewed as the Republican gadfly, like the Democratic Congressman Dennis Kucinich, and never taken seriously. Time would tell.

The next day, Tilsdale met with Karen Littleton at the CIA headquarters. As he walked into her office, he was surprised to find Billings already there. "Karen, I have decided to retire and get married. It's time to move on."

Littleton and Billings exchanged glances, smiling. "What's so funny about *that*?" asked Tilsdale.

Littleton handed him a letter. It was embossed with the seal of the President on White House letterhead. "Brad, the President is nominating you to be the National Security Advisor. He told me to tell you that you can go ahead and get married, but you can't retire. It looks like you have another gig, cowboy."

Tilsdale was stunned. "Why? How did this happen?

There are many people that are better qualified than me. I'm an *operator*, not a staff guy."

"Apparently, Bill Hanlon gave him a briefing before the oath of office, and told him that you were the right guy for this job. Brad, I know you wanted to retire, but you can't turn down the President when he needs you. Between you and me, I think this President is really going to need the help." Littleton continued, with a smile, "Besides, I'm tired of trying to keep track of your activities. You make me nervous!"

"I would only take it if Jeff Billings went with me," grumbled Tilsdale, certain that Billings would want to stay with the Agency, giving him a reason to decline the appointment.

Billings could not suppress a laugh. "Brad, guess what? I got a letter too, appointing me as your deputy. Hey, why break up a winning combination? Someone has to keep your ass out of trouble!"

Littleton looked at both of them, her face getting serious. "Gentlemen, I wish you the very best. Do what you can—and do *whatever* you have to do—to keep America safe."

Tilsdale spoke. "Karen, thanks for that. But you know us. We *always* go by the book!"

The end—for now.

CPSIA information can be obtained
at www.ICGtesting.com
Printed in the USA
FFOW01n2332150215
11097FF